THE
Miracle
Thief

Iris Anthony

sourcebooks
landmark

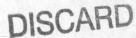

Published by Sourcebooks Landmark, an imprint of Sourcebooks, Inc.
P.O. Box 4410, Naperville, Illinois 60567-4410
(630) 961-3900
Fax: (630) 961-2168
www.sourcebooks.com

Library of Congress Cataloging-in-Publication data is on file with the publisher.

Printed and bound in the United States of America.
VP 10 9 8 7 6 5 4 3 2 1

To my husband, who shares my faith, my hopes,
and my dreams,
and in memory of my cousin, Linda Morris,
who would have liked this book

Autumn 911

The Darkest Hour of the Dark Ages

CHAPTER I

Juliana

ROCHEMONT ABBEY

*S*UCH A WRETCHED WAY TO DIE.

I watched from my knees beside the abbess's bed, hands clasped before me, as she took a shuddering breath. Squeezing my eyes shut, I raised my hands to my brow, pretending to pray. But I could not do it; I had forgotten the words.

She could not die. I would not let her.

The abbess had been more of a mother than the woman who had raised me. Her heart had been more constant than the man who had once loved me. Was there nothing I could do to ease her pain?

Adjusting her counterpane, I shivered as an especially vicious draft stole in through the chamber's high windows and swirled its icy tendrils about my knees.

I felt the heavy weight of a hand upon my veiled head. "Daughter."

Looking up, I saw the abbess watching me. Grasping her hand, I kissed it. "Do not leave us."

A ghost of a smile curled her thin, cracked lips. "I do not think I have any say in the matter."

"What shall we do without you?" How would we go on? Who would lead us?

"Do not fear. God will provide."

"How?" The word escaped my lips before I could catch it. I had not meant to give voice to my unbelief. Surely now she would regret asking me to attend her. "Without you, I do not know how we will…"

"Take heart." She clasped my hand. "Without me, there will still be you."

"Who am I but the least of all the others?" I had come to this mountain-ringed abbey seeking sanctuary, and even after all the years I had spent here, I felt myself a stranger still.

"Trust God. Seize the chance to serve."

The chance to serve? Was I not already doing that very thing?

She released me from her grip, but left her fever-withered hand resting in mine. "Remember—" Her words left off as a spasm gripped her body.

I leaned closer.

After the seizure had passed, she lay back on her cushions, panting. "Speak truth. Stand for what is right." Her hand twisted in mine as her face contorted with pain.

Looking straight into my eyes, she spoke again. "Lead them."

"What?"

"Lead them. There is no one else." She clutched my hand with a strength that stole my breath. "You must do it."

If she did not relinquish my hand, I feared she might wrench it from my wrist. "I will."

"Promise."

"I promise." If only she would lie down and spare her strength.

"You promised."

"I did."

She searched my face for a moment, and then she smiled. After I had smoothed the counterpane around her shoulders, she closed her eyes, and she did not open them again. As she lay there, her breaths becoming more shallow and labored,

I let her expire without doing the very thing she had made me promise. I did not tell her the truth: I did not intend to do as she had asked.

The abbess died along with the sun as the bell was tolling vespers. She went quietly, exhaling her last breath with a lingering sigh.

We mourned her for the required number of days. And then, secretly, I mourned her still. A message was sent to the bishop, informing him of her death. Though we would elect the new abbess, it was he who would induct her. And so we gathered in the chapterhouse one forenoon, after the day's meal, to do that very thing.

As I looked up and down the benches that lined the walls, I did so with a growing unease. I could not see a clear candidate to lead us.

Of the several dozen sisters in the abbey, Sister Rotrude was the oldest and had been at the abbey the longest, but she seemed troubled in her spirit of late. I used to think her full of the joy of the Lord, since she had always been prone to laughter, but she had taken up the habit of laughing during meals at nothing any of us could see or hear. Her warbling, tuneless voice could often be heard singing during prayers, and increasingly, she asked after sisters who had already departed to receive their eternal reward.

Sister Berta should, perhaps, have been the obvious choice. She was sound of mind and body, and none could doubt neither her capacity nor her willingness for hard work. But she lacked a measure of joy. The tips of her mouth pointed toward her chin, and one could not be long in her proximity before being informed of everything that had been done wrong in the past and all that would most certainly be found wanting in the future. Even a dove of peace would soon find himself shooed away for want of a proper place to perch. Were Sister Berta appointed abbess, I feared the abbey would soon become a dull and dreary place.

Sister Amicia? Perhaps not. If Sister Berta dwelt too often on what was wrong, Sister Amicia trusted overmuch in Providence. To hear her speak, God would provide whether the workers tilled our fields or not. If she were to be believed, Providence might be depended upon to cook our food and feed us our meal as well. Although she never lacked a cheerful word, and a smile was constant upon her face, I could not see the abbey long surviving under her leadership, knowing from regrettable experience that great hopes came to nothing if they were not first founded upon practicalities.

Though in generations past, the nuns of Rochemont had been well and truly cloistered, hidden away from the world, we could afford the luxury of quiet contemplation no longer. Even at these perilous heights where we clung to our meager existence, pestilence and famine, cruel winters and wars, had long since thinned the ranks of our tenants. If there was work to be done, we too had to take part in the doing of it. The tasks, which in the abbey's earliest years might have fallen to lay workers, we had taken upon ourselves. And so, I nearly overlooked Sister Sybilla entirely. It was not difficult to do, since she spent her waking hours at the hospice. Rarely speaking, rarely even moving among us, she had never done anything wrong that I had noticed, but I did not know that she could be counted on to encourage any of us toward righteousness either.

Sister Clothild, the abbess's prioress, was kind of heart and beloved by all. A gentler soul I had never met, but for all her generosity of spirit, and despite the winsome way she had with the chaplain, the bailiff, and the household staff, she had never learned to read or write.

Sister Isolda was our librarian. Within her realm and with

her long face and sharp features, she had always been quite fearsome. But books did not an abbey make. I had never seen her out among the pilgrims who made their way to Saint Catherine's chapel. I did not think she had ever labored in the hospice or in the kitchens. She knew Latin, both written and spoken, but I could not say she knew anything else.

The other nuns being too young for the position, that left me.

I considered myself as the others might have. There was not very much to note. I had made such a habit of attaching myself to Saint Catherine's relic, to spending my time interceding for the iniquities of my past, that any of the sisters might have taken me for a misanthropist. That I tended to my duties with great care was undeniable. That I greeted each pilgrim with God's peace was, perhaps, commendable. For eighteen years I had been resident at the abbey, and in all that time, to my great shame, I had served no one's interests but my own. Even the tending of the chapel was a selfish pursuit, so I did not think any of the sisters would hold me in greater esteem than Sister Clothild or Sister Isolda. Although I could write and I could read, none sitting here knew that, and it was too late to make it known now.

It was true I had made a promise to the abbess, but had she meant her words?

And if she had, would I not be remiss if I did not let the others know? Should I propose myself as a candidate?

My gaze swept our number again.

Though my sisters' failings be great, was not God greater still? And why could His strength not be evidenced through their weaknesses?

As I had told the abbess, I was least among them. I knew some of my sisters were not virgins, but at least they had the sanction of wedding vows. When they had joined their flesh to another's, they had been given the blessing of the Church. Widowed now, some still had the comfort of their children's love.

Not I.

Not I, who had abandoned a daughter. Not I, who had indulged in the sins of the flesh.

Lead them.

No. How could I do it when my heart still yearned for another, different, more temporal groom? I had pledged myself to Christ, but I had done so as a last resort, with a faithless heart and suspect intentions.

Surely if I were to be the new abbess, then the sisters would come to that decision on their own, prompted by the spirit of God, without my interference. Was that not the way it should be?

If we were to pray to discern the will of God, then I was content to let His will be discerned.

Sister Clothild stood. "Are there any who would recommend a sister to be abbess?"

There was no sound save the cheerless laughter of Sister Rotrude.

Sister Clothild's smile faltered as she looked at each of us in turn. "No one?" As she waited for some response, even Sister Rotrude fell silent.

"Surely someone would like to propose a sister. We must not look to the bishop to do it on our behalf…"

Sister Isolda stirred. "I would propose myself then."

"And I would propose *myself*." Sister Berta did not look pleased at the prospect, and in truth, neither did anyone else.

"Sister Berta and Sister Isolda. Is there no one else?" Did I detect a plea in her voice?

I put a hand to my mouth, feigning a cough to keep myself from speaking.

"Is there no one?" Her eyes seemed fixed upon me. "We ought all of us, then, to meditate upon these candidates and pray that God would make His will be known." Was it disappointment that had drawn those lines at the sides of her mouth? "We will choose the abbess here, after our meal, on the morrow."

⁂

I tried not to think about the selection of the new abbess as I greeted pilgrims that forenoon and assisted them at the chapel, but the more I tried to concentrate, the more my vow weighed upon my soul. Surely there is a place in hell reserved for those who made promises they did not intend to keep.

In the ancient cavern that was Saint Catherine's chapel, all was light around me. A radiant, flickering, golden light. The glow reflected off the rocks and from the rise of my cheeks, warming the air about me and causing a halo to encircle everything I saw. After our chaplain took pilgrims' confessions and gave them Holy Communion, they stepped forward, one by one, from the newly built wooden church. As their steps left the smooth, earthen floor for the timeworn stone that sloped toward Saint Catherine's chapel, the light embraced them.

Rich and poor; the young and the aged; both the whole and the sick.

Saint Catherine welcomed them all.

"After receiving the mysteries of eternal salvation, we humbly pray thee, that as the liquor that continually flowed from the limbs of Saint Catherine, virgin and martyr, did heal languishing bodies, so her prayer may expel out of us all iniquities." I murmured the prayer in welcome as a weeping woman dropped an enameled cross that had been edged with gilt-work into a chest piled with pilgrims' gifts. She turned with a wail to cast herself before the altar. As she lifted her face toward the rock-hewn roof, the candles' light shone in starry points from her tears. Extending her hands, she whispered a prayer, and then she placed her hands on the golden casket containing Saint Catherine's relic and leaned forward to kiss it.

After caressing the carnelian cabochons that had been polished by the touch of a thousand hands, she rose and stumbled back toward the church as the next pilgrim came to take her place.

"After receiving the mysteries of eternal salvation, we humbly pray thee, that as the liquor that continually flowed from the limbs of Saint Catherine, virgin and martyr, did heal languishing bodies, so her prayer may expel out of us all iniquities." I spoke those words over and over again. A hundred times a day I might say them in the warmer months. Now, as winter threatened to blow its hoary breath down our backs, only a score of pilgrims still braved the mountains to access the valley in which the abbey had been secreted. The time of silence would soon descend. Once the snow began, we could expect no visitors until the melt came in spring.

I helped an aged man to his knees and waited for his toneless prayers to cease.

The sword that from her neck the head did chop, Milk from the wound, instead of blood, did bring; By angels buried on Mt. Sinai's top; From Virgin Limbs a Sovereign oil did spring.

The rustle of pilgrims' tunics, the chaplain's murmurs in the church, the clap of shoes against the stone floor had almost ceased. The candles' glow had gone hazy from the censers' incense, and the air was heavy with expectation and hopes near extinguished. The hour of vespers was near, and the sun would soon be lost to us. Any pilgrim who had meant to reach our walls this day had already come.

The last of them, a round-eyed matron, approached with trepidation as she clutched a gilded leather girdle to her chest.

I gestured toward the pile of gifts.

She started, and then a flush lit her face as she placed it atop all the others. She watched me, waiting I suppose for some sign. But it was not me to whom she needed to make her appeal. I was not the one who could grant her soul's request.

I nodded toward the altar, while keeping my gaze fixed to the floor.

The pilgrim bowed and then, casting a worried glance at me, she knelt. When she did not pray, I said the prayer for her, and when it was over, I touched her hand and then pointed toward the relic.

It surprised me no longer how many pilgrims, after having journeyed all this way, feared to do what it was they had come for. In hope of persuading Saint Catherine to take up their cause, to heal them, to intercede on their behalf, some of the pilgrims came into the church and kept here a night-long vigil. Others prostrated themselves on the floor as they prayed one prayer for every year of their sin-filled lives.

In all of my thirty-three years, there were only two that I cared to remember. The first was stolen, its pleasure tainted by the fact that I had tasted, devoured, and then savored forbidden fruit. The second was bought and paid for with all of the years, all of the days, all of the hours that had followed after it. I was paying for it yet.

Two years, two people.

The first, beloved and complicit in my great sin. The second, wholly innocent and precious beyond measure. The loss of both, I constantly mourned.

But if Providence decreed I must live my life again from the start, I would make those same choices and love those two people in the very same way without once pausing for regret. I would do everything just as I had done it at first. No matter how many times I examined my actions, no matter the perspective from which I viewed my sins, I could discover no other path than that which I had taken. If I had been wicked, if I had taken pleasure in my iniquity, at least I had done so honestly.

Virtuous in my vice; noble in my depravity.

What further evidence did I need of my wickedness? What more proof did I need to doubt the salvation of my eternal soul? Perhaps this is the mercy in God's great plan: that we have life but once for the living.

After the woman left, a clerk stepped forward to make a record of the pilgrims' gifts. The pile had been built earlier in the day upon a foundation of linens with a length of shining silk wound through the folds. It was buttressed by a few pouches filled with coin and a small jeweled coffer, and it was weighted by a gold chain or two. The clerk clucked with satisfaction as he pushed aside the textiles and pulled several candles from the fabric.

Turning my back on such luxuries, I wrapped a fold of my sleeve about my hand and then went around to each censer, lifting the perforated lid and adding incense to fortify them against the coming night. Then I went to each of the lamps and used a pair of snips to trim the wicks. Next came the candles. There were a hundred of them. And just when I despaired one would melt into oblivion, a pilgrim always seemed to present a new one. The wax, which puddled on the prickets and cressets, I peeled up and kept for the abbey. They would be remelted and reformed and put to use once more. The smallest of the splatters and drips I collected in a leaf of my Book of Hours, and then emptied into a handkerchief when I retired to my cell after compline.

Over the course of a year, I could collect enough to make one small candle. I heated the drippings in a small bowl over the top of one of the censers, and once they had melted, I added one precious drop of perfume.

It was a scent come from the Orient, my lover's gift. The one thing I had managed to keep when I came into the abbey. I might have felt it deceitful, except that I did not use it for misbegotten purpose. Each night before I left the chapel, I lit the candle and burned it for an instant as I prayed one last prayer to Saint Catherine. If I closed my eyes at that moment and concentrated, I could discern its smell before the thin trail of smoke commingled with the incense and disappeared into the hazy, golden light.

There were too many memories. Too many things I wished to forget.

But beyond those, there were an eternity of things I wished to remember.

The clerk closed his book with a satisfied grunt and placed all of the pilgrims' gifts into a basket. A second clerk grasped it at the handles and hoisted it to his hip. It would be taken to the treasury to be stored with all of the others. All those lengths of fabric, all the collected jewels, all of the crosses and chains and coins that had been brought to invoke Saint Catherine's favor.

The clerk paused in his leaving, and then he too knelt before the altar.

I tried to find a shadow in which to hide myself. One place where that golden light would not reach me, but I could not. The glow of grace was everywhere and illuminated everything. I feigned indifference and did not move until he left my sacred stone-walled fortress and walked out through the church.

The chill night air snuck in before he closed the door. It raced down the nave and into the chapel, poking at the candles' flickering flames. The light faltered for a moment, plunging the altar into relative darkness, but then the flames rallied with a triumphant flare.

With the wind came a memory, and the sound of a dying breath.

You promised.

I did.

I had.

The abbess's words haunted me. Would that I had promised to gouge my own eyes out or stab myself with a hot poker. The abbess could not have known that on my journey to the abbey, I had promised I would never raise myself beyond what God had intended. That I had sworn not to take for myself any position that belonged to another.

A girl like you has nothing to offer at all. A girl like you can never come to anything. It's simply not ordained.

I gnashed my teeth at the memory of the woman who had spoken those words. But had she not been right about me? I pulled my candle from my sleeve and lit it. With my eyes closed, I saw the abbess's face; I felt the grip of her hand on mine. What if—what if I *did* propose myself? Surely the others would not elect me. And if I did it, if I put my name forward and the nuns did not choose me, then perhaps I would be released of this great burden.

"Please, Saint Catherine, show me what to do."

As I crossed the courtyard toward the church the next

morning, the door of the hospice opened, spilling the sounds of its children. So many of them there were. The healthy and the ill. Both the sound of mind and the dull of wits. Those no parent wanted, or those they could ill afford to keep. Eventually all of those who were scorned by the world passed through our gates.

It was the greatest of mercies the abbess had never directed me to care for them. I could not have done it. Not when I still mourned the loss of my own precious child. As it was, I had not asked to tend Saint Catherine's chapel either. When I had come to the abbey, once I had taken my vows, I had been the youngest of the nuns. Although tending the chapel was a more public task than the other nuns had been given, it was not at all important in this place where the sacred was far more valued than the secular. The other women sought positions that kept them within the walls of the cloister—librarian, scribe, lecturer, teacher, prioress, or sacrist. Although pilgrims may have been the lifeblood of our community, they were a poorly tolerated distraction from prayer, fasting, and contemplation. But it did not matter to me. I reveled in the hours I spent in the chapel-cavern.

How easily we lie to ourselves. How quick we are to believe our own falsehoods. Those first few years in the abbey, after having spent my grief in a frenzy of novenas, I told myself my wounds were salved. I declared myself beset by grace. I renounced the world and everything in it, and I made myself into the image of the perfect nun. One who never complained, never questioned, never doubted the goodness of God's great love. What were wars, what were famines, what was pestilence compared to the Almighty's infinite wisdom and power?

I think I had managed to convince even the abbess of my

great faith when a message arrived that scuttled it all. The king was coming to the abbey that summer. And he was bringing his daughter, *our* daughter, the princess, with him.

CHAPTER 2

*H*OW CAN I DESCRIBE MY FEELINGS? IN AN INSTANT the lies I had told myself gave way to the torrent of emotions I had buried deep inside. I was not stricken with guilt, so much as I found myself adrift in memories of my life before the abbey. They overwhelmed me; they swept me along in their familiar currents. They lifted me up.

They possessed me.

Had I truly contented myself with so little, when once I had had so much?

I tried to remind myself it had all been an illusion. That everything I once held dear had only been borrowed. That this life I now lived was one I had chosen, one that was more fitting to both my nature and my station.

But there, I lied to myself once more. A royal abbey like this one, established by one of Charlemagne's own sisters, would never have accepted the daughter of a simple clerk. Not without the dower the Queen Mother had sent along with me. But the very best and the worst of all was that everything within me longed to be once more at my beloved's side.

The raging war within me drove me to Saint Catherine. After the pilgrims had gone, I beseeched her, I pleaded with her, wept before her on my knees. I had given up all of my past, and done so gladly. Why did it have to follow me here?

Please, you who see and know and care, take this cross from me. Why could my mind not cling to the thought of God?

Why, after all these years, could I not imagine seeing Charles without my heart growing faint within me? And why should the pain still cut like a knife through the cold, dark void that had once been my heart?

God must have known how hard I strove to be good and to do penance for all of my wickedness. Is this what sin did? It laid an egg in the soul, which hatched and birthed a thousand miseries. I would have given my life not to have to remember any of it...all of it. Except for one thing.

Except for my daughter.

At the abbess's behest, I helped ready the chapel for their visit. And then the abbess appointed me to receive them there. For the first and only time, I begged to be released from my task.

The abbess had only looked at me in that wise, still way she had. "Why now?"

"I will do anything. I will even work in the hospice or the kitchens, if you will only release me from my work in the chapel."

"This I have tried to do many times since you first came here. But I must ask you again. Why now?"

I did not wish to answer.

She inclined her head as she considered me. "We have novitiates, to be sure, but I feel they are not yet to be trusted with a guest so important. The stuff of the world still clings to their souls. I fear they may develop too much reverence in their earthly king, and so forget their heavenly one."

But neither would I be able to resist so great a temptation. If truth be told, I could not even say my spirit was willing, though I could vouch—over and over again—that my flesh was very weak. "Please, Reverend Mother, do not make me welcome them." My hands were clasped in front of me, my knuckles gone white from the effort of hoping, praying, imploring she would grant my request.

"Do you remember why you told me you wanted to take your vows?"

I remembered. How long ago that was. How young I had been then.

"You told me you had lost your way in the world and that you wished to serve God as best as you could."

I had. I was. And still it had not helped. The best I could do was so very little, so very rude and mean. There was nothing I could offer Our Lord that was not already half-spoilt, used, and worn. "I am not worthy of the honor. I do not deserve it." Indeed, I had forfeited my right to it long ago in lands far away from here.

"They wish to make a pilgrimage to Saint Catherine. Why should they not be served by the nun who tends the altar?"

How many years I had spent trying to forget my old life; how many years I had prayed to be delivered from those memories. And now their coming threatened to undo all the work I had done. "If I had wanted to be part of the world, then I would have stayed there. Please do not force me back into it."

"I hardly think greeting a pilgrim could be called forcing you back into the world, and the princess has the right to visit the abbey as often as she chooses. It's part of her dower."

I raised my head, heart stuttering in alarm. "Her *dower!*"

"Does this distress you?"

I could not trust myself to speak, only clasped my hands tighter, watching my fingernails grow purple from the strain.

"Why should this affect you so?"

"Because she is mine."

The abbess shook her head, as if I had delivered some

glancing blow. "Yours?" She said it as if unfamiliar with the word.

"The princess is my daughter." I had kept that knowledge from everyone in the abbey. But now that I had claimed my past, now that the abbess was looking upon me with such kindness, such compassion, I wondered why I had not said it to her long before. Where there had been panic and shame just a moment before, great relief had come to take its place. And…a ridiculous joy.

"All the more reason then to see her."

"But—"

"I command it."

"What would—how will—whatever will I say to her?" Now, after all of these long, lonely, desolate years?

"The fact that you have no wish to see her shows me that indeed you must."

There, the abbess was mistaken. I had every wish; all of my wishes, in fact, had always been to claim my daughter, to see the princess, if only for the briefest of moments. It was for that very reason I knew I should not.

But the abbess's command was as good as God's. Though His eyes were continually on us, it was the abbess's gaze we could see. I knew there was no purpose in beseeching her any longer. And so, with fear and trembling, I rose and kissed her hand.

And so it was, despite my many prayers, my growing trepidation, and the elation of my shameful heart, that the king and the princess came to visit the abbey.

The people of the village abandoned themselves to the excitement of the occasion and to the preparations. There were fences to be mended, roofs to be thatched, and the road to be repaired. A ripple of anticipation even filtered into the abbey to diffuse itself among the sisters in the refectory as we ate, and the chapterhouse as we met. There was a notable shifting about during the offices, as well as a flurry of whispered conversations. And finally, the polishing of the bell atop the church and the exceptional gift of new black tunics for us all.

Surely, I was the only soul who viewed the coming of the royal party with dread. As others counted the days with growing excitement, I marked off the hours as one condemned. And then, at the end, I too gave myself over to pride and vanity, giving the lamps an extra polish and fishing the blackened stubs of cut wicks from the depths of the lamps. Saint Catherine must not suffer a loss in esteem for my sake.

∽

In the end, it was just as I expected and exactly as I had feared: I knew her.

Her honeyed hair; her bright blue eyes and finely arched brows; the chin that tipped so slightly forward: all of her was familiar.

The moment the girl crossed the threshold of the church, that sharp pain of separation stabbed at my breast, threatening to rend my heart in two. Though I knew her, the best I could say about myself and all of my actions in the years that had followed her birth is that she did not know me.

I clasped my hands, bowing my head as her maids left her. I stood there at the entrance to the chapel, heart thundering in my ears as she made her confession and partook in Holy Communion. But as she reached my stone-walled haven, I heard her steps falter. And then, they stopped altogether.

I looked up to find her staring at the chapel as if in wonder, light glancing off her cheeks and reflecting from her eyes. And then, her gaze fell upon me.

Reminding myself she did not know me, I clenched my jaw in an effort to keep myself from speaking. I hid my hands within the folds of my robe to prevent my reaching for her.

Her gaze left my face to look around once more, and it came to rest upon the altar. But then her wonderment turned to dismay. She seemed to shrink from Saint Catherine, from that beloved saint I continually implored on her behalf. She took a step backward.

No—do not leave me!

I walked toward her, hand outstretched. "You must place your gift there." I gestured with open palm toward the pile of gifts that had grown throughout that long day.

Her eyes had blinked wide. "I do not have one." Her gaze, gone dark and troubled, met mine.

She did not have a gift? I could assist her in kneeling, I could say for her the prayer, but if she did not have a gift, there was nothing I could do to help.

Her mouth suddenly bent into a smile. "I know!" She put a hand to her hair, which had been plaited with ribands and bound at the end with gold tips. "Will you help me loose them?"

I did not deserve for one moment to touch that glorious creature, but how could I resist her plea? As she stood before me, I pulled the tips from her plaits with trembling hands. Such exquisite torture. I gave them to her and then let my hands linger in her silken tresses, pulling my fingers through the length of them, unknotting the ribands and smoothing her hair across her shoulders.

"Will those do?"

Oh! How I wanted to press my lips to her forehead and

smooth away the care that creased her brow. I only nodded, gesturing toward the pile. Then I clasped my hands together in an entreaty. *Please help me, Saint Catherine. I must not reveal myself.* Not now. Not after all these years. Just a few more precious, miserable hours. Just the span of one long, sleepless night, and then they would be gone.

The girl—*my girl*—had placed her gift in the chest and now, once more, she was looking to me for guidance.

For one who had just days before despaired of speech, I found of a sudden that I had much to tell her. *Do not do as I have done. Value your virtue above your life. Do not let well-spoken words bewitch you.* And yet, if I could have said them, and if I could truly have believed and acted upon them, it would have meant the absence of one whose presence I had longed for my entire life. How our sins do so beset us. And hobble us. And bind us. In the end, I found just one word to say. "Kneel."

She knelt.

And then—bless heaven!—I found more. "Do you know the prayer?"

She nodded and bent her head to pray it as I added my own silent words to her pleas.

So big she had grown. Had I truly thought she would remain forever an infant? I reached out my hand. Did I dare? It trembled as I set it upon her head. I could not bless her as a priest would, but would it be too great a sin to bless her as a mother might? "Bless you, child." May God bless you and bless you and never stop blessing you.

Keep her. Help her. Guide her. Protect her. Save her. *Oh, beloved Saint Catherine, if you would do for her anything at all, please...save her from me.* I would have lit a thousand candles or cast a hundred jewels before the altar; I would have given everything I had to ensure my prayers might be answered.

The girl clutched at my sleeve. "May I?" She was looking at the reliquary. "May I kiss it?"

"Yes." My dear, sweet, beloved child.

She leaned forward and kissed the casket.

And then I did something I had never done before. Something I ought never to have done at all. But I wanted to give her something: something special, something she could treasure, something that could come from no one but me. After making certain no one was looking, I touched the reliquary myself, placing a steadying hand to its side, and then—God forgive me—I lifted the lid.

We stood there, both of us, shoulder to shoulder as we looked inside.

I tipped the golden casket so the glimmering candles' light could reach the depths of the bottom. But there was nothing inside save a mounded pile of dark, granular dirt.

"Is…is that all?" Her words were hedged with disappointment.

Surely there had to be something more, didn't there? Although Saint Catherine had died so long ago… Perhaps this was all that was left. I tilted the reliquary ever so slightly. There!

Besides me, the girl gasped. And then she smiled, candle-light glancing off her even, white teeth. "There it is." She said it so softly, so reverentially, I could hardly discern the words.

When the dirt shifted, it had revealed a small, slender shard of a bone. Saint Catherine's finger.

And then she seized my hand, my own daughter did. "Thank you."

I had thought that would be the end of it, so I found my bed that night, praising God I had not had to face the penance of seeing her father. And I spent those long hours of darkness saying all the prayers I could remember on my child's behalf. But Providence was not so kind as I had hoped. The abbess summoned me the next morning and told me the princess awaited me in the garden.

What madness, what hope, what joy arose in my soul: she wanted me.

But I made myself kneel before the abbess and say what I knew I ought to. "I cannot see her." I had spent the night releasing her into the hands of Providence. How could He then place her back into mine? For just how long would He torment me?

"She asked for you, for the nun who tends Saint Catherine's chapel. She met you yesterday, did she not?"

I could only nod.

"Then there is no other for me to send but you."

"Why could she want me?"

The abbess reached out a hand and touched my shoulder. "She asks not for a mother. She only knows you as a sister. I do not think it would do you any harm."

But then she did not know how much the previous day's encounter had cost me.

Chapter 3

I DID NOT SEE HER AT FIRST. A FOG HAD SETTLED over the garden during the night, and now, warmed by the sun, it was rising in a golden, twisting mist. Putting a hand to my eyes, I tried to peer through that shifting veil.

"Juliana." The word came as if from a dream.

My breath caught in a tangle of emotions.

It was—was it *him*? Was he a memory come to life, my imagination's rendering of my fondest wish? Would he vanish if I turned to address him? I closed my eyes as I turned toward his voice. And then, when I opened my eyes, I nearly cried out when I saw it was he.

But it was a Charles aged and grayed. A Charles with lines etched into his face and deep sorrows in his eyes that had not been there before. I wanted to reach out to touch him once more, but my arms would not move. And neither would my feet. I knew I should step back to remove myself from the temptation of his presence, but I could not do it.

Taking the measure of me, he nudged aside the edge of his mantle, putting his hand on the jeweled hilt of the knife that rode in his belt. Then he placed his other atop it. "You are well?"

No. I had thought myself well once, but I knew then that I would never be well again. "Yes."

Something, some light, some interest, some hope went out of his eyes. "Then I am glad."

Oh, my beloved! If he would speak my name once more, then maybe I would be able to breathe again. What a faithless, fickle bride of Christ I was. "Our…our daughter? Is she well?"

"She is." A smile flickered upon his face and then grew into the mirth I remembered so well. "God has cursed me, for she is the double of you. She is stubborn, and wise…and proud."

Then God had cursed me too. For what had I ever prayed but that she would be as unlike me as day was from night? "She does not know me?" I could not have said how I hoped he would answer.

"She does not." Like a man enchanted, he raised his hand to my cheek.

I closed my eyes. A moment's touch, a lingering caress, and then it was gone. Had I truly felt it? And would I remember it? I had to, for I knew the feel of it would have to last for all eternity.

"My mother raised her. And spoiled her."

Little wonder. His mother had ruined me as well.

"She does not understand she has no choices."

"We all have choices." I was paying for mine every day of my life.

His eyes wandered from me toward the mist-shrouded gardens. "She died, you know. My mother did. Ten years ago."

I had not known. The woman who had saved and raised me, the woman who had mocked and scorned me and then exiled me from court, was gone. Curious strange it was how little that news mattered to me now. "I am sorry for you." I should perhaps have thought of masses and novenas, but all I could think of was the satisfaction on her face as she took my daughter from my arms.

"She asked to talk to you. Gisele did." He gestured beyond me toward the mist.

As I followed the gesture, I thought perhaps I could see her, but then the breeze twisted the fog, and she was gone.

Suddenly, I was afraid to see her again. "I do not—I could not—"

The mist thinned, and we stood, shoulder to shoulder, looking at the daughter we had created. "The abbey is part of her dower. I thought she should have something of her mother's. You left in such a hurry that I..." He shrugged. Then he sighed and turned to me once more. "She asked to come. She wanted to. Said she wished to meet the women who lived here."

But I had nothing left to offer her. Everything I'd had, everything I once was had been subsumed by my life here. By my vows and my veil. And such a poor nun was I that I could not even offer her the benefit of sage wisdom or spiritual advice.

"Are you...weeping?"

What if I was? I was poorer, I was meaner and ruder than ever I once had been.

"After all this time, still, you are so beautiful."

A thousand times I had imagined what I might do or say if I saw Charles again, and none of them had included my crying like a child. Could I not be spared this one last indignity?

He stretched forth his hand. "Juliana—"

I put up my own to stop it. "Do not. Do not touch me." I spoke the words as best as I could through the sobs that choked my throat. My mouth was moving with great, ugly jerks. "Or I will not be able to last this life through."

Ignoring my protests, he gathered me into his arms.

Weeping and trembling, I held myself apart from him as long as I could, and then there was nothing left to do but let him hold me. Hidden from the world by the rising mists of the morning's dew, I like to think we righted whatever had been put wrong between us. He felt just the same as I tucked my head into the spot beneath his chin, and yet, he was so different. "I have heard they call you simple."

"Straightforward. Yes, I know."

"You were not always like that."

"No." He spoke the word as he pressed his cheek to my temple. "I learned it from you. You were never one to say yes when you meant no. After you left, I realized I had lost what I held most dear, because I had been too circumspect. Much better for everyone to know what I am about. Much better to declare my intentions while I still have time, before that chance is taken from me."

The sun, bright and fierce, burned through the last of the mist.

He stilled for just a moment, and then he dropped his hands and stepped away. "I wish you would speak with her."

"What would I say?" What could I offer her that her formidable grandmother and her father could not?

"She is too impulsive."

Too impulsive? That was a fault I could not fix. But I could pray she would become more like her father. That if she did not yet have it, she would come by a will less malleable than mine. I could beg heaven, as I always did, that she would find some kind of peace, some sort of contentment. But how could she not? She was a princess. Her life would be nothing like mine. And that is why I had come to the abbey, why I had left her there with him. I had wanted her to be loved, and I had wanted her to be safe.

⚭

"I wonder what it would be like to live at the abbey. To stay up here in the mountains, away from all the world." She had looked at me with those shining blue eyes that were so much like her father's.

I dropped my gaze, because she was too willing, too eager, wanting, I suspect, to place far too much weight on my opinion. Behind us, I knew her father stood watching.

Pulling my hands up within the folds of my sleeves, clasping myself about the elbows, I thought about what I must say. The reason I had gone was so she could stay with her father. That she might wish to live out her life here at the abbey was a repudiation of all I had done, all I had sacrificed for her, and all I had tried to become. I must not give her any reason to stay. I must not hint at any reason for her to choose my path instead of her own. "A life of contemplation is not for everyone."

"Why ever not?"

I delighted in the fire that shone from her eyes, even though its blaze was directed at me. "It does not suit everyone." It had not, in fact, suited me, because there were some things that should not be contemplated. And in the solitude, in the dark of night, when I had said all the prayers I could say on her behalf, when I had accomplished all the things I could do, it was always those things that pressed in against my soul. "I think, my lady, they must have need of your presence at court."

Her mouth had quirked in a disdain I remembered from her grandmother. "Need of my hand for marriage perhaps." A ray of sun touched her hair, turning it into a gleaming gold.

"They would miss you."

"Not my father. Not anymore. He's taken to wife. A woman of Lorraine." She chattered on for some moments with scorn for the woman.

Agony pierced my heart, but I spoke through the pain. I had looked for so long into the past, I had not ever considered a future for these two people I so dearly loved. When she paused, I spoke the one thing I knew to be true. "Your father loves you, my lady." I could not doubt it. I never had. "Do not despise the life you have been given." Not when it had come at such great cost.

∽

I did not see them again. The bell for prime tolled, and I went to offices with the rest of my sisters. By the time we had finished, they had gone.

Charles had asked me for words of wisdom, but I had given her none. And what had I received? The certain knowledge my child was better off without me. I had been told it before, but it was only then that I came to know the truth of it. I wept along with the pilgrims that forenoon for all I had given up, and all that had been taken from me.

The abbess summoned me after vespers. It was with raw grief and shameful weeping that I entered her chamber.

"You torment yourself, Daughter."

"I do not know how to stop myself from thinking of them. I have so many memories." And now I had these new ones to add to all the rest. Perhaps I loved my memories more than I loved God. How stingy, how sparing my devotion must seem to Him.

"Think on other thoughts."

"But how do you forget the people you love? How do you give them up?"

"By realizing there is One who loves them still more. You must sacrifice your own poor interest in their souls to One whose interests are higher and greater. You must rest in the thought that He can do more for them than you can."

I could not do it.

God help me, I had tried.

✍

Should confession truly free the soul, then I confess I did not hurry to the refectory for the meal on the day of the election.

As always, Sister Isolda read the Holy Scriptures to us as we ate. The table at which the nuns dined was silent. Though I could not discern actual words coming from the novitiates' table, and though I could not have accused any one of them of actually speaking, a restless, ceaseless noise rose from that quarter nonetheless.

After the meal, we who had taken our vows left the others and repaired to the chapterhouse. A clerk waited in the hall, ready to take the news of our decision to the bishop. After we took our seats, Sister Clothild led us in a prayer, and then she stood. "Today we choose a new abbess. I must know, before we proceed, if there is any other who wishes to be considered."

She was the one who ought to have been the new abbess. It was she who had served at the abbesses' side for years, who oversaw the tradesmen and those who worked the fields. It was only for her lack of education that she could not be considered. In every other way she would have been perfect.

I felt an unreasonable surge of anger at her ignorance. She could have managed with a clerk to do her writing, but why had she never learned to read? She had always told me the effort to do so made her ill. She seemed astonished anyone ever could. If she were to be believed, words were sly, changeable creatures, always jumping about the parchment before they could be deciphered. That such an otherwise kind and generous person should evidence such laziness was troubling and—

"Would no one else like to propose a name?" She seemed to ask the question directly to me.

I blinked. Looked to my right and to my left. No one replied.

"Are there no other names we should consider?" There was an edge to her tone that had not been present before.

I had told Saint Catherine I would propose my name if she would take care of the rest of it. I was counting on her to persuade God—and the former abbess—that I had no business accepting the position. But if I meant to make good on my entreaties, now was the time. I lifted a hand, though I kept my gaze fixed to the point at which my robes fell at the turn of my knees. "I think..." Why would the words not come? "Perhaps..." A cold sweat had broken out upon my brow as I remembered what had happened the last time I had taken a position for myself, presuming upon the well-wishes of others.

As I sat there, casting about for words, the sisters stared at me. How could I ever have thought I might be worthy of such a great honor? Why had the abbess even asked it of me? And why had I promised Saint Catherine I would offer myself? "Perhaps...if you would allow me..."

I will never know what I might have said, for at that moment, the door to the chapterhouse swung open, and a man strode into our midst.

Tall and broad-shouldered, he wore a tunic of shimmering silk and a finger ring the Queen Mother herself would have envied.

Sister Clothild stepped toward him. "We are currently holding a chapter meeting. If you take yourself to the hospice, one of the workers there will help you."

"I am not here to stay. I am the Count of Bresse, come with your new abbess."

A gasp rippled through the room.

He pivoted toward the great doors, gesturing to someone who seemed to be skulking there in the shadows.

Sister Clothild replied, and rather sharply. "We have no new abbess, my lord. That is why we meet today: to elect one."

"There's no need. I have already spoken to the bishop. My daughter Aldith will take the position."

Sister Clothild's brow folded in alarm as a hiss went up around the room. "It is not open for the taking. By charter, the new abbess is to be elected from our members."

But he was not listening. He was striding toward that shadowed figure who had not moved from the threshold. Taking the person by the hand, he pulled her forward, toward us, with a frown. "Now then."

The girl was handsome, though still young in years. Her hair fell in waves to her waist, and she wore it uncovered. As we sat, mute with shock, she took us all in through glittering eyes. And then she started toward Sister Clothild.

If I was not much mistaken, she was not too many years older than my daughter. A vision of my girl, on the day she had stood in the garden, rose in my mind. I kept it always close to heart, and during those times when I despaired of life, of ever being able to attain some measure of righteousness, I reminded myself that I was yet a mother, that I had birthed a girl. A girl who, in so many ways, made me almost glad I could not claim her. Should I ever have that honor, I knew I ran the certain risk of vanity and pride.

She tipped her chin up. "Is this where I am to stand?" She asked the question of no one in particular, and the vision of my daughter disappeared. The girl reminded me overmuch of all those thoughtless, grasping daughters of nobility I had known at court. And when Sister Clothild did not move, the girl dismissed her with a wave of her hand. "You may be seated."

Sister Clothild did not move.

The count's daughter pushed past her and sat down in the chair the death of our Reverend Mother had left vacant. She rested her arms on the armrests, caressing the carved ends with her palms. As she looked about the room, her lips crimped in a display of distaste. "I cannot say I like a room as plain as this one, but I suppose it can be remedied."

Her father was still standing in our midst.

She sighed. "I should like some meat and some wine, for I am famished from our journey. And who is charged with supplying you the fire's wood? It is far too cold in here."

Anyone who knew Sister Clothild would have recognized as anger the sparks that lit her eyes. "I think you may have misunderstood." Her head swiveled from the woman to the man. She could not seem to decide who to address. "We cannot elect an abbess who is not from our cloister."

The count did not seem disturbed by that news. "*You* may not be able to, but the bishop had no problem appointing her." He paused to survey us. "You must know your position here is too remote. And quite dangerous. If my daughter is to be abbess, then in return for a portion of your pilgrims' gifts, I will have no other choice but to offer the protection of my men and my many resources to your community."

Sister Clothild's eyes had narrowed as she listened to him. "We have never needed anyone's protection but God's."

"These are troubled times."

The woman in the abbess's chair suddenly leaned forward. "I hope your meals are not as plain as your robes...or this room."

"We have one meal each day at this time of year. And it is—"

"One! That will not do. It cannot be good for the body or for the soul."

Sister Clothild opened her mouth as she turned to the girl. Then she closed it up as she turned toward the count. Finally, beneath a gathered brow, she shot a look at the rest of us and then took her place among us without saying another word.

The girl sat back in her chair with a smile. "I don't know how I am to dismiss you, but I'm sure you all have other things to do. Might I suggest, perhaps, that you go about the doing of them?"

CHAPTER 4

Anna

AUTUN

I TRIED TO MAKE SENSE OF THE WORDS THE PRIEST had spoken, but I could not do it. "She cannot have meant it." How could she have meant it?

My eyes traveled beyond him, across the rush-strewn floor toward the bed where my mother had lately lain. To the curtains she had woven with her own hands and the mattress she had just had restuffed. To that place of refuge and peace, where I had slept with her from my birth, fifteen years before. How could she have intended to cast me from it?

The priest was seated at our table, looking across a parchment at me. Concern was evident in his eyes. "I assure you she did mean it. We spoke of it in great length, and she made provisions for it here in her will."

She wanted me to leave? To go out *there*? Among all those people? "I do not—I cannot—" In faith, I did not know *how*.

"I have already spoken to the bishop, and he is writing a letter for you. He will give it to you tomorrow, in the morning, if you go to confession. That way you can leave early and have the whole day to travel."

So soon? "I do not see how I can leave just now." The servant had not yet even made the bed. The hearth in the center of the room needed to be swept. There was much too much work to be accomplished and too many affairs to be put in order. My hand began to itch at the thought of them all.

I felt the priest's eyes on me.

The room was too bright. I moved toward the window, shivering from the wind that poured in through it, and drew the shutters closed, securing them with a flip of the metal hook. That was better. Only the fire's light remained. A calming, golden, flickering glow. "She has only just died. There are things I must see to. There are people…" So many people. Too many people. Already they had begun to come to the door, keeping the servants busy in tending to them.

"Your mother had debts."

"Then you must pay them. Please. As a priest you must know what to do and who must be paid." My mother had kept meticulous accounts. She was always going over them at night before she retired to bed.

He sighed. "She was quite clear. There is nothing to pay them with."

"But my father was not a poor man when he died. And she herself was an heiress." When they had spoken at such great length, why had she not told him this? I went to the chest and retrieved her accounts. He had followed me, so I placed them into his hands. "She kept a record of everything. If you look, I am certain you will find—"

"Her lands are already encumbered, and your father left debts of his own when he died. I am truly sorry."

"Surely, there must be something." I tried to take the records back so I could look at them. I had never been able to learn how to write, but I knew how to read. Numbers could not be much different than letters.

He placed a hand firmly atop the accounts. "There is

nothing. Which is why she knew this house and all her possessions must be sold. And even then—"

"Sold!"

"Yes."

"But then where am I to live?" My gaze drifted back to the bed. I wanted nothing more than to retreat to its feathery depths, pull the curtains about me, and sleep away my sorrows. "Surely you do not need the bed?"

"Everything that can must be sold."

"Where am I to sleep?"

"The house itself must be sold."

"Then…what is to be done with me?"

He sighed once more. "The pilgrim's way is the only path open to you, and it is what she wanted." He glanced away from her records toward the parchment he had placed on the table. "Once your mother's debts are paid, there will be nothing left. At least on the pilgrimage to Saint Catherine's relic, you will be fed, and your needs can be attended to at the hospices along the way."

I did not understand what he was saying. Was I to leave my home? And if so, for how long? When could I come back? "Even if I went, I could not stay on pilgrimage forever."

"No."

Suddenly, I felt far younger than my fifteen years. "Then what…what am I to do?"

"I think, all things considered, you ought to do as your mother requested. She wanted what was best for you. She wanted you to go on pilgrimage so you could be healed."

❧

The priest left me there with only my memories for company. Mother was gone. And now she wanted me to go too.

I began to tremble. The fire was not hot enough to chase away October's chill. I waited some time for one of the servants to come tend to me, but no one came, so I bent and picked up a piece of wood, feeding it to the flames just the way I had seen them do. And then I added another and another. I stood there for some time in the center of the room before the fire as the flames gorged themselves on a plentitude of wood. But why should they not? The priest had said none of this—not the wood, not the table, not even the bed—was to be mine.

I crouched before it, knees drawn up to my chest as I watched. Its heat enflamed my cheeks. Its smoke furled out into the room instead of up through the hole in the roof, and it set my eyes to weeping. Too late I remembered the dangers of stopping near the fire, and a spark ate a hole through my sleeve. When I stood, I saw my hem had dipped itself into the cinders.

What would my mother have thought of me? The mother who had always insisted that to be deficient in body did not mean I had to be slovenly in appearance. She had always kept me well away from the work of the household, claiming it would only tire me. Even during her long illness, she had never once let me aid those tending to her needs. She had only ever asked me to read to her from the Psalms or recite the prayers she had taught me as a child. To be sure, I had tried to do those things she always had, to accomplish her tasks in her stead, but I could not work the loom, and the spindle and distaff needed a guiding hand I could not give them. I'd had to content myself with my own tasks of feeding the chickens and gathering the hens' eggs, of strewing the rushes and culling nuts for worms.

Why could I not go on as I always had, here inside the house, away from prying eyes? I could find someone to go to market for me. I could ask someone to light the fires and the candles on my behalf. There should be no reason for me ever to have to leave.

Except that I could not stay. My mother had wanted me to be healed. She had wanted me to go pray to Saint Catherine. We had planned to go, together, once she was well.

I went to the window, unlatched the shutters, and cracked one open. On the street outside, people passed as pigs routed in the muck and carts clattered by. There were so many people out there. They were talking, laughing, calling out to one another. As I stood there watching, a pair of them even came to blows.

I opened the shutter a bit wider.

What would it be like to go out there among them again?

I reached up with my left hand—my good one—and felt that hollow, empty place near my right arm where my bosom should be, and then I slid my hand across to the other side. Why should one side be so plump and full while the other was not? What poison lay inside my breast that it had failed to grow?

Perhaps no one out there would notice. Why should anyone find out what I had always managed to keep hidden beneath the folds of my tunic?

As I watched from the window, a child skipped out to cross the street. Midway, he stumbled over a wandering dog. Reaching out, stretching both hands wide, he circled his arms until he had regained his balance, and then he ran off down the road.

Perhaps no one would notice my breast, but how could they fail to remark upon my hand? I held it out in front of me: my useless right hand. Far smaller than my left, only three fingers protruded from it, and those were all misshapen. One, twice as large as it ought to be, had two fingernails at its tip. The second finger had none. And the third finger, pushing up from the middle, was no bigger than my smallest toe. My hand itself was scarred and shiny, the skin stretched too tight, from the time when a priest had plunged it into a kettle of boiling holy oil. And there was a wound that still seeped a clear-colored ooze from the place where the surgeon had cut into my palm, trying to free the fingers he had thought were trapped inside it.

My hand ached with a throbbing pulse in the summer and tingled with a needle's pricking in winter's chill drafts. Never did it let me forget its presence. Always it served as a reminder, as a mark of some sin too terrible to forgive. Fearing that great sin had been her own, my mother had done penance more times than I could count. And now it was my turn to atone for it, to seek redemption from it.

What sort of heinous evil was hidden in the depths of my soul that it had manifested itself in this? This awful, distorted, misshapen body. And why were others forgiven their transgressions while mine forever marked me?

What kind of girl was I that God Himself had scorned me?

And why was my mother making me go out there again?

By myself?

Alone?

That first time, when I snuck out the gate and followed a servant to the market, my mother had not known I had gone. She must have thought me occupied with the chickens. Because she had not noticed my absence, and since no one else had remarked upon it, I did it again. But the third time I was caught. And not because anyone had seen me or stopped me. I was caught because I had wanted to play.

A group of children had organized a game of some sort in front of the church where the market was taking place. I watched for some time, trying to understand how it worked. Once I did, I presented myself to them and asked to join them.

One of them, a girl who could not have been much older than me, looked at my hand and started shrieking. "She has the devil's hand! The devil's hand!"

The other children ran toward the church. From the safety of those heavy, stone-framed doors, they shouted at me. "Go on—leave! Go away!" Only they would not let me. One of the boys came down and shoved me. When I fell to the ground, another one joined him in hitting me. They rained blow after blow upon my head, my back, my legs. A man finally came from the market and drew them off.

He brushed the dirt from my tunic, and then he led me to the fountain and cleaned off my face. When he asked me where I lived and whose child I was, I told him, but he called me a liar. He said my father had no children. I slipped from his grasp and huddled there on the ground by the fountain, bruised and crying, listening to the man berate me for lying, wondering why I had the devil's own hand, until my mother came and found me.

She wrapped me in her mantle, turned me away from the scoffs and the sneers, and took me home. After examining my wounds, she cleaned them and changed my torn tunic for a new one, and then she lay down with me on the great bed. There in the privacy of the curtains, hidden once more from the world, I asked her, Why? Why was I different? Why had the devil given me his hand? And why God had allowed it?

She only wrapped her arms around me and made me promise I would never leave the sanctuary of our courtyard for the city again.

I never had.

After that, everything changed. She must have sensed how different, how closed away from everything I felt, for after that day, whenever she returned from her comings and goings, she took great pains to explain to me everything she had seen and done.

I knew the mayor's wife favored tunics in shades of crimson, with embroidery that circled the hems of the skirt and the sleeves. I knew the baker always kept a bit of my mother's bread dough for himself before he baked it. I knew the mayor's son was hoping to marry the tailor's daughter, and that one of the priests kept an old tabby cat out behind the church. I knew everything about the city, and yet I knew nothing at all. I had been told of the citizens' generosity and foibles, of their births and their deaths, but I had never seen their faces. At least, not that I knew.

Without my mother, how was I to know whether I was talking to the cooper or the blacksmith? Whether I should take great care with my words or whether I could speak freely?

I had kept my promise to her. I had never passed through the walls of the courtyard again. Why, now, was she forcing me to leave?

In all the time I had spent gazing out the window, still no one had come to see after me. Though the house was large and long, it was a single room, and it was clear all the servants had deserted me. I did not blame them; there was no reason to stay. I would have to pack for the journey on my own then. At least it was not difficult to decide what to take. The priest had said everything—Mother's arm and neck rings, her tunics and shoes, our bed, our kettles, the chickens and the cow—was to be sold. I did keep for myself a pendant my father had given her. It was a small cross, enameled in blue, hardly bigger than a walnut. She had other pieces that were much finer, but the pendant was one she had worn always, tucked away on a thong beneath her tunic. I did not think anyone would have noticed it but me. And I did not see how any could begrudge me that one memory.

I found those things that were my own: my other inner and outer tunics, a second girdle, and a handkerchief. My bowl, my spoon, and a cup. A knife. My shoes, a hair comb, and a cloth to place them all in. I wanted to take the psalter from which I'd spent many happy hours reading, but the book might help to pay her debts, and so I left it on the table.

The fire had died as I packed. It felt as if it was time for supper, but no servants were here to make it. I went to the stores myself, but as I looked at the long shelves, I saw there was no food. Perhaps it was just as well. I would not have known what to do with it. I had never been allowed to help in the preparation of meals. My mother had feared I might injure myself. I would have been happy, though, with a bit of bread or cheese.

As darkness fell, I heard the scuffle of footsteps out in the courtyard. A servant come to aid me? My spirits rose, but then the chickens let out a dreadful squawking, and a burst of unsavory language soon followed. Heart thudding, I crept to the door. Wrestling with the bar, I hoisted it up and then pushed it across the door. Opening a set of shutters, I tried to see what was happening, but the angle was wrong, and I did not wish to give away my presence by leaning out, so I pulled the shutters closed, securing them with a hook.

My mother had always warned me about the world outside these windows, telling me I would be safe as long as I stayed behind them. But she had never told me what to do if the world did not respect her commands, if it came inside the courtyard.

I stumbled the length of the house in my haste to fasten

the rest of the shutters. But without the benefit of the outside light, with no fire and no candles, the darkness was complete. When someone banged against the door and then on each of the shutters in turn, I sank to the floor and did not answer.

CHAPTER 5

I DO NOT KNOW HOW LONG I SAT THERE.
Long enough that the voice outside went away.
Long enough that the mice came out of their nests and began
to scamper through the rushes. Long enough that my teeth
began to chatter from the cold. Pushing to standing, I cast
my hand about me, searching for something, anything to
hold on to in that vast expanse of darkness.

Shuffling forward, my toe hit something hard. My hand
quickly told me it was a stool. Arm outstretched, I moved
toward what I hoped were the shelves. Somehow I mis-
judged and walked into the chest instead, striking my knee
upon its corner. But moving on from it, after an eternity of
patting and shuffling about, I found the bed.

I climbed up into it and then slid beneath the counterpane. Pulling it up over the top of my head, I wrapped my
arms about myself, imagining them to be my mother's. And
I began to whisper the prayer we had always said together:
Have mercy on me, O God…have mercy…have mercy. I could
not remember the rest, and so I whispered those few words
over and over until my tongue began to trip itself from
fatigue and I drifted off into sleep.

Though I did not hear the cock greet the morning, a pale
light crept in through the hole in the roof and the cracks in

the shutters. It did not take long for the darkness about me to soften. Slipping from bed, I followed the lightening of the gloom to a window, and then unfastened the shutters, opening them the barest slit.

I shook the wrinkles from my tunic and straightened the braided girdle about my waist, bringing the knot around forward from where it had pressed into my back during the night. Mother had always plaited my hair, for it took two hands to accomplish the task. For this day, I let it fall free. I was not, perhaps, so tidy as Mother would have made me, but it was the best I could do on my own.

When the sun crept higher, I threw on my mantle, and then I went about and opened the rest of the shutters. Pulling the counterpane up, I drew the curtains closed around the bed. I might have left the bedclothes as they were, but it did not seem quite right to leave them in disarray.

All was in order. I had nothing else to pack, but still I lingered.

The last time I had left the courtyard I had come back bloodied and beaten. This time, if the worst should happen or Providence should conspire against me, there was nowhere to come back to. This time, there was no hope of return.

I opened the door and shut it up behind me, then I went to the gate. Pushing it open, I saw it was busy outside, *out there*, on the street. There were too many people and too many creatures and too many carts.

I tried to gather my courage, but I failed miserably.

A pig nosed at the gate, nudging it farther open. A man looked in at me as he passed.

I drew back into the shadows.

The pig squealed as he found the cook's pile of garbage. Another came trotting over to join it.

As I stood there, thinking about leaving, a second man looked in, slowing his pace. Stopping altogether, he put a hand to the gate, drawing it open even wider. Searching the courtyard with his eyes, he sent a furtive glance back over his shoulder before advancing.

And then he saw me.

He started, touched his hat and, mumbling something, moved away, joining the others out on the street.

The pigs moved on as well, snorting and squealing as they went. Knowing I must leave at some point, I followed. As I stepped onto the street, I felt certain someone would say something. That someone would point to me. Laugh at me. Tell me to go on home.

But nothing happened.

Things went on the same way they always had when I had been on the other side of the window, safe inside the house. No one stopped. No one looked. No one even noticed. But even so, it was...different. Viewing the goings-on was not the same as being a part of them. I had not known that a horse was so big or that a child could be so small. I had heard the rattle of carts as they'd passed by, but they sounded so much louder now that I was in the midst of them.

"Hey, girlie. Move!"

I turned around to see a cart coming at me; the man pulling it was red of face, and he seemed not to care that he was about to walk right into me.

Someone grabbed at my elbow and pulled me from his path. But when I turned to offer my thanks, I was nearly knocked over by a horse.

"Are you blind?"

Everything was so loud, and everybody was moving so

quickly. There were too many things to be kept track of. Somehow, I found my way to the side of the road and stood there, trying to determine a safe way to join the throngs. But no one slowed, no one stopped; there was never a break in all the humanity that passed before me. I glanced back across the road at the gate to our house. Going back seemed just as dangerous as moving forward. But in this world beyond the window, I did not have a mother to tell me what to do, and I did not have any servants to assist me.

How did people survive?

Who told them all what must be done?

A man brushed past as if I was not even there, pushing into my shoulder as he went. A dog ambled by and then turned back, pausing to snuffle around the hem of my tunic. Lifting the skirt, I shook it at him. He let out a whine, wagging his tail, and then darted out into the street.

As I stood there, overcome and defeated, bells began to ring.

Was I already late?

Staying as far from the road as I could, I started off in the direction from which I'd always heard bells. Mother had described them to me, the pair of them, sitting high on the roof of the church. If I followed their sound, then I knew I would find the church.

I need not have worried. As I neared the end of the street, wondering which way to turn, a glance toward the sky gave me a glimpse of a steeple. I followed that sight as it bobbed in and out of view, and finally the street opened up onto the market square with its fountain. Reminding myself I had nothing to fear, I walked up the church stairs and then in through the doors, pausing as the light outside gave way to the darkness within.

I took a deep breath and then started forward toward the altar.

Here, at least, I knew what to do. My mother had told me. There, on my right, was the holy water in its stone font.

I bent on one knee, twisted to put my good hand in the water, and then made with it the sign of the cross. There were windows, high above near the roof, but they spread only a feeble light. And even then, far above my head.

It took me a while to find the priest. His dark robes obscured him from sight. When I reminded him I was to go on pilgrimage, he pointed out a second priest, who was sitting in a chair up front near the altar. "You must make your confession before you leave."

I went and knelt before him.

"When did you last confess yours sins, my daughter?"

Relief infused my face with heat. These were the words I was used to hearing. A priest had come to our house each week and listened to my confession. "It has been a week since my last confession. I confess…" I supposed now was the time for truth. "I confess I have great fear." But perhaps life outside the house would be different this time. I was grown now. Perhaps this time no one would mock me or beat me.

"Do you not know what God has said? Fear not, for He is with us."

"But I must also confess I do not think God approves of me."

"God approves of none of us."

Was that true? And if it were, then what was there to hope for?

I confessed to the sin of covetousness, for I longed to keep the bed that would soon belong to someone else. And I confessed that I doubted God's provision, for I still had anxious thoughts concerning the pilgrimage I would undertake. I might have confessed to stealing, but I decided my mother would have wanted me to keep her pendant, and it was so small it could not have mattered very much to anyone but me. As well, I would have confessed to the sin that had disfigured me, but I did not know what it was.

It was not difficult to know why my mother had sent me on pilgrimage to Saint Catherine. No other prayer had healed me. Even so, had she told me what she had written in her will, I would have begged her not to do it. But what else was there for me? No man, no master, would have me with a hand like mine.

The priest assigned the pilgrimage as penance, and then he absolved me of my sins. When I rose, he asked me to stand to the side, where a growing number of people were milling about, waiting on a man who wore a crimson robe. I stood while others presented gifts or made their petitions, and then he turned to me.

"And what of you, child?"

I bowed my head. "I am to go on a pilgrimage to the abbey at Rochemont to pray to Saint Catherine."

"Ah! The heiress's daughter. You have put your affairs in order? You have signed a will?"

"I own nothing." Nothing but what I wore and those few things I carried with me.

"But the poor are always blessed."

I did not feel blessed. I felt sad and lonely.

"Here is your letter." He handed me a folded piece of parchment.

I took it with my good hand.

"Show this to any who ask, and he will know you are a pilgrim."

I nodded.

His brow wrinkled as he looked at me. "Do you not have a proper scrip?"

"A—a what?"

"A scrip. A pilgrim's bag."

"I have this." I held up the cloth into which I had bundled my few possessions.

The priest frowned. "It is not the same."

"I did not know it was required."

His gaze traveled the length of me, from the toe of my shoes to my uncovered hair. "If you are not properly equipped as a pilgrim, I do not know that you can make a proper pilgrimage."

"Please, Your Excellency. It was my mother's dying wish, and I have no home. Everything is to be sold to pay our debts. There is nothing else for me to do."

"Then you must marry." He gazed out around us at the people who were waiting for him, as if looking for someone to agree to take me.

"I...cannot."

His eyes came back to me, his gaze softening. "Have you made a vow to God then?"

"No." God had already made it clear He did not want me. "Please, Your Excellency."

"Your tunic has no cross, you have no scrip. Do you even have a pilgrim's hat? Or a staff?"

"Please. I have none of those, and it is too late for me to come by them now. I could not hold a staff if I wanted to." I lifted my arm and let my sleeve fall back from my hand.

As he saw it, his mouth dropped open, and he shrank from me, making the sign of the cross as he stepped back.

I had deceived myself. Everything was exactly the same as before. Nothing had changed in the world beyond my window. He was just like the rest: he too believed I had the devil's hand. I sank to my knees, letting my sleeve fall down across my hand. "Please, bless me. I wish only to be healed. Perhaps Saint Catherine will hear my prayers and help me."

The people who had been waiting behind me had stepped back at the sight of my hand. The church that had hummed with whispered conversations had stilled. Somehow, this sudden silence was worse even than shouted cries and cruel blows.

I bent, resting my head upon my knees. Was my pilgrimage to end before it had even begun?

A hand touched my shoulder.

I lifted my head and saw the bishop.

"Rise, Daughter. Hand me your pack."

I rose, handing it to him.

Taking it, he walked over to the font. Sprinkling it with holy water, he blessed it. "Lord Jesus Christ receive this scrip, the habit of your pilgrimage, that after due chastisement you may be found worthy to reach in safety the shrine of Saint Catherine, and after the accomplishment of your journey, you may return to us in health." He sprinkled my tunic with the holy water as well, and then he blessed me. I stood there, head bowed, until he stepped away and started back toward the others who awaited him.

"Please, Your Excellency?"

His footsteps paused.

"Where is Rochemont?"

"It is..." He frowned. "Well, it is to the east. In the mountains."

"And how am I to get there?"

"What do you mean *how*?"

"I mean...I mean... Where do I go?"

"You go out through the gate, and you walk. Walk until you get to the hospice at Couches. Spend the night there. Walk until you gain the next one." He turned with a shrug.

I walked out of the church and down the steps into the square. There, I paused. I was far beyond the view from my window now. I had never been past this square before, and I did not know where the abbey at Rochemont was to be found. I did not even know where the walls of the city were. Should I go to the right or to the left?

I went left, away from my misshapen right hand. At length, I saw a stone wall ahead of me. I followed it around to the left and finally found what I was looking for: a gate. As I walked beneath its soaring arches, I left the city and everything I had ever known behind me, knowing only one thing for certain.

I still did not know which way to go.

CHAPTER 6

Gisele

SAINT-CLAIR-SUR-EPTE

*I*T WAS SO BRIGHT. MY EYES CONTRACTED SUDDENLY, painfully, leaving me squinting as sunlight glinted off the river that wound past at my feet. Ignorant of the scores of soldiers who had perished to the north in the battle against the Danes—that vile, evil, wicked race—the River Epte swirled by in lazy currents as birds foraged in the grassy banks. It seemed the world cared not what had happened at Chartres.

I leaned too far forward, and the earth crumbled away beneath my toes and dropped into the water.

A man on the opposite bank came down the tree-lined road toward the river. I stepped back, shrinking behind the willow tree I hoped was hiding me from view. Across the narrow river from our own Frankish camp, the Danes had struck a camp of their own. Only the river's slim, silvered arm separated us from them.

From some distant childhood past, a voice came back to me in a whisper. Along with the memory of a cool hand gripping my arm, and of fingers digging into my flesh.

They'll come back for you if aren't good. Those Danes will come for you like they came to Paris: in the dead of night with seven hundred ships and forty-thousand men. They'll put your father's palace to the torch, and it will be all your fault.

Another voice, another hand. This one gentle, gripping my shoulder, releasing me from the spell cast by those frightful words. I closed my eyes, trying to remember to whom those words and gentle touch had belonged. Not my mother. It could not have been my mother, for I had never known her.

There's no need for fear. The voice had been trying to reassure herself as well as me. *The Danes are gone. Robert the Strong sent them home, to the lands in the north. They will never trouble us again.*

But that woman had been wrong. The Danes were not gone. They *had* come again, bringing strife and death and all kinds of evil with them. They had returned.

I edged away from the tree, just a bit, leaning forward as I held onto a handful of slender branches that had drooped to dangle their tips in the water. I saw the man kneel at the river's edge. In three leaps, I could have joined him. At this place near the ford, the river was that narrow and that shallow. He cupped his hands and dipped them into the water, and then brought them out to clap against his bearded cheeks. The water snaked down his hands and disappeared into the sleeves of his tunic, while the breeze ruffled his fair hair. His ears were a bright, ruddy red, his eyes a light, piercing blue.

The wind skipped across the river, fanning the ripples and bringing with it a curious stench. The smell of dung and something the pagans must have eaten that morn. But underneath those odors was something else. I felt my nose curl. It was something unpleasant.

I let go of the willow's branches, and they closed in front of me. But still, through the leaves, I could see the man splashing about in the water. And I heard him call out. A second and a third voice joined his.

I should not have come. Not this close to the river. And not by myself.

There ought not have been a need for fear. The Danes had been defeated. Robert, the Count of Paris, had taken them at Chartres. They were here to make peace, not war.

I parted the branches and risked another look.

They did not seem defeated. The man was standing now, laughing as he called to the others who stood back by the road, drinking from horned cups. As I watched, they were joined by one I had decided was the chieftain among them, an enormous bull of a man, a veritable giant, whose height was matched only by this girth. His hair was the color of flames, and his beard as well, though it was grizzled with gray. Rollo they called him. It was said that when he attacked Bayeux, he had taken Poppa, one of the noble's daughters, to wife; although in truth, some said she was little more than a concubine. And when they said it, they would send sly glances in my direction and then pretend to apologize when I made it known I had heard what they had said.

Wife or concubine, she had given the heathen two sons. I shuddered to think of being claimed by such a man. Shuddered to think others might ever say those things they said of Poppa about me. In truth, I did not so much care what any *said*... It was their thoughts that wounded me. Their unspoken disdain of a princess born to a king's concubine.

It did not matter. That is what my father told me, and my grandmother as well. But the more they had reassured me, the more I had doubted their words.

A girl without a mother grows up knowing things she should not. As well, she grows up wanting things she could not have. Things no girl could have. And yet, still, I craved them. I would have a proper marriage, there was no doubt of that, but I wanted more than an alliance. I wanted a man who would never cast me aside for another. I wanted a man who would never give me reason to be disrespected. A man about whom none would speak behind their hands. I would not be like Poppa. I ought to have smiled at the thought. I could not be like Poppa, for I was the daughter of the King of the Franks.

As I watched the Danes, contemplating the best way to leave without being seen, a whistle came winging through the air, rustling the willow's leaves. And then something struck the trunk above me with an alarming thump. As I turned, I realized my curiosity had caught me out.

Andulf, my knight, was sitting atop his courser, scowling at me. Though he was older than some of my former knights had been, he would probably still go on to do great things. Beneath his gruff manner, blunt features, and his steel-colored eyes, he had that look about him. Many of my past knights were now in my father's service. I was forever following my father about, and they were forever following me. My father got accustomed to them, and then he came to rely upon them, and soon he had taken my men for himself. There was no quicker way to him than through me, and everyone knew it.

"I was instructed to retrieve you, my lady. And just in time. You look as if you might have wandered across the river to the other side." He nodded toward the opposite bank.

Following his gaze, I realized the Danes had made note of our presence. The large one, the chieftain, lifted his horned cup in our direction.

"Look there, they invite you. Why don't you go? It might lend some interest to an otherwise dull and dreary duty."

Andulf was not the worst of knights. At least he talked to me, even when he did not have to. For a long while, before my father had taken to wife, I was *the* princess. Now I was just *a* princess. One of many…the least of those many. I was a princess no one had need of anymore. Lotharingian blood did not flow through my veins as it did through the others'. I could offer a bridegroom only an alliance with my father, and he had more enemies than he did relations. I could not bring anyone ties to Lorraine, like my half sisters could. No one cared what I did, and I had no honor to preserve. Everyone knew I was common; my mother had been a palace servant.

Even so, at eighteen years, I should have long ago been married, but as loyalties throughout the empire shifted, so did my marriage prospects.

Andulf extended a hand. "We've had word the archbishop is returning."

There would be news of the treaty then! I came away from the willow and clasped his hand so he could pull me up to sit behind him.

He took me back to the villa. As we rode through the palisade, the breeze snapped at the banners that had been hung about, announcing the royal presence. There were horses and squires aplenty in the courtyard, evidence of the counselors who had assembled at their sovereign's behest.

My father's eyes followed me as the horse passed by, and I knew he would speak to me later of my whereabouts.

A shout went up from the gate, and soon the sparkling tip of the archbishop's jeweled miter came into view, followed by his sweat-stained brow, drooping jowls, and then his crimson-draped shoulders.

Andulf gripped my hand as I slid from the back of the horse.

My father did not even wait for the archbishop to approach. He left the villa's colonnaded porch and strode into the courtyard. "Have they agreed?"

I stepped up onto the porch the others had abandoned and leaned against one of the columns.

The archbishop paused, panting, as he grasped his crozier between both hands and clung to it as if he feared to let go. His nephew, a canon, carried the cleric's parchments. They were followed by a fair-haired monk with strangely pale eyes. "They request a three-month truce, Sire."

"A *truce*?"

My father's counselors gasped, and I right along with them. How bold the Danes were to request anything from my father at all! It was their army that had been defeated at Chartres, not my father's.

The Count of Paris scowled. "All the better to rebuild their armies and repair their weapons."

The archbishop was already shaking his head. "They wish to be allowed to return to their families and take in what remains of the harvest before winter."

My father turned toward the count, the jewels of his crown glittering. "You say you cannot fight them, Robert?"

"I cannot." The count said it with such a firm set to his jaw I rather thought he wanted to say, "I will not." But it was my father who was king, not he. And not his brother, Odo. Not any longer. The crown of the Franks had finally come back to where it belonged.

My father replied to the count's obstinate words the way he always did: with a firm and even tone. "Then if we want a treaty, we must believe they speak the truth."

The archbishop stepped nearer. "I think they will agree to a treaty, Sire."

"They will take the lands I offered?"

My father had offered them lands? As if *they* were the victors? I did not understand what was happening. Beside me, I heard a tut-tut. Turning, I saw Andulf. He was watching the proceedings, just the same as I. But I could not care what he thought, for the archbishop was already speaking again. And by the looks of his smile, he was saying something my father would not wish to hear.

"...did what I could, but they insisted they do not want Flanders. They thought it too marshy for their purposes."

I hid my smile in my sleeve before I could laugh outright. Everyone thought Flanders too marshy, the Count of Paris among them. It served no purpose to anyone.

Little Ermentrude toddled out onto the porch, and I sprang forward, looping a finger around the collar of her tunic before she could tumble from it. Her mother, the queen, must not be far. Though constantly breeding, still she was loathe to let my father stray from her side. I pulled the little girl toward me and caught her up around the middle, swinging her to my hip.

She grabbed at the gold tips of my plaits and gave them a tug.

"Not those, little sprite. You will make me immodest."

The count was speaking now. "They should be pleased with your benevolence. After all, it was myself and the other counts who won at Chartres, not them. If anyone should be taking lands for their troubles, 'tis me. Sire."

"But it is not me who pleads for peace, Robert. 'Tis you. I find myself negotiating on your behalf, not my own."

"Then tell them if they do not take Flanders, they will take nothing."

I held my breath. It was not the count's place to tell my father what to do.

"It will not be difficult to get him to agree to a truce." The archbishop spoke the words with a smile, but this time it was a smile of triumph.

My father sent him a sharp glance. "You know this already? How?"

"In exchange for better lands, he will agree to recognize

you as his lord, submit himself to God, forsake his pagan ways, and be baptized."

"All of this? But I have offered him nothing yet to which he has agreed."

I tickled Ermentrude's cheek with my fingers. She squealed in delight, and I followed with a nuzzle from my nose. Was that a smear of honey on her cheek?

"I also promised him the hand of the princess, Gisele, in marriage."

Andulf stiffened as I pulled my nose from the child's sweetly scented skin. What had he said? Had the archbishop spoken of me?

My father was calling him names that would have made even the devils in hell blush to hear. "I want to treat with him, not breed with him!"

The child was tugging at my plait anew, but I could not bring myself to care. What exactly was it the archbishop had said? I hadn't heard him clearly.

"What in the name of God's great throne possessed you to offer up such a prize to that—that—that pagan butcher?"

"He agreed to be baptized, Sire. He and all his men. *All* of the Danes."

"You promised him *my own daughter?*"

My father's counselors had wisely stepped away from him. All of them but the count. He had taken up a position beside the archbishop. They stood together, facing the king, as one man.

The archbishop's smile had not yet faltered. "He said, 'Yes.'"

"He said what?"

"He said, 'Yes,' Sire. He agreed. The terms have all been written." He gestured to the canon, who handed him a scroll of parchment. "He agreed to a treaty, so long as different land than Flanders is given him. *And* he agreed to the marriage."

Why was it that I could not seem to gain my breath? And how was it that it had become so deathly cold?

Andulf glanced over at me and then took the child from my arms.

My father stepped toward the archbishop. "*I* have not agreed to the marriage!"

The count stood between them and placed a hand on my father's chest.

My father knocked it away. "You forget yourself!"

The count withdrew his hand as he inclined his head. "May I remind you, Sire, that I cannot fight them and—"

"If you will not fight them, and if, because of it, I am not to be allowed to keep my own daughter, then you must forfeit something in return." My father, seemingly done with the count, took a step toward the archbishop.

That unfortunate man stumbled back, away from him.

Now my teeth were clattering together. I could not seem to stop them.

Andulf set the child down and pushed her back toward the door of the villa. "My lady?"

My father was still shouting. "You tell that Dane he will find his new lands here, in Neustria."

The count's face went dark as his hand dropped to his knife. "But these are my lands, Sire!"

"He can have all the lands from this river to the Seine and out to the sea. I trust those will be more to his liking." He turned his wrath on the archbishop. "If those are sufficient, then he shall meet me in Rouen three months hence, when you will indeed baptize him and save his piteous, black soul."

The archbishop bowed. "For the glory of God."

My father stared at him for one long moment. "For your glory, Franco. I suspect this has been for your glory all along."

CHAPTER 7

I DO NOT KNOW HOW I MADE IT BACK INSIDE THE villa; my knees were shaking like leaves, and I could not have had my wits about me. Once inside, once I had gained the sanctuary of the royal bedchamber, I waited for my father while my belly twisted with fear. Had I once thought my life sad and sorry? Had I despaired of being forgotten and neglected? How I wished it were now so!

As my father entered the room, I threw myself before him. "Please, Sire. I beg of you, on the grave of your mother, the rightful queen, do not give me to the pagan."

His own queen looked on from her silk-cushioned retreat in the corner of the room.

He sat in his armed chair. When I reached for his slippered foot, he shifted, removing it from my grasp. "What else can I do? I cannot defend my own kingdom, and I cannot control my own vassals. And now I cannot even save my own daughter."

"But the pagan already has sons. He already has a wife! So what would that make me?"

He did not need to answer. We both already knew. It would make me my mother. His face went dark, and I knew I had overspoken. I rose to my knees as I beseeched him. "And—and I was not told. I was not even asked—"

"Nor was I."

"The archbishop cannot expect that—"

"He does."

"But *you* cannot just—"

"What else am I to do?" He passed a hand over his face with a weary sigh. "If I will not agree, they will keep on fighting. Robert may have more men than I do, but in this, he is right. The Danes will keep on attacking. Perhaps not this spring, but surely the next. And maybe the one after that. How many times will Chartres be burned before there is nothing left there to destroy?"

"But it is the count who won the battle. At Chartres *he* was the victor, not they."

"A truer word was never spoken. He won. And now he will never let me forget it. So now he has what he wants, he has a treaty, although I've wrested his best lands from him in forfeit. Lands that ought to have been my own."

My father thought the count's lands and titles ought to be his, just as the count thought my father's crown ought to have been his own. There was no end to the enmity between them. "And what of me?"

He turned a sorrow-filled gaze on me. "You heard the archbishop. He made an agreement."

"Then unmake it, I pray you!"

"And go back on my word? The Danes would mock me. And so would all of my vassals. What man would pledge himself to one who will not keep his own word?"

"But it was not *your* word. It's was the archbishop's—"

"Whom I appointed to speak for me."

"But, wasn't I to marry Rudolph of Burgundy? Or the Count of Vermandois? Is that not what you've always said?"

In her corner, the queen stirred.

"It's what I had always hoped. An alliance with the Burgundians would have been wise. And very profitable."

Would have been? Had he already given me up? A desperate panic took wing in my stomach. "I would rather—I would rather…"

His gaze sharpened as if he were curious to hear what I would say.

"I would rather marry Robert's son Hugh than—"

"Do not say it! Do not even think for one moment I would consent to unite that despicable family with my own. At least the pagan is honorable."

"But, they're—they're *Danes!* They're murderous monsters who do nothing but pillage and plunder. You have not consigned me to some ignominious marriage. You have consigned me to death!"

I had entreated my father to be kind to me. I had appealed to his sense of justice. I had invoked the grave of his mother, the old queen. It had availed me nothing. I was to be offered to the Danes as if it had been my father's idea from the first. Would that I was marshy like Flanders. Then perhaps the chieftain would have no use for me.

My father left me there, prostrate, my pleas resounding from the marble walls. He declared he must dine with his counselors. In truth, I knew he was trying to escape me. He hated me to be angry with him. I could not say I had not used it to my advantage once.

Or twice, perhaps.

I lay there for several minutes, trying to think of what I had forgotten to say, of some other thing I might have used to change his mind, but there was nothing. As I pushed to my feet, I heard something, saw some movement in the corner. Whirling, I expected to see my stepmother lounging there, gloating. But it was not her. It was Andulf sitting upon her cushions, peeling an apple with his knife.

"How long have you been there?"

"Here?" His gaze lifted for a moment from the apple and then went right back to it. "On the cushions? Not long."

I could not decide if I ought to be offended. But how could I fault him for performing the task that had been set before him? Still, shame crept up to warm the tips of my ears, and I wished there were some other society I might seek to join. But there was none.

"They are not married, my lady."

I was too spent to pretend I did not know to whom he referred.

He took a bite of the apple, and then spoke as he was chewing. "Poppa is just a concubine."

Just a concubine. "And you think that makes me feel better? That it should abolish all of my complaints?"

"I did not think—"

"No. You did not. And now you've done nothing but make it all worse. Be gone!"

"You cannot—"

"Go!"

"I can't." He had not even unfolded those long legs of his to try.

A sorry use I was of royalty. Even my own knight would not obey me. "If you do not go now, then you will be full sorry that you stayed." *I* would be sorry he stayed. I would be mortified should he see me give vent to my anger through raging tears and heaving sobs.

"Your father said I was to escort you to dinner when you wished to come."

"I do not wish to dine tonight." I did not want to smile at the Count of Paris and receive the archbishop's blessing as if they had not just sold me for the bounty of a thousand convert souls. I did not want to feel the eyes of all of the nobles upon me or watch the looks they passed me as they wondered what kind of man the Dane was and how ill he might use me.

The knight shrugged as he took another bite.

"Must you eat that here?"

"What else am I to eat? Just because you do not want anything does not mean that I do not."

At such an imminently reasonable complaint, the dam that held back my tears broke, and they overflowed my eyes with the force of fury and desperate fear. "And just because the archbishop promised me to some pagan does not make it right. And just because my father cannot bear to break a promise someone else made on his behalf should not mean I have no opinion about it!" And just because the marriage was part of a treaty did not mean I would become like Poppa... did it? Could it? If she were a concubine, then I would be the Dane's lawful wife, would I not? But as I turned that thought over, I found all I had been clinging to was a flimsy bit of straw. My worst fear was going to come to pass. It did not matter if Poppa was just a concubine. She was with the chieftain just the same. And though he had abducted her, she had stayed with him and borne him sons. She might as well be his rightful wife. And that would make me, in all the ways that mattered, his concubine.

The knight could not say I had not warned him. When I could not staunch the flow of those pitiful tears, he finally picked himself up and left.

∽

My sleep that night was short. My dreams haunted by that

nameless, faceless woman of my childhood and her dire warnings of the Danes. By the time morning dawned and the sun sifted in through the gaps in the shutters, I was famished. Rising before the others, I went out and begged some bread and pickled fish from the kitchen. I ate near the door, out of the way of the servants' preparations, where I could still benefit from the warmth of the fires. I was not the only one about at such an early hour. As I was finishing, I heard the shuffle of footsteps across the courtyard.

They drew near and then stopped just short of me.

It was my father. I could tell by the scents of the lavender that was used to freshen his tunics and the cloves he liked to chew. "I wish you would not weary yourself over the Dane."

It was as close to an apology as I was likely to receive. If I hoped to gain anything, any promise from him, then this was the time to try. I turned and took his hand in mine. "I do not doubt this was the archbishop's idea, and I know it was done without your consent, but I fear for my life. Please. Do not let me become a Saint Lucy or Saint Agnes. Please do not send me away."

We parted, dropping hands, to allow a water carrier to pass.

When he spoke again, his eyes were soft with compassion. "Surely God will defend you."

"He did not defend them."

His face creased with a frown. "There is nothing left for me to do and God could not disagree with this treaty. Why would He not honor a desire to convert the pagans? And in that case, why would He not protect you?" His eyes searched mine for…understanding? Forgiveness? "How could this be wrong?"

The archbishop had brought God into these negotiations, and now my father was doing the same. But I did not want to be used by Providence. "What if it *does* mean certain sacrifice for me? Could we not ask for some sign from God?" For something, *anything*, that would keep me from the Dane.

"A sign?"

"I do not want to act in disobedience, to do something contrary to God's will." I feared that possibility even more than I feared wedding the Dane. To do so would bring swift and certain punishment. "I simply wish to know it *is* the right thing to do." The archbishop had placed the future of Christendom upon my shoulders, and it seemed too weighty a burden to bear. But if this destiny was indeed the design of Providence, then what else could I do but make my peace with it?

"But…how could it *not* be God's will? Think of it, Gisele. The conversion of an entire people!"

"Would you give me leave to inquire of Saint Catherine? At the abbey in Rochemont?"

His frown deepened.

"Just to ease my mind, so I may be certain?" God himself might not deign to reveal His will to me, but Saint Catherine might. "What harm could there be in my going?"

"Why Saint Catherine? Why *that* abbey?"

"I just wish…" I wished, for the first time in my memory, that I was not a king's daughter, that I was not a princess, and that my mother had taken me with her when she had fled the court. I wished I was exactly as the ignominy of my birth should have decreed: I wished I was no one at all. But how could I say that without sounding ungrateful or offending my father, the king? "The abbey is my dower." It was the only thing of value I possessed. "And if I marry the pagan…"

He sighed as his frown eased.

If I married the pagan, I had little hope I would ever be allowed to go there again.

I had traveled there once before. In that place of lofty heights and quiet contemplation, I had known a peace I had never felt before. There, I could pray to Saint Catherine and kiss her relic, she of a noble and pure heart who never ceased to advocate on behalf of maidens and those who died a sudden death. But more than that, I was almost certain if I could just talk to one of the nuns again—not the abbess herself, but the nun who tended the relic—she could calm this fear, soothe this panic that threatened to undo me. Had she not done so before? Had she not had just the right words when I had entertained hopes of abandoning the court? And whether I ought to remain a virgin or sacrifice myself to the heathen, Saint Catherine would not fail to tell me what to do. After that, I would pray for the strength to accept whatever my future held.

"Why could you not just pray at the cathedral in Rouen?"

"Because I want to pray to Saint Catherine." I had cried enough tears the night before. How could I possess still more? And why could I not keep them from staining my voice? "Even if…" Even if. Even if it meant a long journey to the east and the south. Even if the archbishop would not like it. Even if, in the end, it would change nothing. I took in a great breath and tried once more. "The Danes have asked for a three-month truce. Surely I could make it there and back by then."

"It's far too late in the year—" A servant was approaching. Father accepted a cup of wine from him.

I held my breath as he took a drink.

"But then why should you not be allowed to ease your mind?"

Praise God and all His angels!

"I am to meet the chieftain this morning." He took another sip. "You will come with me and—"

"Why must I—"

"Because I say so!"

I took a step backward, away from his wrath.

He closed his eyes for a long moment. When he opened them, he looked even more wearied and worn than he had before. "Because I say so, and it is I who wear the crown and I who sit on the throne of this kingdom. Will no one obey me simply because it is their duty? Must I always and forever explain myself? What other king has ruled a people so stubborn and stiff-necked as these!"

I understood then that it was not I in particular who had incensed him. What other king had had his throne stolen by his father's mistress and then given first to his half brothers and next to a man who had kept it well beyond the day my father came of age? A man who had wanted to give it to his own brother, Robert, Count of Paris, instead?

"My mother, the queen, always said daughters could be of great use." He took another drink from his cup. "But she never told me they could also be so taxing and vexatious."

"You would do well to prepare yourself then, for you have three others, and who is to say this next one your queen is breeding might not be a girl child as well?" I bit my tongue to keep from saying anything more. I had said far too much already.

A warning glinted from his eyes. "You will go to Rochemont, and then you will come back and marry the Dane. If it takes your hand to guarantee his fealty, then it is a sacrifice we both will make."

⁂

Would he have treated his queen's daughters so poorly? Sacrificing them so quickly, so carelessly to a pagan? I returned to the villa and exchanged my linen tunic for an azure-colored silk. The hems had been edged with golden threads that glittered even in the room's dim light. Why should I give the Dane reason to think so easily gotten a treasure was a poor one as well? If he thought me dull or meek, a girl who could be satisfied with careless attentions, then I would show him now, at the outset, he was mistaken.

I stood while my hair was combed and plaited and a golden fillet set upon my head.

Is this how my mother had felt when she'd gone to my father? Had her fingers trembled? Had she felt the same dread? I wondered if she'd had any say in the matter and if anyone ever stopped to ask her how she felt about becoming the concubine of the king. I had never felt a deeper need for her, never wanted her more than I did now. Why had she left me, and where had she gone?

Later that morning, as I left the villa to await my father and his counselors in the courtyard, the archbishop hailed me. I might have pretended disdain or indifference, but my years at court had taught me there was nothing to be gained by making enemies. As I pretended pleasure at his greeting, my father appeared, crossing the colonnaded porch to join us. Together, we walked out past the palisade down to the ford. The heralds trumpeted our coming. And my father's men carried his pennon. His counselors followed behind us.

Across the bank, the Danes were waiting for us, their broad, silver-ringed arms crossed before them. They did not appear to be impressed with the trumpets or the banners. If anything, they seemed...to hate us.

They came in the dead of night with seven hundred ships and forty thousand men. They'll put your father's palace to the torch, and it will be all your fault. In spite of the fine weather and the warming sun, a chill crawled up my spine. I hid my trembling hands within the folds of my sleeves. At the foot of the willow that had screened me just the day before, Andulf was waiting. I accepted his hand as he helped me into a boat; I barely had time to settle myself upon the silk cushion before we had reached the other side. There, we exchanged the sun for leaf-dappled shade.

Behind us, a full contingent of my father's guard crossed the ford on foot, shields in hand, swords glinting.

A grove of trees crowded this far bank, dipping their roots into the water. I was helped from the boat and stood on that foreign shore, blinking, waiting for my father's party to advance as my eyes became accustomed to the gloom.

The trees here were oddly formed. Their branches were misshapen and swollen with large, lumpen cankers. I had never before seen their like. "What are—?" My hand found my mouth as I came to realize exactly what they were. Horses and—and *dogs*? Their throats had been slit, they had been hauled up into the branches, and now they were hanging from the limbs like trussed hams or strings of mottled cheeses.

The archbishop and his party had joined me. Walking behind the archbishop was his nephew, a canon. The monk who accompanied them was introduced as a translator. A Dane himself, he had converted from the pagan religion. He was just as broad as the Danes before us and just as fair, but no fire burned in his eyes save that of the true faith. He spoke in an accented tongue from the canon's side as he followed my horrified gaze. "It's a heathen practice. They sacrifice to their gods to seek favor and blessings."

As I looked around, I realized every tree, and nearly every large branch, dangled some rotting, dead thing that dripped a noxious ooze and buzzed with flies. As the wind gusted from the west, I smelled them too.

My vision spun, and as I faltered. I took a step backward

away from the gloom, away from that dreadful, rancid smell toward the boat.

Toward the river.

Toward the light.

But my father was proceeding beyond us, away from the water. As he struck out, I fell into step behind him. Up ahead, farther down the road, stood a hulking beast of a man: the chieftain, Rollo. He seemed as likely to murder us all as to treat with us for peace.

The translator leaned close. "In our tongue, they call him The Walker, for he is too large to ride even the mightiest destrier."

He was too large for his shield. It looked puny in his hand. He was too large even for a helmet, for unlike the others, he did not wear one.

When my father stopped the procession, the Dane spoke to us in his native tongue. When we did not comprehend, the translator gestured us forward. The guards looked at each other, full of unease. My father hesitated, but the archbishop tipped his crozier in their direction and started out ahead of us all. The trees thinned and soon gave way to a meadow. The Danes had pitched their camp on both sides of the road. There were many more of them, vastly more of them, than I had ever imagined.

Their comings and goings had beaten the meadow into dusty submission. And in the center of that great encampment, a massive fire had been kindled. It burned hot and bright, its dark smoke spreading a stain through the sky and draining the life from the sun, leaving it pale and grayed, a poor imitation of the moon.

That giant-man strode toward the flames. Once there, a second man brought him a bull. Two other men stepped forward to support it as the chieftain slit its throat. Blood spurted forth in a stream that fanned out to either side. Those heathens clamored for it, basking in it, while Rollo took up a bowl and collected some of the blood.

After babbling something over the bowl, he pulled off one of his arm rings, plunged it into the blood and then pulled it out. Thrusting it over his wrist, he shoved it up his arm. It left a dark red smear as a mark of its passing.

Beside me, the archbishop clutched at his crozier as he made the sign of the cross.

Turning from that abominable sight, I pushed through my father's guard and collapsed onto the bent meadow grasses, retching.

CHAPTER 8

NDULF STOOD BEFORE ME, HANDS AT HIS HIPS, blocking me from view of the others. When I was done, he passed me down a handkerchief. It was there the archbishop found me.

"You must get up and show yourself! Do not let fear rule your heart. Remember the faith of Saint Perpetua and the courage of Saint Felicitas."

Saint Perpetua? Saint Felicitas? "But—"

He gripped my hand. "They were pure of body and of heart."

And they had died for it! "They were martyrs!" My intended whisper came out as a shout.

He bent toward me as he looked me straight in the eyes. "And now they have received their heavenly reward."

"For their *earthly suffering!*" Such suffering. Torn apart by wild beasts and then put to death with the sword. "You cannot ask—surely you cannot think that I—"

"It is not *I* who does the asking. It is your father, the king. You must not doubt that you were born for such a time as this. God is sovereign in all things. Even the low circumstances of your birth He has used for His purposes. Just think: your father's other daughters are much too young to be of use. Clearly even the king's youthful indiscretion was meant for good."

But I was not good. I was not even especially devout.

"The chieftain has promised to be baptized. What could be greater than leading a pagan people to God?"

Many things. Everything I valued and held dear was greater than being joined in marriage to such a barbarous brute. "I do not think my faith is great enough to—"

His eyes flashed. "The king is not in a position to dither about this treaty. He is bound by Saracens to the south, while the Saxons are ever restless in the north. And to the east, the Magyars are rumored to be on the move. But if he can count on these Danes to aid him, then perhaps he can triumph after all. You must look beyond what you see. You must fill your heart with hope and faith."

He was right. Surely he was right. I durst not believe he was wrong. Perhaps this was something God, in His mighty Providence, had decreed for me. And for my father.

He grasped my hand in his.

I kissed it.

"Take heart. This is what you were meant for."

"But I am not valiant. I fear what may happen to me once I wed the Dane."

"Better to fear for your life than for your soul."

Were they so very different? Was not the one married to the other? He sent a look back over his shoulder to where two different peoples awaited me. "Is your life so very dear? Do you consider it more precious than these thousand souls?"

Did I? I supposed I must. Was it my great vanity or my small faith that kept me from feeling honored that I could be used in such a way? In truth, my skin crawled at the thought of uniting myself with the Dane. How was it that the archbishop and my father could see my path so clearly, when I could not see it at all?

He gripped my arm, pulling me to standing, and then trundled me back toward my father. "Hush now. The king speaks."

I could not hear my father. Not clearly. But it seemed he spoke no more than several sentences before gesturing through the crowd toward me.

His men fell back, leaving me exposed to the gaze of the chieftain.

Beside the Dane stood the archbishop's translator. "He wishes to marry now, in honor of the agreement."

On their side, the Danes had moved closer to the great fire. One was adding hanks of grass to feed its flames.

Now? "No! I—"

The archbishop tightened his grip on my arm, pulling me forward toward my father, who was speaking in reply. "No. During the truce, the princess will journey to the royal abbey at Rochemont to seek there the will of God. You may marry in three months' time at Rouen, after you have been baptized."

There was no little discussion between the Dane and the translator before they seemed to come to an agreement. The translator spoke. "He says the girl will not make the journey."

My father turned to the archbishop. "I told her she will be allowed to petition Saint Catherine, to assure herself this is God's will."

The archbishop's mouth tightened as his gaze narrowed. "And I told him she will be his in marriage."

"*After* the pilgrimage."

"I gave no such stipulation."

The fire was now shooting sparks and sloughing billowing clouds of smoke. I tugged at my father's sleeve. I would have gone down on my knees if it would not have been unseemly.

"Please. *Please*, do not make me marry him." The Dane's eyes had not once left my face, but I did not care if he saw me begging.

My father glanced down at me and then back to the archbishop. "She will marry him after she has made her pilgrimage to Saint Catherine. It was they who demanded the three-month truce, and so it is they who will have to wait." He lifted a hand when the cleric would have spoken again. "That is all I have to say." He turned to leave, though he paused as he passed the archbishop, speaking to him in a lowered voice. "I have little taste for this. Either they will agree, or they will not."

The archbishop frowned as beads of sweat broke out on his brow beneath his miter. "Wait. Just—just for a moment." He gestured to his translator and consulted the monk in low tones. The translator spoke to the chieftain, who answered with a rapidly rising volume. The translator finally returned and spoke with the archbishop, who relayed the message to my father.

"He says he will wait."

I found I could breathe again, though only with great effort.

"But the princess cannot go to the abbey."

"He has no say in this. Not if he wants a truce. And they will not wed until after he has been baptized. I will not risk God's wrath by wedding my daughter to a pagan."

The count had been silent throughout the negotiations, but now he stepped forward, bowing. "Sire, I have not asked you for money, and I have not asked you for men. But I do ask you this one thing: I must have a truce. I cannot fight them."

"You must have a truce, he must have my daughter, and my daughter must pray to the relic of Saint Catherine."

Sweat had made a trail down the archbishop's face. "I gave my word, Sire."

"And apparently you gave mine along with yours!"

Behind us, my father's guard parted as a page approached. The lad swept off his cap, bowed, and then handed my father a missive. Father broke the seal and parsed it. Then he refolded it and passed it to an abbot, who gave it to a clerk.

After a glance toward the chieftain, he clapped the archbishop on the shoulder. "I shall give the Dane the lands he asks for, but I shall not give him my daughter unless Saint Catherine wishes it."

"But—" The archbishop's protests were stayed by a squeeze of my father's hand.

"The chieftain will agree, or he will not. Go and inquire."

We waited while the autumn sun grew hotter and the birds ceased their swooping hither and yon, preferring their shaded nests to the bright sun. And still the archbishop and his translator conferred with the Dane.

My father finally stopped his pacing. "Enough. If he does not agree, he does not agree." He caught the count's eye. "I will entrust these proceedings to your care, Robert."

"I must beg you, Sire, to consider that—"

I pulled at my father's sleeve. "He comes."

My father glanced over at me. "What is that?"

"He comes. The archbishop comes." And the chieftain with him.

The cleric's smile was triumphant as he lifted his crozier. "He has agreed!"

My father sprang forward as if longing to be gone from that place. "Then they may have their truce, and we will meet in Rouen at the end of December."

The translator passed the message to the chieftain, who grunted. "He agrees."

It had not sounded like an agreement to me. And behind

the chieftain, there was much low-voiced murmuring among the rest of the Danes.

"Then we will seal the agreement." My father stepped toward them and then stood there, hands at his hips, one foot poised before the other.

The archbishop spoke through the translator, gesturing toward my father.

The Dane looked at my father's foot and then shook his head.

The archbishop spoke once more, pointing at my father's foot.

He shook his head again and made a show of putting his hand to his sword.

My father sent the cleric an accusatory glance. "You said he had agreed."

"I assure you he did. He does." As the archbishop was speaking, the monk pantomimed getting down on his knees and kissing my father's foot.

The Dane responded with a barrage of angry words. Then he turned and spoke to his compatriots, pointing to my father and then at his own foot.

A rumble passed through the pagans. They stepped forward as one, hands at their swords.

My father's men responded in kind until my father lifted his hand and addressed himself to the archbishop. "Then he does *not* agree?"

Someone behind the chieftain hooted. Another man picked up the sound, and soon the rest of the men had caught up that strange, wild cheer. It set the hackles at the back of my neck on edge.

Andulf stepped in front of me as he drew his knife from his belt.

My father placed his hand atop it, raising his other as if in supplication. "I have come here freely, and they have treated with me freely. If they have objections, then they must make them known."

The monk ignored the archbishop completely and spoke directly to my father. "The objection is to the gesture of obeisance, Sire."

The Dane had pulled one of his men from the crowd, and now he thrust him forward, toward us. The man turned and said something to the chieftain. That giant of a man unsheathed his sword and pointed it toward my father.

Around us, all had fallen silent.

Though the Dane did not take his gaze off his man, he spoke to the translator with words both clear and slow.

The monk's face flushed, and he cleared his throat before speaking. "He says this man will kiss your foot, Sire, in his place."

"No." My father did not hesitate in his reply.

The chieftain pressed the tip of his sword into the man's chest.

That man lifted his chin, though he held his ground. He looked as pleased with the chieftain's idea as my father had been.

"If the chieftain will not honor our agreement, then neither shall I."

No man on either side seemed even to breathe.

The translator did not bother to pass on the message as the chieftain abandoned the threat of his sword and gave his man a mighty shove.

My father's jaw went tight. "Robert will receive the show of fealty in lieu of me."

The count's face went pale and then flamed with sudden ire. "Sire, I must—"

"You must do what I command if you wish to have your borders protected."

His face devoid of all emotion, Robert bowed to my father and then walked toward the Danes. Sweeping his mantle behind his shoulder, he posed, one foot in front of the other.

The chieftain's man took a long look at us, hate gleaming from his eyes, and then turned his attentions to the count. He took his measure from tip to toe, and then he spit onto the ground.

The chieftain barked something at him.

The man's mouth twisted into a grimace. Just when I thought he would refuse to do it, he bent. But instead of pressing his lips to Robert's foot, he lifted Robert's foot to his mouth.

The count stood there, teetering for one long moment, arms thrashing in desperate search of balance, and then he tumbled backward to a roar of derision on the side of the Danes.

On our side there was laughter also. The archbishop was smirking, and from several of the nobles came outright guffaws. Even the eyes of my knight, who stood beside me, were dancing with mirth.

Only two men, save Robert, found no amusement in the count's humiliation: my father and the chieftain. I hoped it was not an omen of things to come.

The count refused any aid and came to his feet, hand on his sword.

My father caught him by the forearm, though the count tried to shake him off. "There has been enough of this posturing. You wanted your treaty, and you shall have it. Was that not the purpose for all of this?"

Robert bowed and released the grip on his weapon, though his eyes still glittered with rage.

"These pagans do not understand our ways. It will be in your best interests, Robert, to find some tolerance for your new neighbors."

"I will tolerate nothing but adherence to the treaty!"

"Enough! Sometimes overt hostility is better in an ally than hypocrisy and covert treachery. At least you know where he stands."

Robert's gaze dropped, and when my father put forth his hand, he was slow to kiss it.

As I glanced over toward the Danes, I saw the chieftain eye me. I stepped behind Andulf to save myself from his gaze.

My father's guards and counselors followed us down the road, through the trees, to the river's edge. When we reached our side, my father asked the archbishop to join us in the walk to the villa. "I have received a summons from the court in Lorraine. I may be away for some time."

He was leaving? Now? After he'd just promised me to the Dane?

He grabbed the cleric's crozier when the man would have kept walking. "It is you, now, who must find a way to keep all the promises you have made."

"Sire?"

My father nodded back toward the other side of the river. "The terms have been agreed upon. We will await Saint Catherine's blessings, and I shall return in December."

Though I would soon be leaving as well, knowing my father considered the matter settled made me uneasy. But the archbishop nodded assent, and my father passed us both as he strode toward the palisade.

I would have asked him to wait, would have asked him

not to leave so quickly. Indeed, I hurried up the road after him, but I soon realized my entreaties would have done no good. While we had been with the Danes, the household had been hard at work. The queen's cart was waiting in front of the porch, and its silk canopy, buffeted by the wind, shimmered in the sunlight. One of her men was helping her into it. A groom awaited with my father's favorite horse.

As my father mounted, despair and panic scoured my stomach. I had never been left before. Always, I had gone with my father. I had been his constant—his favored—companion. Until now.

"Do not leave me here alone!"

Father turned in his saddle, regarding me with a curious curl to his brow. "I thought you wanted to go to the abbey." He prodded his horse and rode toward me, leaned down and put a gloved hand to my cheek. "The Lotharingians have offered their throne to me. It is what I have been hoping for, and I cannot delay."

Of course he could not. Lorraine was the beloved homeland of my great-great-great-grandfather Charlemagne. If father could take their throne, then he could unite the rest of the empire. Of course he must go.

"Perhaps you should speak to the nun there, at Rochemont. The one who tended the relic. It seemed to do you some good before."

I clutched his hand. "I will."

"May God go with you. I will see you when I return." He left in a flurry of dust, taking all of his men with him.

My father had not been gone long when Andulf found me. I was instructing my maids to pack for my own journey. No good would come in delay. The mountains would soon be ringed in snow.

He made a desultory swipe at a buzzing fly. "The king should not have left before concluding the treaty."

I paused in my task. Was he conversing with himself, or was he addressing me? "He did conclude it." As much as there was to conclude before I made my visit to Saint Catherine.

"Then why did the archbishop summon the Dane, my lady?"

"What do you mean?"

"After your father left, the archbishop summoned the Dane."

I could think of no good reason why he should have done so. And even those reasons were discarded when I left my chamber and slipped into the great hall. The chieftain was there, towering above the others. In some uncanny, heathen way, he must have felt my presence, for he suddenly turned and raised his cup to me.

My knight stepped forward, to my side.

The room was not even half-filled, and even then there were only the count's men-at-arms and a few clerics. The count himself had chosen to stay at the villa. It was not unexpected, since these lands in Neustria had fallen under his protection, but he seemed to have claimed the estate just as surely as he'd tried to claim the throne. His banner now had the place of honor, and his men the best seats at the banqueting tables.

As I walked into the hall, the archbishop's translator had turned from the Dane to relay a message to the count. "The chieftain will wait until December, but the girl will not go to the abbey. She will stay with you in Rouen."

I could not keep myself from speaking. "That was not the agreement! I am to inquire of Saint Catherine at—"

Not one of them acknowledged I had spoken, save the Dane, and he looked at me with such ill-concealed interest that I soon wished I had not. But I could not let them disregard the agreement my father had made. "I am to go to Saint Catherine at the abbey in Rochemont. That's what my father, the king, commanded."

The archbishop's translator glanced away from the archbishop toward me. But it was the count who spoke. "The Dane will not allow it."

Not allow it? "He already agreed to it."

"He fears an early winter. He does not wish to lose you along the way. Nor do we, my lady."

I might have been charmed by his sentiment, but it was clearly an afterthought.

The Dane was staring at me again, and in a gathering where he towered above every man, it was difficult to ignore him. A flush swept me from head to foot.

The count's smile was perfunctory. "We do not dismiss the king's command. In lieu of your journey to the abbey, the relic will be brought to you."

How could it be brought to me if it were in the chapel at the abbey? Besides, I didn't want the relic. I wanted to know God's will. "There's no need. I simply wanted the chance to ask Saint Catherine if—"

The archbishop responded with a pinch of his mouth. "If Saint Catherine blesses the marriage, then she will allow her relic to be moved to Rouen. My nephew, the canon, will be able to go and return much more quickly than you would."

I eyed the canon.

"It will save you the journey."

But I did not want to be saved the journey, and I did not want the relic here. I wanted to go *there*, to the abbey up in the mountains. I wanted to experience, for one last time, the peace that had seemed to reign there, and I wanted to speak to that nun again. In spite of all reason, in spite of her having spent her life at the abbey, I felt certain she would understand.

But the count was already speaking to the translator, and the archbishop was all but ignoring me. The translator's gaze wandered to me as he listened to the count and then, once the count was done speaking, he verified the message he was to pass to the Dane. "There is no reason for the princess to journey to the abbey. If Saint Catherine agrees with the marriage, the baptism, and this alliance, then she will allow herself to be brought here."

Robert nodded, and the translator turned toward the Dane. Had not one of them listened to me? "But—"

The archbishop sighed as he rubbed at a spot beneath his ear, tilting his miter precariously to the side. "Is this not what you wanted? A chance to let Saint Catherine decide?"

"Yes... but I do not think that—"

The Dane was pulling some rust-stained ring from his arm and offering it to the translator.

The monk shrunk from the giant, shaking his head.

The Dane grunted and then moved toward us, trying to give it to the archbishop. It was then I saw it for what it was: that metal arm ring he'd dipped in blood back at the meadow. The streak from it still marked his arm. When the archbishop would not take it, he thrust it toward me.

I side-stepped him as Andulf moved to stand in front me. But though I sought the count's help, he refused to look at me.

I beseeched the translator. "What does he want me to do with it?"

"It is a gift. This means you belong to him. He wants you to put it on."

CHAPTER 9

Juliana
ROCHEMONT ABBEY

I WANTED TO THINK THAT PERHAPS THE NEW abbess's coming was evidence of Saint Catherine's intervention on my part. The abbess might be young, and she might be preoccupied with things other than God's service, but had not the Almighty been known to use just those kinds of people for His purposes? And it was not unknown for churchmen to ally themselves with nobles like her father. As the Count of Bresse had said, these were troubled times.

But the count's presence—his silk robes, his golden finger rings—had returned me to memories of my youth. And a small, increasingly strident voice inside my heart kept insisting men's plans often had nothing to do with God and everything to do with their own gain. But even so, it was not difficult to convince myself none of that mattered…except when I remembered I had not truly fulfilled my promise to the abbess. I had not spoken; I had not, in fact, offered to lead as she had asked me to.

But what was I to do about it now? The new abbess had been chosen. The bishop had confirmed the choice. Both man and God had presumably acted, and done so in concert. Although in between the offices and on the way to the refectory for our meal, quite a lot of words were being exchanged between the sisters. And not one of them saw the abbess's coming as the will of God.

If she were a king or a pretender to the throne, I might have worried. But our abbey was not a kingdom. Our doings did not affect the world beyond our gates. And the abbess herself was not immune to God's great design. If He had let her be chosen, then there must be some reason for it. That is the thought I clung to in order to push the other away: the idea that I was responsible, that I should have spoken. That I should have been the one sitting in her place.

I contented myself with Saint Catherine, trying not to care overmuch for things beyond my control, but the abbess made it increasingly difficult. She was haughty. She was discourteous. She was unkind. And she brought with her to the abbey a type of company we were not used to keeping.

Her family, her father, and her brothers, the nuns might have overlooked. *I* might have overlooked. But there was a young nobleman among them who, if I was not mistaken, looked on her as if she were not a nun. As if she had not given herself to Christ. I might have warned her that God is a jealous bridegroom and man a capricious companion, but she did not seek my approval nor my advice.

I tried to coax myself from my suspicions, and truly, I had almost succeeded, when I came upon them one night after compline. In the darkness cast by the overhanging cloisters, they were entwined in a lovers' embrace.

I closed my eyes, fearing that if I opened them, I would confirm what I thought I had just seen. And then, starved for passion, for the sensation of desiring and being desired, I opened them and watched their frenzied gropings. And I remembered it all then: the birth of desire, of passion…and of love.

✑

Charles caught me while I was going up the stairs with a ewer destined for his mother's evening ablutions. He was coming down with his retinue of nobles' sons. I pressed myself against the wall to let them pass, but he saw me and halted them all.

"Juliana! Did you hear it? Did you hear?"

Not certain how I must respond, I curtsied as normal to give myself time to decide how to reply. "Yes...Sire."

"Sire!" He chortled. "How good it is to hear that word! Finally, I am to be king!" His grin was wide, his tone exultant. He grabbed up my hand and swept me along with them, down into the great hall where they began to dance and drink themselves merry.

I stayed for a while, to enjoy his good spirits and see him rewarded for his many years of hopes and his mother's extraordinary efforts, but then I knew I must leave. I was wanted upstairs, and my absence must have long ago been noted. Skirting the party, I made once more for the stairs, but there, he intercepted me.

"Don't go."

"Charles, I have to. Your mother awaits."

He took the ewer from my hands. "For once, can you not forget about her and please me instead? Come dance with us; come celebrate."

"I did. I have." Perhaps I had not in actuality danced or partaken in the festivities, but I had watched. "And now I must go." I reached for my ewer.

He held it up, just out of reach.

"Charles!" I took a swipe at it, but he raised it even higher at the last moment.

"Please, Juliana." He lowered it, clasping it to his chest. "You of all people must understand how much this means to me. How can I not exult when what we have waited for these many years has finally come to pass? And why should you not celebrate with us?"

My gaze wandered from him to the knot of nobles and hangers-on who reveled just behind him.

"One dance. Please. That's all I ask."

I looked again into the eyes I knew so well. Into that face I'd seen every day for all of my fourteen years. The long jaw. That noble nose. The eyes that so often danced with amusement. Like brother and sister we had always been. How could I refuse him? "Just one."

As the music began a new melody, the circle parted to make room for us, pulling us around the large hall. That first dance turned into a second, and the second into a third. How could my heart not be glad my childhood companion had finally received what was his rightful due?

As the third dance came to an end, I pulled my hand from Charles's.

He turned, reaching after me. "Don't—"

"I must go."

And I should have done so sooner rather than later. His mother was in a state by the time I arrived. The tops of her cheeks and base of her throat had flushed a bright, splotchy red. "Has everything gone topsy-turvy? Does it require a battle now to draw water?"

"No, Your Highness."

"Then where is it?"

"Where is...?"

"My water!" She pulled her lips into a thin, flat line, sending furrows racing from her mouth down toward her neck.

Charles had set it down when we had gone to dance, and in my haste, I had forgotten to collect it. "Forgive me, Your Majesty, but—"

"*Forgive* you? Everybody is celebrating my son's news but me! Even *you*, I suspect."

I put a hand to my reddened cheeks and tried to calm my ragged breath. "But is it not wonderful, Your Majesty?"

"Wonderful? What would be wonderful is if I were down there with them! What would be wonderful is if he had the crown on his head right this instant. Or if he actually had a throne to sit on! What would be wonderful is if my maidservant stopped acting as if she were my equal instead!"

"I'm sorry, Your Majesty!"

"Stupid girl! Sorry is a state of being, and right you are in thinking it applies to you."

Tears stung my eyes. I dipped into a curtsy. "I will go and—"

"Yes, go. Be gone with you! When I took you up, I had hoped you would turn into a fine servant. Now I can see I am destined to disappointment."

"I'm sorry—"

"Then take your sorry self away. Do something useful. Fetch me my water!"

I tore down the steps, tears blinding my eyes. I tried—how desperately I had always tried to please her. One would think on this day, at least, she could not be out of sorts. She had worked, ever since I could remember, to get the throne back for her son. Why could she not just be happy?

I stumbled on a step, and my foot slipped, sending me down the next two steps on my buttocks. That seemed about right and as rude as the position I now found myself in. My sole friend was bound to leave me behind, and my mistress was not likely to improve. And so I indulged in a luxury: I gave myself over, for just a few moments, to my tears.

That's where Charles found me.

"Juliana?" He bent and offered me a hand.

I wiped at my tears with the sleeve of my tunic.

"What is it?"

"Nothing. It is nothing."

"*It* cannot be my mother, can it? I'm sorry. Did she scold you?"

I did not wish to dampen his high spirits, but I could not lie, and so I said nothing.

"Juliana?" He put a gentle hand to my face and tipped my chin so I had to look at him.

I tried to turn my head, but he would not let me. "She did."

He sat on the step beside me.

I felt a surge of furious, perverse anger. "You had to know she would."

"I'm sorry."

A pair of tears slipped down my cheeks as I gathered up the skirts of my tunic, preparing to stand. "You're not forgiven."

"I am not—?"

"She was...*horrible*." My lips wobbled. "You know how she is. You knew, and still you kept me. I told you I could not stay and—"

"I'm sorry. I didn't mean—I did not think—"

"It's fine." I turned away so he couldn't see the tears descending in streams down my face.

But he would not let me leave. He stayed me with a hand to my shoulder. "I said I'm sorry."

"You're always sorry, and still you always seem to get me into trouble."

"It's just that—don't—don't cry. Please don't cry."

I swiped at my tears. "I'm not crying."

"Please don't." He pulled a handkerchief from his belt, took me by the jaw, and tipped my head up toward the torch's light so he could see. And then he dabbed at my tears. "I just—I wanted you there. You're the only one who truly understands. The only one who knows how it was to wait and hope those many long years."

Perhaps. But now there were many to share his good fortune. The palace was filled to bursting with them. "It seems to me as if you have friends aplenty now."

"Don't cry. Please." He'd stopped dabbing and was staring into my eyes. "You're so...beautiful."

A flush rose up and swept across my face. "Beautiful?" I meant to scoff, but the word came out in a whisper.

"Just—just let me—" He bent forward, putting a hand to my neck, and gave me the softest of kisses. That was when I lost my heart to him. It must have been. For when he found me later that week, I followed him out to a dark, deserted corner of the palace, and there we kissed again.

It soon became difficult to find a place to be alone, for every day, more were being added to the numbers at the palace. But our childhood wanderings through that place did not fail us, and most of the time we were able to steal a kiss or two between my tasks.

It was so new and magical, the spell that had come over us. It had to have been an enchantment. I have nothing else to attribute it to. For why else should I have yearned for a boy I had known all my life? How else could what happened be explained?

I had been bewitched, and so had he.

His mother must have suspected, for she kept me busy, running between the floors, going from one side of the palace to the other. But still, somehow, Charles always seemed to know where I was. And before long, where one kiss had suited, when one caress had sufficed, I found I needed more. We both did.

"Don't make me stop," Charles groaned late one night from his cushions as he reached for me.

I pushed his hands aside. God help me, I did not want to, but I knew I had to. "You must." What in heaven's name were we doing? And why did I want so badly to continue with the doing of it?

"I mustn't do anything I do not wish to now. Didn't you hear? I'm to be king at last."

I broke away from his embrace, though I was curiously unsteady in the doing of it, and I could not seem to get enough air in my breathing. "But even kings must care what people say about them." Or at least their mother's maidservant must. I made sure to keep plenty of distance between us.

He pushed up on an elbow and came after me. "Don't go, Juliana. Not yet."

I could hardly dare to look him in the eyes, this boy, my childhood friend now become a man. Was my hair hopelessly ruined? I put a hand up to feel the length of my plaits. "Your mother must wonder where I am." My cheeks were flushed, I could feel it. I hoped she would not notice.

"Just tell her you're attending to your king."

"Charles." Shifting, putting a hand to the collar of my tunic, I tried to straighten everything that had been set askew by the goings-on between us.

He crossed his arms behind his head as he lay back on his bed, grinning at me.

I couldn't help but return it. What a fine expanse of chest he had.

"Don't I need attending to as well?" I could tell he meant the words to be enticing.

Perhaps then I could be forgiven for not having moved quite far enough away, for not reacting swiftly enough when he rose and took me in his arms once more.

"Juliana."

I could not help it. I knew, of course I knew, the thing we did was wrong. I had no doubt it was against God's holy commands. But I could not help myself. Companions we had always been, Charles and I. This was simply another step along life's path we had decided to take together.

After, when our passion was spent and I was trying to decide why I did not feel shamed or even very guilty, he rolled from me and tucked me into his side, planting drowsy kisses on my neck. "When I claim the throne, then you shall be my queen. Make no mistake about it."

I had not. I did not.

Not through the long days of service to his mother, nor through the procession of short, stolen nights spent in his bed that followed. Had I ever even thought to doubt his love, I would have been assured of it when I confided to him my secret hope and greatest fear. I was with child.

He had taken my hands in his. "Are you certain?"

I nodded.

"Oh, my sweet love." He slipped from the bed, bent on one knee, took up my hand, and kissed it. And then he'd picked me up from the bed and carried me about in a merry jig.

I clung to his neck, laughing.

"A prince! We are to have a prince!"

I kissed him full on the lips. "Or a princess."

He kissed me back. "And now my mother cannot keep you to herself. We shall marry at once."

❧

If we had married as he said we would, perhaps things would have been different. But then perhaps he would never have been king at all.

Surely, I had been cursed by my memory of those days long past. And surely I was not a true penitent. If I were, would I not refuse to pull those memories out at night, turning them this way and that, like the finest of jewels? If I were, would I not feel shame at the remembered warmth of those stolen kisses? Would I not have stopped waking in the middle of the night with the feel of Charles beneath my fingers?

I brought them, trembling, to my face. My soul was in such desperate need of salvation. This I knew, and yet I could not seem to find it within myself to submit to saving grace. For if I gave up all my memories, then what would I have left?

"You there!"

The abbess's imperial voice startled me from my thoughts.

She pushed the young man away, letting her skirts fall back into place. "Forget what you have seen."

I could not do that. And I knew she would not be able to either.

Walking back to the dormitory, I tried to push my thoughts of Charles away. As always, they did not go far. They came flooding back to me as I lay down on my pallet and shut my eyes.

Such heady days of sweet love those had been.

I might have expected to be secretly scorned, discounted as a servant simply keeping the king's bed warm, but Charles must have made it known how he felt about me. Dressed in robes of silk and clad in embroidered slippers, I was relieved of my duties as a maidservant and installed in his chamber. But...I did not know what to do with myself. Clearly, I was not expected to wait on anyone anymore—at least no one besides Charles—but I could not bring myself to consort with those daughters of the lords I had once served. I contented myself with waiting for Charles's visits and dreaming about the babe who was to be born.

There was immense competition for position as nobles flooded the court. The order of precedence was constantly changing. And though Charles wanted me always by his side, I had no position at court. No one was sure quite what to do with me. My presence made life much too complicated.

I tried to excuse myself from most of the official occasions, but Charles would not hear of it.

"Why should you not come?"

"I am not wanted, Charles."

"I want you, and I am the king, so it's decided."

In truth, I hated being noticed by anyone for any reason, for I knew what people were thinking. They were wondering why I had been so blessed by Fortune and how long I was going to last. If we had been married, it might have been different, but there was strife on every front. Though Charles had been crowned king by the archbishop of Reims, Odo had no intention of relinquishing the throne. Pagans were threatening every corner of the kingdom. Worst of all, nobles who had pledged Charles their fealty seemed to betray him at every turn.

I had expected we would marry, but with emissaries arriving daily, and meetings that took place at all hours of the day and night, there seemed to be no time, and in the middle of such turmoil, I could see no reason to push for something Charles had already promised.

CHAPTER 10

$\mathcal{S}$INCE I HAD SEEN THE NEW ABBESS WITH HER LOVER, she liked me even less than she had at the beginning. At least she let me serve Saint Catherine in peace. But as I went about my duties one day, a new clerk came to take the accounts.

As a pilgrim came forward, he stopped her. "Where's your gift?"

She presented a length of linen to him.

"Is that all?" He was eyeing her mantle as if he suspected she had something else hidden beneath its folds.

"It is all that I have, all that I brought."

He took it, turned it over once, twice, and then tossed it into the chest. He looked at me. "She can pray, but she can't kiss it."

"She can...what?" I was not certain I understood.

He had already started questioning the next pilgrim. But he spared me a glance. "She can pray. Can't stop her from doing that. But she can't kiss the relic."

"Then how can she expect a miracle from Saint Catherine?"

He shrugged.

The woman clutched my hand and begged me for the chance to kiss the casket, but the clerk blocked her from it. Indeed, half the pilgrims that day were sent on their way without a chance to kiss the relic. And only half of their gifts were placed into the basket meant for the treasury. The other half were bundled into a separate chest.

When I asked where they were going, I was told to mind my own tasks. But as he was sorting the gifts, the clerk grasped at something and pulled it from the pile. It was a candlestick fashioned from silver. "My lord will be pleased with this one."

"And so might *Our* Lord as well."

"Can't fault the count for getting something in return for his protection."

"Protection of what, exactly?"

"Of the abbey."

"From what have we need to be protected?"

He looked up from the candlestick. "From the Saracens. Or Danes. Or the lord's men themselves."

"The count's men?"

"Ah!" He plunged a hand into the pile again and fished around for a moment. "The abbess will like this one." He held a plump white pearl between his fingers.

Outrage quickened my heart. "It was not meant for her. It was meant for the abbey!"

"And she's the abbess, is she not?"

When he was done with his recording, he shut up his records. Tucking them under his arm, he strode off toward the church.

"Don't you wish to pray? Or kiss the relic?"

He hardly paused in his step. "Why?"

"For...for peace of mind? Or healing?"

"Don't want anything. The count has given me everything I have need of."

After he left, I walked about, finishing my work, wondering what kind of world ours had become when everything of value could be bestowed by the hand of men. What need was there for God?

❧

The next day, after the pilgrims had gone, the same clerk returned. He placed atop the altar a large golden box marked with crosses and set with glittering stones. Then he picked up Saint Catherine's reliquary casket, lifted the lid, and dumped the contents inside his box.

"You cannot—!"

"The abbess said the reliquary should be bigger. Grander."

He took the old one and dropped it into his chest. Then he went about collecting fully half of Saint Catherine's candles, hardly pausing to allow me to extinguish their flames.

I tried to stop him. "They are not yet depleted." Most of them still had a good many days left to burn.

"Saint Catherine doesn't need them."

"They were given her by the pilgrims."

"They were given to the abbey." He wound them in a length of cloth and then moved to carry them off.

"But, where are you taking them?"

"Somewhere more eyes than yours can use them." He placed them into his chest and gestured for his lad to take it up.

The glow had gone from the chapel, and it had nothing to do with the decrease in candles. "I must protest."

"Then talk to the abbess." He tossed the words over his shoulder as he walked toward the nave.

❧

Should I say something? And if I should, then what? Even if I should, who would care what I said, and what difference could it possibly make?

A girl like you has nothing to offer at all. To anyone.

The Queen Mother's words were as true now as they had been back when she had first said them.

Besides, how could I fight Providence and ever hope to win?

Only the bishop could approve an abbess. And only an archbishop could approve a bishop, and if the count's daughter was charged with the abbey, then what chance had I of changing it?

What chance had I ever had of changing anything?

Once again, the world had changed around me. I had been swept up in a tide against which I had no purchase. The feeling was familiar, but no less alarming than it had been the last time such things had happened.

⁂

I had not known Charles's crown would ruin forever the possibility he could ever be rightfully mine. Foolish girl that I was, I thought heaven had blessed us both. Perhaps I could be forgiven such things. I had been so very young.

It had taken the Queen Mother to make me understand.

I had no mother or father. They were killed in a raid by the Danes when I was yet a babe. The queen had taken pity on me, the daughter of palace retainers. I was brought into her household, and I had been raised according to her wishes, as a handmaid. She treated me as a plaything. A bauble or a trinket. Betimes she petted me. Other times she beat me. Sometimes she ignored me completely. Those things she had taught to me—reading, writing, embroidery, Latin, singing—were for her use rather than mine.

Perhaps it was inevitable Charles would turn his attentions to me. I had grown up with the prince, though during that time, due to the circumstances of his parents' marriage, a prince he could not be called. And she ought not to have been called Queen Mother either; the pope had refused to crown her. The king's first wife insisted her own two sons, Charles's half brothers, were the rightful princes and she the rightful queen. But Charles's mother had refused to accept it. In her mind and among her people, at least, Charles was the only prince, and she the dead king's only true wife. The rest of the nobles had laughed at her. They had mocked all of us.

But Charles's half brothers had died in quick succession, and then his cousin had taken the throne, only to be deposed three years later. Though Charles ought to have been crowned right then, the nobles gave the throne to Odo, Marquess of Neustria, by reason of the prince's young age. But not all had been lost. The King of East Francia supported Charles, and the Archbishop of Reims had finally crowned him king. Anything, even our love, seemed possible then, had it not been for his mother.

She took to taunting me. "You can do him no good, you know."

I had never liked her eyes. They were small and black. And just then they glinted with ill-concealed rage. "I love him." And by the Holy Mother's veil, though I had tried everything I knew to keep my heart from caring, I loved him still.

"Love! What good is love in a time like ours? What use are promises of forever when he has yet to truly secure his throne?"

"But Odo must give the throne to him, now that Charles has been crowned."

"*Give* it to him! Mark my words: the only way we'll take that throne is by force. And we'll need armies in order to do it."

"But there is the Count of Poitiers. And the King of Burgundy. And the Archbishop of Reims."

"Churchmen!" she scoffed. "If you love my boy at all, you'll see you cannot help him."

"But I believe in him." I always had. Even when everyone else had deemed him illegitimate and did not think him worthy of the throne.

"And so do I. But he needs more than a sentimental heart and kind thoughts. He needs friends."

"I am his most faithful friend of all."

Her eyes had lost some of their heat then, and her mouth had softened. She had taken up my hand in hers and kissed me on both cheeks. "That you are, and that you have always been, but the time for friendship has passed, and the time for allies has come." She gave my hand a squeeze. It was a wonder she did not break my bones.

"I could be an ally."

"Can you bring us armies or empires? By marrying you, will Charles have access to men or horses or weapons? To princes or palaces?"

"No." All I could offer him was one small girl child. The prince he had been hoping for had been born a princess instead.

"No." She agreed with an imperious lift to her chin. "You can give him nothing at all. You are worthless. In fact, you are worse than worthless. Your very kindness keeps him from what he needs the most."

"I do not think that—"

"Clearly you do not. For if you did, then you would understand a girl like you has nothing to offer at all. To anyone."

My vision shimmered as tears rushed to my eyes.

"And now you are crying." She put a finger to my chin and lifted it.

I met her eyes.

"It is for you, my dear, to listen and obey. If God in His infinite wisdom has made my son king, He has also made you a servant. Despite his half brothers' reigns, despite your ascent to his bed, I think the lesson is clear: God always gets His way in the end, does He not?"

I gasped.

"How can you fight Providence and ever hope to win?"

"I—I never—"

She patted my cheek. "That's right. You never will." She drew her hand back and slapped me.

I dropped to the floor, hand to my cheek as I cowered before her.

"A girl like you can never come to anything. It's simply not ordained. Stop trying so hard. If you truly love my son, then give him what he needs the most. Give him his freedom."

I truly believe Charles did not know of his mother's words to me. I never told him, and he never heard her. So far as he must have known, all was well with the world. And still he wanted me to take part in his.

"Come!" Charles had managed to coax me to another dinner, and then he had insisted upon musicians and dancing. Now he wanted me to join him in the dance. The commotion of the conversation and the laughter and the music reverberated from the palace walls.

I shook my head.

"Juliana!" He made a wide, sweeping gesture with his arm. "Come down here. Right now." He was not as cross with me as he was pretending. There was yet a twinkle in his eyes.

No. I mouthed the word. There was no use trying to speak it. My voice had always been soft, and he would never have heard me over the screech of the fiddles and the clashing of the cymbals.

One of his men handed him a cup.

He took it, tipped it to his mouth, and drained it in one long swallow. And then he wiped his mouth on his silk sleeve as everyone cheered. "If she will not come"—he paused, and the hall grew silent—"I shall go get her!"

The men cheered and then stood aside as Charles stumbled toward the dais where I sat.

He stopped in front of it, hand on his chest. "My lady love! Do come. Please?"

I did not like it when everyone stared at me. I shook my head.

"Come dance with me." He held out his hand and started to bow, but nearly stumbled in the doing of it.

"You're drunk."

He gripped the table and steadied himself. "I am! Which is why you must dance with me."

The men were starting to murmur now, and I got the distinct feeling that concubines of kings were not supposed to refuse them dances.

"You do not—" He looked into my eyes. "You do not *want* to dance with me?"

"Not like this." Not with leering, drunken men looking on. A simple circle dance was one thing, but I had not been trained in those more complicated than that. I had been kept too busy fetching things for the queen or reading from her psalter. And there were slippers on my feet, which were far too big, and a fillet atop my veil that kept slipping. I longed to seek the haven of my bed.

"You do not want to dance with me?"

I had said the wrong thing. I ought to have been more clever in refusing him, the way the Queen Mother and his men always were, but I had never known how to say yes when what I truly meant was no. "Come up here. You can sit beside me."

He leaned forward, toward me. "It is time for dancing, not sitting. I have been sitting for most of my life!"

I leaned across the table toward him. "Then I must not keep you from it. And there are many who wish to dance with you."

Taking up my hand, he pressed a kiss into it, and then he held it to his cheek. "You must watch me then."

⁓

I did watch him. For a while. I watched as the daughter of a marquess smiled at him, and the daughter of a count filled his cup. I sat there as his men flattered him and plied him with drink. I smiled when he looked at me. I tried to smile whenever anyone looked at me, but it left me feeling dull and witless. I sat there a while longer still, while my new fillet pressed in on my skull. I stayed while my feet swelled and my slippers bit into my skin.

I stayed as long as I could, and then I made myself stay even longer, even as the Queen Mother's words dogged me. *Stop trying so hard. It's simply not ordained.*

Finally, when I could not stand it any longer, I stole from the great hall, up the stairs to our chamber.

His chamber.

My maid curtsied.

I nearly turned around, for I did not wish to be waited upon. I did not wish to be observed. I wanted only to be alone.

If God in His infinite wisdom has made my son king, He has also made you a servant.

I was not meant for this. Not for any of it.

The maid approached, waiting, hovering, wanting to serve me. But I did not want anything or anyone. Except for my daughter. "Where is the princess?"

"She is with her nurse."

"Bring her to me."

She paused.

"I want her."

She left, and for several blessed minutes I was alone. But then she returned with the nurse, though both were empty-handed.

"Where is my daughter? Where is Gisele?"

"She sleeps."

"Is she well?"

"She is fine."

"There is nothing I can do for her?"

My maid curtsied once more. "She does not need you."

She did not need me. But clearly, eventually, she would need her nurse. I dismissed the woman, and then I let the maid undress me and unbind my hair. And after, I climbed into the bed.

She stoked the fire before she left. Once she had gone, I stared into the dark for a long while, trying to make sense of the life I had happened into. It had proved a better life than my own in every way. But I had come to the conclusion that perhaps the Queen Mother was right. Perhaps the best thing to do was walk away from it. Because one thing was certain: I had nothing to offer anyone at all.

CHAPTER II

Anna

ALONG THE PILGRIMS' PATH
TO ROCHEMONT ABBEY

FTER LEAVING THE TOWN, I WALKED FOR SOME TIME with my eyes fixed on the road beneath my feet, for I did not wish to stumble. It was not the same as walking across the yard to feed the chickens. Here, the way was pitted with puddles. Passing carts and horses had thrown up clods of mud, which made for slippery and treacherous steps.

The sound of hooves and the splat of mud sounded behind me. Remembering my earlier encounters with horses and carts, I moved to the side of the road, not willing to be run down when I had only just begun my journey.

The rider was past and well away before I remembered I ought to have asked where this road was going. As I lifted my gaze to watch him ride out of view, I felt my mouth drop open as I saw something I had never seen before; or perhaps I should say I did not see any of those things I had been accustomed to seeing. The countryside was… It was *empty* as it stretched out before me. I slowed my steps as I glanced back over my shoulder. It stretched away behind me and to either side of me as well. There were no houses and no creatures and no people. It was vacant. And vast…and strange.

As I looked around I realized how very *full* the earth's fullness was. How very splendid was God's creation. I thought I had seen nearly everything there was to see from my window. It was only now, when there was not one of those things I was used to seeing, that I realized how very much more there was to the world. And I had never known it. Never even known to imagine it!

I saw—I saw trees! They had to be trees, didn't they? I had read about them, but never before had I seen one. They were so big. But I had thought... Somehow I had gotten the impression they were supposed to have *green* leaves. The leaves I saw were yellow. As they flapped in the wind, they caught the sunlight, distilling it into gold. How lovely they were!

A soft thrump, thrumping filled the air. Up above my head, a flock of birds wheeled through the sky. I had heard birds chirping, but I had not known their wings alone could make such a soft, loud noise.

So bewitched was I by the sights I saw that I plunked my foot right down into a puddle. I could not help but laugh at myself as I pulled it out. How Mother would have despaired of me! With the sun above me, God's great earth around me, and one of the servant's jaunty songs on my lips, I walked along much lighter of heart than I had been.

And then, from behind me, I heard the chatter of conversation and a shout of laughter. Before long, a group of some dozen people overtook me. My mother's words returned to me as I made my way to the side of the road to let them pass.

She had begun, in her last months, to utter warnings about this thing and that. Her admonitions had always started with "if." *If a person unknown should approach you and find you alone, then go to the nearest church and there appeal for sanctuary. If any should offer you something, do not take it; first demand of them what they expect in return. If any should grant you friendship upon the first acquaintance, you may accept it, but do not depend upon it, for ties of faith and loyalty are proved through time and not through words.*

These people were so jovial, however, I could not help but decide my mother's words did not apply to them. They each had a cross sewn upon their tunic, and they carried a peculiar sort of purse thrown over a shoulder. The men wore broad hats and carried hooked staffs. Perhaps... Were they pilgrims? There were several women among them; I dared to think I might ask them where they were going and where the road was headed.

As they passed, I spoke. "Pardon me. If you do not mind my asking, could you tell me please, where does this road lead?"

The man at the head of the group paused in step and then stopped. The others pooled around him and stood gawping at me. "*This* road? Why, to Chalons!" He looked me up and down. "And where are *you* going? If I may ask?"

"To the abbey at Rochemont. So I can pray at Saint Catherine's chapel."

"And so are we!" They seemed so happy to be doing so.

"So this is the right way then?"

"If it is not, then we shall all go the wrong way together!" One of their number gave a cheer, and the man lifted his staff, pointing it down the road. With a shout, they fell in line behind him.

I stood to the side so they could pass, but one of the women grabbed me about the arm and pulled me along with them. "There's no need to walk by yourself. It isn't safe."

Was she offering me her friendship? If so, should I accept? Mother's warning rang in my ears, but I did not have any other friends, and this woman seemed to be so kind. "I am Anna."

"I am Helda. And very glad to know you." She leaned close. "I have to say these pilgrims are hardly the best of the lot, if you take my meaning." Her drooping chin shook like a cock's comb as she waggled her head.

They all looked fine to me.

"Begging pilgrims' alms from every stranger they meet and hoping for *healing*!"

"That is what I am hoping for too."

"We all hope for something. But there's no need to be so shameful about it, is there?"

"Shameful…"

"You have no idea what a sorry group they are. I joined them only for the safety of their numbers. To hear them talk, they are a disgraceful and pitiful lot, going on about all those things they do penance for and seek healing from!"

"But why would you hide your faults, if a mending of them is what you seek? Would you not then fail to obtain what you seek if you pretend not to need anything at all?"

"What strange ideas you have! They might at least pretend respectability. Why would God give you something when you've done nothing to better yourself? If you have done nothing to deserve it?"

But that was the point, wasn't it? I had done everything I could think of to deserve my healing. I had almost come to think my own poor efforts had nothing to do with my request being granted at all. And that's what I planned to tell Saint Catherine. I was going to cast myself upon her good graces, admit I *was* nothing and could *do* nothing and hope she could intervene in spite of it all. In spite of myself.

"Let me lean on you here for a moment." She proceeded to do so with nearly crushing weight as she skirted a mud puddle. "This is your first pilgrimage?"

"Yes."

"I thought so." She nodded toward my bosom.

I looked down in horror, expecting to somehow see the absence of my bosom made plain, but all was as it should have been.

"You need to put a cross upon your breast."

"I had no time before—"

"If you are going to undertake a pilgrimage, you must make yourself into a proper pilgrim; otherwise, it would hardly be worth the effort, would it?"

"I don't—"

"How can you expect any to treat you as a pilgrim if they do not know who you are? And if you do not take the proper measures, how can you expect God to thank you for your trouble?"

"I confess I do not know."

"Have you a handkerchief?"

"Yes."

"Then when we get to the hospice, we can ask for some shears, and you can cut a cross from it and sew it on your tunic."

I did not think, in fact, that I could. Mother had given up long ago on my learning to sew…or do anything that required two hands. I ought to have said right then I could not, but I did not wish to give this woman, who had been so kind, any reason to despise me.

She sent me another glance, and then she frowned. "I hardly know what you can do about not having a scrip…"

I thought my cloth did well enough, but the bishop had noted its absence as well. Perhaps I ought not have been so quick to make do.

"Maybe you could spare some of the money you would have given to Saint Catherine in order to purchase one. I'm sure God would understand."

I was supposed to give money to Saint Catherine? "I—I have no money."

"None?" She sent a glance to my tunic again, her gaze lingering on the woven trim that circled the hem and the sleeves. "I had thought... I mean... How are you expecting to care for your needs along the way?"

"I had heard the hospices will take care of me."

"They will. But if you had even one coin, or two, they would take better care of you."

I would have thought she might have said more as we walked along, for she had seemed more than willing to before, but for the rest of the day's journey, she was silent. And when we reached the hospice of a monastery that night, she parted from our group without a backward glance.

We were greeted with a warm welcome, and our feet were washed. The monks asked for news, but I had none to give them. The men of the group went on about kings and counts and some great battle to the west, but they were things of which I had no knowledge.

We ate together, a simple meal of bread and gruel, and then we attended a service in the church. I had never been in a place so large. Though I had just eaten with many people, and though we had all attended the service together, the church was so vast it still seemed empty. It was made of stone and was quite cold and very dark, but when the priest began to speak, something happened to his voice. It magnified and multiplied until it seemed to be coming from everywhere at once. At least there were candles burning at the front where he was standing. If not, I might have felt myself lost in the darkest gloom.

After, we were shown to separate dormitories. One for the men and the other for the women. We slept, all of us women, on the same wide pallet. It was hard, and the bugs were many, but I pinched all those I could feel. Then I drew my knees up underneath my tunic and tucked my mantle in about my feet, and before I had the chance to worry about the next day's journey, sleep claimed me.

❧

The next morning, I attended prime. I even made a confession and stopped to pray at the altar of the church, but I did not do so quickly enough. The group I had traveled with the day before went on without me.

From the talk I had heard the previous night, it seemed most of the pilgrims were headed south. Not many were journeying to Rochemont. Although the weather was fair and my town of Autun would not have seen winter for several months yet, already there was some fear of encountering snow in the mountains this late in the year. "Are there any going on pilgrimage to Saint Catherine?" I was inquiring of one of the monks who had given me a bit of bread for the day's journey. "Or do you know which road I must take?"

He nodded toward a group that was leaving. "You might speak with them."

I did not wish to throw myself upon strangers, but I did not want to start off in the wrong direction either. Especially not with the possibility of snow. I tugged on the sleeve of one of the women in the group. "If I wanted to go to the abbey at Rochemont, do you know which road I should take?"

One of the men overheard me and answered in her stead. "The road of repentance and the pathway of peace. Those always lead to redemption."

That is what the priest had always said after I made my confession. "But I am bound as a pilgrim to Saint Catherine, and I do not know the way to go."

The man gestured to the road that lay to the left. "This way. It leads to Besançon."

"Yes, but I am bound for—"

"And after, it goes east and up into the mountains."

"Then this is the way?"

"Indeed! If you are filled with courage and stout of faith, then come with us."

CHAPTER 12

I FELL IN WITH THEM AND, HEEDING MY MOTHER'S warning, I did not seek a friend. But the woman I first talked to fell into step beside me anyway. She looked older even than my mother had. Wispy strands of gray hair escaped her wimple to be bandied about by the breeze. I had noticed her earlier that morning as we were in the church. After the offices, she had approached the altar. Tears had streamed from her face as she knelt before it.

Her dark eyes still held a hint of sorrow and of hopes unmet. But that did not stop her from speaking to me. "You travel alone, then?"

"Yes."

"Your need must be very great."

I nodded.

"You were right to seek companions. Whatever you do, do not take to the road by yourself."

I would do what I had to in order to gain the abbey.

"Is this your first pilgrimage?" She was looking at my tunic.

I covered my bosom with my good hand and nodded once more.

"You'll get the way of it, and you'll know better next time."

Next time? "But, how many times have you been?"

"Oh…" She squinted away down the road for a moment

before she answered. "This is my first to Saint Catherine, but I've been to Conques and Toulouse several times each. There's something about a pilgrimage just makes everything else seem less important. And more dull. And every time I go back home, there's something else that needs to be prayed for special; have you never thought the same?"

"I do have a special request."

She nodded. "Exactly. A special request that only a saint can grant. You'll see. It won't be long before you'll be right here the same as me, telling some other young pilgrim what must be done."

"How…how *do* you do it?" My only cares had been for the journey; I had not thought of what I must do once I arrived.

"Do it?" She cast a startled glance at me. "Well, most of the way, you do just like we're doing. There's a hospice or a monastery or an abbey at the end of every day's walk. And they board you and lodge you. They'll take your confession." She seized my hand. "Don't ever pass up the opportunity to do that. Not like some. What if you meet with your death on the road? Or what if you reach the abbey only to have God decide you did not care enough to make Him answer your prayer?"

I promised I would make a confession at every opportunity.

"Oh! And you must leave your cross at the place with all the others."

Cross? "I have no cross. I did not have time to have one sewn—"

"Not that cross. The one you carry."

"I carry no cross."

"No cross?" She looked at me with pity. "You have *no* cross?"

"I did not know I needed one."

"You *do* need one. But you can buy one. Most pilgrims travel with theirs, but I see no reason you could not buy one."

"I've no money to buy one with."

"*No* money? None at *all?*"

I shook my head.

"Then you can use your alms."

"I have none." I had nothing I was supposed to have.

"That is what I meant. You can *ask* for alms."

"Ask whom?"

She shrugged. "Anyone."

"And...they will just...give them to me?"

"They're supposed to. It's like giving them to Our Lord and Savior Himself. Although, considering how late we mostly arrive at the hospices, sometimes there's never anyone to ask..."

My spirits sank just as quickly as they had risen.

"I suppose...you could make one."

"What with?"

"I don't know. Let me think on it."

This group was not like the other one I had walked with. These people were sober and serious. When they sang, the tunes were hymns, and when they spoke, their words were solemn. Often they recited psalms and prayers together. But it helped to pass the time. When the sun was high and we heard the ringing of far-off bells, we knew sext was upon us, so we stopped for a bit of a rest and ate the bread the monks had given us. The woman talked with some of the men. One of them left the group to search through the grasses that lined the road. When he waded out from them, he held long strands of it between his fists. Grasping the long stalks, he twisted and turned, knotted and tied, and then he came over and handed it to me. "Your cross. My Rosamund said you needed one."

The whole group was watching me. "Thank you." I started to take it from him, but then I remembered my mother's words and withdrew my hand instead. "I have nothing to give you in return."

"Our Lord once said it is better to give than to receive."

I smiled. "Thank you."

"There now." He handed it to me once more.

I tucked the cross into my cloth with all my other things. We left soon after and took to the road again. The woman, Rosamund, walked along beside me. "Now that you have your cross, you can leave it with the others."

"But where? Where am I to leave it?"

"At the place."

"What place?"

"The one we come to where the others have left theirs. There is always one along a pilgrim's path."

"But how will I know it? What if I miss it?"

"You won't miss it. Besides, I'll tell you what to do. But more important than leaving the cross along the way, is what you must do once you gain sight of the abbey."

"What? *What* must I do?"

"Better, I will tell you what I did. All of the times at all of the churches. I will tell you what I have done."

She told me of her first pilgrimage and then her second. After her third and her fourth, I confess I could not keep straight to which saints she had gone and to which she was still hoping to go.

"...and then, at first sight of the church—" She dabbed at her eyes with a crooked finger. "At that first sight, I took off my shoes and I walked that last bit in my bare feet, rocks tearing into my soles, just the same as Our Lord did in Jerusalem..." She broke off with a tremulous cry.

"And then?"

"And then...what?"

"And then what happened?"

"What happened? Well! I got to the church, and I made my confession, just as I was supposed to." She glanced at me. "Remember what I said: Never miss the opportunity to make a confession. That time, I spent the night there in vigil, on my knees. Not once did I allow myself to shift back onto my feet or sway forward. Not that time, though I must say I did the time before. But I stayed there the whole night, praying until the bells rung lauds."

"And then you were healed?"

"Healed?" She touched a hand to her the nape of her neck as if probing for something. "No. But that morning, I was first in line to view the shrine, and it was wondrous! So many candles, so much light! First we prayed together, all of us, and then the priest took the cover off the relic, and there was the sound of tinkling bells—"

"From *heaven*?" Oh!—the joy of it.

She eyed me. "No. There was another priest standing beside the first one. He was holding a strap of bells and shaking them. So we made our offerings, and knelt and kissed the reliquary, and then we left."

"And *then* you were healed."

She heaved a sigh. "No."

"But you did everything right that time, didn't you?"

"Yes..." Though her answer was affirmative, she did not sound very confident about it. "At least, I thought so." She clutched her walking staff more tightly. "But this time, I am going to do everything righter. I won't just take off my shoes when I see the abbey. I'll take off my shoes and go the rest of the journey on my *knees*. And I'll spend *two* nights in vigil if they'll let me, and then maybe...maybe this time..." We walked on for some length in silence, and then she grabbed my arm again. "But let me tell you about my pilgrimage to Toulouse. I was almost certain that time...almost, really quite certain..."

෨

The next day, as we walked along, I rehearsed what I must do. At the place up ahead that we would come to, though I did not quite understand where exactly it was, I would leave my little cross. At the first sight of the abbey, I would take off my shoes, and I would go the rest of the distance on my knees. And then I would make another confession and partake in—in *three* nights of vigil as I prayed. I could not imagine going on another pilgrimage after this one, so I must make certain to do everything exactly right. On the fourth day, at last, I would pray at the altar and kiss the relic. And then, if I had pleased God, I would be healed.

I only hoped I would not forget anything Rosamund had said I must do.

Another group of pilgrims must have left the hospice not long after us. They overtook us midday as we paused for rest at a spring that bubbled up beside the road. As we left that place together, one of their men fell into pace with me. It was difficult for me to keep with the others. My feet quickly tired, having become blistered and bruised, and I had discovered my shoes ill-suited to the purpose of travel. What had worked sufficiently within the confines of my house had begun to crack and tear.

But the man did not seem to mind my awkward gait or my slower steps, and he whistled some jaunty tune as we went along. He looked as if he had long been on the road. The cross on his tunic was fraying, and his mantle had several holes in its cloth. Heedful of Mother's advice, I knew I should not acknowledge him, but there was no church to run to, and it seemed rude to refuse his companionship since we were traveling in the same direction.

Though he had pulled his hood far over his head, he kept glancing at the road we had already traveled as if he were expecting someone. But already we had fallen behind the others, and I could not see how any would fail to recognize him, so I said as much.

He only looked over at me as if startled. "I don't travel with anyone."

"I thought you were with them." I nodded toward the group now well ahead of us.

"No."

"Neither do I travel with anyone."

"So you are not from Lyons, then?"

"I come from Autun and happened upon them as I walked."

"You travel alone?"

I nodded.

"But to whom do you return after all of this is over?"

"No one."

"No one? No father?" He gave me a keen-eyed look behind the fringe of black hair that had fallen across his eyes.

I shook my head. "He died many years ago."

"No brother?"

"I was a child alone."

"You must have a mother."

"She died just last week."

"I am sorry to hear it. But surely you have a husband, a lass as pretty as you."

Perhaps one day, if God was kind, after I had been healed. "I have no one."

He looked at me as if I had misspoken. "Everyone has someone. At least you must have a lord."

"No." None had wanted to claim me. Not with my hand so misshapen and scarred.

"You jest."

"I do not." His questions discomfited me, though I could not think why. He had an easy manner. "And yourself?"

"Me? What about me?"

"Where do you go? Which saint do you visit?"

"Everywhere. All of them." He said it with a broad gesture of his arm.

He must be very holy then, although he did not exactly look it. And he did not have that same determination, that same anticipation the others seemed to have. "And from where do you come?"

His brow rose. "It's been so long now. Let us say I come from everywhere else. There are not that many of us who travel alone, not bound to any lord."

"No lord but Our Lord."

Again he seemed startled by my words, and he sent a glance back over his shoulder. "Of course. No lord but Our Lord." He bumped my arm with his staff. "What is it you wear on that cord around your neck?"

I put a hand to my throat, wondering how he had come to notice it. "It was my mother's."

"I suppose it's just a trinket."

"It's quite nice, really." At least I had always liked it. I drew it out and held it up to catch the sun. It caught the light, making the enamel-work glow.

He reached out and took it up, turning it within his palm.

Now it was my turn to be startled.

"A pretty bauble for a pretty girl."

My cheeks warmed at the compliment. No one had ever called me pretty before. At least no one who seemed to mean it in the same way this man did.

He held it up and watched it spin on its cord for a moment.

I put my hand around the cord and stopped it. Then I let it drop back beneath my tunic.

"I've never seen anything like it. You should leave it out. It suits you."

As I returned the smile he offered, I considered his suggestion. Perhaps he was right. Why should I not appreciate its beauty? I pulled it out and let it settle atop my chest.

The man began to whistle a tune and then broke out into a song that had nothing to do with holiness. But the others soon picked it up, and the cheery melody and sheer exuberance of it made me wish to sing along as well. As I listened, learning the words and then starting to sing along, I looked down at Mother's pendant. Just seeing it flash in the sun put my mind at peace. I did not know why she had worried so. All of the people I had met along the road were so very nice.

CHAPTER 13

WE REACHED THAT EVENING'S HOSPICE RATHER LATE, as the sun was in its decline. The bells for vespers were already ringing, and there was a great knot of people at the entrance to the church. I had still not grown used to the push and crush of thronging crowds, and I was jostled to and fro by the people. I confess I stayed close to the man who had been my walking companion, for at least he was known to me, but the crowds soon parted us, and I ended by standing in the chancel among strangers, clasping my knotted cloth to my chest.

This church had been built of stone just as the others had been. It had the same high, soaring roof and the same sort of few, small windows, which failed to let in light. But I had become accustomed to searching out God in the dark. And how glorious was that service. I closed my eyes as I listened, imagining the priest to be the voice of God. The incense to be the scent of heaven, and the chanting monks to be the voices of angels. The offices were soon finished, and I shuffled into the hospice with the other pilgrims. I did not see the man I had walked with, but I soon located the woman, Rosamund, I had spoken with the day before. She caught my eye with a wave of her hand. As had been my habit, I waited until the others had been seated before slipping along the wall and finding a place for myself at the darkest corner of their table. Thus situated, I had learned that by the time the remainder of the food had reached me, the others were intent upon their own meals and I could eat with my left hand without any of them remarking upon it. Happily, when I sat, it was next to Rosamund.

Unfortunately, I was served first.

"He who is last shall be the first." The monk spoke the words with a nudge and a wink as he set a large kettle of steaming fish and a piece of bread beside me.

I smiled, or tried to, as I shook my head. But he stopped my protests with a gentle hand. "Go on. Take some. Eat while it's yet hot."

The others were looking at me with frank admiration... and impatience if I read their looks correctly.

"I should wait, for the others."

"The others will all have their turn. There is enough here for everyone. To serve the least of you is to serve Our Lord Himself."

Which was worse: to reach for the food with my left hand, to show my misshapen right hand, or to insult the monk by failing to eat at all?

"If you haven't any hunger, then send it on down this way!" The man who spoke the words smiled, but his flash of teeth looked anything but forgiving.

I had to eat; I was famished. And I would not last the next day on the road if I did not. We were all of us pilgrims, were we not? All of us in search of something. All of us in need of saving grace. Lifting my right hand, I let the sleeve fall back, and then I used it to hold the bread trencher still as I dipped my spoon into the kettle for some fish.

Conversation ceased as everyone at the table looked at me, their gazes fixed on my right hand.

I tried to smile, but the monk had pulled the kettle from

me and was wiping the side where my sleeve had brushed it with his own sleeve. Stepping past me to Rosamund, he bent to offer it up to her. She slid down the bench, away from me, before she took the food he offered.

As I put my spoon to the fish, I glanced at Rosamund and braved a smile, but she was intent upon her meal and did not see me. Later, as we filed into the dormitory for the night, I asked after her meal and her day's journey, but she must not have heard me, for she did not reply.

I caught what fleas and bugs I could before the lamps were removed, and then I drew my knees up to my chest and wrapped the hem of my mantle about my feet. Head on my cloth pack, listening to the night go still about me, I put a hand to my neck. At least I had memories of happier days. I closed my eyes and imagined Mother's arms about me. But as I drew the cord from my tunic, I discovered it was severed. Mother's pendant was gone.

I asked the monks the next morning if they had not found it.

"A pendant upon a cord? And you lost them?"

"I lost the pendant, but not the cord."

His face was a mixture of bepuzzlement and bemusement. "If you have the one, then how did you lose the other?"

I opened the palm I held it with. "It was cut."

He took it from me, examining the ends. "If it was cut, then surely someone must have taken it."

"But why would someone take it? They would have had to have known it belonged to me. I wore it about my neck."

The monk closed my hand around the cord. "Child—"

"And if someone took it, then where did they put it?" Why had they not returned it to me?

"When I said someone took it, what I meant was they must have stolen it from you."

"*Stolen* it?" I had heard of stealing before, but never had I expected to experience it. "I do not know anyone here. How could they hate me enough to steal something from me?"

"Hate is not required by a thief. Only opportunity is needed, along with envy and greed. You, dear child, had not one thing to do with it."

"But I need to find it! Will you not help me?"

He patted my hand. "It would be a fool's errand. Whoever has it is probably far away by now."

"But, it was taken from me *here*. At this hospice." I did not know why he would not help me.

"Misfortune finds us all."

"But I have only been among the pilgrims. I have not gone out around thieves."

"Ah, but if we knew who the thieves were, then they would never be able steal from us, would they?"

"It was all I had left of my mother's." Tears began to prick at my eyes, begging for release, but I had been taught tears were useless.

"You have your memories still, do you not? And no one can ever take those from you."

"But my pendant does not belong to whoever took it. It belongs to me!"

He gestured toward the door. "If you do not start soon, the others will leave without you.

I hesitated, wanting to search the place, but I could not deny the cord had been cut. And for what other reason would it have been done than for the purpose the monk had said?

I remembered the man I had walked beside the day before and how he had asked about it. Had he been the thief? But how could he have stolen it from me? I had told him it was from my mother. Why would he have done it? Besides that, he had called me pretty.

Worse...I had believed him.

❧

I found my group, joining up with them as they were leaving the hospice. They must have slept as little as I, for there was not much talk among them. As we walked along, I quickly fell to the back. Only this day, there was no one to walk beside.

As we rested, I hoped to sit beside Rosamund. She had been so kind to me, but there was no room on the rock she chose to rest upon, and the others made no move to accommodate me. I ate the crust of bread I had taken from the hospice alongside the road as I admired the bright, cloudless sky. I had not known it to be so large.

When we reached the hospice that evening, I made my confession and then spent some time before the altar on my knees, praying for the soul of whoever had taken my pendant. I prayed also for Saint Catherine's favor to rest upon me.

That night at dinner, there was no room at the table, so I sat with a different group as they made a place for me among them. The next morning, when one of the monks saw me hobble in my step, he sent me to the infirmary for an unguent to salve my blisters. The monk there washed and dried my feet and then put a cooling poultice atop them.

"You should stay here until the blisters have healed."

"But I am bound to visit Saint Catherine at the abbey at Rochemont, and they say the snows are coming. I cannot afford to wait here."

"Saint Catherine will still be there in the spring when the snows melt."

"I do not wish to wait."

"Your feet may not let you go."

"They've carried me thus far."

He removed the poultices and then dried my feet and salved them. "At the very least, perhaps you could purchase new shoes."

"I have no money. These will have to last the rest of the way."

"Then take this." He handed me the small jar of unguent he had used. "And this." He gave me a length of gauze as well. I went from that place with his gifts in my hands. Though the trip to infirmary had delayed my leaving, many of the pilgrims were still milling about. As I tugged at the knot on my cloth, I saw my group leave. It took me a moment to place the monk's gifts inside, along with my other things, and then I struggled with reknotting it, and as I picked it up, the contents spilled. As always, my efforts at haste were useless.

Despite the monk's treatment, each step I took still chafed. My group must have struck out quickly, for they had disappeared from view by the time I passed through the monastery's gate.

It was lonely, walking the road by myself, but at least I could hear them in the distance. The wind threw snatches of their hymns and recitations back to me.

The road was steeper this side of the city and covered with rocks as it began its climb toward the mountains. By midmorning, I was leaning into my steps, and for the first time, I wished I had a pilgrim's staff. Still though, at midmorning, I had almost caught up with them. I feared to present myself, thinking they might have left me behind on purpose. Although Rosamund had been so kind; perhaps they thought I had left without *them*. In that case, I supposed I should hasten in order to make amends.

But my poor, aching feet would not allow it. The faster I tried to walk, the more they protested. And so I let my pace slow, knowing we would end in the same place that night, and there I could tell them about my visit to the infirmary. At midday I could see them stop ahead of me at the top of a hill.

By that time, I could not take another step, and so I sat along the wayside in a rocky place and opened my cloth to take up the monk's gauze. As I wiped the blood from my feet, I sent glances up the hill. They did not look as if they planned soon on leaving, so I tucked into my bread and let my feet feel the warmth of the sun. It was such a lovely place, situated away at the side of the hillock with a view out into a valley. I had all of the warmth of the sun and none of the chill of the breeze. As I sat there, waiting for the group to start up again, my head nodded, chin falling to my chest.

I blinked awake and stood. It would not do to fall asleep. Not now, not here, so far from the next hospice. But as I glanced up the hill, I saw the others were still there, looking as if they had nothing to do but eat and talk and rest. So I returned myself to the rocks and determined to keep myself awake by reciting prayers.

It did not work.

When I next awoke, the warmth had left the rock I was seated on, and the breeze had wormed its way into the hollow. A shiver brought my wits back to me. Stretching, I dipped my hand to my mouth to cover a yawn.

Was the group still there?

Standing, I shook out my tunic as I looked up the hill.

There was no one. Not one form was outlined against the clear, blue sky.

Fear pulled at my belly as I reassembled my things with a quaking hand. They must have gone while I had been dozing. I started out at a brisk pace to close the distance quickly. The road had not felt too terribly lonely while I had been able to hear them. But now, I confess, trepidation began to whittle at my resolve.

I wavered for a long moment.

Perhaps I should return to the hospice and set out again in the morning with new companions. Or even return this way in the spring. Although I had no other place to go, no home to return to. I had no other thing to do. And besides, the group could not have gone far in the little time I had been asleep. Once I gained the hill, I was sure to see them. And if not, at least I would be able to hear them once more. And as long as I could hear them, they would be able to hear me should I need any aid.

I must accomplish what I had set out to do; I had no other choice.

After leaning into the incline to advance my steps, I finally topped the hill. As I peered down the other side, I expected to see them on the road beneath me. They were not there. But the road curved away down at the bottom and disappeared into a stand of trees. Perhaps they were just hidden from my sight. I stood a moment longer, listening for sounds of prayers or of singing, but I heard nothing save the whistle of the wind.

Descending was far easier than mounting the hill, and it provided some relief to the blisters at my heels. My steps followed each other more quickly as well. I followed the turn in the road as it dove into the stand of trees, expecting at any moment to happen upon my friends, but they were not here either.

The wind stripped a handful of orange-colored leaves from the trees' branches and tossed them in my face.

Quickening my pace left me panting. But beyond the next

turn, the road lay empty, and beyond the one after that, still I saw no one. At least the road had turned toward the sun once more by then. I welcomed its warming rays, though I put up a hand to block them as I strained to see into the distance.

How long had I slept?

No matter my sloth, the sun was clearly in decline. I had to hurry if I hoped to make the next hospice before nightfall. I vowed to affix myself to the group that night no matter whether they accepted my apology or not. Intent as I was upon catching the others, I could not help but pause some time later as I came to a bend at which the world seemed to drop entirely away from my feet. Down in the valley beneath me, I could see a village nestled between the trees, the spire of a church, and the sparkling ribbon of a stream. Between myself and the village, crosses had been placed at the top of every hillock and glen.

This must be the place. The one where I was meant to leave my cross.

If I left off my journey though, for even the few minutes it would take to place my cross among them, I might never catch up with the group. But if I did not leave my cross, then how could I expect Saint Catherine to incline her ear to my prayers?

Surely I would meet up with the others at the hospice. Though the village looked quite distant, it could not be far now. The sun had nearly disappeared behind the mountains, and I had been walking for quite some time.

Loosing the knot on my cloth, I felt inside it for my cross of straw. Leaving the road, I stumbled down the hill. Crosses sprouted from the earth like a grove of trees of various sizes, but all of them were larger, all of them more substantial than mine. It seemed a paltry offering among so many others, but Rosamund had said I must leave it here.

The wind gusted again, battering my mantle about my legs and my hair about my face. I disentangled myself and then walked forward and bent in front of a stand of crosses. I would have liked to have planted mine in the earth, along with the others, but the ground was hard, and my cross was hardly larger than my hand. After kissing it, I set it down between two others.

There. The first step in my pilgrimage had been accomplished.

But as I turned to regain the road, the wind gusted once more, cupping my pitiful offering in its hands and then setting it loose to tumble end-over-end down the hill.

I ran after it, hoping to retrieve it, but it had already disappeared.

There were crosses without numbers surrounding me, but none of them were mine. How could I ever hope for healing now?

I battled my way back up the hill. It was with a heavy heart and sinking hopes that I placed my feet back on the road. As I started down off the heights, I heard a noise rise from the road behind me. As I turned, I was startled to see a creature cross the road.

My heart clattered against my chest before I realized it must be a dog. A big one, for certain, but a dog just the same. I had seen many of them from my window, and all they seemed interested in was rousting the pigs from their forage. As I continued on, however, another creature darted across the road in front of me.

I walked more quickly, knowing I must reach the valley before night fell. As I threw a glance behind me, I saw the dog again. And now he was trotting down the road in my direction.

Unease rippled through my stomach. Though I had seen

dogs, it had always been from a distance; I had no wish to meet one. Though there was no reason I ought to have been worried, I broke into a run.

And then the other one appeared again in front of me. Caught betwixt the two of them, I stopped. There was no reason to be frightened. I was not some discarded rag or rotten piece of food for them to fight over. They must simply have wandered from the village. Perhaps they wanted me only to lead them back home. "Nice dog."

The one in front of me bared its teeth.

Perhaps it was not quite so nice as I had hoped.

I turned around, hoping the other had gone, but he lifted his head and gave a bloodcurdling howl. It was then I noted something I ought to have seen before. Their heads were rather larger than any dog I'd ever seen, and their muzzles and legs much longer.

What if these were not dogs? What if they were—what if they were *wolves*?

CHAPTER 14

I RAN.

But not three paces down the road, I stepped into a hole and fell sprawling, as my knotted cloth fell from my hand. I could not breathe, but I dared not stay prostrate. As I pushed up, I heard the creatures' footfalls cease. Rolling to my knees, I lifted my head with great dread.

The two had joined forces, and they were sitting on their haunches, staring at me.

Facing them, I pushed up from the ground with my good hand. My pack was lying on the road just beyond my reach. Bending, I stretched my hand toward it.

One of the creatures curled up its lip with a snarl.

Leaving the cloth, I straightened to standing and took one slow step away from them. And then another. And then I turned and ran.

Stumbling and sliding on the loose rocks, I went a good ten paces down the road, but when I chanced a glance back over my shoulder, they were still following. Veering from the road, I entered the wood. I had hoped to gain speed in my flight, but there I was sorely mistaken. Fallen branches and a tangle of brush blocked my way. Though I leaped over those I could, more confronted me with every step. And then, once I had finally managed to free myself from those entanglements, the earth sloped sharply away beneath me, and I found myself on the verge of a cliff.

Behind me, the wolves were howling. Off to my left somewhere, a third seemed to answer in return. My only path to safety lay beneath me. If I was very careful, I just might be able to find a way to the bottom.

I grasped the trunk of a slender tree beside me and then stepped out, hoping to pick my way down the cliff. That first step sunk into a thick litter of leaves, and then my foot slid a bit of a ways, leaving my arm stretched out behind me.

I looped my bad hand around another tree trunk and disengaged the first as I took another step downward. My movement started a cascade of leaves and stones. I clung to the tree until it stopped.

Reaching out with my good hand, I stretched forward, hoping to reach another tree's trunk, but it was too far away. I sat down and then, releasing my hold, I let myself slide down the cliff, just a bit, until another tree came to hand.

The howling began again, echoing in the twilight about me.

Standing, I reached farther, for a different tree, but another cascade began, and this time, it carried me along with it. I could not keep my feet beneath me. Tumbling shoulder over shoulder, I careened down the cliff. Only the presence of a large boulder toward the bottom arrested my fall. And that, none too gently.

I lay there for some time, too dazed to move, fearing the wolves would assail me at any moment, but they did not come.

Out in the wood before me I thought I heard the sound of water, though it might have come from the space between my ears. From my prone position, I glanced up to where I had begun my descent. Four wolves stood there, staring at me. I wondered why they had not followed. With my body bruised and my wits scattered, they would have gotten the better of me. And yet...there they stayed.

Night had crept into the wood now, and the wind had stiffened. With it came a fishy, fetid odor. My nose tingled with the stench. I coughed and then winced as the effort set my head to aching.

Sitting, I ran my hands over my tunic, brushing dirt and leaves from the fabric. I wriggled my toes and stretched out my legs. Straightened my arms. They were stiff, but despite the fall, they did not give me any pain. And, best of all, in my wild tumble I had left those wolves behind.

But as I gained my feet, something snapped and crackled through the wood. Something big by the sound of it. A horse, perhaps! "Hallo! Is anyone there?"

The noise stopped.

"Hallo?"

The crackling and crunching started once more.

"Hallo?"

The noise stopped, and an unearthly growl, low and menacing, came by way of answer. It was different than the wolves' howl, longer and deeper, and it made the hairs at the nape of my neck stand on edge.

I stood there, still as a stone, as the snapping and crackling grew closer. They were accompanied by a rhythmic snuffling and the rustle of fallen leaves. By the moon's pale light, I could make out a large, lurching figure through the trees.

Up behind me, the wolves began to howl in chorus.

The thing before me seemed to stand and then let out a lengthy growl.

I sank to my knees in the dirt where I had landed and cowered there behind the boulder. Eyes closed, I recited a noiseless succession of prayers.

The snuffling paused as it passed the boulder.

I squeezed my eyes tighter still as I ceased my supplications. And then...the beast passed on.

By that time, night had come in earnest. I was far from the road; I was stranded at the bottom of a cliff with an unknown beast somewhere in the wood around me and a pack of wolves on the cliff above me. And worst of all my woes, the loss of my cross still pressed upon me. I saw now I should have taken it as a sign.

I had lost the favor of Providence.

The wind shifted directions and came to assault me more directly. Did I dare to leave my boulder in search of some other warmer, safer place? But how could I move without alerting the beasts? And in the dark of night I might well stumble over another cliff or become mired without any warning in another slew of bushes and branches.

Pulling my knees up to my chest, I wrapped my tunic and then my mantle around me as best as I could. After increasing fits of shivering seized me, I used my hands, both the good and the bad, to pull leaves close and mound dirt up around me. And there I kept watch as birds hooted and creatures howled throughout the long of the night.

Morning's pale light did not do me any favors. As I stared up the cliff from which I had tumbled, it served only to remind me why my body ached. And it put to rest any lingering hope I had of ever going back the way I had come.

I knew I must find the road, but which way was I to go in order to discover it?

Although I had been descending to the valley on the road, the countryside was rife with hills, and the road always seemed somehow to mount up before it went down again, and turn right before it curved to the left once more. And besides, my escape from it had been headlong. In any case, I could not climb back up the cliff I had tumbled down, but I also knew I should not advance past the boulder that had stopped my fall. Should I do so, I would be heading away from the road, not toward it. But in my flight from the road, in wading through snags of brush and tangles of fallen limbs, how was I to know if I had turned back upon my own path? Or if I had even advanced any farther down the road than I had been when I had left it?

Had I lost myself in this dark, shadowed, wild place, never to have the chance to pray to Saint Catherine at the abbey?

A sob clogged my throat, swelling it with disappointment and regret.

How could I find a way out of this place I had fallen into?

There was a village at the bottom of the valley. I had seen it. And in that village there must be a hospice. I had already walked a far piece, so the village could not be too distant. If I could only reach it, then I could have my wounds tended, and I could eat, and then I could take to the road once more.

I must go no farther into the wood than the boulder; I could go no higher in the wood than I was right now. That meant starting off in the direction from which that hulking creature had come the night before. Though he had not come back during the long, dark night, who knew that he might not decide to do that very thing now? Though I suffered a moment of indecision, there was nothing to be gained by delay but the misery of another long, cold night. And so, I started off.

At first I turned every few steps to keep the boulder in sight, to make certain I had not strayed beyond it. My suspicions had been well-founded: there was a stream that wound through the wood. I did not mind the sound of water, and so I followed it; its gurgle seemed to lighten my thoughts and lift my hopes, but then it suddenly turned. If I followed it, the boulder would soon pass from view. And if I could not find my way back to it, how would I ever be able to return from whence I had come?

I thought on the problem for some moments before realizing I had been holding on to false hope. What purpose had the boulder served but to mark the place at which I had known myself to be lost? And why should I be so set on returning there? It could do nothing for me but keep me waylaid. In order to be found, I had to be willing to leave it behind.

But which way should I go?

If I followed the stream, I might be wandering farther into the wood instead of coming out of it.

Knowing nothing of my dilemma, the water trickled past, carrying leaves on its current as it ran past my feet, but *that* was something. The water had to be going somewhere, and had a stream ever been known to course *up* a hill?

I had never seen it happen.

But then...I had never seen much of anything.

Reason told me I should follow the water. Would it not always find the lowest path down the mountain? I closed my eyes, remembering home. The way potage dripped from the ladle, and how milk had streamed from the mouth of the pitcher, a mouth that had channeled the milk much the same as this stream's bed had channeled the water.

I would follow the stream.

And no matter where it led, at least I was certain I would find myself farther down the mountain. The water sought what the road and I both did: it sought the valley.

∽

Following a mountain's stream was easier said than done. The wood was a chill and somber place, both dim and drear. I trod from shadow to shadow as I followed every crook and bend of the stream. As I went along, it seemed to broaden, and then at times the water seemed to sprout rocks. It would dash itself around and over them, churning beneath them as if trying to dig them up and push them along. At other times, so zealously did the stream devour the rocky earth that its gently sloping bank became a treacherous cliff. At that point, I had to follow the water unseen, from the heights, being careful to keep the sound of the stream in my ear.

I was walking along, picking my way over rocks and through the brush, when I realized I could no longer hear the water. Looking down into the gulley, I realized I could not see it either.

The stream had disappeared.

∽

I crashed back through the brush as I tried to hue to the track I had just made, listening for the burble of water.

At last I heard it once more.

I coaxed myself toward the great cliff, and then I got on my belly and stretched myself out over the edge, straining to see the stream my ears told me must be there.

Looking back to my left, I could see silvery strands of it slip by. But just in front of me…there was nothing. I crept along the edge of the cliff, back the way I had come until I could see the stream more clearly. Here, I proceeded with great care. The earth had fallen away from the edge in what must have been a great slide.

I could see where the earth had cascaded down to meet the stream, leaving a gaping hole into which the waters poured as they vanished into the bowels of the earth with a great roar and a frothing mist.

The stream was gone.

All my work, all my efforts had been for naught. I had placed my faith in an illusion, and now I had lost my way completely. I would have done better, perhaps, to try to fight off the wolves and cling to the road. At least if I had perished, it would have been along the way. And perhaps if I had been able to beat them back for just a little while, help might have come. But here, in this dark and dire wood, I had only myself.

I could not go back. I had come too far for that. Most of the day had gone. But I could not stay here either. Should I be swayed from my belief the lowest path was best? Was it better to gain the heights farther above and hope for another clear view of the valley below?

After crawling back from the edge, I stood and decided to try for higher ground. At least then I could hope for a vista, for some revelation that would show me where I ought to be. So I turned my face upward to the land I had so recently scorned.

I stumbled through trees and over branches, sliding backwards, more than once, on the leaves the wind had strewn across the ground. Just as I despaired of ever reaching the valley, I heard the sound of bells. Faint and indistinct, they echoed in the wood about me. Though I could not discern their direction, they gave me hope.

The higher I climbed, the more trees gave way to rocks, until finally I broke from the wood altogether and stood on a large, flat expanse of rock that thrust out from the earth around it. There were other crests that were higher still, a series of them that seemed to reach up to the sky. But standing where I was, I could see a steeple silhouetted in the afternoon's sinking sun.

If that was the village, then there must yet be a road. And if I could find the road, then all hope was not lost. Turning my back to what lay behind me, I fixed my eyes on what lay before me.

⁂

I do not know how long I walked. After a while, the sun set and the moon, a poor pale sliver of its fulsome self, rose. It did not give enough light to reveal my steps, but it illuminated the mountain behind me. I did not have to see where I was going just so long as I kept myself from where I had been.

I made noise enough to warn any man or beast of my coming, but at least the sound of my steps made it impossible for me to hear anything else. If any creature were following me, I did not wish to know it.

Hunger dogged my steps. It filled my belly with sharp, insistent pangs. When dawn came and I could stand it no more, I picked up a few chestnuts from the hundreds that dotted the ground. Little solace they gave for I could not crack them with my teeth. I stopped for a moment, and kneeling, sifted through the layered leaves in search of a rock. Upon finding one, I used it to bash the husks and I peeled and then ate several as I walked along.

Even in this wilderness, I heard church bells toll the appointed hours. Terce passed and then sext and none. Whipped by the wind, clouds rose and hid the sun. The air had not been warm before, and now it attacked my face with a bitter sting. Vespers would soon be upon me, and with it, the setting of the sun.

When my path leveled off, I stopped for a moment to find my breath. Looking behind me, I was heartened to see how far I had come, though I did not know how much farther I had left to go.

I descended into a valley for a while and then went up a hillock. I dipped down to a dale before rising out of it. And then I entered an expanse of dead, flattened grasses, sweet relief for my aching feet. The mountain's peak ever behind me, I pressed ahead. As the grasses left off, there rose another stand of trees. But this time, they did not appear to go on forever. And as I approached, I heard…voices?

I stopped.

From the other side of the trees drifted the scuff of footfalls, the whinny of horses, and the clap of feet against the earth. A muttered conversation and then, after a lengthy silence, an especially bitter-sounding exchange.

Voices—they were *voices*! Great God in heaven, was I saved?

CHAPTER 15

Gisele

SAINT-CLAIR-SUR-EPTE

MY SLEEP WAS FITFUL AS I DREAMED OF THE DANE'S blood-soaked arm ring, but even so, I nearly missed the canon's leaving that next morning. He and the translator were leaving ahead of us, so they could be provisioned before starting for Rochemont. Their small contingent would travel much faster than our larger one.

The canon had been present at the audience with the Dane the day before, but I was not certain he understood what I wanted. I was not certain any of them did. Some of the count's men were already about, their squires trying to look officious as they set to packing their lords' goods. The canon was conferring with the cook at the entrance to the kitchen. I waited until he had finished and went to speak with him when he moved to inspect a selection of swords and long knives, which several squires were displaying for him.

A churchman with weapons? "You do not take those on your journey?"

He glanced up, and then his eyes slid toward the ground. "The archbishop says God favors the strong and the prepared, my lady."

Remembering my journey to the abbey through the wilds of the mountains, I could not say it was a poor idea.

"Besides, you should not concern yourself with the affairs of men."

"I would not have to if they would stop concerning themselves with mine!"

"I had forgotten the refreshing candor of your speech." And it seemed he was not amused to be given new evidence of it.

"When you reach the abbey…"

"Yes, my lady?"

"You will inquire of Saint Catherine?"

His turned his attention back to the weapons, taking up one of the swords. "Of course, my lady."

"It must be her choice to come with you."

He touched the length of the blade with his fingertips. "It would work no other way."

"But how will you know?"

"How will I know? Do you mean to ask how I will know what she chooses?"

Somehow, the man never failed to make me feel stupid. I nodded.

He gave the weapon back to the squire and then looked me in the eye. When he spoke, he did so slowly, as if trying to make certain I would understand. "I will try to take the relic. If Saint Catherine allows it, then she must agree. If she does not, then her message is quite clear. Would *you* not agree?"

"When you say you will try to take it…*how* will you try to take it?"

He blinked and raised a brow. "How?"

"How."

"I will ask for an audience with the abbess, and I will tell her the archbishop has requested it."

"And what if they will not let you have it? Will you leave it there?"

He laughed. "I hardly think they have any say in the matter!"
If they didn't, then who did?

"I will explain that the archbishop has commanded a cathedral be built to honor Saint Catherine, and I will appeal to their sense of duty. Surely the saint would become much more widely venerated, and many more pilgrims would visit her if the relic were in Rouen instead of in the mountains of Aquitaine."

"Burgundy."

"What's that?"

"The abbey is in the mountains of Burgundy."

He smiled, but it was perfunctory. He gestured to the lad with the knives, and the boy handed him one.

"So you think she will agree then?"

"I have great faith she could do nothing but. And you should as well."

It sounded as if the decision had already been made. But how could they make the decision without inquiring of the saint? Was there no opportunity for her to have any wishes but their own? "Is there any way in which you might decide Saint Catherine does not wish to be moved?"

He shrugged. "She could paralyze me when I try to take her. Or she could render me mute."

"She would do that?"

"She might." His smirk let me know he did not think so. "It has been known to happen."

Somehow, the idea of the canon being struck dumb made me feel a bit better about everything.

He returned his attentions to the assortment of knives, and soon the archbishop came to pronounce his blessings upon the journey and to give the canon a letter for the abbess. At his gesture, a stable hand brought around a pair of diminutive rounceys, which had clearly served most of their lives as pack horses. They had no particular beauty, and their swayed backs boasted no particular strength.

Several of the squires laughed outright as the canon flushed. "I would think my own palfrey more appropriate for the journey."

"These rounceys may not travel fast, but they travel well. They will see you to the abbey and back. And you must not forget that even Our Lord did not disdain the ass that was given Him."

From the canon's sour scowl, I rather thought the canon believed that poor recompense for the blight on his honor. But he mounted a rouncey and settled in the saddle, feet dangling well below the animal's belly. The archbishop handed him a packet. "A map."

The canon took it out and unfolded it.

"Rochemont is to the east."

The canon's brow furrowed. "I thought it was to the west. And the south."

"To the east and the south. Be on watch for Magyars. We have heard they are on the move."

The canon's eyes had widened with alarm.

The archbishop offered his hand.

The canon kissed the man's ring. "I will do my best."

"Do better." The archbishop slid a look at me. "Come back with the relic."

The canon eyed me as well. "Is it not up to Saint Catherine whether she will go or stay?" He had posed the words as a question, but I knew he was directing the words at me. Telling me, warning me perhaps, what I should expect.

"Of course it is. But why would she not wish the conversion of the pagan? Why would she not want to reside in Rouen? Rather, why would she wish to stay up in the mountains, where few can find her?"

Because it was peaceful there. Because she was loved there. Because she belonged there. I defied them to tell me she could not decide for herself.

"Bring her here, to me, and surely your reward will be great." The canon bowed his head.

"You have been faithful in many small things, Nephew. I do not see why you should not be given responsibility over bigger ones."

After making the sign of the cross, the archbishop bid the canon go. The cleric kicked his heels into his rouncey...or tried to. So long were his legs, so freely did they dangle, that he only ended by kicking himself.

I smothered a laugh in my sleeve. The squires were not so polite, but one of them subdued his laughter long enough to grab the creature by the reins and pull it forward. As the horse began to walk, however, the sound of a great distur-bance arose from the other side of the palisade. And soon there followed a shout as well.

As the gate opened, I saw a black-headed horse. A Frisian with a long, waving mane, it snorted swirling, frosty breaths as it bobbed in and out of view. Close behind it was a second. And then there came a third. And as they rose up and pawed the air with hair-ringed hooves, it was not their odd appearance that disturbed me. It was their riders. They were mounted, all of them, by Danes.

I shrank behind Andulf as I counted them. There were one, two...five of them. The canon stopped the squire's progress. "Are those Danes? What can they want?"

The archbishop cleared his throat as his gaze dropped to the ground. "Their chieftain has sent some of his men to accompany you. They'll ensure you obtain the relic."

Dread settled in my belly. If the Danes accompanied the canon to Rochemont, my sole means of escaping the marriage had just disappeared. For as powerful as Saint Catherine was, regardless of her ability to discern the will of God, to plead with the Almighty on my behalf, how could she stand against them? How could anyone resist the Danes?

∽

The canon rode away from the villa surrounded by Danes. As I watched them, any hope he was going to the abbey to honestly inquire of Saint Catherine, to try to discern the desires of Providence, disappeared. He was going to seize her relic, and the Danes were going to make certain his success. I needed, at all costs, to speak to him at Rouen, to plead my case and appeal to his sense of justice one last time before his journey.

Would that we had followed on his heels, but we did not.

And once the count finally decided to travel, it was the archbishop who played the laggard. First, he could not locate one of his chests, and then he was dissatisfied with the feel of his saddle. It had to be taken off and the embroidered caparison beneath it repositioned. And since, by that time, the sun was overhead, he proposed we dine before leaving.

We were well into the forenoon by the time we rode from the palisade. The count placed my retinue in the center of the procession. The better to guard me, he claimed. All I received from the honor was a throat choked with dust and the certain knowledge that my mantle would never recover from the offense. We rode at a pace more befitting cavalry than royalty.

As my maids' cart jounced along behind me, I could hear them both start to complain. The road was difficult and narrow. When it widened, I broke from the ranks, intending to speak to the count.

Andulf raised a shout as he sped his courser to catch me. The count raised a brow when he saw me, but he did not halt the column.

"I beg you for a break in our journey. My maids tire."

He only spurred his horse forward and fixed his sights on the road ahead. "Perhaps the king travels at your leisure, but you are not in your father's lands. You are in mine. And I say we press on."

I was not used to such insolence. Not even from the queen. It was not my fault the sun had sunk in the sky. Had we left midmorning, we might already have finished our journey. So as the count continued, I returned to my carts. Pulling my palfrey off to the side, along with my maids, I signaled for Andulf to aid us.

He rode up beside me, his courser towering over my palfrey by several hands. "I would not do this, my lady, if I were you."

"If you were I, then I should hope you would understand it is my father who is king, and not the count."

He glanced at the rest of the count's men who rode by us. "It is not for lack of wishing, my lady. And make no mistake: here his word is taken as law."

"Do you say you will not help me?"

"I am only one man, though I am a loyal man. I simply ask you to consider whether this is a worthy endeavor."

"I am not asking for him to pitch a tent and let us pass the night here. I ask only for a short respite."

He glanced up at the sky. "Night will quickly come."

"Someone will tell him we have stopped. He will not leave us here, but he will be forced to slow and to send someone back to inquire. By the time that happens, my maids will have taken their rest."

The count did not send a knight. He came himself. And

when he questioned me, brow flaring, face enflamed with impatience, I played the fool.

"I thought I had told you we continue on!"

I was not some retainer that he should speak to me thus, and when my father returned, the count would be made to remember his mistake. "I thought I had told you we would stop." I dismounted just in case he should mistake my meaning.

Anger burned in his eyes.

"My palfrey seems to be favoring a foot. I did not think I should ride it to exhaustion."

His eyes passed to Andulf and then back to me. "If your horse cannot be ridden, you should ride with him."

I would have demurred, but it was I who had chosen to speak an untruth, and the count did not look inclined to leave us. Even so, Andulf might have dismounted to aid me, but he only reached down a hand, making it plain he expected me to help myself up with a foot upon his stirrup. There is a reason the Holy Scriptures caution against lying.

I settled myself before him as my maids climbed back into the cart, and we took once more to the road. After the count had returned to the head of the column, the knight turned around for a long moment. When he turned back, he spoke into my ear. "Your palfrey does not look lame, my lady."

I refused to answer.

"But my courser might be if it has to bear the weight of us both for very much longer."

"Then perhaps you will have to acquire a new one."

"I might have, and done it long before now, but my monies have dwindled as my time at court has lengthened."

It was not my fault my father had given him to me.

He spit onto the road.

"What else would you have had me do? The count must be reminded he is not the king."

"It is said he thinks of little else."

Even if he did, what good would it do him? My father wore the crown. And if the message he had received were to be believed, he had Lorraine on his side now as well.

I rehearsed the words I would use to entreat the canon when I saw him. It could not hurt to remind him of my father's wish for me to go to Rochemont, or of Saint Catherine's great power. I could not assume she did not want me to wed the pagan, but then neither did I wish to assume that she did. I assumed nothing at all, and neither should he. That was the whole reason for the journey. And in truth, he could do nothing but agree with me. Although, what good would my paltry words or appeal to his sense of fairness do when the archbishop had promised him some great reward?

Stars were beginning to glitter in the gloaming sky as we ascended the hill toward the archbishop's palace in Rouen. After a momentary stop to allow the archbishop to leave us, we descended toward the city.

Beneath us on the river, the sails of a merchant fleet caught and swelled with the evening's breeze, like swans adjusting their wings before bedding down to sleep.

As we rode into the count's palisade, there was a flurry of activity as his retainers came out to meet us.

Once in the courtyard, Andulf dismounted and then helped me from the courser. As I slid to the ground, I requested he take a message to the canon, requesting his presence. I did not dare to wait until morning, for fear he might leave for Rochemont before I could speak to him.

The knight's face was the picture of bepuzzlement. "You wish him to come *here*, my lady?"

"And where else? The hour grows late."
"But he has already made for Paris."

Chapter 16

"Paris!"

"He must be provisioned for the journey."

"I had thought…" I had assumed, in any case, that the preparations would take place here, in Rouen.

"The count's stores are in Paris. With the siege along the river so lately lifted, there can be little here to spare."

My maids were standing beside me, gaping at our exchange. "If the canon is going to Paris, then we must follow!"

"I am afraid I cannot let you do that. Your father gave you into my care."

I whirled around at the voice, to find the count had joined us.

He raised his torch by way of greeting. "But you will not find yourself mistreated here, my lady. Come." He nodded to his men, who dragged my chests, my bed, and my table and stools from the cart. Another of his men had rallied my maids and led them off into the night.

"But where are my maids?"

"They will be provided for. Have no fear of that."

I might have expected to be welcomed by his lady wife, but instead my knight and I followed his men toward the back of the enclosure, where a great wooden tower rose like a mushroom high into the night. Up three stories we climbed before the steward threw a door open at the top.

While his men assembled my bed and put my things about, the count gestured around the room. "Here you will be safe. None can come to you, but they will be seen by my men."

I had not thought myself endangered. Leastways, not by any but the Dane. And up here in the tower, safety seemed to me more of a confinement than a comfort. As the count swept the torch about, I could see no hay had been strewn across the floor. No fire burned in the grate that had been centered in the room beneath the opening in the roof. "Where are my maids to sleep?"

"They will be lodged along with mine."

That was not so very great a hardship for me, for they were neither of them sound of slumber. "And what of my man?"

"He can stay in the guardhouse with mine."

Until then, Andulf had kept a respectful distance, trailing behind us, but at the count's words, he stepped to my side. "My duty is to my lady."

"She will not require your attentions. My own men are adequate for the task."

Maids could be replaced, but a knight could not. "I must insist my man stay here with me."

"Surely not. When your hand has been given to the Dane?"

"It has not yet been given. I await to see what Saint Catherine has to say about the matter."

He bowed as if in apology, but there was no apology, and most certainly no humility in his manner. And his eyes said that he did not consider himself mistaken. "It is widely known your family has quaint ideas of propriety, but what would your father say if word of scandal reached him?"

The knight slanted a glance at me and then bowed toward the count. "I will sleep on the stair outside my lady's door. She can bar it from within and I will bar it on my side as well."

"Sleep on the doorstep? And allow it to be said the Count of Paris would not lodge you? You cannot think me so ungracious as that."

I had not ever liked the man, but I had not known he was so disagreeable as this. "Then you mean to strip me of both my maids and my man?"

"I strip you of nothing. You will be quite comfortable here. You may have anything you like, my lady. You have only to request it."

"Then I request to be served by my own people."

"I am certain you will find my hospitality surpasses even the royal court's." He smiled and bowed, taking Andulf with him.

Though he left the torch in a cresset that had been fixed to the wall, the chests had been deposited on the opposite side of the room. Not able to see for the darkness of the night, I took the chests by their leather handles and dragged them, one by one, toward the light. In the third, I seized upon one of my furs. Pulling it out, I recognized it by the musky smell: my otter mantle. Pulling it on, I bundled myself into its glossy folds and slipped beneath the bed's counterpane. I watched the torch birth shadows that flared and then turned upon themselves to flit about the room.

I had never slept alone before, and I could not decide whether it was better to keep my eyes open and brave the torch's eerie light, or to keep them shut and pretend myself elsewhere. Anywhere seemed a more comforting place than here, so I screwed my eyes up tight and summoned visions of the abbey at Rochemont, comforting myself with thoughts of that peaceful, lofty place and the woman I had spoken with there.

But then a scrabbling sound came from outside the door. Had I secured it?

I could not remember.

Alighting from the bed, I clenched the robe close about me with a trembling hand and crept to the door. Feeling along its solid frame, I found the bar, lifted it, and then let it drop into place.

Fleeing back to the bed, I pressed my back up against the bed frame and drew my knees to my chest. Then I shut my eyes and began to recite a prayer.

As I finished the words, the torch sputtered, throwing flares of light and darkness against my shuttered eyelids. I opened my eyes to see a fluttery, flapping creature drop down from the hole in the roof. The torch flickered bright once more as the creature reeled about the room. And then the flame guttered and died. I screamed, drawing my fur up over my head, and plunged beneath the counterpane as the creature beat about the rafters, but no one came to my rescue.

The count was true to his word. He sent up one of my maids the next morning to help me dress. The room was not dark in the daylight, for the hole in the roof let in no little light. There were windows too, but they were narrow and set just above my head. I could not see from them. Once I was dressed, I followed my maid down the narrow circle of stairs to find Andulf at the bottom.

He pushed away from the wall where he had been lounging and bowed. "My lady."

"I do not wish to stay here any longer."

"We might have some trouble leaving." He nodded toward the gate, where a contingent of the count's men sat their horses. They were staring in our direction.

"Does he mean to make me his ward?"

"He means to keep you in his care until your father returns in December."

"I am not his prisoner, that he should treat me thus."

"And should he allow you to leave, would your father not be enraged to hear his word had been violated? That you were not allowed to travel to Rochemont?"

"Yes!" That was my point exactly. Although… I thought about it for a long moment. "The count cannot let me leave, or my father will know his orders have been countermanded."

The knight's gaze traveled to the count's men, and then back to me, before he gave me a long, slow wink.

"This is madness! He cannot keep me captive, hidden away in some tower!"

"And who will free you?"

"You."

"My lady?"

"You must."

"And how can I? I may be your man, my lady, but I am only one man. And what would you do if you left? Where would you go?"

"I would…" What would I do? "I would ride to join the canon and insist upon accompanying him to the abbey."

"By now he has gained Paris."

"Surely the two of us could travel fast enough to overtake him."

"How would that change anything, my lady?"

"Change anything?"

"You wanted to beg Saint Catherine's blessing upon the marriage. Is not the canon doing the same thing?"

"Yes, but—"

"Then what is to be gained by slipping away from the count? It will only anger him further, and once His Majesty the king is told, it will provoke more enmity between them."

"Precisely so!"

"Pardon me for saying, my lady, but to my mind, the terms of the treaty with the Dane have already been decided, otherwise the king would not have left."

"I am not asking for your opinion."

"I am not offering you my opinion. I am only reminding you of the king's opinion."

"Speak plainly."

"He agreed to allow you to consult the relic."

"Yes, but—"

"So now you must let Saint Catherine decide."

Could no one understand? The canon was not going to let the saint decide. My fate had already been determined by men. I did not think there was anything God could do now to intervene. "You will not help me, then."

"You appealed to Saint Catherine, my lady. If you wish to be saved, then it is to her you must look."

I had been mistaken in his loyalties. Apparently he had already become my father's man.

I did not see any reason to pretend I was anything other than a prisoner. Returning to my tower, I vowed I would not leave it until the canon returned from Rochemont. Pray God it would be *without* the relic. I would have thought the presence of a princess would generate some sort of excitement, or that the household and officials from the city would take pains to entertain me. I had planned on refusing such offers of amusement, but I was not able to, for no one came to extend any.

My dinner that forenoon was brought by one of the count's maids. I unbarred the door for her. When she would have lingered, I dismissed her. That evening, a boy came with my supper. He set out the food and the drink upon my small table, and then he went to fasten a new torch to the wall.

"Have you another?"

"My lady?" He paused in his work.

"Have you another one of those?" I did not fancy entertaining a second nighttime creature in the dark. "I wish to have enough that they will last until dawn."

At least one person was eager to do my bidding. He scampered off, thumping down the stairs. At length, I heard footsteps coming back up. But when the door pushed open, it was not the boy. It was the count.

"What am I to do with you, my lady? You refuse to grace us with your person."

It seemed I was not quite so forgotten as I had thought. "I am not in the habit of having to find my way through unknown parts, wandering about like some poor beggar in search of sustenance or welcome."

"Forgive us. We had thought you might be in need of rest from your travels."

"I have recovered."

The ends of his lips crimped into a frown. "My lord, the king, sent a message to the mayor, informing him of your stop here before journeying to the abbey, and inquiring after your welcome to our city. The mayor regrets he was not previously aware of your presence. He hastens to organize a fete on your behalf."

"And I regret I will not be available."

He smiled, though it was perfunctory, without pleasure. "I have not yet told you when it will be."

"You cannot hold a princess as your prisoner and then command her to display herself at your whim."

"You are not being held anywhere. You are free to

go about the palace and the grounds. If you complain of restraint, then you have chosen it for yourself."

"And what of the city? May I wander about the streets? And what of the countryside?"

"I am sure they would not please you."

"Being lodged in an ill-kept room such as this does not please me either. Nor does the absence of my people. So I do not see why I should take such pains to please your people."

"You do not seem to understand that your father's name holds little importance here. He has done nothing to succor us in our tribulations. I have done everything."

"Do you not understand that your meaning could be taken as treason?"

"Your father himself would agree with me. Did he not approve the terms of the treaty? Did he not cede the Dane lands in exchange for help in protecting his borders?"

"He exchanged your lands, if I am not mistaken."

His brow darkened as rage glimmered in his eyes. "He has taken a policy of protecting his own men in return for me risking mine. A policy that has bred no little feeling of ill will here in Neustria. So forgive me if I do not seem properly grateful." He paused, taking a deep breath and steeling his jaw. "You will accompany us to the fete and give these people, whom your father seems to have forgotten, the honor of your presence. My lady."

He was, perhaps, not wholly wrong about having done the bulk of the work in protecting this western edge of my father's empire, though he might have been more gracious about it. There could be no harm in trying to establish my father's good name among these people. And so I inclined my head by way of acquiescence. "Then perhaps your lady wife would care to attend me."

His jaw tightened. "Of course. You do us great honor."

❧

The fete took place two days after my conversation with the count. I'm certain it must have galled him that I had to be given the place of honor.

As I picked at my food, talk swirled of the hunt and the animals with which the count had stocked his park. He had taken my attendants; he had placed me in a tower. Why should I be denied the pleasures of the hunt? Especially when they could be used to my advantage? For what better way could there be to distract his attention. If I could manage to remain at the outer edges of the party, then I might be able to escape when no one was watching. "There has been a hunt organized?"

He spared me a glance as he nodded. "The day after tomorrow."

"May I accompany you then?"

The count's lips pursed as he contemplated me. "What would I tell the Dane if you were to come to injury, or if you should lose yourself in our deep, dark wood?"

I raised my voice as I answered. If he would not let me ride, there were others present who might advocate on my behalf. "I have survived many a long ride in woods more dense, and with trees much thicker than yours."

Several of the nobles grabbed at their cups and took deep, long draughts. Only the trembling of their shoulders betrayed the laughter that had seized them.

I recognized that sort of laughter. I had said something I should not have. And now the count was scowling. I felt my cheeks pink as I considered what to say next. I must be allowed to join the hunt! "The royal demesnes are the finest in Christendom. Perhaps you fear I shall best your men."

His smile flashed briefly, though I could have sworn it mocked me. "I have no fear of that."

I decided to try a different tack. "Though I can hardly credit the reports, it has long been rumored your lands are the equal of my father's. If that were true, then I should very much like to see them."

One of the local nobility banged his cup against the table. "Let her ride!"

Another joined him. "What harm can it do?"

His eyes probed mine. I only hoped I betrayed none of my thoughts. Finally he nodded. "Then see my lands, you shall."

CHAPTER 17

VER THE NEXT DAY, I SAVED WHAT I COULD FROM my meals. I would have warned Andulf, but I considered the less he knew the better. Once away, speed would be to our advantage. After we cleared the count's lands, we could survive on what we hunted. Only one day, perhaps two, would be needed before we could declare ourselves away from the count's lands and out of his reach. And the farther east we traveled, the more friends I might find.

On the morning of the hunt, I wrapped the food—a wedge of cheese and some bread—in a cloth and tied the ends about my thigh. When I descended, I found my palfrey waiting for me, my gilt-embroidered caparison glinting in the sunlight. Though the day was cool, I knew the riding would soon warm me.

While the count's men formed up beside me, Andulf remained at the count's side.

"You would keep my man?" As I fled to my father, I would need his help.

The count rode close. "I wished to observe him and see if there is not something I can learn and—"

"He is not yours to command!" I spoke the words louder, perhaps, than I had meant to.

"—*and*, since you do not know my lands, I thought it prudent to send with you those who do."

Had he managed to discern my plans? Again I was caught between my suspicions and his eminently reasonable prudence. To do anything other than accept his considerate concern would seem strange indeed. "Your forethought is much appreciated." I tried to smile. I do not think I succeeded.

He gestured toward the gate. "Shall we?"

We rode through streets both narrow and twisted before leaving the city behind us. Spread about us were fields. The peasants were plowing, cheeks gone red from exertion. Sweat seeped down their dust-lined brows into their eyes. At the far edge of the fields, a hedge of trees had laid a boundary betwixt sky and the upturned earth. The count's men kept a respectable distance, and they let me set my own pace, but never did they leave me, and never did their attention stray from me.

As we rode into the forest, awaiting the bark of dogs or the signal of a horn, the air shed its scent of dust. The horses ventured forth onto a cushion of fallen leaves, releasing the odor of decay with each step, and cracking the acorns that littered the ground. The taller oaks had already given up their orange mantles in exchange for scarlet. Parti-colored leaves spun down upon us as we went deeper into the wood. Already, sky could be glimpsed through limbs gone bare at their tips and trees gone bald at their tops.

A horn sounded.

Time stopped for just an instant as it hung in that space of mottled darkness and light. Then all the earth seemed to shift. Fallen leaves took flight as horses were spurred into a canter. Shouts rose and joined the horns in chorus as we set out with merry abandon. My palfrey leaped forward at my urging. I fed her more rein, and she stretched out her neck as she veered around brush and sprang over fallen trees. My hair fanned out behind me, tugging against the constraint of my fillet. I searched the wood before us, straining for a sight of the prey that awaited.

And then I remembered what I must do.

The horn sounded once more. It was closer this time, but off toward the left.

As the count's men adjusted their course, I too adjusted mine, ever so minutely. I could not delay leaving, so I would have to do it without the luxury of my knight. I would make for the royal abbey at Chelles, where I could claim sanctuary. From there, I could send a message to my father.

As the count's men thrashed through a coppice, I let my palfrey carry me away from them, though none too quickly, for I did not wish to raise alarm.

"My lady!" The shout came from the count's men. Too early they had remembered me. I had not gone quickly enough. Turning a full shoulder to them, I raised a hand in reply.

The horn sounded again, still farther to the left.

As the count's men reeled to the chase, I spurred my palfrey forward in the opposite direction, and this time I did not dally in the doing of it. Though twigs snapped and my horse's hooves thundered, I could only pray they were masked by the noisome hunt. Though I took care to duck low-lying branches, one of them reached out and tore off my fillet.

Behind me, the horn sounded. Once. Twice. And then a long, wavering note. They had cornered the prey, then. I tossed a glance back across my shoulder, envying them the thrill of the hunt.

When I turned back, Andulf was there before me.

Providence had conspired to reunite us! But as I careened toward him, he did not move.

I jerked at the reins. The horse arched her neck, chafing at the bit. She danced sidewise to arrest her flight, slipping across the acorns that blanketed the ground. As we jounced by, the knight reached forward and grabbed hold of the reins, wrenching them from my grasp.

"What do you do?"

"I am trying to protect you, my lady." The effort he exerted in mastering the horse showed as a thin white line above his lips.

"I do not want your protection. Come and quickly, while they are not yet with us. We shall make our escape."

He drew my horse to a standstill.

"Release me!"

"No, my lady."

No? "Have you forgotten whom you serve?"

Around us, there was a rustling in the underbrush, and then, to our immediate right, a hound began to howl.

"My lord the king has entrusted your safety to me, and it would not be safe to go deeper into this wood alone."

"But I am not safe anywhere in the count's grasp."

"You may not be safe, but at least your life is not in danger."

I kicked at my palfrey with my heels. She tried to spring from the knight, but he held the reins fast, so I put out a foot and kicked at his courser. The creature snorted and rose up on its hind feet. The knight dropped my reins so he could take a firmer grip on his own. Fisting my hands in my horse's mane, I kicked at her, urging her forward.

But the count had appeared from the wood in front of me like an apparition in that mottled light.

He took us both in with a glance, lifting his chin and peering at us through narrowed eyes. "What happens here?"

His men rode up in trio behind him, dashing whatever hope there might have been of fleeing.

Andulf answered. "My lady thought she saw a hare farther on, just there." He gestured toward a jumble of large stones that had been piled atop one another to form a sort of mound.

The count's gaze shifted there, to one of the most unlikely spots for a hare I had ever seen. "Is that true, my lady?"

Why had Andulf stayed me from my course? If he had not stopped me, we could both have been free of the count by now. "It is as he said."

The count frowned as he peered at the mound. "I have never known a hare to favor such an exposed position." His gaze swung back to me. "There are not so few creatures here that you must weary yourself in the process of hunting a single hare." He handed my fillet to me.

I took it from him. "I was just going back to retrieve it when my man found me."

"And such a long way back it was." His gaze lingered on me. Then he turned his horse toward the nobles who trailed him. But not before instructing his men to stay with me for the rest of the hunt.

When we returned to the palace, I excused myself from any further activity and made for my tower.

Andulf had difficult work keeping up with me. His shoes slapped along the packed earth of the courtyard as he jogged to catch me. "My lady. Wait!"

I spun on my heel, throwing my mantle out around me. "Wait? For what? For you to stay me once more? So that you can keep me from gaining my freedom?"

"The count was riding right behind me. I wanted only to help you."

"Help me! You ruined my best chance of escape."

"You said you would wait for Saint Catherine. If you leave now, it would put into question the king's honor."

What could I say to that? How could I admit to my fears? To my suspicions that the saint's power could be counted as nothing compared to the wiles of men?

"If you wish to allow Saint Catherine to decide, then you must give her leave to decide, my lady. Or some might think you have lost your faith."

"Can you not see? The decision has already been made." I started for my tower once more.

"Yes." He called out after me. "By God Himself. So you see you can change nothing. Even your leaving would not alter the outcome."

I did not slow my step, but threw my words over my shoulder. "It would if I were not here in December to wed the Dane."

"Ah. But when you ask something of the Almighty, you must first be certain you do not ask with an answer already in hand."

What gave him the right to speak to me thus? I changed course and rounded on him. "How simple this must seem to you! How easy it is to trust in God when you do not have to trust Him for your life."

"On the contrary. I think it would be far more difficult to trust if nothing depended upon my faith."

"So you believe then? That Saint Catherine will decide?"

"I believe when I should need it, I will have faith to believe."

"What sort of belief is that?"

"The most sturdy of kinds."

I did not understand him at all. Tears of frustration

swamped my vision. "You tell me I must wait? That I must put up with this insolence and stay with this group who wants only to see me given over to the pagan?"

"I think you can do nothing else."

"What good are you to me then? And what gives you the right to decide? Be confident in this: next time I set my eyes on escape, I will not stop for you."

❦

My dinner had been sent up to me, but my hunger had vanished, and so I left it on the table, undisturbed. I had determined to put my exile to use and work a border around one of my tunics in gold thread. I had not yet grown used to sleeping alone, and so I lit three torches that night, hoping the light would help me in my work. I soon regretted the decision as the smoke served only to darken the gloom as it smudged the lines between shadow and light. Gathering my furs about me, I was bound for my bed when a boy suddenly appeared on the far side of the room.

I crossed myself, whispering a hurried prayer, and then called upon the name of Our Lord for deliverance.

The smoke parted in wispy swirls as he advanced. As he approached, I could see him more clearly. He was thin and short of stature, with a mop of unruly dark hair. His right cheek had been split and was marked by a green-colored bruise. Two paces from me, he stopped. "Are you the princess?"

"Who—who are you?"

He dropped to one knee. "I am Hugh, my lady."

Hugh. "Hugh?"

"Yes, my lady."

"The count's son, Hugh?" The one whose name I had invoked to my father? Had the count sent the boy to spy on me? I could not seem to gather my wits, nor to keep my knees from knocking together at the nobs. "How did you get here?"

"It's for me know." He glanced around, then fixed his gaze back on me. "So...you are the princess?"

"Yes." I tried to gather myself to my full height, but I fear I failed at that as well. "But what are you doing here? What gives you the right to approach me thus?"

He rose and then stood looking at me, hands clasped in front of him. "I came to meet you."

It was to this runt of a lad the count had wished to wed me several years back. Having seen the boy, I could take it as nothing but an affront. "Now that you have met me, you may leave."

He glanced over at the tray that sat on the table. "Are you going to eat?"

"No."

"May I have it then?"

"You may do as you wish."

"Thank you." He bowed and then sat on a stool and made quick work of the food.

I looked away as he chewed. It made me hungry.

When he was done, he simply sat there, scuffing the toe of his shoe against the floor. "I suppose I shall go then."

"You should do what you like." I had not invited him, though now that he was here, the gloom seemed much less frightening.

"I could stay, if you want. Nobody's looking for me."

I wouldn't either. He was such a small and puny boy, I wondered that anyone ever noticed him at all.

He was watching me, brow quirked, waiting, I suppose, for an answer.

"You can stay. For a while. As long as you tell me how you got here."

He had gone back to the tray and was picking at the crumbs. But at my demand, he jerked an elbow at the wall he'd come through. "By the stair."

"The stair is there." I nodded in the other direction toward the door.

"I meant the other stair."

"But there is no other stair. There's only one way in."

He'd gone on to quaff his thirst with my wine, so he dried his mouth on his sleeve before he answered. "There are two of them."

"But there's only one door." If there were a second, I would have noticed. There was only one way into the tower, and there was only one way out of the palace grounds.

He seemed to think on my words for a moment as he took another drink. "That's true. Just one door."

"Then, pray tell, how can there be another stair?"

"You probably wouldn't call it a stair, my lady. It's not a proper one, in any case."

"Then show me the improper stair, please."

I followed him toward the wall through which he'd come. But this time, he did not walk through it.

"There is no stair here!"

"It's not on the inside. It's on the outside."

"Outside?"

As I stood there, perplexed and befuddled, he jammed his toes into a crack in the wall and vaulted up, curling his hand around the window's opening. And then he pulled himself up onto it.

"Where are you?"

He lay on the ledge and reached a hand down. "If you just put your toe in that crack there, my lady…"

"You want me to—to come up there?! There's no room for me."

His wiggled his fingers as he reached for my hand. "If you want to see the stair…"

"I cannot just—" do what it was he seemed to expect me to do.

"It's not much different than mounting a horse. Only it's a bit higher. And you would not wish to put too much force into it, or you might just throw yourself through the window. And if—"

"Yes, I see." I put the toe of my shoe into the crack and then stretched up, grabbing at his hand.

He tugged on my arm, but it did little good. "You're heavier than you look, my lady." He released my hand, and I fell back to the floor. "I can't hoist you." He pushed to sitting, letting his legs dangle over the edge.

I pushed up onto an elbow as I swept my hair from my eyes. "But you say there's a stair out there?" If I could exit the tower without being seen, then perhaps there was a way to exit the palace grounds as well.

"I'm the only one who ever uses it."

I picked myself up from the ground and shook out the fur that had fallen from my shoulders. There had to be some way to reach that window… Ah! "Come down and move my bed over here so I can climb up on it."

"The bed?"

"That way, if I fall, I won't come to any harm."

He jumped down and scrambled over to the bed. Crawling across it, he fixed himself between the bed and the wall. But no matter how he pushed and heaved, he could not move it. Finally he came away from it and stood before me, panting, hands on his knees. "You're going to have to help, my lady."

Shedding my fur, I applied myself to one side of the frame. When pulling did not get us anywhere, I moved to the other end and pushed. But still, even the two of us could not budge it.

The boy finally gave up. "It's no use."

I agreed with him, though it pained me to say it. "Then get my chest. That will have to do."

The boy made short work of pushing it over to the window. We ought to have used it from the first.

He hopped atop it and then leaped up to the window ledge.

"Come on, then!" He was already lying on the ledge, arm extended.

I stepped up onto the chest and grabbed his hand.

"Jump."

"Jump?"

"Jump!"

I jumped. He gave a mighty tug on my arm, and soon I found myself kneeling in the window beside him, though it felt as if he had wrenched my arm from my shoulder.

The moon had bathed this side of the tower in silvered light. I could see now there was nothing behind the structure but the palisade that enclosed the palace grounds.

Leaning forward, I looked out over the edge. First to the left, then to the right, but I saw no stair. "Where is it?"

"There."

I looked beneath us to where he was pointing, but I could see nothing. "Where?"

"Right there." He'd leaned rather farther out than was prudent and took a big swipe at a sort of peg, which seemed to protrude from the wooden walls.

"See? Look at them."

"*That* is the stair?" I used the term loosely, for his stair appeared to be made of stubby pegs shoved into the tower between the boards at irregular intervals. "That's not a stair." And it wouldn't help me.

"I made it myself. I wanted a place just for me, where I could go whenever my father—" He broke off speaking.

"Whenever your father...what?"

He shrugged. "He does not seem to like me much, my lady."

"Was it he who did that?" I put a finger to his cheek.

He winced, though he said nothing.

I considered that I ought to let him keep his pride, since he had very little else to show for himself. "You could not use the real stair like everyone else?"

He gave me a knowing look. "Sometimes you don't want anyone to know where you are. And I can climb it quick as a squirrel. Want to try it?"

"No." I did not. I had not suffered from my time here, only to lose my life by pitching myself from the tower's window.

"It's not so difficult."

As I watched, he turned and rolled onto his belly. Then he slid out the window and dangled by his fingers as he felt along the wall with the tips of his toes. Finding the first stub, he beamed up at me. "See? First one's the worst."

"They all look bad to me."

"It's easy. There's hardly any sport to it."

I leaned out farther to watch as he climbed down, hopping this way and that to follow his stair. He jumped the last bit, leaving me gasping when he fell. But he soon bounced up like a court tumbler. Collecting his hat, he doffed it as he bowed. And then he gave a cheery wave as he ran toward the front of the tower. For the first time since I'd arrived, I slept without once waking in the night.

CHAPTER 18

Juliana

ROCHEMONT ABBEY

A S I WALKED TOWARD THE CHURCH, EAGER TO reach my sanctuary of golden light, a great wailing arose from the hospice. As I watched, the door was flung open and the abbess's new bailiff appeared. He was dragging a woman behind him. As soon as she passed the threshold of the door, he pushed her out into the muddied courtyard.

Astonished, I came to a halt.

He soon reappeared, arms filled with a wriggling man whose feet were bound in rags. He proceeded to pitch the man into the mud beside the woman.

Striding toward him, I held out my hand, anxious that he should stop his abuse. "What happens here?"

"They're to leave."

"But why?"

"The abbess's orders." He drew me aside as another man, one of the laymen, pushed several other people from the door.

"But they're not well."

"Harvest was lean this year. She said there's no stores for those who don't deserve them."

"Don't deserve!" We none of us deserved any good thing. I watched the eviction with growing horror. "This is *not right!*"

The abbess's men paused to survey those who sat on the ground, gazing about with befuddlement. "We're just doing what the abbess said."

Just doing what the abbess said had become synonymous with unseemly parsimony and an appalling lack of good sense. These pitiful men and women had not the where-withal to help themselves, and now the men were adding children to their number.

Not the children!

Anyone but them. Anything but those. "Stop." I put a hand on the arm of the man who transported several of the youngest into the yard.

"Abbess's orders."

I fisted my hand in the fabric of his tunic. "But this is madness!"

A child, eyes shimmering with tears, reached for me with outstretched hands.

As I felt those old cords of guilt and shame draw tight about my heart, I retreated, grasping my black tunic tight about the throat. "You cannot cast out the children."

"Don't have any choice in the matter." He dropped the children to the ground and then turned to go back inside.

They stood there, bare feet sunk into the frost-scarred mud. I might have expected one of the men or women to gather them up, but no one moved. They all seemed ren-dered witless by their rude dislodgement.

And then one of the children began to cry. It was not a shriek. I might have remained unmoved by a display of umbrage or anger, but the child whimpered. That piteous, heartfelt cry crumbled every defense by which I had hoped to buttress my wounded heart.

I snatched up the mite, clasping it to my chest, and went in search of the abbess.

∾

"Who?" The abbess looked up at Sister Berta, her new prioress, as I stood in the entrance to her chamber.

I set the child down beside me.

Sister Berta's frown deepened as she glanced at me. "Sister Juliana. She tends Saint Catherine's chapel."

The abbess's gaze sharpened. "The one who takes in all the pilgrims' gifts?"

I took it upon myself to reply. "Among other things, Your Grace."

"Why are you here?" The abbess pulled a dried date from a tray that rode her lap. She rolled it between her fingers before putting it into her mouth.

I stepped across the threshold. "Women and children are being evicted from the hospice, Reverend Mother."

Her brown eyes looked at me with neither surprise nor apology. "Yes."

"You must put a stop to it." The child slipped its cold, bony hand into my own. Glancing down, I saw its gaze fixed upon the abbess's tray. "The men said you had ordered the eviction."

Her eyes flicked from me to the child. "I did."

"Why?"

"Because we cannot afford them." She plucked another sweet from the tray.

"But it is not for us to decide. We are keepers of the poor, sanctuary for the weak, and solace for the brokenhearted."

"Yes. All of whom expect to be housed. And fed. Those who can leave should do so. Somewhere, someone must be eager to put an able-bodied child to use." She pronounced the words without inflection or emotion. "The pilgrims can stay for one night and pass on. And then the sisters who keep the hospice can apply their efforts elsewhere." She paused, and then looked up toward the ceiling where someone had begun pasting gold leaf onto the beams. After sighing, she continued. "For us to keep those who cannot contribute to this community is not possible. The harvest has been poor."

"And yet, you eat those?" I do not know how I dared to speak those words.

She glanced down at the tray. "I had them brought special."

I advanced and took a date from it and then gave it to the child.

"What!"

"In a year of lean harvests, the poor must eat whatever food can be found."

Her mouth dropped open. "I shall have you—I shall have you—"

I felt my brow quirk.

"—you—!"

"This place is not here for your service. Your position is supposed to be used in the service of others."

"If you have such grave concerns about the welfare of the hospice, then you shall be the one to care for those who are left."

I had walked into a trap of my own making. "Not the children, Your Grace." I had avoided that fate thus far. I would beg if I had to in order to be released from it now.

"The children? You mean the young ones? Like that?" She gave a pointed look at the urchin by my side.

I nodded.

"No. I did not mean them. They're to be put out to those in the village. I meant the others. The dull-witted."

The dull-witted. This abbey, like all the others in the realm, collected them. Those not fit for earthly duties were always given to us so we could fit them for the heavenly realms, or at least look after them until they stepped from this life into the next.

She looked at me, lips pursed as if reconsidering. But then she nodded and picked up another date. "Yes. I think I would like you to look after them. That should keep you busy enough not to put my commands to question."

"But what will happen to Saint Catherine?"

"I'll have one of the others, one of those novices, look after her."

"But they don't know—"

"They don't know what? How to light a candle? How to trim a lamp? We both know that's not what you've been after down there. My father always wondered why the abbess didn't have more funds at her disposal."

"Are you speaking of the pilgrims' gifts? Because they aren't collected for the abbess. They are collected for—"

"Why do you stand there gawping? You have charges to be looked after." The Queen Mother herself had never been so imperious as this young girl who had taken on the duties of abbess. She shooed me away with a hand as she contemplated her next selection of sweetmeats.

Taking the child with me, I returned to the hospice. None were left of the dozen that had been rudely cast out not long before. As I drew the door open, a scene of chaos greeted me. If I had once thought the abbey plain, this place was even more austere. But now the pallets had been overturned, and the stools had been tossed about. The table sat on its side.

"Sister Juliana?" Sister Sybilla stopped setting the room to rights long enough to pause beside me.

"The abbess sent me to you."

Her brow peaked. "Then who is tending Saint Catherine's chapel?"

I might have answered, but at that moment, a hackle-raising screech rang through the air. We turned to see a girl screaming at…nothing at all.

"What—what's wrong with her?"

"She can't speak." Sister Sybilla gave her a sharp glance. "Or she won't."

A certain gleam in the girl's eye made me think perhaps the latter was the case.

"And this one hardly ever stops." She pointed to a boy who might have seen a good dozen years. He was sitting on one of the righted stools, bobbing his head to some melody only he could hear.

His dark eyes were slanted at the corners, and as we passed, his mouth tipped up into a smile. "Hardly ever stops. Hardly ever stops. Hardly ever stops."

"A right mimic, he is."

The boy stood and slipped a hand into Sister Sybilla's.

She pulled hers away, took him by the shoulders, turned him around, and pushed him back onto the stool.

She pointed to a boy who stood in the middle of the room, flapping his arms up and down. "That one there hasn't the sense God gave a goose."

"Yes, he does." A boy nearly fully grown rose from the floor to defy the nun.

She seemed to cower under his gaze. "He's never said one blessed word to me."

"It's only because you always grab at his arms and try to make him stop. If you would leave him be, then he might say something."

The boy in question took a deliberate step away from us

196

and then a hop. A step and a hop. Another step and another hop, all the way to a corner.

The older boy gave us a scowl and then joined the younger one in the corner at the other side of the room.

"Who is that?" The young man's clothes seemed too fine to be one of the workers, and he held himself more like a young lord than a peasant.

She crossed herself. "He's the young abbess's brother, and the devil incarnate! He may look as if he has his wits about him, but just as soon as you think it, the demons come to possess him again."

"Then why does he stay?" I would think those with demons would flee the work of Our Lord.

"Where else can he go? Their father entrusted him to our care. The heir he is, though he'll never inherit. We can do nothing else but look after him and hope he won't eventually murder us all."

I eyed the boy over my shoulder. He did not look like one possessed. He was sitting now beside the girl who had been screeching, patiently spooning gruel into her mouth.

"And those?" I nodded toward a group of children who reclined upon the packed earth of the floor, boys and girls together, not unlike a litter of pups. As I discerned one from the other, I saw their limbs were twisted and bent.

"Lame, the lot of them." She went over and picked through the pile, separating one from the rest and dragging him out by the elbow. "But they have to be toileted now and then." She slung an arm around his waist. "Help me."

The lad was meager and frail. As we walked him to the outhouse, a cough wracked his slender body.

"Ought to have died, this one. Still might. But at least she can't throw these out." Sister Sybilla spoke the words with no little satisfaction. "Where else would they go? If they cannot come by aid at God's house, then where else will they find it?" Having said that, she grimly went about the task of helping him, and then we walked him back to the hospice and returned him to the pallet.

The hours passed slowly, and without the benefit of workers to aid us, and because our charges needed constant attention, we could not both attend the offices. At midday, I went at sext. Sister Sybilla went later, at none. Upon her return from the church, as she entered the hospice, her eyes widened as she let out a bellow. "Stop him!"

CHAPTER 19

*S*TARTLED FROM MY WORK, I TURNED AND THEN FOL-
lowed the direction of her outflung finger. Over by
the hearth in the middle of the room, one of the boys was
on his hands and knees, sifting through the ashes.

"Take it away from him, I tell you!"

As I walked over to the lad, he fished a charred twig from
the hearth.

Poor lad. He could not have been more than six or seven
years old, and in a place like this, he must have been in want
of amusement. I could not find it in my heart to blame him
for that. I put a hand to his shoulder. He flinched at my
touch, threw an arm up over his face, and backed away from
me. And then, as I watched, he put the twig to his mouth
and took a bite.

"Stop! You cannot—!" I reached for his hand.

Sister Sybilla joined me, face purpled with rage. "Do we
not feed him? Do we not lodge him? And this is how we are
thanked?" She grabbed him by the arm. "Out with it!" She
put a cupped hand to his mouth.

He closed his fist around the twig and shoved it behind his
back as he screwed his mouth shut.

"Out with it!" She grabbed hold of his ear and gave it
a twist.

His mouth dropped open as his eyes filled with tears.

Applying the heel of her hand to his back, she gave a mighty whack, and the bit of twig flew out of his mouth. "Now give me the rest!"

He gave his head a solemn shake.

"Give it to me! Or I shall—I shall—" She wrenched his arm from his back and pried his fingers apart. Scraping the twig from his hand, she threw it into the fire. And then, taking up a broom, she pushed all the rest of the ashes and charred wood back toward the flames.

Clamping his palms to his ears, he began to scream.

I put a hand to his arm.

He kicked at me and then sprang away toward the door.

"Stop him!" Sister Sybilla shook her broom at his back.

The young lord looked up from a book he had been reading and scrambled to his feet, but by then the lad was long gone.

"Sweet Mary, Mother of God!" She clapped a hand to her mouth, looking as shocked as I was those words had come from her lips. "I give him bread. I give him gruel. And he insists on eating—!" Her words were choked by her frustration. Her face sagging with exhaustion.

"I am sure he does not mean it as ingratitude."

"What else could it be? For what other reason would he insist upon doing it? And before my very face?"

"Are there not things to which all of us cling? Even when, by their very baseness, they cannot be good for us?"

She looked at me for a moment, mouth slack with incomprehension. And then she lifted her chin in umbrage. "The next time he comes to me with a splinter stuck through his tongue, I'll send him to you to remove it. Eating things like that! If he does not stop, he will surely die. And then he'll know I was right. And so will you!"

"He cannot know what he's doing."

"Cannot—! How could you sift through the ashes of the hearth and sneak out a burnt twig, *from the ashes* mind you, and then hide it in your hand and not know what you're about?"

"He cannot mean to offend you by it."

"Me! Better to worry about the offense he gives to his creator. Wood was not meant to be eaten! Spurning God's good food for a—a—a piece of wood!" She spluttered away toward the others, but I could not help thinking we all spurned God's good provision at one time or another for things just as vile and incomprehensible as that boy's burnt piece of wood.

℘

At vespers, the abbess stopped me as I left the church to return to Sister Sybilla.

"Are you still here?" It was clear she had rather hoped I would not be.

I did not answer.

She smirked. "Do you find the hospice amusing? Are you happy with your new position?"

Was I happy?

Another woman in a different place had once asked me that question.

Both women had known I was not.

The other woman, the Queen Mother, had reached out to pat my cheek after she had asked her question, but I had stepped back, out of her reach into Charles's chamber.

She had followed me into the room. "I cannot blame you if you are not. It's rather gloomy here, shut up in the city. But summer should be better. We'll go to the countryside then. You remember. You'll be able to ride with Charles in the hunt every day. That should be amusing."

I had never liked horses, and I had not ever been trained to hunt. As the queen never went, there had been no need for me to go either.

"I had forgotten. You don't like to ride. Not to worry. It won't seem long, and then we'll be off to Compiègne, and after to Laon. I heard Charles say he might even want to spend some weeks at Verdun this year."

The talk of travel wearied me. "Why do you hate me so?"

"*Hate* you! You flatter yourself."

"You seem to despise me."

"It would be hard to despise someone I so rarely think of, would you not agree?"

"Is it his love you begrudge me?"

"Love. Hate. Two of the most tiresome words I know."

"He can love us both. We do not have to be in competition for his affections."

She turned and came at me. "Love us *both*! How generous you are. How gracious you seem. But how could that ever be? How could he love the woman who would tie his hands, as well as the woman who wants nothing but to see him succeed in reuniting the empire? Can you not see he must choose?"

She thought I would keep him from his fondest dream?

"Losing his heart to a base, common woman, placing his passions above his duties! At last, he is in a position to reclaim the kingdom his forbears lost, and yet he is bewitched by you. Like father like son. And I will see you in hell before I let you ruin him the way that daughter of a whore ruined his father!"

I began to see the foundation of bitterness that lay beneath her humiliations. The hurt that stoked her fury. And then I understood: it wasn't me she hated. What she hated was the love I'd been given. "You are jealous of me." I possessed what she had always wanted. She may have gained Charles the throne, but I had gained his heart. I was loved.

"Jealous? Such nonsense. How could I be jealous of you? I will make him be the king his father was not. You can only degrade him. You are nothing. You have nothing, and you can bring him no honor. He will listen to me; he *needs* me." She seized me by the arm. "I am the queen, the rightful queen. I always was. I always will be. Can you not see? There is no place for you here."

"I never asked for a place. I do not want one. I want only to be with him."

"God in heaven!" she scoffed. "As if that were nothing. You ask for everything! How completely noble that sounds. And how utterly selfish you are!" She left the room in a whirl of Tyrian purple-colored robes, and I did not see her that evening. She sent word down to the great hall that she was ill.

But that did not keep her words from echoing in my thoughts. Was I as selfish as she claimed me to be?

As the concubine of the king, I had gotten into the habit of avoiding the archbishop, but the next week, I sought him out. And when I found him, I asked him whether the Queen Mother was right.

"I only ask, Your Excellency, because I want to do what is right."

"For whom?"

"For...for everyone."

"Then you must cease your sinful pursuits. No good can come of them. You must know God cannot approve of you."

I did know, and it shamed me. But there was no undoing

what had been done, and Charles said we would marry. So what else, pray heaven, was I to do but wait? "Am I...*am* I being selfish then?"

"We are all of us selfish."

"But am I being selfish by being here. The Queen Mother says I am distracting."

"Woman is ever distracting to Man."

"But she says if I stay here, then the king can never fulfill his duties."

He peered at me more closely. "How so?"

"She says I have no family, no influence. That I can do nothing for him."

"Are you saying he means to *marry* you?"

I did not understand why everyone always seemed so surprised. We hardly spoke of anything else between us, and yet, it seemed no one else had heard of our plans.

I asked Charles about it that evening as he changed his tunic for supper. I had just returned Gisele to the arms of her nursemaid. "Have you told anyone about us?"

He laughed as he nuzzled the babe's smooth, plump cheek. "Do you not think they may have already guessed?" She squealed as he tweaked her nose before sending the nursemaid away.

"I meant have you told anyone about our plan?"

"What plan?" He kissed me. It was a deep and lingering kiss, which made me struggle to hold onto my thought.

As he edged me toward the bed, through great effort I pulled myself from his arms. "Charles? Have you?"

"What? Told anyone what?"

"That we are to marry."

"I had thought…" He advanced upon me once more.
"Had I not told you? I thought for certain I had…" His
words broke off as he grinned.

I might have returned his smile as I usually did, but I
wanted an answer.

He tried to tickle me with the silk tasseled tip of my girdle.
"Why? Have you?"

"I told the archbishop today, and he seemed bothered by
the idea."

"Ah." Leaving off his pursuit of me, he opened the door
and stepped into the hall. Summoning his valet, he asked
the man to fetch one of his crowns, and then he returned
his attentions to me. "I hate to wear them, they pinch like
the devil at my ears, but some Lotharingians are here and—"

"Charles!"

He took up my hand and held it to his heart. "These
things…they take time. I do intend upon telling him. I plan
on telling everyone. But not yet. Things are so unsettled just
now. In autumn …maybe then…"

"But we *are* to marry?"

"Of course we're to marry. Why would we not?"

"I just… I think… People think… I do you no good."

"You do me no *good*? How can you say that?"

"I can do nothing for you but—"

"Who is it that says these things?"

"I think people were hoping you would marry for alliances or for armies or—"

"Then these people will be doomed to disappointment."

"But I am no one, Charles. I have no influence: no father
and no uncles. And you need people to help you if you
hope to—"

He laid a finger across my lips. "I do have people to help
me. And there are plenty of men who come here offering

alliances, but I have no one else to love me. Not the way you do."

I might have believed him if his mother had not kept harping at the idea. She appeared at my door one night when I had slipped from the evening's amusements early to take solace in my bed. She swept into the room and dismissed the maids who served me. Then she stood by the fire in the center of the room, hand at her hip as she surveyed the place.

"I thought I might find you here."

I fumbled with the counterpane as I pushed myself to sitting.

She raised a hand. "Do not bother yourself. I know how you feel. It's never pleasant to be where you are not wanted."

"It is not that I am not wanted, it is that *I* do not want..." I sighed. It's that I did not wish to be reminded, by the look in people's eyes, that they did not want me there. She was right.

She had come toward the bed, brow raised. Now she was looking down at me with something quite close to pity in her eyes. "And Charles did not stay you?"

He had not.

"He is too much like his father. If you are to survive here, then you will have to make them accept you. And then, once you have done it, they will want you. And eventually, he might too."

He already did want me. He had never made me feel as if he did not. That is how I had come to be in his bed. Charles had never been the problem. "He never said—"

"Has he not? But he should. He must. He ought to make clear what he expects people to think of you. Do you really believe they would snub you as they do if the king had spoken on your behalf?"

I had not thought on it before.

"Or perhaps I am mistaken. Perhaps he already has."

It was true the court had turned itself inside out trying to please their new king. The moment he made known his wishes, there was a veritable rush of nobles trying to meet them. "What if?"

Her eyes narrowed. "What if...what?"

"What if you are right?"

For once she did not mock me. If she had, perhaps I would have chosen a different path. She put a hand to the curtains that hung about the bed, running a finger over the gold embroidery. "If you cannot bring yourself to believe me, then ask him. Ask him what it is he wants. And then you will see for yourself whether there is a place for you here."

I lifted my chin, for I did not like the way she presumed to know me. "I shall."

"Good."

And I did not like the way her lips lifted at the corners as she left.

CHAPTER 20

I DID NOT SEE CHARLES FOR THE NEXT WEEK, AT LEAST not long enough to talk to him. The war with Odo for control of the kingdom had consumed his attentions, and he spent all of his time with his counselors.

Feeling rather neglected and not willing to wait any longer to speak to him, I decided to accompany him as he rode one afternoon, exchanging the muddy, winter-worn city for the budding spring in the countryside outside the city's walls.

"Juliana!" He smiled when he saw me approach the stables.

My heart leaped to witness his regard. Surely his mother was mistaken.

He sent his men out ahead of us so we could ride together. And then he dismissed the grooms so he could help me mount. He cupped his hands, stooping forward so I could lift myself up. And then he handed me the reins. "You do not usually ride."

"No. I do not like it. But, I do like you."

He took up my hand and kissed it. "I saw Gisele this morning. She smiled at me."

Who would not smile at him, so brave, so noble, so handsome was he?

"You should ride more. You would learn to like it."

I did not think that possible. As we passed through the

city's walls, I saw that ahead of us, at the crest of a hill, his nobles were waiting. If I wanted to ask my question, I needed to do it quickly. "I wish to ask you something."

"Ask of me anything you like." These past months of wearing a crown seemed to have given him a newfound confidence.

"What is it you want, Charles?"

He eyed his waiting nobles. "What do I want?"

I nodded. "More than anything, what is it you want?"

"I want to put the empire back together." He nudged his horse toward mine, extending his hand toward me.

I put mine into it.

"I have the support of Burgundy and Aquitaine, and once I have Lorraine, then I will know I am surely blessed. Can you imagine it? Taking up residence again at the palace in Aachen as the great King Charles did so long ago? I was named for him, you know." As we approached the hill, he continued on about the empire in general and Lorraine in particular, but already I had heard enough. What he wanted more than anything was nothing I could give him.

The Queen Mother might be cruel, and she might be jealous of my claim to Charles's affections, but she was right. And she had been right all along.

Once I had made the decision to leave, I could not go quickly enough. There had been nothing at court, save Charles, to keep me, so there was no point in staying. Only, I did not know where to go.

My father and mother had perished in an attack by the Danes. The Queen Mother and Charles had been my only family. The obvious choice would have been to seek out an abbey, but I had a daughter now. And so, I made the last of my great mistakes. I told the Queen Mother of my plans.

"You wish to take the child? Are you mad? She is the only thing of worth you've ever brought him. And now you wish to undo it?"

By the time she had finished talking, she had convinced me to leave the babe behind with her. How could her words have failed to move me? She told me that to have any hope of a future at all, Gisele needed to cease being *my* daughter and start being the king's daughter. It was the only way to save her from a life like mine. And besides, what would a girl like me, unmarried with a child, come to in the world outside the palace walls? What could I offer my child, daughter of a king, that could compare with the court's comforts and luxuries? Could I raise her in golden cloth and silks? And then marry her off to a noble? What was a mother's love, after all, when beset by the practicalities of a cold, cruel winter? And besides, if I left her at the palace, the child would always be a princess. She would always be safe.

If I left without my child, the Queen Mother promised to send me with a dower to the royal abbey at Rochemont. And there no one would know about my past unless I chose to tell them.

I agreed to everything, agreed to it all, and I might have managed to leave without any trouble if Charles had not intercepted me at the palace gate. He was there waiting for me, holding our daughter in his arms.

The noble who rode with me aided me to dismount. His squire held my horse's reins.

Charles strode toward me. "You cannot leave. I will not allow it." Anger and hurt warred in his eyes.

"I must go. It's for your own good."

"Why can't I say what's for my good and what's not? I'm to be king, after all. Just as soon as I can get Odo to agree."

The child stirred in his arms.

"Hush! You've woken her." I had already kissed my babe good-bye. I did not know if I could do it again.

"Take her." He thrust the bundle at me. "If you will not stay for me, then stay for her."

"I—cannot."

"How am I—how am I supposed to rule without you?" His brows were twisting as his eyes promised things I should never have hoped to believe in.

I took in a great sniffling breath and tried to smile. "You won't be able to rule with me. You have not got any allies. And you need those more than you need me."

"Who told you that? They lie!"

A great tearing sob of a laugh broke from my throat. "It was your mother, my lady the queen."

"You cannot leave. We are—we are going to be married!"

"I did not think, in fact, that you wanted to."

"Did not want to! How can you say such a—?"

"I shame you."

"How can you even think—!"

"You never planned a wedding. You never told anyone at all."

"Because I wanted them all to love you the same as I did."

I did not know what to believe. I wanted his words to be true. I yearned for them to be true, and yet the things the Queen Mother and the archbishop had told me made the most sense.

As I hesitated, he seized my arm and forced the child into the curve of it.

I tried to refuse her. "Charles—!"

"Don't you love her? Don't you love me?"

"I can't—don't make me—" I broke off as I gave voice to the sob that had gripped my throat. "I can do nothing for you. Can you not understand? You need—oh, you need so much more than me!" The babe was crying now in earnest. We'd woken her with all of our jostling. I raised her to my breast and bent to kiss her soft cheek and breathe in her sweet scent. And I feared then I could not do it. I could not leave them. I thrust the babe toward him. "Take her!" I fairly screamed the words at him. "Take her from me! Give her everything I cannot."

"And what do you want me to do with her?" Unshed tears had brightened his eyes. He had sunk within his mantle and stood there looking far younger than his age. He clutched our infant child to his chest as she squalled against him. "What am I supposed to do?"

I could not stay. Not if I wanted to leave. I backed away from them both. "Keep her. Love her." I could speak no longer for the tears that had gripped my throat and were now cascading down my cheeks.

Love her for me, on my behalf. Love her twice as much again as I would have. That's what I had wanted most to say. But at that time, like so many others that had been and would later come, words had failed me.

I do not much remember the journey to the abbey. My escort was small. Just the one noble and his squire, and the noble paid me little mind. It was the squire who fetched what I needed as we made our way from inn to inn. Did it take a week? A full fortnight? I do not know. My heart was numb; my soul was dead; my grief had nearly rent my mind in two.

I had fifteen years when I left my beloved and gave up

my daughter as well. I want to think I would choose differently, having grown older and presumably wiser. But I knew myself better now, and still the Queen Mother was right. I could not have been what Charles needed; it had not been in my nature. I had not been enough.

I could not fault him for taking me into his bed. I was to blame as much as he. And never once, after I had given myself to God, had I overstepped my bounds. Never once had I tried to take for myself a position that belonged to someone else, or to ask for anything I did not deserve. In fact, I asked for nothing, save the tending of Saint Catherine's altar. And so I tried to content myself with the life I had been given. And surely, my troubles were not so weighty as some. In a world tormented by wars and famines, anger and strife, my life at the abbey could have been considered a veritable paradise. I was not unaware of my blessings.

Charles would have fought for me. Of that I was now certain, just as I was certain I would not have been worth the fight. Had I been someone else… Perhaps then. If I had not been me, then I might have stayed. But there was no use mining old regrets.

As I went about my new work, I tried to put away all thoughts of the young abbess and did my best not to despair of the days to come. While I went about my tasks, I whispered prayers to Saint Catherine just the same as I always had. And in between prayers, I assigned names to my charges, who did not have them. The girl who would not talk, I called Ava. She did not seem to mind. The boy who hopped about so sprightly, flapping his arms, I named Pepin. The mimic I called Otker. And he who insisted upon eating twigs, Gerold. The heir I simply called Young Lord, since he ruled the hospice as if it were his own domain.

Sister Sybilla insisted I wasted my time. She said they hadn't the sense to know their own hands from their feet. But I paid her no mind, and I added their names to those I brought before Saint Catherine.

I asked for no miracles. In this place to which the least habitually came, these were truly the least of all. But I did not fault them for it. Neither did I have the impudence to wish them other than they were. What we were was God's business. If these ills they had been given were a penance, then they must endure like the rest of us. And if they had managed to find themselves here, it must be for some reason. For some eternal purpose. If they could not understand the benefit of righteousness in this life, we were to pray they might be able to do so in the next. And so I pleaded for an ease of body and mind. And a stillness of spirit to those who did not have it.

As I walked in from attending the office of compline one night, Sister Sybilla found me. She seemed to have been lurking by the door. "There is a problem with our young lord, and the only one who ever dares to approach him is you."

It was true I had taken to speaking with him. In spite of Sister Sybilla's dire warnings, I had never seen any evidence of a demon's possession. And his manner of speaking and his way of being brought back memories of my former days. Of time spent in a court filled with nobles and their courteous pleasantries. I had not found his wits lacking at all.

"He keeps kicking at the back wall, and he's bloodied his foot."

"Why have you not pulled him away?"

"He will not let me. He threw me to the ground when I tried. And now all the others have grown frightened."

Inside the hospice, pandemonium reigned. Pepin was walking in circles, flapping his hands. Ava had stopped up her ears and was wailing. Gerold had dropped to the floor and was rocking back and forth as he whispered words I could not understand. And Otker latched on to me as I passed, peering up at me through those curiously slanted eyes. "Poor lord, poor lord."

Sister Sybilla had spoken the truth. The young man was kicking at the wall as if he hoped he might break through it.

I whispered a prayer as I approached. "Young Lord?"

He twisted his head, regarding me with a wild-eyed, panicked gaze. "Don't make me stop. Don't make me stop."

"You're hurting yourself." His shoe had fallen off, and kicking at the wall had made a bloody pulp of his foot.

"I can't stop. Don't make me." His handsome face twisted into a grimace. What spirit was this that possessed him? In spite of his menacing words, his tone was frantic. "Why can't I stop?"

I turned to Sister Sybilla. "Keep the others in the corner."

"Don't make me stop. *Don't* make me stop!"

I put a hand to his sweat-soaked brow. His head lurched beneath my palm as he kicked out again at the wall. "I won't. I won't stop you." I couldn't. I wasn't strong enough. "I want only to keep you from hurting yourself."

"I can't stop. I *can't stop!*"

Searching for some way to protect him from himself, I drew a blanket from one of the pallets, rolled it into a cushion, and held it up in front of the wall.

His next kick nearly wrested it from my hands.

I made my grip more secure, turning my face from the path of his foot. "There now. Is that not better?"

The strain on the boy's face seemed to ease. By turns, his kicking slowed. And then, finally, it ceased altogether, and he dropped to the floor, panting. When he looked up at me, it was through shamed, guilt-ridden eyes. "I could not keep from doing it, and I did not want to hurt Sister Sybilla, but I just... I could not stop."

I stooped to kneel beside him. "What makes you do such things?"

"I don't know. I tried not to, truly I did, but after a while, I just had to. I could not keep myself from it."

Poor, tormented soul.

He sprawled against the wall, spent and panting, his fine tunic rent at the bottom into shreds. "You won't send me away?"

There was no place to send him to. He and all the others were our charges just as surely as they were our prisoners. Their bodies entrusted to our care, and their souls... We tried to redeem their souls as well. "No. We will not send you away." I would pray for him, as I did for them all.

Pepin had wandered over. He sat down beside us and stroked the young lord's silk embroidered sleeve, running a finger up and down the twining braid and across the silver threads. Though the young man's sister had never once come to see him, at least his family still had the decency to clothe him well.

Pepin lifted the sleeve to his face, where he rubbed it against his cheek. And then he rubbed it against the young lord's, smiling as he did it. He lifted it to mine as well.

Silk.

With such a smooth, soft hand.

I used to wear robes made of silk. Magnificent robes trimmed with gold and silver, embroidered with multicolored threads and scented with rosewater.

Like the young lord, I tried to push my thoughts away. I tried to ignore them. And like him too, I found myself bewitched by them. If he was possessed by some tortuous spirit, then perhaps I was possessed by my memories, which had bruised my heart, leaving it bloodied and torn.

∽

Do what is right; do not be afraid to speak.

I had done; I was not.

But look where my promises had gotten me. As the snow on the mountains' tops began to creep toward us, the gloomy winter's days seemed to bring the young lord darker moods. Though the spirits that seized him were terrible to behold, were it not for him, were it not for the times when he was in good humor, the hospice would have been a dreadful and cheerless place. As often as I had been able to ease his torments and calm his mind, another spell always seemed to come in its place.

He tore great fistfuls of hair from his head.

He battered himself against the table one night.

He tried to stick himself with a knife, but Sister Sybilla and I wrestled him to the ground before he caused himself too great of harm. But instead of thanking us, he only lay on the floor, weeping with misery, as if we had not just saved him from himself.

Perhaps I was a fool to think I could offer more to these poor souls than a place to sleep and a bit of food to staunch their deepest hunger. While I struggled at my new work, the abbess had her rooms refitted with hangings and draperies. She gave the most treasured of the library's manuscripts to her father, and she ordered the illumination in Saint Catherine's chapel cut again by half.

Had I saved my life by coming to this place only to see it destroyed by selfishness and greed? But what could I do? I could not leave. I had pledged myself to Christ, and I could not revoke my vows without risking excommunication. There was no escaping the abbey's gates.

It was then I first began to wonder how God could work his will when man seemed so set against him. Did no one else see what I did? Did God Himself not even care?

CHAPTER 21

𝒜nna

ALONG THE PILGRIMS' PATH
TO ROCHEMONT ABBEY

HAD I TRULY HEARD VOICES? COULD IT BE THAT I was saved from my wilderness exile?

I broke through the trees at a run and came upon a group of travelers. They were men, all of them. Unhorsed, they were standing in a loose circle about a fire. Falling to my knees, I clasped the feet of the first man I reached as a great sob tore from my throat.

A hand seized me at the elbow, pulling me away from him, and I was yanked to standing.

Turning, I regarded this second man through tear-washed eyes. It was only then I began to wonder what kind of people I had come upon. They looked like no men I had ever seen. They had mustaches, it was true, but they curved upward into sharp points instead of drooping. Their chins were not clean-shaven either; each of them wore a beard. And their dress was strange: their mantles longer and secured at the waist, with furs thrown over their shoulders. Their stockings were not cross-gartered, but wrapped with swathing bands, and the man who held my arm even wore a metal helmet.

Shaking my hair from my eyes, I tried to free myself, but the man who held me only tightened his grip.

"If you please…" I tried once more.

The first man, the one whose feet I had taken hold of,

seized my other arm and tried to wrench me away. I might have been glad for his aid, only the two of them began exchanging words in an unknown tongue. And the longer they kept at it, the more heated their conversation became.

"I did not mean to——" I wished they would stop pulling at me! "I am only a pilgrim."

The first man tugged me toward himself. The second took a firmer hold on my arm and pulled back.

As I began to appeal to the others, who stood watching, for help, a third man approached. He looked stranger still with his red tunic split open all down the front, its wide edges splayed upon his shoulders. But he put a hand to each of the men.

Snarling, they both released me to turn on him.

Using my newly gained freedom, I backed away, though my knees were quaking beneath the folds of my tunic. In my distress, I looked to the others, and my eyes fastened on a familiar sight. Two clerics. "Help me!"

The younger of the two turned at me, blinking, as if noticing for the first time that I had spoken. His eyes shared the same peculiar hue of the two men who had seized me. They were a light, bright blue.

"Please, save me."

"You are saved. They will let no harm come to you. At least not until they determine who you are."

"I am Anna. From Autun."

"The one man believes you to be a *troll*." He pointed to the one who had jerked me to standing. "A *dwarf*."

"A troll?" I did not know what that was.

"A spirit. A fairy. The other believes you are a *huldra*."

"But, I am not either of those things!"

He nodded toward the third man, the one in the red tunic, who was beginning to check the assault of the others.

"That's what he said. He says you're just a girl. But the other two are sure you must be some sort of troll."

"But why!"

"It looks as if you must live in a cave or under the rocks somewhere."

I looked down at my soiled tunic as I put a hand to my leaf-spangled hair.

"And you *did* come from the wood." He spoke as if their fighting was my fault.

"Please!" I beseeched the other man, the older one. The one whose tunic was bound with a jeweled belt. "I am a pilgrim on my way to the abbey at Rochemont."

The younger one, who wore a monk's dull robe, stepped between us. "You don't wear the clothes of a pilgrim, but if you have a letter from your bishop?" He held out his hand as if requesting to see it. "If I can show it to them, I can explain who you are."

"I did have one, but some wolves chased me from the road, and I—I dropped it. I left it behind with all of my other things."

"That would have been helpful, for they are trying to decide what to do with you, whether to keep you or let you go."

"Pagans!" The older man was sending dark looks in their direction.

"What kind of people are they that they would think me some spirit? All I want is to—"

The monk looked down into my eyes. "They are Danes."

"*Danes?*" But…but the Danes were wicked and evil, murderers and thieves!

The man in the red tunic was holding up a hand now, as if to stay them. He wiped at the sweat on his brow with a forearm. I glanced at the men who ringed the fight. There were three of them, all dressed in those strange garments, cheering in that strange tongue of theirs.

I tugged on the older man's sleeve. "Is the road nearby?"

He gestured beyond the men. "Just there."

"And it goes to the abbey? At Rochemont?"

"Eventually. We're bound for the abbey as well."

"The *Danes* are going to the abbey?" If the Danes were going to the abbey, then they must be intending to plunder it. God help Saint Catherine! If I wanted to pray to her, then I would have to reach the abbey before they did. As the clerics and the other men watched the fight, I withdrew. Slipping around them all, I went toward the horses and what I hoped would be the road. But at my approach, they whinnied.

Behind me, there went up a bellow.

At that great shout, I turned, but I was too late. One of the Danes had already grabbed me by the collar of my tunic. Now he pressed the tip of his knife to my throat.

As I clawed at his hand, the man in the red tunic put his own hand to the knife, seeming to offer himself in my place.

Everyone else had followed, and now they circled around us. My eyes found the monk. "What does he want?"

"He's the one who thinks you a *huldra*. He wants to cut out your tongue so you can't sing and seduce them all away into the forest."

I shut my mouth, clenching my jaw.

The monk spoke for a moment in a quiet, even tone to the Dane who was holding me. With a malevolent look, the pagan put his knife away, and the man with the red tunic let out a great breath.

But if I had thought the Dane done with me, I was mistaken. He went around behind me and then began to pat the length of my spine.

Fearing for my life, I stood there, trembling.

The Dane grunted and then spoke.

"Your back is not hollow." The young monk spoke the words as if some great judgment had been made, but I did not know if that was good news or bad.

The Dane returned to stand in front of me and then drew his knife again.

I dropped to my knees, hands clasped to my chest, closing my eyes for fear of what might happen next.

Someone grasped my shoulder.

I flinched.

"Rise." It was the monk. "He wants only to see if you have a tail."

A...tail? I gave my head a jerking shake, and then, clasping his extended hand, I stood.

The heathen circled me once more, and I felt a sudden breeze as the hem of my tunic was lifted. He said something and lifted my skirts higher.

The others laughed as the man in red protested.

Though the Dane snarled at him, nothing more was said to me, and I felt my skirts drop back into place.

The monk shrugged. "You have no tail; therefore, you are not a *huldra*."

Now the other Dane approached, barking words at the man who held the knife.

The monk frowned. "He says you might still be a dwarf."

"I am not a dwarf."

"She's just a girl!" Though he seemed to be defending me, the man in the red tunic looked more frightful than all of the Danes put together; his black hair was in wild disarray, and his eyes were as raw and as red as his garments.

The Dane who thought me a dwarf came close, giving me a sidelong glance. He murmured something to the monk as he put a hand to my face.

"He says if you are truly just a girl, then you're a comely one."

The heathen grasped me by the chin and swept my hair from my face, and then he forced me to look into his eyes. He said something to one of the others, and was soon given a cloth onto which he spit. He used it to scrub at my face. When he was done, he stared at me as a smile slowly spread across his face.

The man in the red tunic laid a hand on the Dane's arm. "She said she was a pilgrim." When the Dane did nothing, he directed his words toward the monk. Outrage colored his voice. "Pilgrims are to be protected, not molested!"

The Dane grabbed me by the hair as he said something to the monk.

I gasped from the sudden pain.

"He asks to whom you belong."

I answered what was true. "I belong to no one but myself."

The older cleric's lips twisted. "You call yourself a pilgrim, but you have no letter. And now you claim to have no lord. Everyone has a lord. If you claim none, you must have run from one."

"I did not."

The monk relayed my words, and the Dane replied.

"He says it does not matter. He will be your lord now, and you will be his bed-slave." The Dane's hand slid from my face down beneath my mantle to the collar of my tunic. As I twisted from him, he pulled me toward him. I wrenched away; he jerked me back. The motion tore my collar, and as he pulled at me, the tunic ripped, leaving my undertunic exposed.

I had been able, through all of the tumult, to keep my useless hand hidden, but now I struck out with it, trying to push him away as I used my good hand to gather the edges of my torn garment.

The man dropped his hold on me and staggered back with

a gasp. As he pointed to my hand, the others began to mutter. Even the monk stepped away from me as he translated.

"You *are* a dwarf! You have only three fingers on that hand."

"I was born this way." I appealed to the older cleric, but he too fell back from me. My tunic was useless, torn beyond redemption. No matter what I tried, which way I turned, my undergarments were made plain for all to see. I dropped to the ground and bent over my knees, trying to keep myself hidden within my mantle.

The man with the red tunic stripped off his own mantle and dropped it atop me. "She's nothing but a girl. And if she's a pilgrim, she has as much right to travel to the abbey unmolested as you or I."

As I pulled his mantle down and around me, I glanced up to see his hand, white-knuckled, gripping his knife.

The Dane saw it too, but he laughed. And then he spit into the dirt near my face and said something in a scoffing tone.

The monk helped me to standing. "He says he does not want you now, but they cannot release you. You might go back to your troll-father and put a curse on us."

The Dane came close and murmured something into my ear.

I flinched.

The monk translated his words. "He wants to apologize. He did not realize who you were. And he promises they will let you go once they've gained the abbey."

There was some discussion between several of the Danes, and then the one wearing the helmet broke from the others and addressed the monk.

The monk passed his message to me. "He asks: 'Do you still claim to be a girl?'"

"I *am* a girl."

The Dane had been watching me intently. Now he sprang

forward and sliced my good hand with his knife. The man in the red tunic pushed at him as I gasped, clasping my hand to my chest. But the Dane dodged and lunged toward me, grabbing my wounded hand. Seizing it, he squeezed.

I screamed.

When blood bubbled forth, he held it high as he called out to the others.

As I reclaimed it, crying out from the pain, the monk stepped closer to examine it. "Your blood is not black. You're *not* a dwarf."

Oh, how it stung! I cradled it against my breast. "I was born this way. It's why I journey to the abbey. To pray for healing."

One of the Danes gave a shout, and the others followed him, leaving me for their horses. The clerics broke from me as well. As the man in the red tunic wrapped a strip of cloth about my hand, it was clear they all meant to ride away, leaving me there in the wood.

"Are you...are you going too?"

He looked up from my hand, his red-rimmed eyes awash with apology. "I must. I'm sorry. When you reach the village, stay. There should be someone there who can care for your hand."

"But I can't. I can't stay."

He stepped back from me. "I must go." The sun had almost disappeared behind the mountains, and out in the wood somewhere, a wolf howled.

Another answered back.

"I have to reach the abbey!"

His mouth moved as if he wanted to say something, but in the end, he only bowed and then went to mount his horse.

As they rode, I sprang toward them. "Do not leave me here! I'll do anything." I had to reach the abbey. And if they left me alone on this lonely road, then the wolves would find me again, and I did not know what they would do to me this time.

The Dane wearing the helmet lifted a hand and consulted the monk. Then he stopped his horse and said something to the man who had once claimed me for his slave. That man nodded, and the chieftain called out to the monk once more.

The monk rode from his place at the back of the column toward me. "The man who first claimed you will take you as his slave. When they have returned to Neustria, he will sell you. If you promise to hide your hand until the sale has been completed, then at least then he will get something for his trouble."

I would enslave myself to anyone who was going to the abbey. And if Saint Catherine were pleased with me, then perhaps she could intervene to have this misfortune removed from me as well. I nodded my agreement.

At my nod, the man who had claimed me pitched a parcel over to me. It was wrapped in a hide and secured with leather thongs.

"He says to carry that."

Though it was heavy and though both my hands were now useless, I gathered it to my breast as the others laughed at me.

The man in the red tunic rode over and leaned down to take it from me, but the Dane took up his spear and threw it in our direction. It landed with a vibrating twang.

The man backed his horse away from me.

In spite of the throbbing of my wounded hand, I clasped the parcel more firmly, using the pressure to keep my mantle from slipping to reveal my immodesty. As they moved out toward the road, I prayed my feet would last the journey. I must have walked several dozen paces, following along behind them, before the world began to crumple at the edges and dissolve into a bright white haze of nothingness. And then, I knew no more.

⁓

When I woke, I was no longer alone. I was no longer cold, and I was no longer walking.

"When is the last time you ate?"

I might have started at the voice that whispered in my ear, but the words were spoken in the accent of the man with the red tunic. By the light of the moon, I saw I was riding nestled into the crook of his arm. "Two days. Or three."

He gave me some bread to eat.

At some point during that long night, we passed a city as church bells rang. It could have been the midnight office or matins, for all I knew. A Dane rode close, hand on his knife until we were well by. The village had been set in a valley between mountains. After we passed it, we began to climb in earnest. The gentle lurching of the horse and the rhythmic clop-clop of its steps sent me into a stupor of sorts, but always I woke as my chin dropped to my chest.

As dawn glimmered, brightening the night sky, the Danes parted from the road and led us to a depression in the land, where they dismounted and began to set up a camp.

The man in the red tunic slid from the horse and then reached up a hand for me.

When my skirts lifted up during my descent, he averted his eyes. He was not like the others. He did not stare at me like the Danes, nor did he avoid my gaze like the clerics.

"I am grateful to you and your horse. I am Anna from Autun."

The corners of his mouth lifted, though the gaze from those red-rimmed eyes was sad. "I am Godric of Wessex."

I did not know where Wessex was, but of one thing I was certain. "You are not a Frank."

"I am Saxon." He was regarding me with hooded, watchful eyes.

Saxons were nearly as bad as Danes. My mother had told me Charlemagne had slain many thousands of them during the wars.

"I am from Britain, a land bedeviled and beset by Danes like those." He nodded toward the group of them.

I did not know where Britain was, but if his words were true, they made no sense. "So, you are not one of them?"

"One of the Danes?" He threw a glance at them. "No."

"You are with the monk, then?"

"No. I'm going to the abbey, like you. And at this time of year, it's better to go in numbers than to go alone."

"If you are not of them, and you do not approve of them, then why do you travel with them?"

"I have my own reasons for inquiring of Saint Catherine."

"You do not wear the pilgrim's hat. And you do not have the pilgrim's scrip."

"No, but then neither do you."

I did not. Without the warmth of his chest and the support of his arms, the cold slipped through my tunic and seeped through my skin down into my bones. It was markedly colder at these heights. The chill of the air stung my nostrils. Leaves had frozen into clumps where they had fallen, and frost dusted the branches of the trees, where it sparkled with the sun's rising.

The Danes passed around a costrel and filled their cups with it. One started some sort of song, and the others joined in. The older cleric looked on with a sour face. Behind me, Godric from Wessex unpacked his horse. When he finished, he came to stand beside me. "They will stop singing soon.

Though there are few travelers so late in the year, they seem not to want their presence known. As soon as the sun fully rises, they will sleep. And so should you." He gestured toward a bed of blackened, frost-bent ferns.

I lay down on the ferns, my mantle tight about me, but I could not bring myself to close my eyes.

Godric sat down beside me, one leg drawn up in front of him, an arm looped about his knee. "I never sleep, so have no fear. I will not let them harm you."

CHAPTER 22

I WOKE WITH A CRY AND THE SENSATION OF BEING stabbed in the chest.

As I flailed, Godric fell back onto his heels. "I am sorry, I was just—" He held up a...a needle?

My eyes contracted with pain as they took in the day's light. Dazed from the sudden abandonment of slumber, I put my hand to the place where I had been stabbed. It was above my flattened bosom at the place where my tunic had been torn. I collected the torn edges with my bandaged hand and held them tight beneath my chin.

"I was trying to repair it. I did not think you could do it with your..." His gaze dropped toward the hem of my right sleeve. The fabric had slipped, exposing my bad hand. The skin had gone blue from the cold. Resisting the urge to warm it with my breath, I folded it in on itself, pulling it back up into my sleeve. Over in the glade beyond us, the Danes were snoring.

"...I did not think you could...that you would be able to..."

I released my hold on the tunic, and then fingered the fibers that had sprung free about the torn edges of my collar. "No." I could not repair it. In fact, I could do nothing that needed doing.

"Do you wish that I continue?" He held up the needle once more.

I nodded.

He blinked hard, bringing water to his reddened eyes. Then he reached toward my neck and took up the two pieces of rent material, folding them together. His breath brushed my skin.

Trembling, I turned my eyes from his work.

He pressed the fabric down and pushed the needle through it. It slipped, scratching into my skin once more.

I pressed my lips together.

He took a deep breath and then blinked hard once more. "I am not used to such fine work."

I turned my head away again, burying my chin in my shoulder and closing my eyes against the tears that had begun to leak from them.

"Truly, I am sorry. I did not mean to hurt you."

He had not hurt me. He was the first person, in a very long time, who had been kind to me. The first person since my mother had died who had taken care of me. Who had touched me with the intent of offering aid instead of guile. I would have stopped my tears if I could have, but the more I tried, the more I trembled.

At last he finished, knotting the thread, and then, lowering his head to my chest, he took it between his teeth and broke it off, though not before my cheek was brushed by his soft and wildly curling hair.

My tunic hung strangely from my neck now. I put a hand to his work. The stitches were long and uneven. But though clumsily done, they would probably hold. "Thank you, Godric of Wessex."

His gaze had dropped from me toward the sleeping Danes, but at my words, it swung back.

I was trembling still.

He unfastened his mantle and put it about my shoulders.

I moved to give it back, but he stayed me, placing his hand on mine. "You need it more than I."

It was a generous thought, but the weather made it impractical. His fingers had been frigid as he had worked at my tunic. "I think, perhaps...can we not share it?" I sat upon the ferns once more, and then opened out one side.

He stared down at it for a moment, and then he glanced off toward the Danes again.

"Please." It was not right that I should benefit from the mantle he had brought for his own warmth and comfort.

He sat beside me, back straight, gaze fixed upon the Danes, keeping a distance between us. I did not blame him. Others who had seen my hand had kept themselves farther away than he. Securing my end of the mantle around my arm, I drew my knees up beneath my tunic. Resting my cheek atop them, I turned my head away from him. I had just closed my eyes when he spoke.

"Do you truly have no one?"

I opened my eyes and looked off into the wood. There was no end to it. It seemed to go on and on forever. I had not known a forest would be that way. "I was a child alone, and my mother has just died." But I did not fear the wood now. Not the way I had, back when I had been alone, fleeing from the wolves.

"But what of your father?"

"He is long dead."

"There is no one who would claim you?"

"With my hand?" Not even my father had wanted to claim me. "I belong to no one. No one wanted me."

He was silent for some time. Tired of staring at the trees, I had let my eyes flutter shut, and I had almost found sleep, when he spoke once more.

"I will not let them hurt you."

Though he whispered the words, he had such a sure way of speaking. I turned my head, laying my other cheek atop my knees so I could see him. "Thank you."

I saw his gaze stray from the Danes toward me. It lingered on my hair, my eyes, my nose, and by then my eyelids had grown too heavy to stay open, and my arms began to twitch with sleep. As I slipped from wakefulness to slumber, I wondered where exactly Britain was. And why he had chosen to leave it behind.

That forenoon, the Danes began to stir. They were restless and ill-tempered, uttering their words in vile tones as they stalked into the wood to do what was necessary, and then stalked back. They set up a board to play at some game or other. One of them took up a piece of wood and began to whittle on it. But always, one of them watched me.

The clerics kept to themselves, hands pulled into their sleeves, sitting upon a rock in sullen silence. At the appointed hours, we could hear bells tolling from several directions, signaling the offices. The canon and monk observed each one, and I asked if I could join them. They seemed surprised at my request and not as pleased as I would have expected, but I did not wish to miss any chance to impress upon God the earnestness with which I would be making my plea to Saint Catherine.

As the sun hid itself behind the mountains, and all danger of encountering pilgrims had passed, several of the men went out into the wood with their weapons. They came back, carrying a hart, which they proceeded to skin and then roast over the fire. The sizzle of its flesh and the scent of it made my stomach churn in anticipation.

Godric added some salt to their meal, and they gave him a joint of venison, which he shared with me. We sat together on our bed of ferns as they ate and drank and then drank some more. And still they did not let me long leave their sight. There were five of them. Even when I took my turn in the wood, one of them followed me. That night, it was the youngest of them, he whom I liked least of all. His eyes protruded from his face, and he always seemed to look overlong at me. Upon my return from the wood, he stepped toward me, halting my progress. And then he lurched and fell into me. Murmuring some pagan words, he gave my left bosom a sharp squeeze. Then he grabbed me about the waist and pressed himself against me.

I tried to push him away, but he only gripped me tighter.

As I began to fear I would never escape his grasp, someone grabbed him at the shoulder and threw him far from me. It was not Godric who had saved me this time, but the older cleric.

The young Dane snarled something at him, but the cleric grabbed him by the ear and dragged him over to the fire where the others were playing at their game.

"You will not do this—this—*despicable* thing! We journey to acquire a holy relic, and I will not have the journey profaned by your pagan ways!"

Their chieftain could not have understood what the man was saying, but he rose as the cleric was speaking and went to stand in front of him, staring at the man through unblinking eyes. When the man had ceased his tirade, the chieftain drew his knife and reached out to grasp the cross that dangled by a silken cord from the cleric's neck.

The man went ashen.

Wrapping the cord around his fist, drawing it taut, the Dane severed it with one quick slice. Stripping the cross from the cord, he threw it into the fire. And then, clutching the silver hammer he wore around his own neck, he showed it to the cleric, uttering something in his heathen tongue.

The monk had come near, and now he translated. "He says, when your words can save your cross, then he will do what you tell him. Until then, the girl is a slave, and it is for her master to decide her fate."

 ℘

Godric fairly pushed me toward his horse that evening. "Do not *ever* stray beyond my sight."

"I won't."

"How can I protect you if I cannot see you?"

"It was not your fault."

He gripped my arm even tighter.

"You hurt me."

He dropped my arm as if I had been the one to hurt him. Such shame showed upon his face that I tried to comfort him. "The cleric was there. He saved me."

"But churchmen cannot always be present. And what happens if the Danes come upon you all alone?"

"I have lived my life alone." It seemed to me now as if I had always been alone.

He helped me up onto his horse and then mounted behind me. "I had a wife once, but my lord called me to his counsel, and while I was gone, the Danes came. They murdered her. I should not have gone. If I had been there, then I could have saved her."

"It was not your fault."

"Then whose fault was it? God's?" The accusation was spoken without passion, as if it were a familiar refrain. "They tell me God can do anything, so why then did He not save her? Her faith was very great. If anyone deserved His favor, she did. But He abandoned her when she needed Him most."

"Perhaps He was there with her."

"Doing what?" His cry rang through the wood. "What did He do while the Danes raped and murdered our mothers and our sisters and our daughters? Nothing!"

We rode on in silence for a while. When Godric spoke again, it was in a low tone, though his words were no less vehement. "The priests said the Danes were sent as punishment for some great sin of ours. But my Winifred was kind and good. It should have been me. I ought to have died in her place."

He had his Winifred, and I had my hand. Both evidence of some sin great enough for God to punish, but not important enough that we had ever been told what it was. It seemed a great injustice.

"If I were God, then I would reward those who loved me and punish those who did not."

"Who is to say your Winifred has not received her reward? And who is to say the Danes will not receive an eternal punishment?"

"But what about me? What about me, who loved her? And how can I hate the God who took her and yet long to be with her in His presence?"

"Maybe it was not God who did the taking."

"He allowed it."

He allowed it. He had allowed it. My heart ached with sorrow for him. "But that does not mean He approved of it. And no matter what she suffered from them, they could not have stolen her soul."

"N–no." He spoke the word with tear-choked grief, and he did not say anything more.

The road was difficult, and the way was steep, but the stars shone down upon us. How could they have been there all this time without my knowing? And how could there be so many of them? I marveled at their blinking brightness and great number as we rode.

When dawn broke, we repaired to the wayside, where Godric and I shared his mantle again. As I drifted to sleep, it was, if not in peace, then at least with a sense of safety. But I woke to muffled cries, the twitching of a leg, and the thrashing of an arm.

It seemed Godric had finally succumbed to sleep.

In my own slumber I had curled myself into his side, and at some point, he had turned toward me and slipped his arm beneath my waist. But now, with his other one, he seemed to reach out, to try to grasp something only he could see.

The Danes slumbered on, shaking with great snores.

"*Winifred!*" Godric spoke the name with great anguish as he kicked out at…nothing. And still his spirit was not eased.

I sat and put my good hand to his flailing arm, patting it, stroking it, telling him it would be all right. That whatever ills assailed him would be gone when he woke.

As I whispered, his agitation eased. His hand grasped mine and pulled it close. And then he pressed my head to his chest. I could not have moved from his embrace if I had wanted to, but perhaps he had need of it more than I.

"I slept." Godric spoke the words with great wonder as I eased myself from his grip. His eyes were clearer; the redness had lessened.

"Yes." I smiled at him.

"And you…" He glanced down at the arm he had wrapped about me. "I did not…?" His eyes searched mine. Did not? "Oh! No. You did not assail me. But you suffered from your dreams."

"I have not slept a night through. Not since Winifred…" Grief and guilt and shame pooled in his eyes. "I said her name… I remember it… I remember saying it." He passed his hand before his face and then stared out into the distance. "I was saying good-bye."

Long before evening, the rains began. The sky threw down handfuls as the wind blew it first this way and then that. I had known rain before, at home; by times it had chased me from the window and threatened the fire, but I had not known just how very wet and cold it could be. How relentless raindrops were in finding a way to worm beneath my tunic. Nor how one raindrop atop another and another and another could saturate my mantle, bringing the weight of the world to bear upon my shoulders.

I took refuge with the young monk beneath the overhang of a rock as the others readied themselves to leave.

The rain seemed to cloak us from the others, and he soon became quite loquacious. He told me he was converted by a priest who had wandered to their clan, performing miracles. "When not even our witch could repeat them, I realized Odin and Thor and Freya could not stand against the god he served. And so I asked myself why should I not worship this most powerful of gods. When they let him leave, I went with him."

"Our God is not just the most powerful of gods, He is the *only* God."

"So the priests say. But what does it matter whether He is the only one or simply the most powerful of many? But I know you must understand this. How is it you can worship someone who cursed you?" He nodded toward my right hand. "You would not do it because you wish to. It must be that you believe there is no one else powerful enough to help you." He spoke as if he was trying to convert me to his strange beliefs.

"I believe, because I should."

"People *should* do many things, but rarely do they actually do them."

He seemed disappointed in me, but then I was disappointed in my own answer as well. I had spoken truth, had I not? I had set out on the pilgrim's path because I knew I should: my mother had wanted me to. But even so, that did not mean I had to do it with the hope that burned within me. "I believe because I must."

"You *must*? But who can make you?"

"Then perhaps…perhaps I believe because I want to." That was the truest of all of the answers I had given him. I believed because I wanted to hope I was one of God's creatures; that not only the strong or the brave deserved the best eternity had to offer. I wanted to think that somewhere, someone did not despise me; that God, perchance, might even love me, if I could prove myself deserving. I believed because of the things I had seen. And because of those I had not.

"What was it like"—he gestured toward the hand I had drawn up within my sleeve—"when you were cursed? What did you do that you deserved it?"

"Nothing." I had done nothing. Nothing I could remember. Nothing I could beg forgiveness for. Nothing I could confess to a priest.

He glanced out beyond the rain to where the Danes were

preparing to leave. "They disdain you because of it, but they will not hurt you. At least not in the worst of ways. They plan to keep your hand hidden and sell you as a bed-slave; for that they will preserve your chastity. So do not fear." He sounded as if I should be grateful.

"Why do they seek the relic?"

"They don't. It's the canon who wants it."

"But why?"

"To take it back to Rouen. A marriage depends upon it. But mostly, the archbishop wants it for his cathedral."

"What if the abbey won't let him have it?"

He smiled. "That's why the Danes come with us."

"But, what do they plan to do?"

He looked out once more to a world that had gone gray. "Whatever they must."

"They would not harm any in order to take it?"

He did not answer.

"What if Saint Catherine does not wish to go?"

"I do not think she has a choice in the matter."

"But I need to pray before you take her relic. It's why I've come all this way. To seek healing."

"I can promise nothing."

"Can you ask the canon, then?"

"The canon? They will not listen to him. They do not understand prayers or weakness, only war and death. They would *prefer* to have to seize the relic, for it's by fighting they prepare for life after death, for Valhalla, where only the bravest of warriors will go." A glaze had settled over his eyes, and he stared into the rains as if he were looking beyond them. "And the bravest of those brave warriors are the berserkers, they who beat upon themselves and eat their own shields in their lust for blood."

"But...but...what of Paradise?"

He blinked. "A place of rest and peace?" He turned to look at me. "They would forfeit Paradise without a second thought. They would spurn your angels and wait instead for the winged Valkyries." He leaned close as he stared into my eyes. "They fight, you see, to have a place among the worthiest of warriors, for only those will be taken to Valhalla. And there, each day they fight, and at night, they feast."

It seemed a strange eternity, spent in endless war. "Surely they do not fight each other."

"Only each other."

"For amusement?"

"Never for amusement. They fight to prepare for the last great battle, so though their limbs be lost and their heads be severed from their bodies, each night they are made whole so they can feast together. And they begin their battle anew each morning."

"But what of love and charity?"

"There is no place for them there. Nor for the meek or the aged. They care nothing for angels. Upon his death, what every warrior hopes for is a Valkyrie. You see then why they do not accept this message of grace or this God. They do not want to."

CHAPTER 23

E STARTED OUT LONG BEFORE NIGHT HAD FALLEN, when the rains seemed to lessen. At times they stopped altogether, and we saw glimpses of the sun's decline. But soon they returned with more force and such conviction I feared the rest of the day's light would be lost to us.

The road was steep. The Danes halted our procession and conferred, then led us off the road toward a rocky cliff that rose up toward the sky. There, we each took shelter where we could find it within the crags of the rocks.

Godric took me by my bandaged hand and led me some distance from the others before he drew me into a shallow cave where we were protected from the rain. He took the mantle from his shoulders and transferred it to mine. Though it was wet, it was warm, and it still held his scent.

Kneeling beside me, he drew a bundle from his belt and placed it before me. Unknotting the cords which bound it, he opened it to reveal the contents. A collection of small pouches and tiny phials lay within.

I looked over at him. "What are these?"

"A hair from Saint James. A filing from Saint Peter's chains. Oil from a lamp that burned in the church of Saint Andrew. Dust from the tomb of Saint Denis. A piece of cloth upon which once rested the crown of thorns. A thread from the veil of the Holy Mother. A sliver from the true cross." He touched each pouch and phial in turn.

"They are...relics?"

"I am a relic hunter for my lord." He was looking at me as if weighing the impact of his words.

"A relic hunter?"

His gaze slipped from mine, though he nodded. "My lord collects them. And each time I find one, I keep a small piece...a thread from a veil or a few sprinklings of dust..." He placed several of the phials into my hand. "Perhaps if you prayed to them, you might be healed."

"Why do you offer me these?"

He looked up once more into my eyes. "I joined the Danes because I also travel to the abbey. But it is not for prayer, nor is it for healing. It is so I can take Saint Catherine's relic myself, for my lord."

I did not know what to say.

"You must not doubt that when I have the opportunity, I will do it."

Everything he said I understood, but still it did not make any sense. "But why do you keep *these*?"

"For Winifred." His voice broke as he swallowed. "She died without the last rites. They all did."

My heart lay heavy within me. It was only the fact that my mother had been visited by a priest in her last hours that gave me any comfort in her death. Because she had received absolution, I knew she had gone on to Paradise. But Godric had no such knowledge. Indeed, there was nothing for him to hope for.

"If I say enough prayers, if I collect enough relics, then maybe..."

He did not have to finish his thought. If he collected enough of them, if he said enough prayers, then maybe the saints could intervene and save her soul. And then she could rest in peace.

"She used to come to me every night. But last night when you...when I slept...she said good-bye. I think the prayers have finally worked. So perhaps these relics can help you as well."

"My way lies toward Saint Catherine."

"But these are all here, right now, in the same place. You would not have to go all the way to the abbey, and if there were an opportunity to leave, for you to escape..." There was hope and desperation in his eyes.

I collected the pouches and phials and gave them back. "I am bound for the abbey because my mother wanted it. She had it written into her will. I have to go, or she will have no peace." And neither then would I.

As he gathered up his collection, he did it as one ashamed. As if he had shown me his weakness.

"Your offer is very kind, but if prayers on my behalf could work, then they would have done so long ago. My mother sent me to Saint Catherine because she thought it was my only hope."

He looked over at me. "I am trying to save you from the same kind of Danes who murdered my wife. I would help you escape."

"But if I choose to save myself, then I might lose my only chance at healing."

I thought he might speak, but he only hunched his shoulders up toward his ears, and he squatted there beside me, staring into the rain that spewed out from the cliff over the mouth of our shelter.

I held out a corner of his mantle.

He looked first at the mantle and then at me.

"I wish I could do as you would like, but I cannot."

Finally, he nodded. Accepting the mantle, he leaned back against the face of the cliff, pulling me close and tucking my head beneath his chin.

I turned and curled into his side, and there we slept until morning.

❦

"Saxon! Where are you?"

The words startled us out of our reverie. The rain had been so plentiful, a veritable stream had formed, and now it fell in a chute from the cliff.

Godric lifted his chin from my head. "They cannot see us through the water. We could stay here."

We saw the monk stop in front of our shelter. He cupped a hand to his mouth and called out again.

Godric pressed my head to his chest as if to hide me from the world beyond the cave. "Say nothing."

"But I must go." Though I wanted nothing more than to stay within the circle of his arms, I could not renounce my journey to Saint Catherine.

His arm tightened about me for a moment, but then he sighed and released me from his embrace.

As he stood, I clutched at his fallen side of the mantle and wrapped his warmth about me. Rising, I went to stand beside him.

He held out his hand to me. "If you are sure…"

I was.

Together we slid past the cascade and stepped away from it.

The monk blanched at our appearance as if we might have been some apparition. Godric pushed past him, and we met up with the others.

Not long after we started out that evening, we rode into snow. At first, after the stinging, pelting drops of rain, it seemed a wondrous thing. It sifted down around us like the smallest of feathers, reminding me of the great bed I had left behind at home. I had not been out in snow before. My mother had feared I would do myself harm; she had lived with the constant worry I would damage myself more than I already was.

Though it was dark, we rode through a world become softer and brighter. But then the snows began to come down faster and thicker, and the wind changed, throwing it into our faces. It piled up on my lashes and my nose. The flakes that had seemed so light now collected on the shoulders of my mantle and at my knees.

I pulled my mantle up around my neck and buried my chin in its depths. The path, which had unfurled so plainly in front of us, became cloaked in drifts. It was then I understood snow's menace. Whiteness was no blessing. Its brightness was a curse. It covered hummock and hollow with perfect equanimity, pulling up the depressions and pushing down the peaks. It was then I understood how great was our peril.

We battled snow all the night long. At length, it began to lessen, but by then the horses had wearied from the work of walking.

It was cold. A cold such as I had never felt before. One that sank through my skin and into my bones. The world shrank until it was smaller even than my mother's bed in Autun. It existed between the top of my mantle, into which I had sunk my chin, and the tips of my shoes. And it survived within the space of my heart's beat, the one place in which I still retained a degree of wavering warmth.

Godric pulled me closer against his chest. "You could still escape. I would help you."

"You would come with me?"

It might have been several minutes before he answered me, or it might have been an hour. Time had ceased to have any meaning.

"I cannot."

My thoughts had slowed. It took great effort for them to congeal and then to transfer them to my tongue. But it did not matter. There was day and there was night. Light and dark. And constantly, there was white, unrelenting snow. "Where would I go?" Where in this snow-swept, white-washed world could I flee?

"Home."

"I have no home." As I pondered the idea of being from nowhere at all, the Danes pulled off into the shelter of a group of trees with long, swooping, low-hanging branches.

We dismounted and followed after them, ducking beneath the limbs, letting them sweep the snow from our backs as we went. But though we had stopped, it was not restful. We huddled together for warmth and watched the snow blow by. I was almost thankful for the wound the Dane had given me. Bound as it was in a cloth, at least that hand was warm.

"You truly have no home?" Godric continued the conversation as if we had never stopped talking. The Danes did not care anymore if we spoke. And I did not care if they heard us speak of escape. It could not matter. Our footsteps were obliterated, torn from our feet almost before we had finished making them. There was no path for us to take. No road by which to make an escape.

"I have nothing. Just the hope that I can reach the abbey." Even if the Danes took the relic, if I stayed with them, perhaps they would let me touch it. What would they lose by doing so? And if Saint Catherine did heal me, would I not be more valuable to them whole? "I wish to be healed."

"And what if you are not? What will you do then?"

I did not know. I had not thought on it. "I will go where the Danes take me."

"And what if you are healed?"

If I were healed, then I would be healed. But still I would have no place to go and nothing to return to. "I do not know."

"I will help you." His words were as futile as the driving snow. He would help me. It was a useless offer, for what good, in a world gone white and fraught with Danes, would his help do me now?

What miserable days we endured to reach the abbey. The mountains became steeper, the valleys deeper, and the summits higher. In our travels by night, the moon's light turned the snows into a pale, shimmering blue. The night before we gained the abbey, our journey ended beside a massive fall of snow that had tumbled from the heights down into the narrow, steep-sided valley we were traversing. Our road clung fast to the side of the mountain, and so the fall had blocked our way.

One of the Danes started up and over the slide, but the snow began to give way beneath him, and he barely avoided being swept down with it into the abyss. Beyond the slide, we could see the road continue on. The distance to it was not very great, but with the slide intervening, it was lost to us.

The chieftain strode to the edge of the road and peered down into the ravine. Another Dane stood, hand on his sword, looking up behind us where some snow still overhung the cliff. They began to dispute, the one pointing to the slide, the other pointing up at the cliff.

The monk sat his horse, listening, while the canon gazed at the road beyond the snow. "If there were another way to reach the abbey, they would not have built the road here." He spoke the words to no one but himself.

The chieftain left off arguing and pulled his spear from his saddle.

From behind me, Godric pulled his own knife from its sheaf with a jerk.

The monk raised his hand. "He will let the gods decide what we should do."

The canon spurred his horse forward, crying out, "Saint Catherine has already decided. We will not be permitted to take her. She wishes to stay where she is."

My heart leapt within me, but then my hope died as I realized, if the Danes could not reach her, then neither could I.

The chieftain, ignoring the canon's cry, let fly his spear. It flew through the night, tip flashing. It must have found a rock beneath the snow, for it pitched backward before it came to rest. The Danes dismounted and followed their chief through the snow to find it. By the time Godric and I reached them, they were gesturing at it. Though the shaft of the spear was pointing toward the cliff, its tip was bent toward the snow slide.

The chieftain gestured at the slide.

The other Dane pointed up at the heights.

Gathering together at the edge of the ravine, the Danes conferred with many words until the chieftain finally broke his spear in two and then tossed it over the edge.

Godric raised his voice so it would reach the monk. "What do they decide?"

"They will try to cross here."

"Through the slide?"

"They will leave the horses, and we will go on by foot."

"This is madness!" The canon broke in to their conversation. The chieftain strode up to the monk and seemed to make a demand.

The monk turned to the canon. "He asks, 'What does your god say?'"

"It's clear what God says. He tells us to go back. We cannot have the relic."

The monk translated. The chieftain spit an answer back at him.

"Then your God does not know Rollo, and Rollo wants the relic."

Before any more could be said, the youngest Dane, the one who had accosted me, started off into the snow slide.

The chieftain let loose a shout, but he continued on.

After several steps more, he turned around with a grin and a wave, and then he started off again. But as he continued, a great crack ran through the slide, and the snow began to crumble before starting a slow drift toward the abyss. He threw his arms out, trying to balance, but he could not keep his feet. As the snow plummeted toward the ravine, he rolled onto his side. Stretching his arms out to us, he shouted something.

The chieftain ran toward him, but there was no way to arrest his fall, and he went over the edge in a flurry of snow.

The chieftain stared into the abyss for a long while, and then he turned and made some pronouncement, which caused all the Danes to turn and look at me.

I shrank against Godric as he threw an arm about me and tried to turn his horse. But the chieftain strode toward us and grabbed me by the arm, dragging me from the horse. Then he shoved me toward the slide.

"I do not—"

He did not seem to care what I did not want to do. Pushing at my shoulder, he kept edging me toward that great pile of fallen snow.

"I cannot—"

When I tried to stop, he drew his knife and pressed the tip to my cheek.

"Don't—please don't!"

Godric had run up behind him and was reaching for him, but somehow the chieftain seemed to know it. He grabbed me by the hair before turning and slashing at Godric with the knife.

"I will do it. I will go!"

The chieftain released me as he grabbed Godric around the neck with his arm.

I walked out onto the snow slide.

"Anna, don't do it!"

Turning my back on them both, I placed my attention on what lay ahead. The new slide had not cleared all the snow from the road. The top had simply fallen away to reveal a lower layer. Unlike the snow we had been traveling through, this layer was topped by a glaze of ice. With each step, my feet broke through the crust. The farther I walked, the deeper the snow became.

From the slope high above me, a trickle of snow began to fall from the overhang, gathering in both volume and fury as it came. I retreated to let it pass, praying it would not take me with it. As it swept by with a rumble, it ruffled my hair and assaulted my ears.

A cry from behind made me turn.

The Dane had forced Godric to his knees and was holding the knife to his neck.

Trembling, I started forward once more. The slide had filled my footsteps and added depth to the snow. As I advanced this time, plunging my feet into the slide and then pulling them out, the snow reached well above my gartered stockings, halfway up my thighs. Soon I was panting from the effort. But as I took another step, the snow separated beneath me in a great spreading crack.

I stopped, closing my eyes in anticipation of death.

But it did not come.

Opening my eyes, I saw the crack had gone around me through the snow, and as I watched, that portion slipped away toward the ravine. As it fell, I moved as fast as I could and eventually gained the other side.

My triumph was short-lived.

It was not Godric who followed in my footsteps. The Danes sent the clerics across first, on foot. And then, after leaving their horses, they took up their weapons and crossed as well. Several times, more pieces of the slide broke off and cascaded into the abyss. Finally only Godric and the Dane who had claimed me for his own were left.

As Godric bent to shoulder his pack, the Dane kicked him in the stomach and then kicked him again as he fell to the ground. As the heathen ran through the slide, just short of the middle, the rest of the overhanging snow on the cliff above him broke off in a thundering cloud and slid down the hill, taking him with it. His screams echoed through the night.

As the snowy mist roiled and then blew away, I saw the form of Godric in the moon's light as he advanced through the remains of the slide. As he reached us, I caught up his hand in my own, and I did not let it go.

*

It took me hours to stop shaking. When my trembling would not cease, Godric pulled me close and shared his mantle with me. We walked on for some time together, ragged of breath, struggling to keep to the path.

I concentrated simply on putting one foot in front of the other, stepping neither to the right nor to the left, trying to keep free from the encumbrance of the drifts. We walked and walked, and it seemed we hardly went anywhere at all.

The world was white and only kept getting whiter.

Eventually, when the road turned, we found shelter from the wind and the snow. Though we stopped there, we did not sleep; it was too cold for sleep. But we rested. And there, I listened to a conversation between the Danes and the clerics.

"They say the best is to attack with no warning. Then they will have no time to prepare."

The canon was scowling. "Tell them this is an abbey. They are nuns and—and laypeople. They must be given the chance to give us the relic of their own volition."

"This is not the way they prefer to conduct their raids."

"But this is not a raid! And we will *ask* for the relic, we will not just take it."

The monk translated and then listened as the chieftain spoke. "You may ask if you like, but he will still plan on taking it."

"That's not the way it's done!"

"Not your way, perhaps, he says, but this is his way."

"He must at least give me a chance to warn them!"

As dawn came, the snow stopped, and the winds slowed. We could hear quite clearly now the ringing of church bells. And as the sun crept over the mountains, down at the bottom of the hill, we could see the abbey's snowcapped palisade, a church's spire rising from within it.

At a nod from the chieftain, the canon started down the snow-swept road.

And so, we sat there in our shelter, and we waited.

CHAPTER 24

Gisele

ROUEN

"YOU MIGHT HAVE LEFT THE CHEST THERE, MY LADY." I was finishing my supper as Hugh's voice broke into my thoughts.

I looked over to find him at the window.

"I did not wish to betray your secret entrance." My knife trembled as I applied more butter to my bread. I had not been expecting him. I had been expecting no one at all.

"Why don't you eat with the rest of them?"

"Do you want to come down from there?"

"Are you asking me in?"

I was, in fact, though I did not wish to admit it. In my solitude, I had found myself poor company. "I fear if you sit there much longer, you might topple from your perch."

He made a show of pushing away from the window and sailed through the air, arms stretched above his head. He landed with a grand flourish like some tumbler. Then he came over and stood, staring at me as I ate, as if he were some poorly fed hound.

"You aren't going to eat it all, my lady?"

"I was planning to." But I could hardly bear his sorry face. "You can have the bread if you wish."

He reached out and took it from me before I could give it to him, and then leaned over to inspect the rest of my plate. "That meat looks rather spoiled."

"I suppose you wish to test it for me." I pushed it toward him with the tip of my knife.

He shoved it into his mouth and chewed. Then he shook head quite violently. "It's no good. You won't want it."

"I am grateful for your concern."

Once done with eating, he took a tour of the room, standing at length in front of an embroidered panel I'd had hung from the wall. Turning his head this way and that, he studied it. "What is it?"

"Charles the Great."

"What's he doing?"

"Converting the heathens."

"What for?"

"Because they're *heathens*. They have no faith."

He frowned. "They don't seem very happy about it."

"It was either that or be executed. But now they all have eternal salvation."

He turned toward me. "They say the Dane you're to marry is going to convert."

"How did you hear about that?"

"Everyone knows about it. So what will you do?"

I blinked. "About what?"

"I mean…where will you go? What will you do after? Once you're married?"

"I suppose…I suppose I will do what I do now. Only I shall do it elsewhere." I had not thought on it before.

"You do not seem very happy about it."

"How would you like to be married to a pagan?"

He stooped to poke around at the ashes in the middle of the room where a fire should have been. "But he won't be a pagan when you marry him. He'll be a Christian."

"I rather suspect he'll be a Christian pagan." I could not imagine him kissing the archbishop's ring or kneeling in front of the altar of a church. I could not envision him humbling himself before anyone.

"Or maybe he'll be a pagan Christian."

"There is no such thing as a pagan Christian. One either is or is not."

"But you just said he'll be a Christian pagan."

"That was not what I meant. What I mean to say is…well, I meant it, but not in the way you understood it."

"What else was I to have understood by what you said?"

I wished he were not so vexing. "I do not wish to discuss the marriage any longer."

"But *you* should have the most to say of anyone, and everyone has been speaking of it for days."

I returned my attentions to my plate. I was sorry I had let him eat the rest of the food.

"Danes do terrible things."

"So I have heard. And as I told you, I do not wish to speak of it any longer."

"Why not?"

"How would you feel if you were betrothed to marry some foreign woman who did such terrible things?"

"I should think I might sleep with one eye open."

"Yes. And so you must understand how I fear for my life."

"The archbishop says it's for the glory of God."

I might have thought God had enough glory, if I did not know it would put my eternal soul at risk. "It is not he who has to marry, is it? It's quite easy to tell someone else to go risk their own life while you spend yours shut up in a cathedral."

"I should think you would feel honored to be so blessed, my lady."

"But then you are not me, are you?"

He fell silent as he seemed to contemplate my desperate situation. "I suppose you cannot appeal to my lord, the king."

"Can you suppose I have not already tried? But he says it is a question of honor."

"But what if you were *already* married. Then you could not marry the Dane."

For the first time I did indeed wish I had already married.

"Why could you not marry me instead?"

And to think, I had already made that very suggestion. Had it been only several short weeks before? "You're hardly of an age, and—"

"I've thirteen years already. I don't think my father would mind."

Mine would! "We cannot be friends, and I cannot ever marry you. Our fathers are enemies. They would neither of them approve. Besides, if I were to marry someone other than the Dane, it would be Rudolph of Burgundy or the Count of Vermandois." Though they being nearly the age of my father, I hardly thought them much better than the Dane.

"No, you wouldn't."

"Yes, I believe I would." My father had long talked of both men as matches.

"My oldest sister is to marry the Burgundian, and the other is to marry the count, because you're to marry the Dane. It's all working exactly as they planned."

There was a plan? "Are you certain?" How could there be a plan? My father had been as surprised as I when the archbishop told him I'd been promised in marriage.

He nodded.

"But how do you know?"

"Because I was with them when they were speaking of it."

They? "Who? Who was it you heard talking? Because my father—"

"*My* father and the archbishop."

They had planned it? How could they plan it without my

father's knowledge? "But how would they know what the Danes would—?" I felt my jaw drop as everything became clear. And then I gasped. There was treachery afoot! I'd been offered to the chieftain like some piece of bait. He had not *asked* for me, he'd been *given* me. And with me promised to the pagan, the count's daughters could marry whomever he wished, forging alliances, which for my father were now impossible. The queen's children would not be ready to marry for years. If any grand unions were to be accomplished before then, my father had need of me in order to do it. Did my father even realize what they'd done? He couldn't. Otherwise, he would not have allowed it.

"My father says I'm to be a king one day."

"King!" Could he not be silent for even one moment? "I'd like to see you try."

"You don't think I'd be a good one?"

"I think you've no chance of becoming one. How would you do it? Your father would have to be king for you to become one. And your father is not the king; *my* father is."

"That's what my mother says."

"Your mother is right. But why are you telling me these things?"

His gaze dropped from mine. "Because I wish to help you. And because my father doesn't like it when I ask questions. And besides, your father being the king, I thought you should know."

"Do you know my knight?"

"The big one? With the face that looks as if it were hewn with an ax?"

"Yes." That was him. In a man of lesser stature, his rough features would have been considered faults. "Can you tell him I wish to speak to him?"

"Why can you not do it yourself?"

"Because we aren't speaking."

"Then how do you plan to talk to him?"

"Can you do it or not?"

His chin lifted. "Of course I can do it, but my father won't let anyone come up here."

"*You* do."

"I'm not supposed to. But I've thirteen years now. I ought to be able to do as I please."

That's what I had once thought. I had thought that everyone else ought to do as I pleased as well.

Hugh had left off playing with the ashes to sit on the stool beside mine, interrupting my reverie. "Everyone says you're not the king's real daughter."

I pushed my plate away. "Then everyone lies."

"You *are* his real daughter?"

"I was his real daughter before he started having daughters again with the queen."

His brows folded. "Then why does everyone say—?"

"Because everyone doesn't know what I do."

"Even my father says it."

"And your father hates mine. What else could he be expected to say?" I wished the boy would stop talking. I was trying to think!

"Why would everyone say such a thing if it wasn't true?"

"What they mean to say is my father never married my mother."

He colored. "Why not?"

"She ran away before he could." I had to tell my father what I had just discovered. But how could I leave the palace without being seen?

"Why?"

"Why what?"

"Why did she run away?"

Because she hadn't wanted me. Wasn't that clear? "I have no idea."

"Well, I don't mind that you're not the king's real daughter. I think you're very beautiful." Now he was blushing even more.

It was vexing how easily he went from being a boy to being a man. I never seemed to know to whom I was speaking. "You are very kind, but that cannot help me. I'm still to be married to the Dane."

We sat there some, the both of us thinking, chins in our fists.

He stirred. "If I were king, I would not make you marry him."

I gave him a sidelong glance. "Thank you."

"I would give one of my sisters to him instead."

"I do not think she would thank you as well as I."

"No. But she's sour and mean. She's not like you."

Truly, I needed to think, and he did not look as if he would soon be departing. "Will someone not soon be missing you?"

"No. They're all with the Danes."

"I thought the Danes went back home to plow their fields."

"They may have. But they're here now. They're encamped outside the city. My mother says it's blasphemy, but my father doesn't seem to mind."

"They're *here*? In Rouen?"

Truly, I had to tell my father all Hugh had told me. Had he known the count colluded with the pagans, he would not have been so quick to agree to the treaty. Andulf would not help me, of that I was certain. He was too concerned with obeying my father to understand sometimes the only way to honor a command was to break it. If I went to him with my news, I feared he would only tell me Saint Catherine must have knowledge of this treachery, and God in His heaven as well, and why could I not just wait for the return of relic the way I had been told to in the first place? And then he would most probably watch me even more closely.

Hugh was right: the only way to avoid marrying the Dane was to marry someone else first. Someone of my own choosing, a marriage that would be irrevocable and unimpeachable. What I needed was an abbey where I could marry myself to God.

If I were going to leave—and now I was certain I had to—then I would have to manage it on my own. But how could I find a way out of this place, which had only one entrance and exit? And that, always guarded?

I asked Hugh the very next day.

His brows rose in alarm when I spoke of escape. "But, you want to leave? I might never see you again!"

"Never is a very definite word."

"Then when?"

"When what?"

"*When* would I see you again?"

"I could not say." Never, if I had my way.

"*I* can rescue you. As I have said before, you have only to marry me."

Was ever anything more vexing than a boy who considered himself a man? "And who would marry us? The archbishop? The same man who has been plotting with your father?"

"No."

"And neither would any of the priests dare to do what he will not."

"We could...we could run away!"

"And how would your father reward you for scuttling all his plans?"

From the look on his face, I imagined his only reward would be a very great punishment. The memory of that bruise was still stamped upon his cheek. And there was a mark now on his forearm as well.

"I truly don't see why you cannot marry me."

Now he was pouting! What I would have done for such a luxury. But there was no time. "Because both our fathers would disapprove. And if we do not have consent, we have nothing."

"When I am king, then I shall forbid people to force their children into marriage. Especially their daughters."

"Hugh."

He looked up into my eyes.

"If you're going to be a king one day, then you must always keep your promises. And do you remember? You said once you wished to help me."

He dropped to one knee and took up my hand in his. "I will. And I promise I will always love you." Having said the words, he pressed a reverent kiss onto my palm.

There was a sort of certainty to his words that made me think he meant them. But that was foolish. "Love is tiresome and tricky, and no one ever says what they mean about it."

His chin tipped up with a stubborn tilt. "I do. I said it, and I meant it." He blushed, the flames licking the tips of his ears. "What do you want me to do?"

"Is there any way through these palace walls other than the gate?"

He shook his head.

"None at all?"

His gaze slid away from mine. "No."

There was. There had to be. I decided to ask my question in a different way. "If you were trying to leave without using a gate, how would you do it?"

His gaze tried to meet mine, but dropped away at the last moment.

"Hugh? Please."

"You truly will not marry me?"

"I cannot. But you were clever when you said I ought to marry to keep from being wed to the Dane. I am going to take the veil as a nun."

"A *nun?*" He said the words with great doubt. "Where?"

"At Chelles. To the north. They will not refuse me there. But first I have to escape from here."

He sighed as his shoulders drooped. "You could disguise yourself and pass by the guards."

I was shaking my head before he had even finished. "The guards might not recognize me, but my knight probably would."

"We could create some sort of distraction that would make them all look the other way."

"But I would not want to count on the chance that they would."

He shrugged. "You *are* the princess…"

"I am."

"It seems like that ought to be worth something."

"It should be."

"What if you said you were going to see the Danes?"

"But I don't want to see them." I'd be happy if I never saw them again in my life.

"My father and his men go to their camp all the time. What if you just rode up to the guard and said that's where you were going?"

"Then my knight would insist upon going with me."

"Not if he were indisposed."

"*Someone* would have to go with me. They would not let me go alone."

"I would go with you."

"But I still don't understand what you would do with my knight."

"Just leave all of that to me."

Knowing how to descend Hugh's stair outside the tower was not the same as doing it. Not even when Hugh went first to aid me. As I dangled from the window's ledge by my fingers, I knew my first regrets.

But then Hugh's hand seized my ankle. "Just here, my lady." He placed it on one of his wooden pegs. It was only thanks to his guidance I reached the ground at all. And then we still had to take care of Andulf.

"Are you sure this will work, Hugh?"

"Of course it will work."

"But how do you know?"

"Because the only thing he cares about is you. He stands at the bottom of the stairs all day and then sleeps there through the night."

He did? When he could have slept in comfort with the count's men?

Hugh reached the end of his stairs, dropping to the ground, and walked toward the courtyard. "Remember: listen for my whistle, and then come around and join me."

For a small boy, he did quick work. It was not long before I heard him signal, and then I walked from the shadow of the tower to join him in the courtyard. "It worked?"

He nodded. "I told him my father had need of you, and could he get you to come down. It was easy. I followed him up and then barred him in."

I glanced back over my shoulder at the tower from which drifted his muffled shouts, and I prayed no one would hear his cries.

We went to the stables, where Hugh demanded our horses be saddled, and then we rode right out of the gate. It was just as he had foreseen. No one stopped us. No one gave us even a second glance.

Hugh went with me through the city's gates and then out along the way for a while, until I persuaded him that I really must begin to ride in earnest.

He passed me a small pouch of food. "I wish—" He bit his words off as the apple in his throat convulsed. "I wish you would kiss me before you go. I should like to know what it feels like, to be kissed by a princess."

I had never kissed anyone before, no one besides my half sisters, but he had been my friend, and he was helping me to escape. If he wanted a kiss in return for his efforts, then why should I not give him one? "All right then." I guided my horse toward his. "Lean this way."

"I—I have never—I have never kissed a lady before."

"It's probably the same as kissing one of your sisters."

"I've never kissed them before either."

I could not afford to sit and listen to him dither. Seizing his hand, I pulled him toward me, and then I pressed my lips to his.

"I shall never forget you, my lady."

My horse had been spoiled by its time in the count's stables. It took me some dozen miles, but then refused to go any farther. And when I kicked my heels into its sides, it simply flipped its tail at me.

"I swear by the saints, if you do not move, I shall see you butchered!"

It only stepped off the road to forage.

I pulled on the reins, but the obstinate beast only winked at me and then dipped its head to take another mouthful of food.

How long would it take for the count's men to discover Andulf?

I tried the reins once more with a similar result. Sliding from its back, I took up my pouch, girded up my loins and started off along the road by foot.

✐

It was my habit of looking back over my shoulder that saved me. I saw the riders long before they reached me. A cloud of billowing dust marked their coming. Moving from the road, I took shelter among a stand of bushes, kneeling to hide myself among their changing leaves.

The count's pennon flicked in the air above their heads, announcing their allegiance. As they galloped past me going east, the thunder of the horses' hooves kept cadence with my heart.

Soon, I would turn north. As long as the count's men kept going east, they would not find me. I had almost decided they were well and truly gone when another set of hooves sounded upon the road. I hid myself once more. Pushing back my hood, I lifted my head just high enough to see past the bushes' limbs. It was Andulf. And he was leading my wretched horse.

CHAPTER 25

*A*S THEY CAME ABREAST OF ME, THE DAMNABLE creature suddenly balked and then stiffened its legs, refusing to be led any farther. When Andulf stopped and gave the horse some rein, it came wandering down toward my bushes to graze.

I might have shooed him away, but I feared such a gesture would betray me.

The knight squinted into the bushes where I was hiding, and then his lips screwed up into what I took to be an especially painful smile. "Would you care to come out, my lady?"

I did not answer.

"The next time you decide to take cover, you might think to hide your golden tresses as well."

I drew my hood up over my plaits, though it was too late now to do anything about them.

"I have your horse."

"Little good it will do you." Little good it had done me.

"Are you coming out?"

"No."

"Then I shall have to come there for you."

I stood. "You did not help me in Rouen. You cannot help me now."

"I have no wish to help you. I want only to keep you safe."

"If you let me go, I shall be as safe as ever you wish. You were the one who urged me to trust myself to Providence. That is what I am doing."

His eyes narrowed as if he suspected me of mischief. "How?"

"I am going to wed myself to God."

His brow lifted.

"I cannot see how that would displease Him or Saint Catherine, and if I am married to God, then I cannot marry the Dane."

"Even the Almighty is not so long-suffering that He could gain much satisfaction in becoming your bridegroom."

Had I once thought it pleasant that this knight offered to speak to me? I changed my opinion. "You can have no say in the matter."

His jaw tightened.

I lifted my skirts and began walking through the underbrush, taking care to keep the bushes between Andulf and myself.

He spurred his courser into motion, but my palfrey bent its head to nibble at another bit of grass. As I kept walking, he tried again with the same result. Then he made a sort of clucking sound, and the creature fairly gamboled after him.

Had I not already decided it for a devil's spawn?

If only I could figure out how to get rid of Andulf. Then I could get myself well and truly gone, with the count's men no more the wiser. Which made me wonder... "The count's men passed some time ago. How did they know where to find me?"

Andulf's lips collapsed into a straight, firm line.

"You did not guess."

"I did not need to, my lady."

He'd been told then! And only one person knew of my plans. "Hugh was not to tell. He *swore* he would not tell."

"That whelp? He did not want to."

I could not keep a blush from staining my cheeks. "What did they do to him?"

"Did he pledge you his love?"

"What did they *do!*"

"Why do you care?"

"They did not hurt him?"

"Not very much."

I had not meant for Hugh to bear any consequence for my decision. I had not meant for any of this to happen at all! "Whose man are you? Why do you continually align yourself with the count's interests?"

"The princess had gone, and it was I charged with her keeping. What should I have done? Waited there until December, so I could tell your father I had lost you?"

"Yes!"

"It's my reputation at stake, along with your fair head."

"You've found me. I am safe. And now I would thank you to be on your way."

"And leave you here alone? When the sun will soon be setting?"

Lifting my chin, I turned my head from him and walked on. "I would not wish to be you when the Danish chieftain hears you lured me out into some deserted wood." Though it caused me no little shame to even think of perpetrating such a false report, I knew it would not take much to create the story, and very little effort to push it into motion.

Chancing a glance at him, I saw his face flush. When he answered, his words were stiffly spoken. "Nor would I wish to be you when your father finds out you have deliberately chosen to disregard him."

In my anger, my pace had quickened. In my indignation, I failed to guard my steps, and so my next one was placed squarely into a hole set some good way beneath the ground. My foot twisted as pain shot up my ankle. But I did not wish to give Andulf reason to gloat, and so I continued on as if it were of no importance, even though my ankle begged me to reconsider.

"Look here. If you will not ride your horse, then ride mine." Andulf had stopped both of them and was extending his hand toward me.

Gritting my teeth against the pain, I refused his offer, keeping instead to my path, albeit much more slowly. I kept my attentions fixed to my gait, trying to make it seem as if I did not yearn to cry out with every step.

"What is it you are trying to accomplish?"

If he were so set on conversing, then why should I not stop, for just a moment, to oblige him? I halted, leaning heavily on my other foot. There! Sweet relief. "If you must know, if you cannot guess, I wish to be freed from my obligation to marry the pagan."

"Which is why the canon was sent to the abbey for Saint Catherine's relic."

"And the Danes sent along with him! Tell me: do you expect they will inquire docilely of the abbess and then wait with patience to hear what she will decide?"

He snorted.

"I wished to inquire, to pray, to beg for divine guidance in the matter. To assure myself what I undertook was in accordance with heaven's will. But the Danes are no respecters of our faith. They will simply steal it."

He shrugged.

"They are going to steal *me*. So I have decided to make my own freedom."

"Freedom! Who are you to speak of freedom? I tell you this: no man on this earth is free. Every peasant bows to his knight, and every knight to his lord, and every lord to his king, and even the king himself bows to God. Who are you to want what none of us ever has one hope of having?"

I walked on, and still he followed by the road.

"Who are you to even think you have the right to demand such a thing?" His voice was tinged with outrage.

I gave no answer. Indeed, I feared I could not open my mouth without loosing a scream.

When he next spoke, it was in the sardonic tone with which I was familiar. "Are you planning to sleep this night, or are you going to keep walking?"

I kept walking.

I walked until the sun went down, and then I could walk no longer. Not without lurching. As well, my stomach had long since tired of being empty. I stopped at a convenient boulder, pulled Hugh's pouch from my girdle, and set about eating a meager meal of bread and a slim slice of cheese.

The knight dismounted, tied up the horses, and then rousted about gathering wood. Once he sparked it to a flame, he unsaddled his horse and my own, spread the caparisons upon the ground, and then got out his own meal: a pouch of smoked meat, a large red apple, some bread and cheese, and a costrel of wine.

He raised his cup in my direction. "Do you wish to join me?"

In fact I did. Even more than envying his food, I envied the warming flames of his fire. But now that I had stopped walking, I could not conceive of the unbearable pain standing once more would require. "No."

He looked at me then, as if daring me to change my mind.

I wanted to, dear God, how I wanted to! But even if I did, how would I get myself over to him? I was no longer certain I could walk, even if I wanted to. So I ignored him and went on making the best of my poor meal.

By then my ankle felt as if it had become a sausage ten sizes too large for its casing. I did not dare to move it. I did not dare to hardly breathe.

"Are you going to ask me to help you?"

I looked up at him, across the fire. He was watching, eyes knowing. He held my gaze for a long moment before dropping it to my ankle.

"I do not know of what you speak." I wished the pain did not sear so.

"You have so little faith in me then?"

The accusation shamed me. "Faith seems to be a thing in which I am decidedly lacking of late."

"Faith, my lady, only means knowing when you have come to the end of your own efforts. And faith needs only the barest permission to begin its work."

Is that not what I had realized when I had asked to appeal to Saint Catherine? But then the archbishop and the count and the Danes had crumpled up my poor hopes and thrown them all away. "And what if there is nothing—no one—to have faith in?" Tears began to leak from my eyes before I could stop them. And once they started, they would not cease.

Andulf began to busy himself with poking at the fire, though he cast a darting look at me now and then.

The misery of being found, the pain of my ankle, the injustice of my having chosen for myself a spot just beyond the reach of the fire's warmth conspired to undo me. I curled into myself, seeking to bind up all those offenses to keep them from tearing a hole through my soul. "I fear." The words came out not so much as a statement, but as a plea.

He paused in his doings for a moment. "We all fear, my lady."

We all fear. As I contemplated his response, I came to the knowledge that the most reasonable act would be to simply turn around, go back to Rouen, and abandon myself to despair. But I could not do even that. I could do nothing. I had ruined my ankle, and now I could not even depend upon myself. "Help me. Please, help me."

He came swiftly, dropping to his knees before me, taking up my foot with hands too gentle for one so large. Though his fingers probed with the lightest of touches, at my heel, my ankle's bone, and farther up on my calf, they left no little agony in their wake. And when he suddenly pushed my foot up toward my knee, I could not help but scream for mercy's sake. It echoed in the wood as bats rose from the trees and flitted away into the night.

"It's not broken, my lady. It's just been overbent."

He slipped my shoe back onto my foot. And then he picked me up and carried me over to the fire. After settling me on my caparison, he handed me a strip of meat. "We should seek an inn before our return to the palace. There your foot could be rested."

"No."

He did not seem surprised by my answer, only folding his mouth into a grim frown. "Then you should sleep."

"And what will you do?"

He rose from the fire and stepped back, outside of the reach of its light. "Try to keep you from being molested or murdered."

I would like to say I stayed awake and provided for him some sort of company, but it did not take long for sleep to find me; for the first time in many days, I did not have to sleep alone.

∽

The sun rose in jest the next morning, bringing neither light nor warmth with its presence. A mist had spread through the air before dawn, cloaking the road and frosting the grasses.

The knight shared some bread with me and then sat me on my horse. But he did not give the reins to me; neither did he mount his courser. "If I may be so bold as to ask? What is your plan?"

"To live."

"A worthy undertaking." He lifted his eyes from the reins to me. "But do you have any specific instructions, my lady?"

I glanced away.

"Any abbey in particular you were riding for?"

I said nothing.

"So you just…you ran away? Without any plan? In no certain direction?"

"Did Hugh not tell you that as well?"

"You told me yourself you were bound for a nunnery. He told me you were headed north, though he would not say to where."

I cheered my friend's loyalty. "My father must be told the Count of Paris and the archbishop have betrayed him." Perhaps I could convince Andulf to deliver the message on my behalf, and then I would be free to travel to the abbey on my own. "They conspired in advance with the Dane in order that he ask for my hand and—"

"I know."

"You—you know?"

"Yes."

I had thought myself alone in all of this. A feeling of amity infused me, and hope warmed my breast. "So you have sent

276

for my father, then?" Had I fled in vain? Had I sacrificed the
good faith of poor Hugh for no purpose?

He shook his head.

"You know all this, and you've done nothing?"

"What is it I'm to have done?"

"You've said *nothing*? Sent no messages?"

"I have been watched since I first came to Rouen. As
have you."

"You've men watching you, and yet you followed me.
They will know by now you have left them. They will soon
turn back to find you."

"They know I've come to find you. They let me come."

"They let you? But why?"

"I'm to bring you back to the count."

"Back to—! But you're my father's man."

"Yes. And his good name and your safety depend upon
your keeping the agreement he has sworn to uphold."

"An agreement made through treachery! They are to
be honored for their deceit, and I am to be sacrificed to
uphold it?"

"You're to be sacrificed to uphold your father's honor."

"Then I will thank you to leave me here, tell them you
could not find me, and be gone."

"I cannot."

"I shall tell no one I ever once encountered you. If you
do not speak of it, and I do not speak of it, then no one shall
ever know."

"My lady, the best thing you can do is to return to Rouen."

"No!"

He grimaced. "Perhaps I misspoke. What I should have said
is that I think the only thing you can do is return to Rouen."

"No." My whisper was as hollow as a reed. "Do not make
me go."

"Your father has made an agreement. The count awaits.
And so do the Danes. What else is there to do?" He pulled
my horse over toward his courser and mounted. But when I
reached for the reins, he would not give them to me.

"Am I to be taken back as if I am your prisoner?"

"No, my lady. As if you are my charge."

"I command you to release me."

He turned and looked at me over his shoulder, a sad smile
on his face. "I have pledged my allegiance to your father. I
am not yours, my lady, to command."

I did not fancy being led about as if I were some addle-
brained girl too dull to know her own way. "At least do not
parade me about. Spare me the indignity of that."

He passed a sideways glance at me.

"Let us not stop at the taverns or the inns. I would not have
it said the princess was being led as if she needed a nursemaid."

He did not answer, but late that morning, he slowed his
courser as we passed a clearing in the wood. "Will this do?"

"For what?"

"For a place to take a repast. I've little liking for the
count's men either."

He had decided to listen to me then! "Perhaps... Can we
stop away from the road? If I must be returned, then I wish
for you to do it and not the count's men."

Another look he gave me, as if wishing to take my measure.
I stared right back.

He steered us past the clearing until we found trees once
more, which screened us from the road. There he unfastened
his mantle from his shoulders and spread it upon the ground
before lifting me from the horse. There we ate, and there we
rested, and when he moved to lift me, I stayed him with a
hand to his arm. "I've need of a few moments in the wood.
If you could help me to stand..."

He ignored me, lifting me into his arms instead.

"I do not think—"

"I know what you need, my lady." He set me down some distance farther, where the trees were thicker. "I will return at your call."

I watched him retreat before I made any move. The trick would be to work my way back around to my horse before he decided to return for me on his own. I tested my ankle, finding it not much improved. I would simply have to do what I must quickly; this opportunity was too providential to ignore.

Taking great care with the placement of my feet, keeping one eye trained on the knight's broad back, I prayed I would be fleet enough to accomplish my goal.

My horse was in my sights when I first took note of a rustling in the wood behind me.

Fearing it was Andulf, and not daring to slow my pace, I pressed on. Two paces, three. I had not much farther to go when I heard a distinctive grunt and snuffle, those sounds that struck fear in the heart of every mortal man.

Chapter 26

*S*LOWLY, I TURNED.

Not ten paces from me was a boar. Its long, protruding snout and large upward-curving teeth were unmistakable.

Behind me, the horses snorted, pawing at the ground. So close I was to freedom, but I feared an attempt to reach them would only provoke the boar into charging.

The beast lowered his head. With a snorting squeal, he started toward me, and I knew my attempt at escape was finished. I only hoped I would live to see the morrow. As I closed my eyes, not willing to witness my own death, a hand seized me about the collar of my mantle and tossed me aside.

I landed on my belly, struggling for breath, as I watched the boar head toward the horses. But just as I whispered a prayer of thanks, the beast changed his course and turned instead toward me.

Pushing my fists against the earth, I scrambled to my knees. And then, realizing I hadn't the ability to save myself, I threw my arm over my face and prepared for death.

The beast's breath scorched my face, its grunts assaulted my ears, and then, as I steeled myself for its attack, it fell into my lap.

"Sweet Jesus!"

And it just…lay there.

Breath caught twixt my soul and my throat; I hardly dared move. When I gathered the courage to look down, the boar gave one last gasp, and then its eyes rolled back into its head as its lifeblood poured out onto my tunic from a gash in its belly.

Andulf staggered into view, took it by the ears, and drew it away from my lap onto the ground.

"Is it?" Was it dead?

"He—" Andulf's mouth was working to form the next word, but then his face went white, and he collapsed beside me.

I waited for him to recover himself, but he did not move. Nor did he open his eyes.

He had saved me, and now I was free! Scrambling to my feet, I gave him wide berth and then limped toward my horse. Grasping the reins, I moved to mount, but then I thought the better of it.

Had Andulf moved? He wasn't…he could not be dead, could he?

I peered around the horse's neck to get a look at him. His position had not changed. Neither had the boar's.

Taking a tighter grip on the reins and putting a hand to the saddle, I told myself he did not matter. He'd wanted to return me to the count and had refused to listen to my entreaties.

I put a foot to the stirrup.

But if he had perished, then it was on my account.

I stepped down.

Although I had not asked for him to save me, had I?

I put my foot back and pulled myself up, sucking in my breath as my bad ankle took my weight.

I cast another look at Andulf as I grasped my saddle. With any luck he might remain senseless for an hour or two, if he were not dead, that is.

I struck the saddle with my fist. If he had indeed died, then it was in the act of saving *me* from certain death.

Although he had not saved me for my benefit, but rather for my father's.

But it could not hurt to find out if he were truly dead.

Abandoning the horse, I limped back to kneel beside him, putting a hand to his jaw to turn his head toward me.

His breath fanned my face.

He was alive then. Elation took wing inside me. If he was alive, then I could leave without guilt. But, could I leave without shame?

By God and all His saints!

Cursing myself for a fool, I decided to stay until he awoke and I could make certain he could care for himself. At that point, I could still slip away and make for the abbey. That decided, I took him by the hand and dragged him away from the boar.

Or tried to.

His hand slipped from my grasp before I could shift him. My faith, but he was heavy! I took up his hand again and heaved, putting my back into it to spare my poor ankle. But I fell to the ground when a scattering of acorns caused my heels to slide out from under me.

If I could not move the knight, then perhaps I could move the boar. I knelt and put my hands to him. He did not move.

Was I to be afflicted by both man and beast?

Resigned to having to look at the both of them, I ignored the tangle of guts that spilled from the boar's belly and looked instead at Andulf's wound.

Wounds.

Three long, deep, dirt- and leaf-filled gashes from the boar's tusks.

It could not be good that there were more than one or that his blood had made a trail down his thigh to the bottom of his knee, where it was pooling at his gartered hose.

Unfastening the girdle from my waist, I moved to fix it about the wounds, pushing and pulling to guide it beneath his hulking thigh and then knotting it tight. It seemed to stay the bleeding, although the wounds still gaped. I pulled the bloodied, torn fabric of his hose from them and then tried to push the skin closed.

It wouldn't stay.

Finally, I gave up and sat on the ground beside him, waiting for him to wake.

As the air grew colder and the shadows grew longer, I unfastened my mantle and placed it over him, deciding he needed the warmth more than I.

Eventually, he woke with a sputter and a start, full face toward the boar. Giving a great cry, he lurched from the beast, and then he started again, clasping a hand to his thigh. He looked down at the girdle I had wrapped around it and then looked over at me. "You're still here."

"I could not leave you. Not after you had saved me. I would not have wished you to perish on my account."

He grunted.

"Does it pain you?"

"Everything pains me." His gaze moved beyond me to the horses.

"I tried to move the boar, and I tried to move you, but I could not do it." That's what he got for collapsing after he'd saved me. "You fainted and then..." He looked quite angry and not very grateful for my help. But then, if I had not tried to escape him, he might not have been wounded at all. "I just...want to say...thank you for saving me."

Out in the forest around us, creatures were about. I heard the hoot of owls, and underneath them the brush of leaves out of synch with the wind, and then, the distinct sound of a footfall on the leaf-littered ground.

The horses blew out a long breath and shook their heads, as if to rally their senses as they pulled at the reins that bound them to a tree.

Andulf put an elbow to the ground, rolling onto his side, and sent a piercing look into the wood. "Whatever is out there must smell the boar. It wants the meat." He fell onto his back, covering his wounded thigh with a cupped hand. "We must do what you ought to have already done: get away from here."

"I tried! But you're too tall and much too heavy, and you wouldn't move!"

"Bring the horses."

I hobbled toward the horses and made quick work of untying them as I eyed the twilight-shrouded wood in front of us.

Out in the brush, a twig snapped.

Andulf pushed to sitting and reached up toward the reins. "If I could just—" He leaned forward and tried to leverage himself up.

I bent to help him.

With a groan, he rolled onto his knees. "Get on the horse."

"I can't. My ankle." When I had ridden before, he had helped me to mount, but now he was on the wrong side of the horse.

"Draw the horse around, and I will help you."

I tried to turn the horse back in the other direction, head toward the wood, but it shied. I tried once more, but the horse nearly jerked the reins from my hands.

Andulf was scarcely able to sit; he could not be expected to walk around the horse to help me, though he looked as if he were contemplating that very thing. "You'll have to mount on your own. If the creature comes, the horse can save you."

"And what of you?"

"I have my sword."

"Little good it will do you! I am not leaving you to die after sitting here the long of the forenoon waiting to see if you'd live."

"And I will not have you perish after I've given my blood trying to save you!"

A snuffling squeal came from the wood.

"We need fire."

We needed many things, the first of which was to get us far from here!

"In my bag on my horse, I have a fire-steel and flint"—he left off for a moment as he took in a long breath through his teeth—"and touchwood."

Standing on the tips of my toes, I tried to retrieve them, but the falling gloom made for difficult work.

"At the bottom."

I seized upon them, pulling them from the bag, and then I handed them to him.

He reached for them, wincing, and then gave up, dropping his hand. "You will have to do it."

Though my hands shook, I managed to lay the strip of touchwood atop the flint and then to strike the rock with the fire-steel. Once. Twice. At the third try, a spark finally arched to the touchwood, but it died as it struck. It took a fourth and a fifth time before the touchwood began to smolder. But a hair-raising growl came from the wood before us as a snuffle came from behind.

There were more creatures out there in the wood than just one.

Keeping the touchwood to hand, I scrabbled about the ground for something: a stick, some fallen leaves. Scraping the ground with the bottom of my hand, I assembled a small pile and put the wood to it.

It did not take.

"Blow on it."

"Blow on...?"

"The smoke. Blow on the smoke!"

Thinking him mad, but not knowing what else to do, I blew upon it. As if by magic, the smoke birthed a flame that devoured the tinder.

"A limb! Find a limb and hold it to the flame."

Leaving my smoldering fire, I searched around us for a fallen branch or a large twig, something we could burn. As I came by a short, stubby branch, the fire guttered for a moment.

I felt my breath catch.

But then the flame flared.

A shadow darker than the surrounding forest emerged from the trees before us.

Holding my branch to the fire, I prayed the flame would take. As the shadow moved closer, the branch burst into flame. Rising, I stepped in front of Andulf and then brandished the flaming branch in front of us. Sweeping it to the right and to the left and then back again.

Andulf had shifted and was crouching now. "You cannot do that forever."

"I will do it as long as I have to."

A rippling shriek echoed through the forest.

The horses blew out a deep breath and took a step closer to us.

"If you can help me to standing, we should leave."

Holding the branch out before me, I knelt at his side. Fixing his arm across my shoulders and grasping his hand, I heaved to standing. He hung from my shoulder for a moment and then rallied, gaining his feet. Releasing his hand, I took up the horse's reins. "Can you advance?"

"I will try."

The fire had shortened my vision to its flickering flames, but the horses were growing more anxious by the moment, and that shuffling snuffle was getting closer.

I started out, away from the approaching beast.

With every step, Andulf shuddered.

"We must stop. You are not—"

"Keep on. I've more planned for myself than to finish as some beast's midnight feast."

I took more of his weight as he seemed to slump.

When he next spoke it was into my ear. "Walk on."

"To where?"

He raised his head, took a look about, and then nodded toward a large tree that beckoned through the moon's light. "There."

It took many steps and much effort. We nearly fell, the both of us, when I stepped into a hole, which wrenched my already throbbing ankle, but we made it to the tree, where his arm slipped from my shoulders and he slumped into me with a loud sigh.

Gripping the flaming branch with one hand, I threw the other about his waist, trying to keep him standing. "You cannot die!"

He sagged against me, and I fell to the ground. As I clasped my arms about his chest, the branch tumbled to the ground as well. "Do not die. Please. Do you not die!" I buried my head in that thick neck of his and held on.

In the distance, back from where we'd come, I could hear the tearing of flesh and the grunting of beasts.

He put an arm up over mine, clasping me to himself. We stayed there for some time as he took in a series of long, deep breaths. Then he set me aside. "Sit there." He indicated the tree trunk behind him with a violent jerk of his chin. "With the tree behind you, and me before you, at least you will be able to sleep unmolested."

"I will not sleep. I cannot! That beast may follow us if he smells the scent of you."

"He'll be plenty satisfied with the boar."

"What if—what if—" I could not bring myself to speak the words I feared and so settled for a different thought entirely. "What if you fall asleep?"

A hiss escaped from between his teeth. "I could not sleep right now for all the gold in the archbishop's treasury."

"But I do not know if—"

"You are the most stubborn girl I have ever had the displeasure to try and save. *Get behind me!*"

Picking up the skirts of my tunic, I stepped into the space between him and the trunk.

"Sleep."

I would not do it, but it would do no harm to let him think I might. That way, should anything come for us in the night, then I would know it, and he would not have to fight it off alone. Not having any cushions or a counterpane, I settled myself as comfortably as I could into the curve of the tree's roots and then drew my mantle around me.

The knight pushed himself back toward me, gasping as he did it, and pressed me against the tree. Then he threw his mantle out over his shoulder, letting it pool onto my feet. And there, God help me, in spite of my best intentions, I must have fallen asleep.

CHAPTER 27

Juliana

ROCHEMONT ABBEY

*I*NCREASINGLY, THE ABBESS HAD BEEN ENTERTAINING her guests at our meal—her relations as well as her lover—and the refectory had become a kind of provincial court filled with singers and mimes and tumblers and all manner of amusements, which we sisters tried in vain to ignore. Though in previous times Sister Isolda had always read scripture to us during the meal, her readings had been set aside for more worldly delights. The careless discipline of the abbess bred laxity throughout the novitiate, and now even my fellow sisters were speaking to one another in plain voice. When the guests began to flirt with the nuns, I wondered that some of the sisters might even try to put off their veils.

In spite of all those things, I could not bring myself to hate the abbess completely. I understood what it was to be thrust into a position that was not of your own making. But while I had forfeited my rights for my duties, she seemed to prize the former over the latter. I did not doubt she had a keen mind. I did, however, doubt her happiness. Even her lover did not seem to be able to assuage her moods. And mostly she retreated to her rooms when her presence was not required at the offices or at our meal.

I had once told a girl much like her not to despise the life she had been given.

Would that I could tell the abbess that very same thing. She could do much good here if she would but use the power and the influence she had been given. The thought lay so heavily upon my heart that I went to see her one morning after terce, before I returned to the hospice. She was gazing out a window at the white-topped mountains that rose behind the abbey. Her veil and wimple had been removed, and her hair lifted in the breeze that sifted in through the opening. At my entrance, she turned. "There is snow already. I did not think it would come so soon."

It always came this soon, but though it was always expected, it was never celebrated.

"I suppose we will be trapped here for the winter."

"It is not a bad place to have to stay, Reverend Mother."

She sent a speculative look at me as she sat in her armed chair, drawing a fur up over her shoulders. "Perhaps not for you, who are used to being enclosed in such a place."

"You are not happy."

"I do not think this place was constructed for happiness."

"There is contentment to be found here, if one has the faith to look for it."

The glance she gave me was wary. "I have faith."

"Then why can you not use it for our benefit, Reverend Mother?"

Her smile, when it came, was sardonic. "Because I am already using it for my father's benefit."

"But the nuns have need of you. And so will the pilgrims, when they return in the spring."

"Then they shall have to stand in line."

"You could do much good here."

"*Could* do? I am *doing*. I am doing much good for my father. It was he who installed me here. Should my first thought not be for him?"

"But what of God?"

"Why should He not approve of me?" She had lifted her chin as if daring me to answer.

"I do not think you have the…*temperament* of a nun."

She slouched in her chair, putting her elbows to the armrests and steepling her fingers beneath her chin. "Ah. You speak of my lord, the Marquess of Belfort. I do wish you would keep your sentiments and your observations to yourself."

"I, too, was once young."

The corners of her mouth lifted. "But even so, I doubt any suitor you might have had could compare to mine. You, who have chosen to deny your body for your soul, cannot know how it feels to yearn for something, some*one*, whom others have said you cannot have."

But I did. And so I gave her the advice the old abbess had given me. "You must think on other things. You must sacrifice your own poor interest in his soul to One whose interests are higher and greater. You must rest in the thought that He can do more for my lord, the marquess, than you can."

Her chin seemed to tremble. "If only it were that simple."

I went and knelt before her. "It is. It may not be easy, but it is not very complicated. And dwelling upon your losses will only prolong your pain." As I spoke the words, I realized at last I had come to believe them. And though the abbess soon dismissed me, I left her rooms with a gladdened heart. Perhaps my salvation was not quite so far off as I had once despaired.

That forenoon, as we sat in the refectory for our meal, the door suddenly swung open, and our chaplain appeared. He was flush of face and panting, cap clutched in his hand. "There are Danes—" He wheezed and then doubled over in a cough. "There are Danes out there! I saw them. I saw them with my own eyes!"

The abbess had paused in her eating at the chaplain's appearance, and the novices had stopped their ceaseless chatter.

"You must come. There are Danes—" His voice seized once more.

An uproar ensued, and the abbess rose from her armed chair, hand at her throat. "Did you—what did you say?"

"Danes! There are *Danes!*"

A canon wearing robes that must once have been quite fine appeared beside the chaplain. He raised a hand. "There is nothing to fear. They have promised me they will not hurt you as long as you give them Saint Catherine's relic."

The abbess had bolted from her table as the men spoke, and now she ran forward, tunic flapping around her ankles. She grabbed the canon about the arm. Sinking to her knees, she released her grip on him. "Danes? Are you certain?"

"Of course I'm certain. I came with them. Rather, they have come with me."

Her face creased with fear. "Save me. You *must* save me. I cannot die!"

The canon spread his arm wide as if in supplication. "No one will die. I promise you. Just give me the relic."

She let loose a long, loud wail. "The Danes are going to kill us all!"

At the far end of my table, Sister Rotrude had not stopped laughing since the chaplain had first appeared. Toward the middle of the table, Sister Amicia was rocking back and forth, whispered words tumbling from her mouth, while the whole front half of the table was taken in furious conversation.

"The relic? May I have it?" The canon's appeal was put to no one in particular.

At the head of the table, Sister Berta stood. "If we give you the relic, they will leave us? They will turn around and go?"

The canon clapped a hand to his chest as he looked toward heaven. "I promise you. I swear on the veil of the Holy Mother herself."

"We are all going to perish!" The abbess still trembled at his feet. "Please, save us!"

Sister Berta turned to Sister Isolda. "Go to the chapel, take the canon with you, and give him Saint Catherine's relic."

"No." The word leapt from my lips before I knew I was even thinking it. "Stop!"

For one long moment there was complete and total silence.

Rising, I addressed myself to the canon. "Who are you? And what right do you have to demand our relic from us?"

His mouth gaped wide for a moment, and then he shut it up. "You do not understand. They are *Danes*. If you do not give them the relic, they will come here and take it by force. And I cannot guarantee they will not take whatever else they want as well."

As he spoke, I closed the distance between us. "But in whose name do you come to us?"

"The—the Archbishop of Rouen."

"And why should we give him what he asks?"

"What *he* asks? It's the Danes who want it now. If you wish to save your lives, you'll do as they request."

Beneath us at our feet, the abbess moaned. "When have Danes ever kept their word? Whether we give it to them or not, they will kill us. They will murder us all!"

"We're to give you the relic because the *Danes* want it? What do you have to do with the Danes? Why should something holy be demanded by those who are so foul?"

"If you would only—"

Ignoring his pleas, I turned back toward my fellow sisters. "We must not do this. We must pray, all of us." I sank to my knees as I spoke. "And we must ask God to save us."

The abbess had listened to my words. Now, chin quaking, she looked up at me in terror. "Ask *God* to save us?!" She stood then and looked around at us all with crazed eyes. "Run! All of you. Save yourselves!"

I raised a hand. "No, please!" But I might as well have asked the wind to cease its blowing. No one listened. Leaving benches overturned and the tables a-kilter, the sisters had fled. And the abbess had followed on their heels.

Only the canon and I remained.

He clutched my hand. "Just tell me where it is. In the name of God, just tell me so I can take it!"

"You call yourself a man of God? How can you be a part of this? How can it be right for you to lead the heathen here?"

"If Saint Catherine wishes to leave, then nothing you can do will stop them from taking her."

"And why would she wish to go anywhere with the depraved and the wicked?" But then why would she wish to stay here, when the abbey had been turned into a brothel?

"They don't want it for themselves. It's for the archbishop."

"And why does he want it?" From the courtyard came shrieks and bellows and other sounds of panic.

"Because…" He sighed. "It's for the princess."

"The princess? Gisele?" My daughter? "Then why did she not come herself?" Why had she sent Danes to take it from us?

"She wanted to, but then…"

"Please. Tell me!"

"The princess has been promised to the chieftain of the Danes. She asked the king for leave to come to the abbey and inquire of Saint Catherine herself."

She would not have asked to come if she had wanted to wed the Dane. Of that I was certain. "And the king?"

"The king agreed to allow it, but then he was called to

Lorraine. They want to make him their king. So he left the princess in the care of the Count of Paris, and *he* did not want her to make the journey. The archbishop suggested the relic would be better housed at the cathedral in Rouen, so I was dispatched to bring the relic to her."

"He had no right!" None of them had.

"And the Dane sent his men along to make certain I did not fail. So all has turned upon itself. What started out as an expedition to inquire of Saint Catherine has been overtaken by the pagans."

A great rage burned within my breast. It was not right that they should demand what did not belong to them, that we should be forced to forfeit what we held most sacred. And it was not just that my daughter was not to be allowed to inquire honestly of Saint Catherine. I did not suffer from delusions: if the saint wished to leave, there would be no stopping the Danes from taking her relic, but that did not mean I had to offer it to them. "They cannot have it." My daughter had wanted Saint Catherine to decide. In this, at least, I would try to grant her wish.

"But they will sack the place. No one will be safe! Not one. We did not have to warn you. Indeed, even now, we could just take it, but I persuaded them to allow me to ask you for it. To try to obtain it without damage."

"But we cannot leave. We cannot let you take it. Surely you must know that. If we flee before the vile and the wicked, will God not find us lacking in faith? If we cannot trust God, then why should we ask Him to save us? And besides, do we not have Saint Catherine on our side?"

"What good is Saint Catherine in the face of pillage and rapine! She is—she is *dead*! And these Danes are not god-fearing men! I have done what I can, but if you refuse my request, I cannot be held responsible for their actions."

"They cannot have it."

"And you are going to stop them?" His tone was incredulous. "How? Look around you. The rest of the sisters have fled."

Speak truth; stand for what is right. "Then their faith has nothing to do with mine."

"The Danes will have no mercy."

"If God is for me, then who can be against me?" That is what I had always been taught. I could only hope it did not matter that the men like him who had done that teaching did not seem to believe the words they spoke.

"If you refuse, I will not be able to help you."

"I do not look to you for salvation." I hoped I sounded braver than I felt.

He simply stared at me, shaking his head. And then he turned and started toward the courtyard. "The sisters said it was in the chapel. I'll just take it myself and save them—and you—the trouble."

"For *shame!*"

He turned, a cynical smile twisting his lips. "If you think to offend me, then you are mistaken. I have lived with shame for quite some time now."

"For God's sake!"

"For God's sake I have perverted justice, I have bowed to every request of my uncle the archbishop, and I have thrown in with the Danes. For God's sake I have done a hundred things I have begun to think have nothing to do with Him at all."

"But you're—"

He looked down at his robes, throwing his arms out. "A cleric. A canon. Yes, I am. But I am also a man of so little faith that—"

"Our Lord has said, 'Though our faith be so small as a mustard seed...'"

Rage erupted in his eyes. "Yes! 'Though it be as small as a mustard seed, still I can move mountains.' But I care nothing for mountains! My faith is worn and beaten and so exceedingly small it cannot see any other way than this."

"Then it must never have been faith at all."

A wave of great sadness swept his face.

"Or if it was, you must have placed it in the wrong thing."

"The wrong thing." His eyes met mine. "The wrong man."

"Otherwise, you would not be so eager to give our treasure to the pagans."

"No." He blinked as his mouth dipped and his brow convulsed. "I would not."

"Then do not take Saint Catherine from us."

A tremor crossed his face as if there was great pain within him. "If you insist upon your own destruction, I give you my word, which is all that is left of my honor. I shall not keep you from it. I will go and tell the Danes they cannot have it."

Once I gained the courtyard, I saw there was no one left. There was not one sign of the sisters, nor were there any workers about. The smith had abandoned his workshop, leaving his fires burning. The cooper had left his task, and a barrel still stood on its splayed staves. Pigs were rooting through the mud with no one to stop them.

Soon it might all lie in waste.

A terrible, desperate fear washed over my soul. Surely I was mad. How could I ever have hoped to save the relic by myself? If I hurried, perhaps I could still escape with the others. Lifting my tunic, I ran toward the gate, following the path they must have taken.

But why should we have so quickly abandoned a place meant to be a refuge? My steps slowed. It had been built to keep those within its palisade safe. By closing the great gate, we ought to have been able to keep the pagans at bay.

But our defenses would not work if they were abandoned.

The heavy gate meant to protect us lay unmanned; those thick doors that ought to have defended us had been left wide open. How could we keep those safe who would not stay within our walls?

As I stood there, I surveyed the buildings that lay around me, this place where I had spent half of my life. The hospice and the kitchens. The workshops and the workers' houses. All were lost now. If the canon was right, all of them would soon be turned to ashes. As I swept my eyes to the east, toward the mountains, I heard a cry lift from the hospice.

Sweet Mary! Was that—?

CHAPTER 28

UNNING OVER TO THE DOOR, I FOUND WHAT I prayed I would not see. They were there, all of them: the young lord, Ava, Pepin, Otker, Gerold, and that wriggling pile of the lame.

The abbess had been right. If we stayed here, we would all be killed. Even these would not escape that fate.

"Young Lord!" I held my breath as he turned toward me, hoping against hope he might be free of his tormenting demons.

Stretching forth his hand, he approached me. Solicitous, eager, with every mark of the nobleman about him. "Sister Juliana?"

I seized his hand. "You must help me."

"Of course, I shall help you."

"We must get all these here into—" Where? Where could we possibly find safety in an abbey filled with wooden buildings? My eyes lifted to the highest point in the place. To the roof of the church from which the spire projected. I remembered then that not all of this place was wood. It would not all burn. Saint Catherine might preserve us yet. "We must take them to the chapel." Surely even godless heathens would respect the sanctity of the church.

"Why?" His eyes were clear, his mind lucid. Did I dare to tell him the truth? His brows lifted in question.

No. I could not risk his placid mood. "Because it is necessary."

"Would it not be better to do it later, perhaps? Once Sister Sybilla returns?"

"No!"

Ava shrieked, and then she wrapped her thin arms about her chest and began to cry.

I tried to soften my tone. It would do no good to alarm them. Any unease would only slow their progress, and if nothing else, I needed them to move quickly. "No. We must do it now." I stepped closer to him, deciding I must reveal my secret after all. When I spoke, it was beneath my breath. "We are in great danger, and none of us is safe here. The chapel is our only hope."

His brows tilted in alarm, but then he nodded and took the cheerful Otker by the hand. I gestured to Gerold, that eater of twigs, asking for his hand, and then put an arm around Ava. These I led to the young lord. "Otker, you must hold Ava's hand." I peeled her arms from her chest as I spoke. "And you, Ava, must hold Pepin's hand." I went to him, ignoring his flapping arms, and took up his hand, walking him over to the girl. Placing their palms together, I folded their fingers about each other. "Quickly now." I nodded at the young lord. "You must take them. Take them all the way to the front of the chapel, to Saint Catherine herself. Go up and beyond the altar even. Do not stop until you reach the stone wall."

When I joined them there, just this once, I would snuff out the candles and the lamps. In the dark shadows, perhaps the children would not be noticed.

Merciful Father in heaven… If I did not deserve his mercy, these poor ones did not deserve his wrath. I turned to the young lord. "Stay with them, there. I will bring the others just as quickly as I can." I wanted to protect the relic, but were these little ones not more important? Saint Catherine could fend for herself, but they could not.

"You should go with them, Sister Juliana. I can bring the others over."

He looked as if he could, but should I trust him? Could I hope the demons would not come over him as they had in the past?

Those who remained were the lame and a few babes who had recently come to us. Those too feeble or too young to walk.

Perhaps... I took up the babes in my arms. "If I take these, can you manage the others?"

"I will do what I must."

✑

"Come now." I told Otker to take the sleeve of my robe between his hands, and we crossed the courtyard like a goose and her goslings. Pepin dawdled, stretching our procession to the point of breaking, and pausing to flap about, but finally, I ushered them into the nave of the church.

"Come now. Come now. Come now." Otker whispered, but the echo of his words vaulted up to the ceiling and then back down toward the floor and vibrated everywhere in between.

I put a finger to my lips. "We must, all of us, be silent. There are bad men who are coming, but God will protect you. And I must protect Saint Catherine."

"Saint Catherine. Saint Catherine. Saint Catherine." Again, his words vaulted up to echo around us.

I laid a finger on his lips. "Do what I say, and no harm will come to you." I prayed the words I spoke were true.

Down at the end of the church, Saint Catherine's chapel glinted with the shimmering candles' light.

"Quickly now!" Passing the font of holy water, I led them straight through the nave and down the stone incline into the chapel.

Ava paused at the threshold. Dropping Otker's and Pepin's hands, she held up her own, entranced at the play of the candles' light against her palms.

Grabbing one of them, I pulled her forward, not stopping at the altar.

"I am going to put out the candles. All but one. It will be dark here. Once the light is gone, you must all be silent."

Otker nodded and then sucked his lips up over his teeth and clamped down on them. I placed the others behind him, leaving him in front, since he was taller and broader than the rest.

They watched, eyes wide as I snuffed out the candles and extinguished the lamps, and soon with only the one candle for light, I could not discern their features from the shadows.

I breathed a prayer of thanksgiving, and then I turned my attention to the relic.

It could not stay atop the altar. It was still much too easy to see—and to seize. There was no time for confession or for kneeling in prayer. I hoped Saint Catherine would forgive my boldness as I took her box up between my hands.

But where could I hide it?

I glanced out toward the church. The floor had been swept clean, and there was no place to put it. I could hide it behind one of the wooden pillars that supported the roof and hope the Danes would not venture deep enough into the church find it, but why would they not do so?

The canon might have promised not to take the relic from me, but that did not mean he would keep silent about where they might find it. He already knew where the relic must reside. And if these Danes had ever raided a church, they must know as well.

I looked up at the open windows of the nave; if only I could reach them! But they were high above the floor, well beyond my reach. Beyond even them, the beams at the roof beckoned. Up there the relic would surely be safe, but I did not have the means to reach them.

"Sister Juliana?"

The young lord had come with the lame. They were clinging to him, about his neck and around his chest. He carried two of them in his arms.

"To the chapel." I turned and hurried before him, and then made a place for them on the floor near all the others. "Are these the last?"

"There's one more. But she's the last." The young man started back toward the church.

I followed him out into the nave. "There's no time!"

"But you asked for me to bring them all."

"I will keep the door open for you."

"If there is danger, you must bar it."

"They are Danes, the men who are coming! This is the only place to hide."

The color drained from his face, but he squared his shoulders as he started off. "Then I must hurry."

Turning back toward the children, I thought, for a brief instant, of entrusting the relic to them and urging them to flee, but I had already delayed too long. Whatever was to happen, they could not now escape. Why should I put their lives in further danger by giving them the relic?

The problem was the box. It was far too large. If it were smaller, if the abbess had let us keep the old one, then I could hide it as we used to do, in the alcove beneath the altar.

Outside, there rose a shout and then a great thumping noise.

They had come.

Pray God the young lord would keep himself hidden.

Did Saint Catherine want to go to Rouen? Was all my work, all of my effort for naught? Perhaps I should just let them have her. If I did, then maybe I could still save the others. But then my daughter would be lost.

Smoke curled through the windows high above me as foreign tongues filled the air with their cries.

Speak truth; stand for what is right.

The abbess had trusted me to do what was right. And my daughter had trusted Saint Catherine would tell her what to do. If the Danes wanted the relic, then they would have to first find it. I retreated back toward the chapel.

I did not have much time. If it weren't for the box, then I could hide it beneath the altar, where no Dane, at least, would think to look for it. The box itself was nothing. The true treasure lay inside it. The *true* treasure! I opened the lid and emptied the contents into my hand. Then I fished the shard of bone from the dirt.

Forgive me, Saint Catherine.

Placing the bone beneath the altar, I poured the dirt on top of it, covering its telltale shape. Satisfied with my deceit, I set the box in its rightful place.

"It's too dark." Otker's voice came whining through the gloom.

Someone, Ava perhaps, began to whimper.

I rose and put a hand to each of them in turn. "But did you not know? Even darkness is as light to God. He can see you just as clearly as He could before." Though I would have much preferred to stay in there with them, trying to hide myself in the gloom, my object was not to spare myself. It was to save Saint Catherine and to protect the children from the Danes.

I might have given the pagans the box itself, but it was empty. And what if they discovered my subterfuge? In their rage, might they not murder us all? I needed something to place inside it. Something that would substitute for a bone.

There were candles aplenty, but those would not do. They were the wrong shape, most of them, too squat and stout. The lamps had wicks, but those were much too slender.

Lifting that last of the lighted candles from its holder, I used its light to search the floor for something, anything, that might work for my purpose. But the floor here had been swept clean as well. And so had all the crevices of the walls. In this one area at least, the abbey was being well cared for. I needed something thin and sturdy. A bone. A quill pen. A...*twig*.

Gerold!

Setting the candle back into its holder, I went to the children and knelt in front of the boy. His gaze crept toward mine, and then it dropped away. He jammed his fist into the folds of his tunic.

Taking hold of it with what I hoped was a gentle hand, I tugged it away from his side. "What have you got there?"

His jaw clenched as his brow folded. He pulled his hand to his chest.

"I have tried to help you these many days. I have tried to give you good food to eat." I covered his hand with my own. "I have tried to make certain you have everything you need."

He was looking down at our hands, his lower lip extended in a pout.

"This time, I was wondering, if perhaps, *you* might be able to help *me*."

Slowly, his gaze rose. It did not meet mine, not exactly, but it was not far off.

"I need what you have in your hand. And I am not going to throw it away. I am not going to scold you. I just want to put it in this box." I let go of his hand and held up Saint Catherine's reliquary.

Just the single candle was lit, but still the jewels somehow captured its light. The rubies glowed. The emeralds glinted. And the gold reflected back the light. Red and green flickered across Gerold's face as he stood there, gazing at the reliquary.

I took off the lid.

He leaned forward and looked inside.

"There is nothing there right now. Would you not like to put your twig there?"

His fist clenched.

"You could do it yourself. Here: I will hold the box, and you can put it inside."

He looked down at his hand.

"You can even put the lid back on top if you want to."

Opening his palm, he revealed a short, splintered shard of wood, which he must have pulled from the hearth before we'd taken him from the hospice. It did not look too different from the bone I had hidden beneath the altar. I wanted to force him to do it. I wanted to snatch it from his hand and drop it inside, but I could not risk his tear-filled cries. The Danes must never suspect the children were here.

"If you put it in this box, then I am going to show it to some other people—"

His fist closed.

"But only so they can admire it too. They have traveled so very far to see it. Everyone who comes here wants to see what's in this box. Did you know that? And now, if you wish it, you can put your twig in here. Would you like to?"

He was gazing out across my shoulder.

"Can you help me?"

He blinked.

"Please?"

Looking down, he held his fist over the box and opened it.

I heard the twig clatter at the bottom, and then handed him the lid.

He took it, rubbing at the rubies with his thumb.

"Can you put it right there? On top?"

He held it up, staring into the jewels as he turned it first this way and then that. Finally, bless heaven, he pushed it down onto the box.

Leaving the children huddled against the back wall, I stepped out into the church, box between my hands, and I waited.

I did not have to wait long. The door flew open, slamming against the wall, causing the building to shudder. The birds that nested in the beams squawked and rose to flutter about the roof. Men filed in, one after the other. They were tall and fair, clad in strange costumes and cloaked with furs. Their faces were bearded. The tallest of them, the man who wore a helmet, led them toward me as I stood in the middle of the nave. And there they came to a halt, axes glinting.

I had never known such terror.

The canon had come with them and stood now, just inside the door. They had a second cleric with them as well. A monk. After the man with the helmet had spoken, the monk translated.

"They are here for Saint Catherine's relic. They have already put the rest of the abbey to the torch. There will be no escape if you refuse to give it to them."

Trembling, I held out the box. The sooner they took it,

the sooner they left, the better. As long as the children kept quiet, they might never be discovered.

The monk stepped forward to take the box from me as the Dane himself walked right past us.

"No!" I grabbed hold of the Dane's arm. "I give the box to you."

He wrested his arm free and continued on toward the chapel.

I appealed to the monk. "I gave it to him. I gave him what he wanted!"

The monk shrugged. "They know there is always treasure at the altar of a church."

"But there is none. The box was all we had. There is no gold. There are no jewels. I gave him what he wanted!" Running to the Dane, I threw myself at him, grabbing hold of his arm.

He rebuffed me with a blow of his hand, and I struck my head against a pillar as I fell.

As I lay there on my back, I saw spirals of smoke curl down from the roof and the spark of flames at the pitch of the eves. Smoke was billowing through the windows now, and the birds were circling in earnest, squawking as flew.

Rolling onto my stomach, I threw out a hand and grabbed hold of his foot. He must not find the children.

The Dane stopped and turned, lifting his ax above his head. But at the moment he would have brought it down, he paused, glancing back at the entrance.

Rolling away, I scrambled to my feet.

The door was opening, fresh air swirling with the smoke. From the threshold stepped the young lord. But he was not the same nobleman who had left me. His demons had returned, and he was beating his breast and thumping his head with one of the cooper's staves. As he stepped forward, I could see blood had begun to trickle down his cheek.

"Go away! Go away!" The strain of his cries had raised the tendons that bound his throat.

The Danes shifted as they turned toward him, and one of them cried out, "Berserker!"

The cry was lifted up and repeated. "Berserker! Berserker!" The Danes tried to push one of their own forward toward the young lord, but he refused to go.

As the young man advanced, they began backing away from him toward the man with the helmet.

Down the nave, the young lord strode, beating his breast and striking his head with the stave.

"Is he mad?" The canon yelled at me across the smoke that had swirled around us.

I could not contain my smile. "Zeal for the Lord has consumed him!"

As the boy came abreast of me, I fell in with him, following as he led toward the chapel.

One of the Danes let out a shout, pointing a shaking finger beyond us at the mouth of the chapel.

Through the spreading smoke, I could see my Pepin outlined by the candle's flickering light. He had ascended toward the church and was flapping his arms, hopping about the entrance to the chapel. In that eerie interplay of light and shadow, his figure was veiled, his features distorted as his silhouette was cast up onto the smoke. He seemed a giant bird, wheeling first this way and then that.

"Valkyries!" The Danes' cry was jubilant. Triumphant.

The young lord loosed a cry of rage so noisome even the timbers of the church trembled. An eerie shriek drifted out from the chapel. It rose and fell in a strange cadence. And then Otker appeared beside Pepin. "Valkyries. Valkyries. Valkyries." He joined the lad, hopping about, and his laughter echoed through the smoke.

The monk threw himself upon his knees, pleading the protection of heaven. But the helmeted Dane let out a bellow and pointed his ax in our direction.

I hurried behind the young lord, collecting the children and pulling them along with me. As we went, there was a resounding crack, and one of the eaves fell into the nave, sending out a shower of sparks.

Before our descent into the chapel, the roof, eaten by flames, crumbled to the floor atop the Danes. And then the beam that had held it up toppled down upon them.

In the church, all was afire. But the smoke had not yet completely overtaken the chapel. I coaxed the children down toward the floor where the air was still clear. Beside me, the young lord slowly ceased his tormented cries and let the stave fall to the floor.

Ava crawled onto my lap while Otker and Gerold watched on their bellies as the church was consumed by flames.

A girl like you has nothing to offer at all. A girl like you can never come to anything.

I had nothing to offer, I would never come to anything, and around me were gathered the least of all of God's children. But I had spoken the truth. I had stood for what was right. And together we had saved the relic.

Saint Catherine had chosen to stay.

Saint Catherine, glorious virgin and martyr…implore for me progress in the science of the saints and the virtue of holy purity, that vanquishing the enemies of my soul, I may be victorious in my last combat and after death be conducted by the angels into the eternal beatitude of heaven. Amen.

CHAPTER 29

Anna

ROCHEMONT ABBEY

WHEN WE FINALLY CAME TO THE ABBEY, WE ENTERED through an unattended gate and found ourselves in a courtyard devoid of people. Buildings lined the square with the church itself at the foot. A rocky cliff seemed to serve as its back wall. Carts stood waiting to be unloaded, and craftsmen's fires burned as if they still expected to be of some use. Somewhere, out among the buildings that lay before us, a door slammed.

The canon was pleading with the Danes as we approached. "I'll just—let me talk to the nun one time more. I can't think she understood what I was saying. She'll give it to us, and then we can leave, and we won't have to trouble them at all." He spoke the words as if he did not quite believe his own pronouncements.

The Danes had not even stopped to listen to the monk translate the words. They began shouting and beating their shields with their axes.

One of them strode toward a fire that burned unattended. He broke up an unfinished barrel and put it to the flame. The others took pieces of it and turned them into faggots. The chieftain took one up and flung it into one of the buildings.

It did not take long for smoke to start roiling from the door.

Another Dane threw his faggot through the church's high window. A second dipped his into a cart filled with straw and then threw it atop the church's roof. The flames sputtered for a moment, but then blazed as fire swept out from it in all directions.

The canon slipped and slid across the muddied snow as he ran toward them. "Stop! You cannot just—! What good will it do if you burn down the church before we can even find the relic?"

The monk grabbed at the chieftain's arm and spoke, gesturing toward the smoking roof.

Pausing a moment, the chieftain barked answer. "He says, 'They will take the relic and be gone, but these people will know forever what a grave mistake they have made in not giving it to us.'"

The chieftain threw open the door of the church while the canon followed, protesting. "You cannot—" He appealed to the monk once more. "They cannot do this! This place is a *sanctuary!*"

To those who believed, perhaps. To those who knew what the word meant.

"In the name of God, I beg you!"

The Danes ignored him as they stalked past him into the church.

Godric placed his arm about me, and I turned into him, throwing my arm about his waist. But we were not the sole witnesses to the church's destruction. Just after the Danes had entered the church, a man ran across the courtyard, beating his chest and pounding his head with a stave.

Was this one of the monk's berserkers? It could not be, for it was not one of the Danes. But he lurched by, eyes wild, as he told us not to make him stop. As he reached the church, Godric drew me away from the scene. "There's no reason to watch this. We should wait outside the gate. I will find a way to take the relic from them later."

"But what if they do not find it? What if it's destroyed?"
The roof was in flames, and the church itself could not last
much longer. If the relic was in there, then I had to go to it.
Slipping from Godric's arm, I joined the canon at the doorway. Flames shot through the windows, and sparks drifted
down from the roof. The church was filled with fire and
smoke. If I hoped to find healing, I must do it now.

The canon tried to stop me. "You'll be killed!" He tugged
at my arm, but I wrenched free.

Stumbling, I walked down the nave.

Up in front of the church, beyond the Danes, had gathered a winged heavenly host. And the sound of a wordless
hymn drifted out over the smoke and the fire.

"Valkyries!" One of the Danes shouted the word, and the
others picked it up and repeated it, but I could not see those
pagan spirits here. I saw only holy angels, and I heard only
that amazing melody of grace. And then the roof collapsed
atop the Danes and their translator monk. The bell came
with it, clattering in protest as the fire sent grasping fingers
up the pillars and pulled them down too.

The canon dragged me from the church by the collar,
despite my protest, and deposited me in the arms of Godric,
who held me fast when I would have bolted toward the
flames. We stayed in that muddied courtyard, the three of
us, and watched as the church burnt down. In time we were
joined by others, residents of the abbey, who began to trickle
back in through the gate.

Once the walls collapsed, it did not take long for the flames
to tire of themselves. When they met the snow-damped
ground, they retreated back to the center of the structure,
where the roof had fallen in, and there they smoldered.

Using some of the craftsmen's abandoned tools, Godric
and the canon prized the rafters from the Danes and the

monk. The others joined in scattering the glowing coals so they would cool. It was not difficult to identify the chieftain with his metal helmet. But melted across his chest was a pool of bright, shining gold.

The canon, seeing it, paused. "Saint Catherine's relic."

The relic? "Is it…?" Stricken, I looked at him. "Is it destroyed, then?"

He only shook his head. "I told him she did not wish to leave."

I wandered from the center of the church forward, to where it had once met the rocky cliff. My journey, all of my trials, had been for nothing. But what other end might I have expected? I had done nothing I was supposed to. Nothing the other pilgrims had told me must be done.

Though I was standing, as I had long hoped to be, in Saint Catherine's church, my feet were still shod. I had not honored the sanctity of the place. I had not prayed my way down the mountain to the abbey. My poor straw cross had been blown from its place in the valley. I had not kept a nightly vigil. I had not made my confession. I had no gift to offer Saint Catherine, no reason to interest her in my affairs.

I wiped a tear from my cheek as my feet left the earthen floor for what felt like stone. Looking down, I discovered the ground sloped down and into the face of the cliff, where there seemed to be a sort of cave.

There in the gloom before me was an altar.

Kneeling before it, hands clasped to my forehead, I could think of no words to say. I was left with no one to intercede on my behalf, and I knew any petition I could make for myself would be poor indeed. Weeping, I placed my hands on the altar and then lay my cheek atop them.

I could not think why I had ever expected God might heal

me, or why I had ever hoped to be found worthy of such unmerited grace. Surely I deserved no good thing.

"God, help me." I could barely whisper the words for my tears.

"The sword that from her neck the head did chop, Milk from the wound, instead of blood, did bring; By angels buried on Mt. Sinai's top; From Virgin Limbs a Sovereign oil did spring." The words seemed to inhabit the very air around me, as if an angel's voice had spoken.

As I lifted my head and stretched my arms toward heaven, my devil's hand unfurled itself. The skin around it had loosened, and there were fingers, which had grown to fill it. New ones.

Real ones.

Whole ones.

And there was an expansiveness in my chest, a new, all-encompassing fullness that made me know I had been healed. I sat there, exulting at my great fortune, laughing as I opened and closed the hand that now looked just like its pair, and feeling with wonderment the bosom that had bloomed from my chest.

I was whole!

From the walls of the cave about me, there appeared a great host of angels. Stepping forward, one of them welcomed me in the name of Saint Catherine, extending her hand.

I placed mine into it. "I am healed this day!"

She smiled as if she had already known it. And then she knelt beside me. "After receiving the mysteries of eternal salvation, we humbly pray thee, that as the liquor that continually flowed from the limbs of Saint Catherine, virgin and martyr, did heal languishing bodies, so her prayer may expel out of us all iniquities."

Beside me, one of the host began flapping his arms. And beside him, a small girl began to intone a song.

The woman clutched my arm. "Are the Danes...?"

"They are all dead."

She smiled through her tears as she lifted her arms toward heaven. "Then we are saved!"

After the fire's embers had cooled, Godric was enlisted to pull the bodies from the ruined church and take them to a cellar where they would be held until spring, when they could be buried. He suggested the Danes might have preferred their bodies to be put to the flame once more, but neither the nuns nor their chaplain nor the canon could countenance such a thing. Not even for the pagans who had rained destruction down upon their heads. Afterwards, Godric aided some of the others in clearing the church while I helped the nun, Sister Juliana, who had spoken to me in the chapel. She left me in care of her charges, those I had mistaken for angels, while she went to find food for all of those who worked to clear the rubble from the abbey.

The sun had fallen behind the mountains before I had a chance to speak to Godric. I had wanted to tell him of my healing, but as I fell in beside him on the way to the refectory, I found I lacked more than just opportunity. After all the time we had spent together, after all of our hours with the Danes, I did not know what to say to him.

And so I slipped my hand, my whole one, into his.

He wrapped his own around it. But then he glanced down, opening his hand to display mine. The corner of his mouth lifted as he looked over at me. There was gladness in his gaze, but as I watched, a sadness crept in beneath it. He squeezed my hand and let it drop. And it felt as if, somehow, he had let me drop too.

The Danes' fire had burnt the abbey. Before it sputtered out, it raced through the cloisters to the pilgrims' dormitory, the baths, and the laundry. After our meal, the nuns turned the refectory into sleeping quarters and invited Godric, the canon, and I to lodge there.

The room, located inside the complex and hidden from the winds and the snow, was much warmer than it was outside, and the nuns brought us furs from their treasury to recline upon and to throw over our mantles, but still I could not sleep. I kept marveling at the wonder of my hand, and I missed the man I had slept beside along the road. I would have gone to him, but somehow something had changed between us, and I did not think it right.

The next morning, Godric and the canon vouched as witnesses before Sister Juliana to the former state of my hand, and then the canon announced he must leave to journey back to Rouen. The nuns tried to present him with a horse, but he refused it. "I came here, desiring to take the relic from you, and found I was in error. You owe me nothing, and I do not wish to compound my shame."

Godric stayed, helping the craftsmen as they began to frame the church. I stayed as well, looking after the children as Sister Juliana concerned herself with the running of the abbey's affairs. The workers continued to return from their mountain hiding places, but the abbess was not among them. She did not appear that next day or the day after, either.

On the third day, one of the laypeople who had been tasked with helping in the kitchens found her. In her haste to flee from the Danes, she must have slipped in the snow and fallen headlong into the well in the courtyard.

Sister Juliana recounted the grisly news for us all as we sat together for our meal.

The man who had pulled her body out stepped forward to lay the abbess's pectoral cross in front of her.

Sister Juliana fingered it for a moment, and then she glanced up around the room. "Again, it has fallen to us to elect a new abbess."

One of the nuns got up from her seat at the table, picked up the cross, and put it around Sister Juliana's neck. "You are the only one of us who stood against the pagans. You are the only one of us who deserves this."

She put a hand to the cord from which it hung. "You must not do this. Not this way. The abbess must be elected by a vote."

The nun looked out across the tables. "Then all who agree with me may stand."

Godric and I stood along with the rest of the sisters.

Tears were falling from Sister Juliana's eyes. "I do not deserve this. I have nothing to offer you. I came to you a girl of fifteen years, who had given herself over to fornication and then left behind the child of that union. I came as one who had no other place to go, and not as one who wished to make atonement. I sought to enshrine my past, not to seek peace or redemption."

"And yet you stayed when the rest of us fled. So why can we not say those words Our Lord once spoke: 'Your faith has made you whole.'"

∽

After offices the next morning, the new abbess came to visit the hospice. "I have always wondered why God has not chosen to heal them."

"Perhaps they serve God's purpose just as they are."

She smiled as she looked at them. "Perhaps they do."

A shadow darkened the door, and Godric appeared, pack in hand.

The abbess greeted him and then slanted her gaze at me. "So I see you leave us today."

I shook my head. "Not I." I had not decided yet what I should do or where I should go.

"I thought you came here together."

Godric sent a look my way before he answered. "We were companions of the road, swept up by the Danes."

"Can I not convince you to stay until the snow melts in the spring?"

He inclined his head toward her. "Thank you for your offer, but my lord awaits." Godric came forward to the table. Reaching into his pack, he brought out his collection of phials and pouches and presented them to the abbess. "For the abbey."

She took up one of them. "And what are these?"

"A hair from Saint James. A filing from Saint Peter's chains. Oil from a lamp that burned in the church of Saint Andrew. Dust from the tomb of Saint Denis. A piece of cloth upon which once rested the crown of thorns. A thread from the veil of the Holy Mother. And a sliver from the true cross." He looked up at her and then looked away toward the fire. "I had sought from them something they could never give me, and I've come to realize I don't need them anymore."

"Perhaps you'd like to take with you some dust from our Saint Catherine?"

"No." He had been gazing into the fire, but now he looked at the abbess directly. "No. Possession makes prisoners of us all; the benefit is in the coming, and the blessing comes through faith. Keep your relic. Saint Catherine's place is here." He turned, and we followed him out the door and to the courtyard, where one of the abbey's horses waited.

He affixed his pack to the horse and then took hold of the reins.

The abbess touched my sleeve. "Do you not think your place is with him?"

Neither Godric nor I could pretend we had not heard her, but he was the one who answered. He shook his head. "The road is no place for her, and I must travel far before I reach my home."

She turned her gaze upon me. "And what of you? Where will you go?"

"I do not know." I had reached the abbey; my body had been healed. All my dreams had been fulfilled, and yet, still, I had nothing.

"Have you no family to return to? No lord to take you?"

"I have no one."

Godric's gaze rested upon me. "You could stay here." He glanced at the abbess. "I do not think she would mind."

But *I* would. I did not wish to hurt the abbess's feelings, so it was to her I made my first reply. "There is so much of life I still need to learn, and much I wish to see." I hoped she would understand. I turned toward Godric. "I don't want to stay here. I want to go with you."

"I am a relic hunter who no longer wishes to hunt relics. I have nothing to offer you."

"But I already have nothing, and I've discovered that is more than enough, just so long as there is you."

Through days of rebuilding the church and nights of heavy sleep, his eyes had lost their redness, but still there was sorrow lurking in their depths. "There are Danes in Britain, just like here, and I could not protect the last woman God gave me."

"I am not afraid of them."

He came to me and put a hand to my face.

I leaned into it, placing my own atop it.

He stroked my jaw with his thumb. "But why would you want me?"

"Because I wish to love you."

His brow bent, and he pressed his forehead to mine. "A stronger man would leave you to better prospects, but I find I am not so strong as I have feared."

I looked up into his eyes. "Then perhaps you could love me too."

He smiled. "I already do."

The chaplain married us, and the abbess prayed for us, and then together we set out on the long road toward our home.

CHAPTER 30

Gisele

ALONG THE ROAD TO CHELLES

I COULD NOT MOVE. I COULD NOT FEEL MY HANDS, and I could not move my feet. Even breathing seemed impossible. As I opened my eyes, I saw why. Andulf had surrendered to sleep the same as I, and at some point, he had toppled back on top of me. I nudged my shoulder into his back to no avail. Was he—? Had he died during the night?

He jerked in a spasm and then snorted as he jabbed me with an elbow. But at least my hands were freed.

I tried to trap his arms to keep from being pummeled by his wild scramblings, but they escaped me. "Stop!"

Immediately he ceased, and then he rolled onto his side. "I am sorry. I did not mean—" As he glanced down toward his thigh, I followed his gaze. The torn skin that ringed his wounds had flushed an angry red, but at least the night's rest had stopped the bleeding.

Bared to the brunt of the morning's cold wind, I gathered my mantle about me.

He tugged at the girdle I'd bound around his thigh and then picked at the knot for a moment before giving up entirely. "You shall have to loosen it."

I did not work for long before I realized his blood had dried upon it, fixing the knot in its place. "I cannot do it."

He edged up on his hip. "Take my knife."

Pulling it gingerly from his belt, I slipped it beneath the girdle and sawed until it tore.

He probed the gashes with his fingers, sucking in his breath between his teeth. "You are going to have to look at it for me."

"Look at it?"

He set his jaw, glancing over at me, and then resolutely fixed his gaze upon the horses. "If there's pus, then I need to know it. But first you may have to cleanse it."

A scab had formed about the leaves and dirt that had filled the gashes. There was no help for it but to scrape it all out. Kneeling beside him, I used the tip of his knife to pry at the edge of a leaf. As I pulled it from the wound, ooze began to seep.

He jerked. "Son of a skiving whore!"

"There's no need for such words."

He said nothing more, though a sweat had broken out upon his brow.

I put the knife to the wound once more and continued with my work.

"Bleeding, bloody *Christ!*"

I set the knife down upon my thigh. "Are you quite done?"

He shied from me and bent himself nearly in half, as if trying to protect his wounds from me. "Good God. Why not let the pagan have you? You'll be a blight and a curse to him and all his house."

I folded my arms across my chest.

He glanced up at me, loathing in his eyes. "You may finish."

"There's half the floor of the forest in there, along with an acorn or two."

"Then you'll have to get them out."

"And what do you think I've been doing?"

"It hurts."

"You saved my life. Now, I'll thank you to let me reciprocate."

He grunted.

"I've nothing to wash it with but wine from your costrel."

"Then use it." He folded his mouth around a frown.

I rose and took the costrel from his courser. The hem of my tunic was black with dirt, so I poured out a measure of wine on the edge of my sleeve and used it to dab at the wound.

"Son of a scummy, bosky, traitorous—!" He bit off his protest as I ripped a leaf from one of the scabs. The look he sent me through narrowed eyes was pure malevolence.

I poured more wine onto my sleeve and tried again to cleanse the wound, but the forest litter clung fast. Sighing with frustration, I poured some directly onto his thigh.

He writhed like a fish thrown from water, and wrenched himself away from me. "By the wounds of Christ!"

I peeled another leaf away from the bloody mess. "One would think you a heathen for all the reverence you accord Our Lord."

"I'm not." His scowl was deep and sullen. When he spoke, it sounded as a growl. "Go on. Finish."

Surely his was a dark and degenerate soul. As I scraped some more, he reached over and tore the sleeve from my hand, jerking me toward him in the process, and then he bent to scrub at the wound himself.

"Stop! You're going to—"

"Might as well get it over with."

"But look!" He had provoked the wound to bleed again.

"If we don't move along soon, we'll have more than this to worry about." Great beads of sweat broke out on his forehead before he finally released my sleeve. "Help me up."

I put a hand to his thigh. "They're bleeding again. All of them."

"Help me up, damn you."

"Don't you damn *me*, you ungrateful, sorry brute! If you don't stop cursing me, then I won't help you at all."

He'd gotten to his knees with a grimace and then shoved himself back onto his ankles. Now he stood glaring down at me. "You haven't helped me yet!"

"I was the one who stayed by you after you fainted and—"

"I did not faint."

"And I was the one helped you away from the boar when you could hardly stand on your own two feet and—"

"I could have managed."

"If it weren't for me, that boar might have made a mince of you!"

"And who was it that led me on a merry chase from Rouen in the first place? And then tried to run away again yesterday? I wouldn't be saddled with turned ankles and beset by wild boars if you had just done what you were supposed to!"

"I did not ask you to come after me. I could have managed on my own."

"Managed! You might have managed getting your heart torn from your breast." He scowled and then winced as he drew in a great breath.

"Since you do not seem to appreciate how you have placed yourself in mortal danger, and because you seem to be quite capable of surviving on your own, then I shall be leaving now." I could not say why I had not left earlier. He clearly had his wits back, and he was not in danger of dying, except by *my* hand. I hobbled to my horse, trying to be as dignified about it as I could.

"Wait." He put out his hand to stop me, but thought the better of it, letting it drop to his side instead. "Just...wait."

"Why should I?"

"The count's men are still out there. You would not want them to find you."

Then it did not matter whether I stayed with Andulf or whether the count's men happened upon me. The consequence would be the same: I would be returned to Rouen where I would have to marry the Danes' chieftain. There could be no other outcome. Not when that band of pagans had gone along with the canon to obtain the relic. "But if you left with them, then will they not be searching for you as well?"

He shrugged.

"I must surely leave and do so now."

"Can you not understand? There is no escape. My fidelity to your father ensures I must return you. If, by chance, I had not found you at first, then I must have continued until I found you at last. I cannot return to court unless I have you. And if by great misfortune I return without you, then you must be dead, and I must have proof, or I must know where you have gone. And if I know where you have gone, then your father will come and find you, and even your new abbess will not be able to stand against him. You cannot take your vows predicated upon a lie."

I did not care.

He lurched over, muttering profanities all the way, and snatched the reins from my hands. "If you leave, then you are most certainly going to be responsible for my death."

"*Your* death!" He was as near to death at that moment as I. Though he was mean and querulous, he had none of that gray pallor I had come to associate with a mortal wound.

"I might be fine now, but come nightfall, I expect those beasts will return."

"I shall leave you with a limb, ready to put to the flame."

"And what will I do when it burns itself out?"

"The beasts did not come last night when the fire burned out."

"Because they found other meat. But they are here. They lurk in the shadows beyond those bushes."

They did? I eyed the bushes with newfound suspicion.

"And I am easy prey, for man or beast. I cannot move. They will wait as long as they have to."

"A knight like you can take care of himself." And if I were about the wood in the day's light, surely the beasts would not attack me…would they?

With a grunt and a wince, he pulled his sword from his scabbard and offered it to me. "If you are going to leave, then you might as well finish the job: kill me now."

I shrank from him. "*Kill* you!"

"Even if the beasts do not finish me, then I will come after you and I will find you and I will return you to your father. It is my death or your freedom."

"Then why should I stay? Why should I not seek asylum at the abbey, as I planned?"

"And bring destruction and shame on the abbess at Chelles for sheltering you?"

"Who says I am going to Chelles?"

"Where else would you go? The abbeys here are controlled by Robert, and if you venture north of Chelles, you are in danger of encountering more Danes."

He was right. Those reasons were exactly why I had chosen Chelles. "The church must always provide a refuge to a virgin being forced to marry without her consent."

"Yes. But princesses are a different matter entirely."

"Once I take my vows, then who but God can claim me?"

He broke his posture as he sagged against his horse. "Who would want to?"

"What did you say?"

"I said, You're as unlikely a princess as ever there has been."
As he stood there, hand clamped around the reins, I
made my choice. I would stay with him one night more. It
was the least I owed him, given it was my actions that had
wounded him.

☙

We rode slowly that day. Andulf did not want the count's
men to lay claim to the honor of escorting me back to
Rouen, so we kept ourselves hidden from other travelers
upon the road. Neither of us wanted to stop at an inn for
the night. So once more, despite misgivings, we headed for
the wood.

After handing me down from the horse, Andulf dismounted, though he groaned as his feet found the ground.

"You have pain."

"Of course I have pain!" He fairly snapped at me. "I've
been gored by a boar."

"And riding all this day cannot have helped you." I
reached a hand around him in support, but he brushed it
away. "You must let me see your wounds." I did not exactly
know what to look for, but his hands had grown damp and
his forehead sweaty, even though the winds had been cold
and cruel. I put a hand to his chest.

He looked down at it and then up into my eyes.

"Please."

He dropped to the ground with a thump and flung his
tunic to the side as if I were some goose to be concerned on
his behalf.

Even before I had knelt beside him, I could see his thigh
had swollen to almost twice its size. And an evil-looking pus
had coated the wound. "I don't know if…"

He took a look for himself. And then, as he probed at the wounds with his fingers, a line of perspiration bloomed above his lip. "Start a fire."

I found his fire-steel with trembling hands, and then gathered a pile of twigs and leaves.

He gestured for the flint and the touchwood, using them to birth a spark. "Get my sword as well."

As I drew it from its sheath, I was startled by its great weight.

He fanned the sparks with the hem of his mantle and roused them to a snapping flame. "Lay it in the fire."

"In…?"

He held out his hand. When I gave him the sword, he placed the length of it on the fire himself, and then left it there for some time as I fed the flames more leaves and twigs.

"Can you get my costrel?"

I gave it to him.

Taking up his mantle once more, he poured wine over it and then used it to scrub at his wounds. He did it so fiercely that drops of sweat broke from his brow to course down his neck. And in the process, he rubbed the scabs right off and set the gashes to bleeding once more.

"Don't—"

"I want you to take the sword from the fire."

I lifted it, using both my hands.

"Now place it on my leg." He bared the wounds to me. "If I try to do it, I will like as stab myself." He nodded toward the gashes. "You must do it for me."

I took a deep breath and knelt beside him. Lowering the sword… I could not do it.

"Go on."

"I cannot." I whispered the words, for courage had deserted me.

"You must."

"It will hurt you."

"I must hurt in order to heal."

"I cannot do it." As my hands faltered, he wrapped his own around them and, fighting my resistance, pressed the flat of his sword to his thigh. His skin sizzled as the stench of seared flesh rose from it, and still he left it there. I tried to move it away, but he only strengthened his grip on my hands and held the sword in place. He did not succumb to profanity this time, which I took to mean it hurt twice as much again as it had when I had scraped at his wounds earlier that morning.

By the time he released my hands, tears were coursing down my face. All of it was my fault: the boar, his wounds, his sword-scarred flesh. I let the sword tumble from my grasp and pushed myself away from him. "If you had just let me go, none of this would have happened!"

"I have sworn to protect you."

"Then let me go, and you won't have to worry about me anymore."

"I have been entrusted by the king with your care."

"He could hardly fault you for not doing what he is not willing to do himself."

"His Majesty the king cares more for you than any father I've ever seen."

"If he did, then he would not have let the count and the archbishop pledge me to a pagan!"

"Has your life been so good that you should fear to lose it, my lady?"

"I do not know anything else. And how can anyone fault me for clinging to what I know? For not wanting to give it up for strange ways and pagan lands?"

He grunted.

"The archbishop spoke to me of sacrifice and the souls

that may be won, but it is not a very great sacrifice if I am forced into it, is it? If I could go to the Dane willing, if I might be allowed to place my own self upon the altar instead of being bound to it, then perhaps I could find peace." He did not seem to be swayed. "But what do you know of sacrifice?"

"I was torn from my mother's arms by my father when I was only three days old. I had not been baptized; I had not even been named. And once I was weaned, I was delivered up to King Carloman, to be raised in his court as a sort of ransom to ensure my father's friendship. Our estates were on the borderlands in Aquitaine. My father had been a loyal retainer of King Carloman's father and had kept the Saracens from crossing the mountains."

I knew this story, for it was partly my own. "But King Carloman never trusted his father's friends." He had been one of the pair of brothers who had stolen my father's crown. Their father, King Louis, was my grandfather.

"When I was old enough, the king placed me as a squire in the household of the Count of Bresse."

An evil and grasping man.

He sent a wry look in my direction. "I see you must have heard of him. While I was in his service, King Carloman died, and then so did Charles the Fat. Then Odo came to hold the throne. While we were at court, the Count of Bresse impugned my father's honor."

I could hardly bear to hear what had happened next.

"My father was seized by Odo and held for many months before he was finally executed."

"I'm sorry. I did not—"

"During his long absence, my mother took on a great many debts to try and rescue him and to keep me in all of the horses and weapons a knight requires." He spoke with much bitterness. "And after my father died, his estates were co-opted by the Count of Bresse for our *protection.*" He fairly spat the word.

"And your lady-mother?"

"She is yet in Aquitaine and threatened with penury, while our retainers languish under the count's control. A man can fight, but my mother never did anything but wed herself to a man well liked by his king."

I did not know what to say.

"I have not ever met my mother, but it is my hope I may one day do so, and that we can return together to my father's lands."

My hand had found its way to my throat as I had listened, and now it lay clasped within my other.

"I served King Carloman with great loyalty, and next I served King Charles the Fat, and Odo, and even the Count of Bresse. And finally I was called here. Your father, the king, being no admirer of Odo or of his brother, the Count of Paris, I have been hoping to gain his ear long enough to ask for our estates to be restored."

"But you must do it! Surely he would understand."

"I hope so, my lady. I pray it with all my heart. But first I must gain the honor of serving in his contingent."

His admission made me feel very humbled and quite small. "I am sorry."

"For what, my lady? Misfortunes befall us all." He stared at me as though daring me to say anything at all about the tale he had just recounted.

"Yes, but—"

"I am afraid we have nothing for our meal this night but wine and a few crusts of bread."

How I longed to put a hand to his cheeks and smooth away his cares. How I wished I could carry, if only for a moment, the hurt and the bitterness that bent his brow. "I only meant that—"

"If you will look in my bag, then you will find them."

I tried once more to extend to him my sympathies. "I wish the world were just."

He looked up at me then with great sorrow in his gaze. "But then what would be the use for faith?"

We rode that next day between fields newly plowed and trees stripped of their leaves, disturbing vast flocks of birds that wheeled as they lifted into the sky. It was well past midday when we came up over the rise of a hill to find a group of men strung across the road at the bottom. It was too late to turn: they had already seen us.

One lifted his pitchfork as another approached, brandishing the sharp edge of a hoe.

Andulf stopped his courser some way off and called out to them. "What do you want?"

"We've been asked by the Count of Paris to look for a pair: a knight and the princess." The man approached, spiderlike, as he spoke.

"And what are you to do with them?"

"Send someone back to Rouen for the count's men. Are you them?"

I held my breath as I waited for Andulf to reply.

CHAPTER 31

*W*E ARE NOT THE PEOPLE YOU SEEK."
　　Another of the men had come over to peer up at us. "He hasn't got the look of a knight about him."

"He's got the horse."

"But she doesn't look like a princess."

Andulf repeated his pronouncement with calm authority. "We are not the people you seek."

The first man squinted up at him. "Whose people are you then?"

"I'm to deliver the girl to the abbey. She's to take her vows."

"Which abbey?"

There was barely a pause before he answered. "The one just down the road."

"You have papers then."

"I have."

He hadn't. Not that I had seen. He would never have had need of them. Normally his horse and his weapons, as well as my father's pennon, would tell any who saw him whose man he was. But his tunic was torn and bloodied and he had no standard. He looked to be an ordinary man.

The peasant had reached out and grabbed at my leg with his hand.

I kicked at him, trying to free myself, but he only cackled

and held on, pulling at the reins of my horse. "You're a comely lass, aren't you?"

Andulf swung his horse toward the man. "She's to pledge herself to God. Leave her be."

"Maybe I can change her mind."

I cannot say what might have happened had they not stepped aside when a short, stout man came walking up. He touched a finger to his forehead as he came to stand before us. "Pardon us for the delay, but as mayor of these lands, I've been asked by the Count of Paris to intercept all travelers."

"I have already told these men we are not those you seek."

If only he could say who he was. If only I could say who I was! But then we would be collected by the count's men. Andulf's honor would be impugned, and I would be placed back into the tower to await marriage to the Dane.

"Whose man are you then?"

"I am bringing this woman to the abbey where she is to take the veil."

He turned a suspicious eye on me.

I tried to look devout.

"Not even the nuns at Chelles would want such an offering as that."

Pity I could not bring down upon his head the wrath of my father the king!

The man seemed set on misbelieving us. "You have not told me whose man you are."

Andulf tensed, repositioning the reins in his hands.

The others must have seen it as well, for they pointed their pitchforks at us in earnest.

I spoke. "We're on God's business."

"You wear no habit. And he has no cowl." A man stepped up to his side, glancing at me. "But, she cannot be the princess, so he cannot be her man."

"But they are not Danes, nor are they Saxons." The short man glanced up at us. "Surely the king would want to know his people drift across the countryside like chaff blown before the wind." He nodded toward the spiderlike man, who came forward. "We'll keep them while we send out word. Whoever is missing this pair might be glad to hear of our tidings."

ご〜の

They confiscated our horses, as well as Andulf's sword and his knife, and threw us into a barn, securing it with a bar thrown across the door.

From the smell, the place had been lately used by goats. The walls let in shafts of light, and the roof gaped at the sky, but at least we would have plenty of hay to bed down on this night.

I hobbled to a mound of hay that had been piled beside the walls of a stall, and sat upon it. Andulf strode to the door and struck it with his fist, rattling it against the frame. The bar held firm.

The injustice of the situation incensed me. And so did the thought of Andulf's mother, waiting for news from her son these many years. "How your mother would despair to see you imprisoned in a place like this, in service to a princess like me."

His mouth turned up in half a smile. "And what would your own mother think?"

"I cannot care what she would think. One thing I have always known: that I would never be like her, consenting to be some man's whore; only now I am to be forced to wed a man who already has a wife."

"I would not say the Dane is *rightfully* married." He settled himself beside me and lounged against the wall as he examined his wounds.

"I suppose that's what people said about my mother as well. And that's why she went off." It must have been. "She was not rightfully married, and so she went and left me behind."

"You would that she had stayed? What kind of life would that have been?"

"*My* life. It would have been what my life was destined to become."

"Then why should she have wanted it any more than you?"

"Is the Dane all I am allowed to hope for? Will I forever and always be unworthy of anything else? Of anything more?" God must think me too mean a creation to be put to greater use. Perhaps becoming a martyr was the best I could hope for. "Was I born simply to save someone else, some other poor girl, from dying at the Dane's hand?"

"What is this you say?"

I scrubbed my tears off onto my sleeve. "How else am I to make sense of all of this? My mother took herself away before I even had the chance to know her. My father abandoned me without a backward glance, for his beloved Lorraine. What else am I to think? What more could there be to know about me than this: there is within me something that does not deserve more. Some base, vile thing I will never be able to change." I thought I was brave enough just then to look him in the eye, but I was not. Whenever my gaze was intersected by those gray eyes, they seemed to probe my very soul. "Why am I not enough?" My chin trembled. I tried my best to stop it, but my pain and the rage only dove deeper inside me, causing my shoulders to quake.

There he sat, a knight so true and noble I did not deserve his regard either. Oh, God, was there ever any soul more wretched than mine?

"My lady?" He opened up his arm to me.

As I shoved off propriety and took the refuge he offered, I could not keep from weeping. That fact only added to my humiliation.

He pulled my head to his chest and then let his hand linger on my hair. "Your mother loved you."

"How can you say that?"

"Because I knew her."

"You—" He had *known* her?

"The Count of Bresse was he who escorted her when she left the court, and I was the squire he took with him. You must believe she mourned you. Every night when she supposed us to be sleeping, she wept."

She had mourned me? "But, if she loved me, then why did she leave?"

"Your grandmother drove her away."

"You know where she is then?"

"I took her there myself."

I pulled myself from him. "Then can you take me there as well?"

When he looked down at me, his brows were knitted in puzzlement. "I thought… I thought that's why you wished to go."

My brow now mirrored his own. "Go where?"

"To Rochemont. That's where she went. I thought that's why you wished to go there."

My mother. At Rochemont.

Oh, God.

Oh, God! I had sent the Danes to her. Sweet Jesus in heaven, have mercy on my soul. Have mercy on *her* soul.

I had worried to think myself a martyr, and all of this time I should have been worried for her sake instead. If she should be killed, or worse, because I sent the Danes to her…how could I ever forgive myself? But why had no one ever told me? Why had I not known?

"My lady?"

"I have murdered her." I turned into myself, keening with guilt and regret.

He enfolded me within his arms. And when I thought I might go mad with the thought I had killed my own mother, he held me still.

"Stop that bellowing in there!" Someone, some man, banged against the door.

Leaving me, Andulf strode to it and kicked at it, rocking the frame.

The man only shouted again. "If you had not run away, you would not be in such a state!"

The truth of those words only made me cry the harder. I would not be here, Hugh would not have been harmed, Andulf would not have been wounded, and my mother would not have been placed in mortal danger if I had not been afraid. If I had not lacked faith. If I had trusted in Providence, as I had started out by doing, then none of those would have happened.

Andulf came back and sat beside me.

I leaned against him as my breathing slowed and my tears stopped. Through sorrow-glazed eyes, I watched as the light grew dim and the scents of food began to waft through the cracks in the barn. Though the people did not feed us, they did let the goats back in. And then they barred the door again.

Andulf shooed the animals away, and then he took up his place on the pile of straw once more. Lying down, his back against the side of the stall, he gestured for me to join him.

I hesitated, overcome by a sudden sense of propriety. But we had already slept side by side, and I had already helped to press the scar of a sword into his thigh. I lay down, pulling my knees up into my tunic and tucking it around my feet.

He reached out his great arm and pulled me to his chest, wrapping a side of his mantle around us both.

"I do not think—"

"Don't. Just sleep." I tried to move from him, but his arm imprisoned me. "Do not think—"

I tried not to, but I could not help it. "What was my mother's name?" Had I met her when I had visited the abbey?

"Juliana."

Juliana. Sister Juliana. Keeper of the relic. She who had once told me: Do not despise the life you have been given. But the only thing I had ever done was despise the woman who had given that life to me.

We lay there for some time as the goats settled themselves into the hay for sleep and the townspeople shut themselves up in their homes.

"I do not think I can do it. I cannot marry him." I whispered the words. "Not even, God help me, for the winning of ten thousand souls." Surely no one had ever been more lacking in faith than I. "I do not think I am brave enough."

"There is not one other woman in the kingdom who would dare to do the things you have done. And I will be there at your side."

"But I am not strong enough."

"I will be strong when you cannot."

"I do not have faith enough."

"Then I will have faith when you have none."

I glanced up at his hand, which he had wrapped around my forearm. "You would—you would come with me? When I marry the Dane?"

"I have pledged to serve the king wherever he would have me serve, and he gave me charge of you."

"But what of your mother?"

"I can look after her interests as well as your own. I have done so these many years."

"But—"

"She would tell you my first duty must be to my king."

"I cannot think that—"

"Do not think. Sleep."

He settled his chin atop my head and proceeded to do just that. And soon, lulled by his deep, slow breaths and comforted by his warmth, I surrendered to sleep as well.

The next morning, I listened to the fluttering of birds and the rustlings of goats for I could not say how long before I became aware that Andulf had wakened as well. I had held myself still for his sake, but now I relaxed against him.

His breathing stopped for a moment, and then it began again. My arm lay pinioned by his, neither tight enough that I felt bound to him, nor loose enough that I considered myself free of him. I could have reached out and taking hold of his arm, secured him to me, or I could just as easily have pushed him away, but I did neither.

Hold me.

I could have sworn I had not given words to that thought, but slowly, gently, his arm enfolded me as he pulled me to himself. "I do not know what you wish, my lady." He whispered the words in my ear.

Neither did I. And so I said nothing, and we lay there, together. The town was slow to wake, and I could not say I minded.

When we heard someone approach, his arm tensed, and he pushed up on his elbow. When the bar was withdrawn, he seized me and thrust me behind himself.

All the warmth we had accumulated between us wasted away into the fetid air. The chill that swept me was not unanticipated, but I had not known I would feel so bereft. They tossed some bread to us and then left us alone once more.

He retrieved it, handing half to me as he came back to sit beside me.

"How long can they keep us here?"

He sighed. "As long as they wish. They have no reason to let us free."

"Then I must tell them who I am."

He gripped my hand. "If you do, all hope of escape will be gone. As you are now, you could be any woman hoping to take the veil. If I can speak to the mayor alone, I can barter for your liberty. But if you tell them who you are, you can be no one but yourself and then they will have to summon the count's men."

And all the trials and all of his wounds would have been for nothing. Except… "Then you will be able to take me back to the count with good reason for our delay, and no one will know what I had once wished to accomplish." My hopes would have been lost, but his honor would be preserved, and he would retain my father's esteem. He would still be able to ask for the return of his family's estates.

"Do not do it. You once asked what kind of sacrifice it would be if you were forced to marry the Dane. You wanted the chance to decide for yourself. I am giving it to you."

"But I am not forced to make this sacrifice. This one, I choose." I pulled my hand from his, flung myself at the door, and beat upon it. "Come! I have something to say!" Andulf took me by the shoulders and swung me to face him. "Do not do it, my lady. I beg you. They think you are trying to take your vows. Their inquiry will yield nothing, and we will be freed, and then you can do as you wanted. If you tell them who you are, then you will be returned to the count, and there will be no hope of escape."

"But one word will put this all to rights."

There was a pounding of feet and a sliding of the bar, and then the door stuttered against the earth and finally opened. "What is it?" Three men stood in the doorway, looking in upon us.

"Don't!" Andulf lunged toward me.

I threw myself at one of the men's feet. "I am Princess Gisele, daughter of King Charles, and this is my knight. It is us for whom you search."

Andulf pulled me away from the man and took me up in his arms. "Do not do this!" He retreated to the depths of the barn. "She is not the princess. Do not listen to her."

It took two of the men to loosen his grip on me. And once they did, they dragged him out and away from the barn.

I followed at their heels. "Where are you taking him? This is my knight! He is returning me to the Count of Paris at Rouen."

Andulf broke from them for a moment and wrenched around to look at me as one betrayed. "Do not listen to her. She lies!"

One of them struck out at him with a goad, while another captured his arm and twisted it behind him.

"Unhand him! I *command* you to unhand him. Now!"

When the men would have let Andulf go, the mayor walked up to us and stopped them. "How do we know you are who you say you are?"

"Send for the count's men, and they will tell you I speak the truth."

The mayor stepped forward, and then he waved his hand toward Andulf. "Put them back into the barn. We'll do as she said."

As they let go his arms, Andulf grabbed me about the shoulders. "Why do you do this?"

"What would you have me do? Allow you to fall into dishonor for not bringing me back? If the king will not keep you, then who will have you? How would you gain back your estates? And what kind of life would I live with your dishonor on my conscience?"

❦

The mayor could not quite bring himself to believe my claims, but he could come to no other explanation for my boldness in proclaiming to be the princess. We were moved into his house and given his room. We were fed meat and sweets and wine. After days of traveling without those luxuries, I could not say the gestures were unappreciated, but as we waited in relative ease, our sense of doom grew greater with each hour that passed.

Three days later, the count's men came for us.

The whole town turned out for our leaving. The mayor made some pretty words about generosity of spirit and the virtues of forgiveness, hoping, I suppose, I would forget the manner in which we had been treated. The man who had grabbed me at the first was there as well, but his eye was blacked, and he had a rag tied around his head. Our horses were given back, and Andulf was returned his weapons.

We were not taken from the town as captives, but we did ride with men both behind and before us. There was no chance to deviate from the road; neither was there much opportunity to talk without being overheard.

We spent a night at one of the count's villas, and then left the next morning, breaking for dinner at an inn midday. The count's men made time for sport outside after their meal, but I could find no pleasure in their antics. Soon my father would return, the Dane would come, and the relic would no doubt be presented to us.

Andulf knelt beside me, peeling an apple as we watched the men. "Come away with me. There is yet a chance for escape. Especially while they distract themselves."

"You said yourself that there is not even one man on this earth who is free. Who am I to want what no one has ever had one hope of possessing?"

"But—"

"You may be a knight, but you are nothing without a lord. And I may be a princess, but I am nothing without my father, the king. We both owe allegiance to the same master. And how could he be pleased by my flight?"

"If you go back, the pagan will have you."

"Only if God wills it."

He was gripping his knife so tightly his knuckles had gone white. "God has willed famine and calamity and all manner of misery. How can you hope He would spare you what He does not spare everyone else?"

I felt my resolve begin to wobble. But then I remembered the words of Sister Juliana—of my mother—at the abbey. "I must not despise the life I have been given."

"Then I shall come with you. I shall ask to be given to your guard."

"And forfeit your life at court? And your chance to reclaim your estates? I will not allow it."

He severed the apple with a slice of his blade. "You have no choice in the matter."

I laid a hand on his arm.

He flinched at my touch.

"You have pledged your allegiance to my father, have you not? And he has need of men as noble and honorable as you."

"You wish to be rid of me."

"I shall always be your friend."

His lips twisted in a mockery of a smile. "I have many friends and no need for more."

I stiffened as if he had slapped me.

With a violent twist of his wrist, he threw the apple into the grasses that lay before us. "I have never considered you a friend. My duty, yes. My lady...my love. Friendship has never had one thing to do with it."

One of the count's men passed near. When he was gone, I spoke my words quickly beneath my breath. "Then I am grieved, for what I need most is a friend. And if I go to the pagan, you would not be able to help me anyway."

"I would protect you."

I put my hand on his. "And he would kill you for it. I will not have you give your life for my sake."

He turned his hand to capture mine. "Not even after you have given up your freedom for my own? How could I offer any less than you have given me?"

"I did not do it with hope of gain. Two should not sacrifice themselves together, when only one is required."

CHAPTER 32

$\mathscr{A}$ ND SO I ARRIVED BACK IN ROUEN AT THE COUNT'S palace, where I repaired to my tower and refused all company. Andulf stood watch on my door, but it was from across the courtyard instead of at the tower's base below me. It seemed the count trusted him even less than he had before.

I had expected Hugh, my boy champion, to appear at the window ledge, but he did not come. Not that night or the one after or the one after that. And when, finally, I dragged my trunk to the window, I saw his stairs had been wrenched from the wall.

He was gone.

To Paris said one maid when I asked. To Orléans said another.

And so I waited to see what would become of me.

But I did not wait in vain. I prayed Saint Catherine would protect my mother, and I also prayed God would grant me strength to endure what was to come.

The canon had not returned by Christmastide. And neither had my father. He sent a message to the count: he had decided to stay in Lorraine.

Epiphany came, and it went, and still there was no word from either man. My hopes had become twisted around a spindle of despair. Was I to think the canon had been delayed in his journey, or dared I to hope he was not coming at all? I hardly knew whether to pray for the impossible or to resign myself to what was most probable. Hope and desolation warred within me until I was tired to the point of exhaustion and despondent of ever having mentioned Saint Catherine to anyone at all.

It did not help that the Danes who encamped outside the city rampaged through the countryside at will. I heard the chieftain, Rollo, often numbered among the count's company. And when he came, it was with Poppa. If they had not married in the Danish way, as both the count and the archbishop insisted they had not, I was told they certainly acted as if they had.

I had no visitors, save the maids, until there came a knock upon my door one forenoon.

"Who is it?"

"It is I, my lady."

Andulf. I removed the bar and pushed the door open.

"Your father comes." After he had finished speaking, he turned on his heel and descended the stair.

I spent a few hurried minutes combing my hair and exchanging my tunic for a silk one. I dug through my chest for my jeweled golden girdle and then looped it around my waist.

My father and the queen entered the palace yard with a flurry of banners and the fanfare of trumpets. Instead of his usual advisors, he was surrounded by strangers. I tried to approach him, but everyone jostled for a place beside him, and I ended by being pushed back into a pile of snow. Before I could extricate myself, everyone had repaired inside.

Everyone save Andulf.

As he looked at me, he nodded and then lifted his brow as he gestured toward the palace.

I stiffened my resolve, squared my shoulders, and determined to speak to my father at once. Even then I might have been relegated to the very back of the hall, but Andulf proceeded with me, allowing me the honor of walking before him, but also keeping me within the expanse of his arms. Still the strangers and the count's men seemed to conspire to keep us from my father, but by both embracing me and propelling me forward, Andulf passed me through the crowds to the dais. And then he stood in front of it, arms crossed, as if daring any to try to breach him.

"Gisele!" My father opened his arms to me, and I dropped to my knee and kissed his hand.

As I rose, he gripped my hand and had me come up to stand beside him. "You are well?"

I nodded.

"Did you enjoy your journey? What did Saint Catherine say?"

"I was not allowed to go."

He gave off searching the crowds that had gathered and rested his eyes upon me. "But I gave you permission before I left."

"The archbishop decided to send a canon instead. And then the Dane sent some of his men along as well."

"To consult the relic?"

"To bring it back to Rouen."

All the blood seemed to drain from his face. "Good God in heaven, they will have murdered them all. I thought... I had hoped..." His gaze was anguished, his words heavy with sorrow. "What have I done?"

"I have come by other troubling news. I have heard the Count of Paris and the archbishop spoke with the Dane prior to the treaty."

He looked at me uncomprehendingly. "Yes, in order to come to terms."

"But they did it long before that." I stepped closer to him. "The Dane did not request my hand in marriage. They *offered* me to him."

353

"The archbishop already told me that."

Why could I not make myself understood? "It did not have to do with the treaty. They wanted me wed to him so I could not be wed to another. They wished to block an alliance."

His eyes left mine and came to rest upon the count. "How do you know this?"

"Because...because the count's son told me so."

His gaze had turned from the count to me. Puzzlement furrowed his brow.

I took care in explaining my flight from the palace. Although I emphasized my rude treatment at the count's hands, I did not dwell long on my detention in the country-side, and I did not mention the incident with the boar at all.

"And you did all this by yourself?"

"I was with her, Your Majesty."

It was a great relief when the weight of my father's attention shifted from me to Andulf.

"You say I have been deceived, then."

Andulf merely bowed his head.

Father looked at those gathered around and pinned the archbishop with a stare. "I treated with the Danes according to your counsel, because I trusted you."

The cleric blanched and came forward, stammering.

"And you—Robert!"

That nobleman appeared as if conjured, when the crowd about him melted away.

"Why, in all of your speeches and all of your dealings, did you not happen to mention you had promised my daughter to the Dane long before talk of the treaty?"

The count's eyes sought the archbishop's.

"Why was I given to believe you spoke with me in honesty, that you were loyal to my throne when, in fact, you sought to block my alliance with Burgundy or Aquitaine?"

The count bowed his head. "I do not know, Your Majesty, how you have come by such information. The pagans are not to be trusted. They must have misrepresented—"

"Enough!"

The count swept forward, dropping to one knee at my father's feet.

"Explain."

As he tried to account for himself, my father broke in. "And why did you keep Gisele from her pilgrimage?"

"It's so late in the season, Your Majesty. I did not think that—"

"And you allowed the Danes to go as well!"

"The idea was not to keep the princess from her inquiries. If Saint Catherine approved, we knew she would not mind leaving the abbey for the cathedral at Rouen."

"And how could you believe the Danes would not destroy the abbey in their zeal to come by the relic?"

"It was not my idea, sire. It was the Dane who suggested it." Robert stayed there, bent in two, hands clasped on his knee, looking for all the world as if he expected some blow to fall upon his shoulders.

But finally, my father sighed. "What is done is done. What has been promised has been promised." I cried out in protest, but he only put out a hand toward me. "I will send a messenger to the abbey to see what has become of them."

From his position on the floor, I saw the count exchange a glance with the archbishop.

My father seemed oblivious to the depths of their treachery. He was exulting that he had returned from Lorraine as King of Lotharingia. I tried once more to speak to him, but he only pushed my concerns aside. "If I can get the Burgundians to come over to our side, then I will have no more need to rely upon Robert and his contingent. The Count of Paris's days of influence are on the wane." His thoughts had clearly left me and had taken up residence in the fabled land of Charlemagne. I despaired they might never return.

In the days that followed, Andulf certainly proved himself my friend. He escorted me, he waited upon me, he dogged my every step. What he did not know was that he tortured me with his every glance, his every word. But did I pray for the misery to stop?

I did not.

The Dane grew restless. Each day he demanded a private audience. Each day, the request was granted. And each day, he insisted he must leave to return to his lands and that he wanted to take me with him.

My father contended that we must wait for the canon's return.

I began to think the cleric might never come and that I had been freed from the treaty, when one evening, without any warning, the canon walked into the hall.

The counselors ceased their talking, and the knights ceased their carousing, and soon, the only one not aware of the canon's presence was the juggler. He kept on with his antics, throwing up one ball after the other until he turned and saw the hall had gone still. Then all the balls dropped at once, as if whatever magic had kept them floating had collapsed beneath them.

This canon was a man much changed from the one who had left. He who had started down the road toward the abbey was vain and much given to arrogance. The man who came down the hall toward us looked weary and worn. His habit was torn, his face dirtied, and his shoes were missing entirely.

To my father's right, the Dane shifted, his gaze sweeping the empty hall behind the cleric.

My father gestured toward the canon.

The archbishop stepped forward and offered his hand. The canon grasped the man's fingers and kissed his ring.

"Rise. The Lord has blessed you."

But the canon did not move, nor did he release the archbishop's hand.

My father leaned toward them. "Tell us: are we to welcome Saint Catherine?"

The Dane, still gazing beyond the canon toward the back of the hall, pushed to his feet. "My men?"

The canon rose, clasped his hands before him, and gazed at the bare toes that peeked out from the hem of his habit. "Saint Catherine did not wish to come. The rest of the men who accompanied me are gone—burned up in a fire."

Had he—what had he just said? My father turned to the archbishop. "Saint Catherine did not wish to come. There will be no wedding."

"My men!" The Dane pounded the table with the flat of his hand.

In the midst of the chaos and general uproar, as all eyes focused on the Dane and his venomous rage, the canon was forgotten. He simply turned and walked away.

But I was not about to let him go so easily as that.

Slipping from the table, I caught him at the back of the hall. "What happened?"

"I do not yet have the words to speak of it. But know this: there were miracles and signs and wonders. The weak were made strong, and the proud were humbled…myself among them."

"But Saint Catherine?"

"Saint Catherine stayed at the abbey."

And my mother? That was the question for which I truly wanted an answer. "Were any others harmed?"

"The abbess met her death, but a new one has been elected."

"And the abbey?"

"It is being rebuilt."

Which meant it had been damaged. Guilt plucked at the chords of my soul. I had not wanted to destroy the only place I had ever truly loved.

⁂

The archbishop ground his teeth at the news, even as my father marveled at the wonder of it all; Saint Catherine had vanquished even the mighty Danes. And then he congratulated me, commending me for my great faith.

That spring, the Dane was baptized, and the Count of Paris's land was ceded to him. As we left Rouen in March, not one of our household looked back. My father and his counselors rode ahead as the rest of us followed, more slowly, behind. And I was not surprised when my father did what he always had done. He took my knight to be his own.

I did not stop him.

Andulf found me the morning my father and his retinue were to ride on into Lorraine without us. After a glance about the courtyard, he caught me by the hand and drew me into the stables. "Forgive me for taking such liberties, but are you unhappy with me, my lady?"

"No." I closed my eyes. To the contrary, I was deeply and profoundly, most assuredly, blissfully happy with him.

"And yet you send me away. I do not wish—"

I put a hand to his lips to silence him. I wished he would… do I know not what. Take me into his arms? Kiss me?

He did none of those. Dropping to one knee, head bowed, he cupped his hands around his other knee. "If I have done anything to displease you, only tell me what it was, and I will correct it."

How I longed to feel his arms about me once more. "You have done nothing but—"

He lifted his head, searching my eyes.

"Nothing but—" There was no word for everything he had done. "You have...you have protected me and rescued me and...and loved me."

He bowed his head again at those last words.

"So how can I expect you to stay with me? If it is not the Dane I marry, it will be some other man. I would not want you to there, to be party to my shame in giving myself to another."

He stood, holding my eyes with his own. "I ask you, I beg you, to reconsider. One word from you, and I know the king would replace me with another."

"As you were forever reminding me, you are my father's man. It is only proper you should go with him." I tried to smile. "You will gain his esteem as you have gained mine, and he will see you deserve to be given your father's lands. And then you can go to your mother." I could not bear to look into his eyes, but yet I could not deny myself that final pleasure. To be known, to be loved, if only for a season. "I would like to be remembered, by just one person"—I took a ragged breath as I attempted to stop the pain that stabbed like a knife within my breast—"by *you*, not as a princess, not as the natural daughter of the king, but as myself."

"How could I ever think of you otherwise?"

Dear God in heaven! This was not going to work. I was not going to be brave enough. I was not strong enough. "Better yet, perhaps, not to remember me at all."

"Do not sacrifice yourself this way."

"You mistake me for some virtuous maiden. I am being most selfish. If you stay with me, if you go with me when I wed, do you not see that I would only diminish myself in your eyes?"

"You could never diminish yourself—"

He must not talk. To hear his voice, to gaze into his eyes, would only sway me from what I knew I must do.

"My lady, you ask the impossible."

"But you have done the impossible. You have given me faith when I had none. You have returned to me my honor." How I wanted to stroke that fine, strong jaw, to kiss that beloved cheek. But I would not do it. Not now, not at the last. I could not ask him for more than was mine to demand.

Nostrils flaring, he gazed into the distance above my head, past the door into the morning's sun. Though not so bright as the sun of summer, still it had the ability to dazzle. Perhaps that's why there were tears in his eyes when he returned his gaze to me. "If you wish it, my lady."

My chin trembled as my throat bobbed with tears unshed. I did not wish it. I did not want it. "I cannot see any other way." No other plan would allow him to keep his honor and me to keep my virtue. If he stayed with me, he would give up the chance to ask my father for his estates. He would forfeit everything that mattered to him, and in the end, he would not even gain me for his efforts. He would sacrifice everything, and I would sacrifice nothing, and we would both be debased by the result.

Bowing swiftly, with a nod of his head and a swirl of his mantle, he took himself away.

Saint Catherine may have saved my life, but I had lost my heart in the end.

The queen came into the stables as I was standing there, mourning the vision of a bleak future, where Andulf would most probably often be present but could never again be mine.

She gave me a keen look. "Do you miss Rouen already? Is that why you cry? We can return. You should not distress yourself so."

"What other reason would I have to weep?"

"Your father spoke of you before he left. He thought perhaps you might journey to the abbey at Rochemont this summer, since you did not get to go this autumn past. Would that please you?"

"Yes." Tears began to stream from my eyes once more. "That would please me very much." I would write a letter to my mother and enclose it with a note to the abbess. Perhaps she would not mind passing it on for me. I wanted to tell her…everything. But most of all, I wanted to thank her. She had been right. In spite of everything that had happened and anything that might come to pass, I knew I must not despise the life I had been given.

"I do not know what the appeal is. It's very remote, and the way, I have been told, is treacherous. I offered that it would be better for you to stay in Lorraine with us, but your father thought it might profit you to visit."

"He was right. I think it will."

She eyed me with a dubious frown. "I cannot see how."

The beginnings of a smile stirred within in my heart. "It will. I know it will. I have great faith."

Character Notes

THE WOMEN

Juliana's character is fictitious, but if the old stories are correct, King Charles had a natural (illegitimate) daughter quite early in his reign. If the child's mother was not Juliana, then it was someone very much like her. But by 907, King Charles was apparently free enough from romantic attachments to marry the Lotharingian, Frederuna.

Anna's character is also fictitious, but obvious deformities were considered a punishment from God during the period. Pilgrims like Anna trod the roads during the Dark Ages, visiting shrines in search of a miracle that would heal them. Records from those shrines record hundreds of miracles, some perhaps easily explained by coincidence or modern science, but others are of such an astonishing nature that "miracle" seems the only term to apply.

The queen mother, Adelaide of Paris, had many reasons to be bitter. Her husband, Louis the Stammerer, was forced to repudiate the woman whom he had secretly married at age sixteen (Ansgarde of Burgundy, who was *twenty* years his senior and by which he had four children) in order to marry her. When Louis was crowned king, the pope refused to crown her queen. And when Louis died, a battle for the throne ensued. Ansgarde called Adelaide an adulteress, while Adelaide called Ansgarde a whore. Soap opera is a modern term, but the concept stretches back to the dawn of history. Combine the fact that Adelaide was not her husband's first choice, with the possibility that she saw her son follow in her father's footsteps, and it is little wonder the queen mother hated Juliana, who was both chosen and loved. And how ironic these patterns would assert themselves once more in the possibility of Gisele's marriage to a man who already had a wife (in the most practical sense of the word). I could not have plotted these relationships better if I had made them up!

French records don't record Gisele ever marrying Rollo, while the Norman histories do. One theory holds that Norman chroniclers confused an earlier Gisele with Rollo's Gisele. This "real" Gisele, they claim, was a daughter to an earlier king and was also married to a Dane. For centuries, the chief argument denying the existence of King Charles's Gisele has always been the age of the king. He was born in 879. At the time of his meeting with Rollo, he would only have been thirty-two. For Gisele to have been of an age to marry at that point, she would have had to have been born early in her father's teenage years. Earlier centuries, apparently, found this inconceivable, but I had no problem imagining the possibility. In any case, no one knows what happened to her after Rollo's baptism, and she figures in no genealogy from the period. If she did indeed exist, she would have been a natural daughter conceived from a relationship Charles had as a youth.

THE MEN

It might surprise you, as it surprised me, that Frankish kings weren't French at all. They were German. If there was any capital during those troubled times, it was not in Paris. It was to Charlemagne's old palace in Aachen that King Charles the Simple aspired. In the interest of not confusing the narrative of the story by recounting the tumultuous politics of the time, I simplified the tale of Charles's ascension to the throne. Suffice to say that Charles had the misfortune of being in the wrong place at the wrong time.

It's unfortunate King Charles III has come down through history to us with the moniker "The Simple." He was straightforward, honest, and sincere, but he was not stupid. With a fractured empire and numerous enemies—Magyar invaders approaching from the east, Danes from the north, and the threat of Saracens ever constant in the south—it was impossible to fight on all sides at once. And Charles did not just want to preserve the kingdom he had been left; he wanted to restore it to the glorious empire created by Charlemagne. He let his nobles defend the edges of the empire, and then he did what many men in similar situations have done: he made a bargain with the devil. And he followed a pattern well established in the ancient world by seeking to seal the agreement through the irrevocable bonds of marriage.

Charles achieved what previous kings had not: he reunited Charlemagne's beloved kingdom of Lotharingia with his own kingdom of West Francia. He must have considered that year of 912 a good omen of things to come. After having been crowned King of Lorraine, he moved his court and his entire attention to its affairs. But as he rode away from Rollo's baptism in Rouen, he had unknowingly given away his destiny. The future of Europe lay not with him but with Rollo, the father of the future dukes of Normandy, and young Hugh, father of the future Capetian kings. The bargains Charles made and had been forced into allowed his nobles to build empires of their own, which would not be surrendered until a painstaking reconsolidation undertaken by a later dynasty of kings.

In 922, nobles who were tired of King Charles's obvious affection for the Lotharingians gave his crown to Robert, the Count of Paris. In 923, with the support of the Normans, King Charles was captured in battle as he fought to retake his throne. He was literally left to rot in a prison and died there in 929. His only truly loyal retainer of that period turned out to be Rollo, who fought faithfully against every advance by the Count of Paris against King Charles's kingdom.

Originally Viking denoted an excursion, not a people. From their homeland in current Scandinavia, sometimes men would go on a viking, sailing off to foreign lands, seeking gold and treasure as they sowed fear in the hearts of people everywhere. For centuries, they were known as Danes. But this designation was not technical. Danes during that period might have come from Denmark or Sweden or Norway. In fact, the actual nationality of Rollo (as well as his lineage and his very name) is still debated. Rollo's descendants became the dukes of Normandy, and his great-great-great-grandson William became known as the Conqueror in 1066. Perhaps most ironic of all, Rollo became a relic collector himself. He was not, however, a convincing convert to Christianity. Legend has it he ordered the beheading of one hundred Christian men upon his death bed.

Robert had many titles: Count of Poitiers, Marquess of Neustria and Orléans, and Count of Paris. Later, he took the crown from Charles the Simple and gave himself the title Robert I. For the sake of simplicity and consistency, I chose to refer to him as the Count of Paris. His brother, Odo, also Count of Paris and Marquess of Neustria, had been appointed King of France during Charles's minority but refused to relinquish the throne without a fight. The agreement between the two rival kings left Robert with Odo's lands, but bereft of the royal crown.

The boy, Hugh, may very well have been in love with Princess Gisele, as he fancied himself to be. His father, Robert, Count of Paris, took the crown from King Charles in 922. When Robert died, just a short year later, the throne was offered to Hugh, his son. He refused it, and it was given to his brother-in-law (his sister's husband, the Duke of Burgundy) instead. And when that king died in 936, Hugh was instrumental in bringing Gisele's half brother, Louis d'Outremer, to France to claim the throne. Though he and Louis subsequently had a falling out, after the king's death, Hugh was the first noble to support Louis's son, Lothair. What better reward, then, for a faithful subject to become the founder of a royal dynasty himself. Hugh's son was Hugh Capet, from whom sprang the Capetian kings that shaped the destiny of modern France.

As so, we come to Andulf. What can I say about this knight who was so noble and true, but that he, more than any other character in the novel, was a product of my imagination? During that time of tumult and turmoil, there were no knights in shining armor. There were no castles as we think of them today, and there was no code of chivalry. There was only survival. If you imagine the world existing within the decaying moldering ruins of ancient Rome, you are closer to a picture of the times than if you read a fairy tale. The story of woe he recounted to the princess, however, was true. If you read *Handbook for William* by Dhuoda, you will hear, in his mother's own words, the tragic tale of his family, and you will discover just how closely faith was woven into daily life. Though it was written a generation before the events in this book, and though more than a thousand years have passed since the words were first penned, you can hear the longing and the fear and the pride of a woman who sought to give her two sons all of the wisdom she could think of. She probably never saw her youngest son after he was wrenched from her arms shortly after his birth.

Author's Notes

CHRONICLERS OF THIS AGE WERE FEW, AND THERE ARE no contemporary histories that remain from the late ninth and early tenth centuries. Those who later recorded the events sometimes relied on unproven oral histories or bent the facts to fit their biases. Some historians of this period claim relationships between historical figures, which other historians take great pains to disprove. And while some ancient records are quite clear on the existence of certain people, other records claim the same person never existed at all. This period is rife with kings named Louis and Charles and usurpers named Robert, all of whom played a part in the dismantling of Charlemagne's Holy Roman Empire. Any given name from the period might be referenced in modern histories by three or four different spellings (Latin, Frankish, Germanic, and old English) according to the author's preference. Place names sometimes suffer a similar fate.

I went cross-eyed tracing family trees, trying to figure out who was related to whom and to what sort of degree. Like nearly everything about the Dark Ages, family lines are rather obscure, with genealogies sometimes skipping entire generations and mixing up those of the same name but of different eras, for who knows what reason, which quite vexingly leads to claims of relationships that are ridiculous upon further investigation.

One thing is clear: the great Charlemagne left many descendants, both legitimate and illegitimate. It was not unheard of for second or third cousins to marry in that tightly knit court, and what might merely raise eyebrows in our time would have been scandalous in an age that would not tolerate marriage within seven degrees of kinship. (Which simply means the bride and groom could not share a great-great-great-great-great-great-grandparent.) I hope you will understand—and quite possibly sympathize!—when I admit that when I did not know for certain, I cherry-picked the facts I wanted, or I made things up where they didn't exist. I only hope for those not acquainted with the era that my fiction mixes seamlessly with the historical record.

In one of those strange coincidences that sometimes befall historical writers, after I had decided which saint should be the focus of Anna's pilgrimage and which part of her body I wanted the reliquary to hold, I discovered that Saint Catherine's finger was in fact brought to Rouen in the eleventh century. It was placed in an abbey that sat atop a hill on the east side of the city. Though the abbey was destroyed in the fifteenth century, the hill is still called by Saint Catherine's name. In the fifteenth century, Saint Catherine was one of the saints who urged Joan of Arc to fight the English, and it was in Rouen where Joan was tried and executed for heresy.

Although in the modern age wolves are not generally known to attack people, the Middle Ages recorded many accounts of wolves preying upon people. With all of the famines and diseases and wars that swept the continent, generations of wolves were raised to believe humans were easy prey. And although no bears currently exist in Europe, there were plenty back then.

Poland Syndrome, exhibited by a deformed hand and an underdeveloped breast on the same side of the body, was named for the doctor who documented it in 1841, but it must have existed for centuries before that. Xylophagia is the type of Pica disorder describing those who eat paper or wood. Pica can be exhibited in children who have developmental disorders or who have been neglected. Tourette's Syndrome, while commonly envisioned as a person uttering profanities at inappropriate moments, more often manifests itself in uncontrollable behaviors, like the young lord's. Arm flapping is a classic symptom of autism spectrum disorders. Children with Down's syndrome often repeat or mimic words or sounds. That the abbey at Rochemont found itself the guardian of children exhibiting these sorts of behaviors would not have been uncommon. All of these disorders would have made children unfit for normal life, and therefore unwanted, during the period. Marked malformation of the body was often viewed as a judgment from God or as a punishment for a grievous sin. Still, in contrast to the region's pagan religions, Western Christian culture actively organized care for those who could not care for themselves.

Reading Group Guide

1. How do you define a miracle? Do you believe in them?

2. Everyone puts their faith in something. What do you place your faith in?

3. Juliana counseled her daughter not to despise the life she had been given. Do you think this was good advice? Would you have said something different to Gisele instead?

4. Was Juliana right in leaving Charles?

5. Juliana believed that by retreating to live at the abbey, she had left the world behind. She says, "Our abbey was not a kingdom. Our doings did not affect the world beyond our gates." Was she right? Have you ever retreated, hoping to leave the world behind? Did it work?

6. In some ways this book is set up as a battle between God and men. Gisele states, "My fate had already been determined by men. I did not think there was anything God could do now to intervene." At another point the queen mother says, "God always gets his way in the end,

does He not? How can you fight Providence and ever hope to win?" With which of those ideas do you agree?

7.   Contrast the descriptions of Paradise and Valhalla. How did each culture's view of death affect their actions?

8.   When Anna is lost in the woods, she tries to find her way out. At one point she thinks, "What purpose had the boulder served but to mark the place at which I had known myself to be lost? And why should I be so set on returning there? It could do nothing for me but keep me waylaid. In order to be found, I had to be willing to leave it behind." What did each character have to be willing to leave behind in order to move forward?

9.   Anna had been told her disability was a curse from God. Was there any way in which it might have been a blessing?

10.   Why do you think Anna was healed when so many other pilgrims were not?

11.   At one point, Gisele states, "How easy it is to trust in God when you do not have to trust Him for your life." Andulf replies, "On the contrary. I think it would be far more difficult to trust if nothing depended upon my faith." Which character do you agree with?

12.   Did Gisele make the right choice in terms of her relationship with Andulf? What other ending would you have written for her?

13.   Would you rather live in a world without faith or without hope?

14.   Who was the miracle thief?

A Conversation with the Author

IRIS ANTHONY

Q: Let's get this question over with right away. Do you believe in miracles?

A: Of course I do! Don't you? Who wants to live in a world where the miraculous could never occur? Art critic Bernard Berenson once said: "Miracles happen to those who believe in them." I also think it matters who you put your faith in. If you place all your faith in yourself, all of your efforts at improvement begin and end with you. If you place your faith in something beyond yourself, then the door to other possibilities swings open.

Q: Speaking of faith, that seemed to be a prevalent theme in this book. But this isn't the Dark Ages. Weren't you worried you might turn some readers off?

A: It would be difficult to write a book about the Dark Ages that didn't involve some aspect of faith. Life was steeped in Christianity. People saw the hand of Providence everywhere. It's often stated that a person is composed of the mind, spirit, and body. Those in the Dark Ages would have agreed. The idea that some people in the modern era deny their spirituality altogether would have been

completely shocking to them. Everyone back then—
pagans included—worshipped someone or something.

People of the Dark Ages asked the same questions
about life and death, purpose and meaning, that we do
today. What I wanted to discover is whether we have
arrived at different answers, whether an interval of a
thousand years has changed anything about the way we
view the interaction between what is sacred and what
is secular.

Q: I'm fascinated by this idea that novelists write to answer
their own questions.

A: It's a rather selfish undertaking, isn't it? Holding readers captive for a hundred thousand words and however
many hours it takes to read them in order to discover the
answer to a question they might never have even wanted
to consider. It would be so much more efficient if I had
the ability to write short stories!

Q: So what did you discover?

A: One of the most basic tenets of Christianity is the concept of grace—the undeserved favor of God. But one
thing that seems to have remained constant across the
ages is humanity's unwillingness to accept that grace at
face value. You can see that need to prove worthiness
scrawled across the history of the faith. By definition,
however, that undertaking is futile.

I discovered the doors of the faith are wide open to all
kinds of reprobates…but only if you're willing to admit
that you are one. You can understand how that would
be a big blow to the ego. Hence the need to prove that
you have somehow earned God's favor…which brings

us back to the original definition of grace. The whole concept is ingenious!

Q: Did you do research on miracles? Or maybe the better question is *how* would you go about researching miracles?

A: During the period, miracles had to be vouched for by witnesses. It was no good to show up at a church and proclaim yourself healed…or your missing ax found or your child suddenly healed. You had to have witnesses swear to the fact that your ax was actually missing or your child had truly been ill. Some of the miracles attested to back then were things that we, in our modern age, can all agree were coincidence, but some were truly inexplicable. Beyond that, in preparation for writing the miracle scene in the novel, I wanted to know what it would feel like. I talked to people who have experienced miracles, asking what it felt like and how they knew they had been healed.

Q: Was there anything that surprised you about the time period?

A: Everything! Here's a secret: I procrastinated in starting this novel because I had such a difficult time imagining the world about which I was supposed to be writing. The Dark Ages didn't look like the world of the high Middle Ages, with knights in shining armor and tur-reted castles, but neither did it look like the world the ancient Romans left behind either. There were castles in the Dark Ages, but they were mostly motte and bailey construction of solitary wooden towers built on top of a mound of earth. There were walled estates, but often the fortifications were wooden palisades, not sturdy stone walls. And there were knights, but there was no code of chivalry. It might sound odd, but the hardest thing for me to remember was that there were no chimneys. Fires vented through holes in the roof and they were kindled at the center of rooms, not along the walls. More than one scene had to be rewritten or repositioned because I imagined the fire in the wrong place.

Q: How did you come up with the idea for this story?

A: Like most of my novels, the idea for this one came as I was researching a different book. I came across a mention of the book *Furta Sacra* by Patrick J. Geary that talked about armies of monks setting out to steal relics from each other. During this period, the concept of stealing relics was approved of and even encouraged. But odder than that was the belief that the relics themselves would decide their fate. If you were successful in your theft, then the relic wanted to go with you. If you failed, then obviously it wanted to stay right where it was. It was such an interesting belief that I began to wonder, "What would happen if..." The story developed from there.

Q: I love History's series *Vikings*. Your Danes aren't portrayed in the same way.

A: There were so many things I discovered about Vikings during my research that I hadn't known and so many things I came to admire in their culture. But my Danes are the villains in this story, not the protagonists. They're also seen through the eyes of people outside their community who don't understand their language, their culture, or their religion. If they act like thugs, it's because, for all intents and purposes, that's the way they appeared to the Franks of the time.

Q: What was the big deal about relics?

A: Relics, which are objects used as memorials of saints, became part of the practice of the Christian faith in the first century. The church quite clearly says they are not to be worshipped, but only venerated for the purpose of commemorating a saint. The idea of the relic is fore-shadowed in the Old Testament. Clothes, kerchiefs, and even the shadow of the Apostle Peter are spoken of in conjunction with miracles in the New Testament. In the Carolingian period, every church was required to have a relic for its altar. Since the supply of saints was limited, the options for acquiring relics were also limited. You could buy one from a relic dealer, you could steal one from someone else, or you could go out and look for a relic that no one else had previously found. A fairly brisk market in what I think of as "secondary" relics arose: dust from the tomb of a saint, filings from a martyr's chains, and other objects of that nature.

Q: So was there really a Saint Catherine?

A: There were several Saint Catherines venerated by the Church. Like Princess Gisele, Saint Catherine of Alexandria is one of those obscure figures of the Dark Ages who may not, in actuality, have ever existed. Her feast day is in November, and she is numbered among the Fourteen Holy Helpers. In the eleventh century, one of her relics was, in fact, brought to Rouen, and a church was built to house it.

There are several hagiographies of her life, according to which she was a pagan princess (or daughter of a wealthy man) who was martyred in the fourth century at the order of Roman Emperor Maxentius (or Maximinus or Maximian). Devoted to scholarly pursuits, she converted to Christianity at the age of fourteen. She then visited Emperor Maxentius to try to convert him as well. Though he pitted the empire's greatest philosophers against her, she confounded them with her arguments, and they converted to her faith. Maxentius promptly ordered them executed. She converted the empress as well…who was also executed. After the emperor imprisoned Catherine for her impertinence, she converted two hundred soldiers who were then immediately killed.

Enraged, Maxentius had her tortured. When she would not denounce Christ, the emperor offered her a royal marriage (whether to himself or some other noble is disputed). When she refused, he tried to have her broken on a spiked wheel, but it mysteriously disintegrated, and she was beheaded instead. Her body, from which sprang a perpetual flow of oil, was later discovered on Mount Sinai.

Catherine is the patron saint of maidens, students, scholars, the dying, wheelwrights, mechanics, craftsmen who work with wheels, librarians, theologians, preachers, orators, and philosophers.

Acknowledgments

To my agent, Natasha Kern, and my editor, Shana Drehs, who not only allowed me to write a book about miracles, but also encouraged me to do so. And to K, who never tired of asking me to tell the story of my story.

About the Author

Iris Anthony is a pseudonym. The writer behind the name is an award-winning author of over a dozen novels. Disguised as her alter ego, Iris has lived on three continents and traveled to five. She has given up on keeping a diary, buying a château, and liking tea. She stills hopes one day to be able to knit a sweater, play golf on the Old Course, and visit Antarctica. Iris lives in the Washington, D.C., metro area in a house decorated with French antiques and Flemish lace. Learn more about Iris at www.irisanthony.com.